THE FIRST DAYS OF
AUGUST

AD HOMINEM: NEVER JUDGE A MAN BY HIS COVER

THE FIRST DAYS OF
AUGUST

ALAN FRONING

ARCHWAY
PUBLISHING

Archway Publishing books may be ordered through booksellers or by contacting:

Archway Publishing
1663 Liberty Drive
Bloomington, IN 47403
www.archwaypublishing.com
1-(888)-242-5904

Because of the dynamic nature of the Internet, any web addresses or
links contained in this book may have changed since publication and
may no longer be valid. The views expressed in this work are solely those
of the author and do not necessarily reflect the views of the publisher,
and the publisher hereby disclaims any responsibility for them.

Any people depicted in stock imagery provided by Thinkstock are models,
and such images are being used for illustrative purposes only.
Certain stock imagery © Thinkstock.

ISBN: 978-1-4808-1333-5 (sc)
ISBN: 978-1-4808-1335-9 (hc)
ISBN: 978-1-4808-1334-2 (e)

Library of Congress Control Number: 2014921747

Print information available on the last page.

Archway Publishing rev. date: 6/8/2015

1.

FRIDAY, APRIL 15

Mrs. Angela Jackson had been healthy for more than forty years till early Friday. Preparing breakfast in the kitchen, she swayed, grabbed for the counter, exclaimed "Oh, God, my head," and then dropped to the floor in front of Mr. Jackson and their three children.

With sirens blasting the paramedics had arrived in eighteen minutes. At All Saints Memorial nine minutes later, a CT scan had shown a bleeding aneurysm in her brain, and within another five minutes Mrs. Jackson was in the neurosurgical operating room suite with Dr. Steve August, aided by an anesthesiologist and three nurses, fighting to save her life.

This was a particularly difficult operation. At the moment Steve could not see his fingers, which were reaching into a small crimson pool filling the cranial cavity of his patient.

Steve needed to clamp the artery feeding the aneurysm, but blood was pumping into the space around Mrs. Jackson's brain faster than the suction tubes were pulling it out. Beneath the surgeon's mask he felt a bead of sweat collecting on his upper lip. Salty. His mouth was dry.

With his right index finger, invisible in the little red bath, he traced the edge of brain tissue around to the pulsing warmth – the bleeding artery. In his left hand he balanced a clamp, letting its weight move along the edge of the living brain, into the darkening pool, down to the tip of his finger. Now only touch and faith could guide him. He lightly moved his left hand forward, relaxing his grip on the clamp.

He held his breath.

The operating room door squeaked. His eyes, mind, and heart were focused on the patch of blood, yet behind him he sensed the arrival of Marion Phillips, one of neurosurgery's living legends. His presence was comforting, familiar, and Steve found himself breathing again.

And as though on cue the vessel beneath his finger was no longer pulsing. The clamp had worked.

The voice was soft, yet steel, "August, what's the situation?"

"Under control, Dr. Phillips. Small aneurysm off the anterior carotid. Bleeder. I think the clamp's holding."

Indeed, the bleeding had stopped. He stared at the pool filling the base of Mrs. Jackson's skull, willing it to go away … and, as if by magic, it dwindled. The suction tubes drew out the blood. Within seconds the surgeons could look inside and see the base of the brain, and there they saw the offending artery, securely clamped.

With the blood flow stopped, the aneurysm was now safe, but parts of brain were being deprived of their blood supply. Within a couple of minutes brain damage would result unless the vessels could be repaired.

"Not bad, Dr. August. Not bad at all. Shall I continue, or would you prefer I first-assist?"

The old man was always good for a laugh. "Thanks, Dr. Phillips, but if it's all the same to you, I'll just back you up."

Phillips chuckled, "Someday, August, you'll make a damn fine neurosurgeon."

He held out his hand to the scrub nurse, who with a practiced maneuver slapped a loaded needle-holder into his palm. With relaxed twists of his wrist Phillips sewed a new, artificial graft into the clamped artery and shunted the graft around the aneurysm, joining it to the blood vessel on the other side. He then opened the clamp, and the blood flow resumed its normal course around the aneurysm site.

"Well, Steve, I'd say that looks acceptable. You mind closing up?"

"No sir, be delighted."

And Steve was delighted. The operation had saved Mrs. Jackson's life.

~

A half-hour later Steve was back in the OR lounge sipping a cup of black Java, eyes closed, feet propped up on a vinyl couch. He loved operating – there was nothing like walking out of the OR knowing you had touched another human being's life for the better. Maybe you couldn't control everything, but there were moments when you did move things in the right direction, and they were sweet.

"Nice work in there, August."

He opened his eyes to find Phillips lowering his bulk into the chair next to his. The old man was famous as much for his gentle warmth as for his brilliance with a scalpel. In the last several years he had operated on no less than five heads of state, more than any other neurosurgeon in the world– but even with the international fame, his compassion was how he won hearts. He kept little candies and chocolates in his lab coat pockets for his littlest patients, who adored his hospital visits and would brighten when he entered the room, even when they were battling the worst diseases.

Phillips took a sip of coffee.

"Good instincts, son. There's hope for you yet."

Steve blushed lightly.

"Thanks, Dr. Phillips. Got lucky. Whole thing could've gone south."

"Could have – but didn't. Good instincts. Smartest guy in the world isn't worth a lick in the OR without good instincts."

The praise made Steve uncomfortable. He didn't mind being watched when he was handling a scalpel, because then what mattered was the work. But when people made him the direct object of conversation, he tended to get flustered.

"I had some trouble finding the source of that hemorrhage. Would've been nice to have better exposure of the field. Just too much blood."

But Phillips would not be deterred, "It was good work."

He shifted his weight, turning his full gaze on Steve. "MacGregor tells me you're making excellent progress at Angion. Sounds like this Angiotox project is going gangbusters: blood vessels melting, brain tumors shrinking. He tells me your work is solid."

Even more uncomfortable, Steve had no immediate response.

Fortunately, Phillips didn't seem to want one. He heaved himself out of the vinyl chair and with a wave of his hand disappeared past the vending machines.

Steve sat quietly, considering the conversation, the morning, and his life in general. The operation had been a home run, and Marion Phillips, MD, one of the world's greatest neurosurgeons, had praised his work. He savored the moment: he was lucky.

But still ... without knowing it, Phillips had touched on the problem. The clinic was straightforward: you saw your patients, took care of their problems, and at night went home exhausted but satisfied. However, the laboratory, Angion, was another matter.

He grimaced, drained his cup, and looked around the empty lounge. 11:30 AM. Everyone was at work in the thirty-two operating suites at Saints – replacing hips, repairing hearts, transplanting kidneys, removing tumors – correcting the aberrations with which nature challenged mankind on a daily basis.

Steve loved the idea of being an instrument of health, a means for restoring the natural order. That's how he'd described his work to Morgan, back when they were together, even though she'd then typically only laughed and kissed him.

He had never told her the whole Angion story.

Unlike Steve August, Dida Medicia was not having a good day. In her corner office on the twenty-first floor of Angion's corporate headquarters, giant windows offered sweeping views of historic Beacon Hill, the skyscrapers of the financial district, and sparkling blue Boston Harbor and Massachusetts Bay. Sunshine warmed young couples walking hand-in-hand along the pond in the Public Garden, their shirts and sundresses bright spots of color against the verdant green of trees and shrubs. But these views of life and youth and beauty were lost on Dida. Her back to the window, she was yelling at her speakerphone.

"Goddamn it! Silverstein, what do you mean – 'Wait?' We can't wait! You keep talking about data, but we don't need data. We need money. And to get money, I need FDA approval. We need less testing and more progress. Push back the FDA application another three months? Goddamn it!! We don't have three months. We have three days. I'm in the board room Monday talking to those Swiss guys with millions in their pockets, and they want to hear about an FDA application."

Her voice went up another octave. "Goddamn it, Silverstein! Do you know what my uncle will say?"

Actually, Dida already knew what her uncle would say, as they'd talked just last night, but Silverstein didn't need to know that little fact.

For several seconds there was silence. Then Silverstein's nasal tone came back, "It doesn't matter what you say, or your Uncle Tony, or even the President of the United States. The last set of experiments turned out a wash. We'll have better animal data in three months. Meanwhile, we only have proof in principle – not in practice – of a tremendous product."

"What happened?"

"George gave that young doctor Steve August the mouse project, but he's fallen behind. When George finally told me that without the mouse data we'd need a stopgap to keep the investors on board, this past week I ran SAGA to test Angiotox against cell-types from several other species."

She interrupted, "Silverstein, if I'd wanted a lecture, I'd have called a Harvard professor."

"Let me remind you that I was offered a Harvard professorship, but I turned them down, instead to develop SAGA – this my own, my very important creation …"

"GODDAMN IT!! Go on!"

"We've been patching together SAGA data for cell lines from mouse, rat, rabbit, dog, pig, chimp, and human. This should have been a trivial exercise – because the original rabbit data were so very clear. However, the current results are unexpected."

He paused.

Dida growled, "So?"

His voice dropped to a near whisper, "For some species the molecule localizes to several endothelial cell types, not just brain. There is greater variety than expected – an interesting result. Very interesting."

The bastard sounded happy!

"Silverstein, in plain English?"

His voice turned flat. "This means we can't conclude the *toxicity* effects in humans from the SAGA rabbit experiments. Instead, we must extrapolate more from a variety of other animals. This makes the mouse experiments doubly important – they give us toxicity as well as efficacy in living creatures, not just cell-lines. And this means McGregor made a serious mistake bringing in this neophyte. If August has garbled the mouse data, then he's set us back months."

At this second mention of Steve August, Dida took a deep breath. She had become a CEO not through the indulgence of hot-blooded passion, but through the exercise of cool intellect – along with several other talents. August was merely a tool, as was Silverstein. And besides, she was not sure how much Silverstein knew. She needed him focused on the task at hand.

Her voice leveled. "I agree, David. Bringing in August was a mistake. He's not a team player. George was sucking up to Phillips. The whole thing's backfired. So what can I tell these investors?"

"Tell them we're making progress, but give them no details. Tell them we have every indication our results will prove Angiotox works in humans, but the data are not yet complete. Tell them … tell them three months for the FDA."

"David, that'd be a hell of a lot better coming from you than me."

His nasal whine returned on the speaker, "I knew it would come to this. What time?"

"Monday morning 10 AM sharp, our board room. Please include coat and tie. You okay with that?"

"Well, Dida, I am okay with the time and place. Please wear whatever you like. I shall do the same."

The speakerphone clicked off.

Dida fumed in silence: *What a prima donna!*

She often wondered how smart people could be so stupid. Maybe Silverstein would be less offensive if he got laid; however, she had to draw the line, *somewhere.* Silverstein was a bald, 350-pound, egg-shaped 48-year-old man lacking the sex appeal of a love-starved rhino chasing a jeep on safari. She'd gladly set up a revolving door to her bedroom, if that were what was needed to get ahead. Still, Silverstein would have to fend on his own. Or maybe he was married? If so, poor woman.

A knock on the door broke her train of thought. Very few people could get past her secretary without first being announced, so this was not a good sign. But then, it had not been a good morning, so why change now?

"Yes?"

The door opened. Michael Riker stood in the doorway, his long, gaunt, pinstriped frame dividing the space neatly in two. A chill ran down Dida's spine. He always reminded her of a razor.

"Riker! You're back fast. How'd it go?"

His grin showed pointed canines. "He agreed. You may now call me Mr. Smith, proud client of Nathan Spear, Private Eye. Our problem will be addressed."

"Remember, Riker, I go first."

"You will have your turn. But I assure you, one way, or another, all loose ends will be eliminated."

He walked to the window and looked out onto the Boston Public Garden.

"Really, Dida, don't you find this light too bright?"

He reached up and turned the blinds, casting the room in shadow. "The dark's so much more comfortable."

He smiled, nodded, and left.

She felt ice cold.

Steve stepped out into the warm noon sunshine, took a deep breath of fresh air, walked down to the corner of Cambridge Street, and then turned back to look at his place of work. All Saints Memorial Hospital glistened, modern towers set atop hundred-year-old historic gray buildings, reflecting the golden sunlight.

"Mecca," he chuckled, and turned back towards the River. He would take the long way this afternoon, a stroll along the Charles, then a turn back to the Back Bay and his little apartment. He had much to think about.

He passed the Hatch Shell, home to the Boston Pops. To his left were the brownstones of the Back Bay, to his right the blue of the Charles River dotted with white sailboats from the MIT boathouse, college kids practicing their racing turns. Although it was only April, the air was warm. A few seagulls flew overhead. He enjoyed the moment.

A duck at the edge of the path was looking at him. Steve paused, motionless, and returned its gaze. After a moment, with no food forthcoming, the bird turned and waddled into the Charles, but good fortune smiled – a bread crust on the water! Triumphant, the duck paddled away, the crust in its bill.

"That's right," Steve murmured to no one in particular. "Do not contend, but do not concede."

Staring at the river, from nowhere he remembered a verse from the *Tao Te Ching*, one Master Lao Huang had quoted often:

> *The highest good is like water.*
> *Water benefits ten thousand beings,*
> *Yet it does not contend.*
> *Nothing under Heaven is as soft and yielding as water.*
> *Yet in attacking the firm and strong,*
> *Nothing is better than water.*

He smiled, amused when Chinese philosophy came to mind unbidden, as it sometimes did. He straightened, looking across the Charles to the Cambridgeport side of the river. There was the neighborhood of Angion, the world-famous angiogenesis laboratory of George MacGregor. He murmured again, "The highest good is like water."

Two young women, maybe college girls, walked past him. They giggled and glanced at him, and the one cooed, "No darling. The highest good is not like water; it's like champagne."

Pulled out of his reverie, he had no quick answer. The best he could do was flash them a grin.

God, I love this town!

Again, he softly repeated, "The highest good is like water," and resumed his walk towards home.

2.

MONDAY, DECEMBER 13

Four months earlier, George MacGregor, former MIT professor and current principal owner of the Angion Corporation, received a phone call.

The timing was inconvenient, as Dida Medicia had been massaging his neck as he sat at his desk, and her hands had just slipped forward to unbutton his shirt.

"Georgie Porgie, don't answer that. We've only a few minutes."

She was nibbling on his earlobe.

He noted the caller ID. "Bugger! It's Phillips."

He leaned forward, away from her hands, and picked up the phone.

Moments earlier he had been entertaining more carnal notions, yet he managed to keep his delivery smooth, "Marion! Glad you called. You know I'm still waiting to meet those Swiss friends of yours."

Phillip's patrician tones were crisp, "George, so glad to catch you in. I know you're busy. Yes, those VC boys are quite excited about your newest paper in *Nature Medicine*."

Dida had walked around to the front of the desk, lips in a pout. She settled into one of the black leather chairs and crossed her legs, the high-cut skirt revealing olive-tanned thighs.

"Thank you, Marion. Yes, the project's purring. Angiotox is the real stuff, pure gold – brain tumors cured in mice and rabbits. Next step: human beings."

As he spoke, MacGregor smiled at Dida, his jowls folding into layers of decadent satisfaction. International financiers were throwing millions his way, a world-famous neurosurgeon was massaging his ego, and a caramel bombshell was flashing her candy legs across his designer furniture. He was on top of the world.

But the mood broke quickly. Phillips was saying, "Very exciting indeed! It's time we bring this full circle, don't you think, old man?"

"Certainly, Marion. What do you mean?"

"Why, our conversation at the Dean's Holiday Party. Indeed, you have your grad students training for careers in laboratory science, but we need to think ahead, to make sure there will be physicians, clinicians, who will carry your brilliant work from the laboratory into the clinic. Translational research, man – bench to bedside!"

MacGregor looked at Dida and shook his head. Marion Phillips was known for his extraordinary demands on people – though always with the most noble of intentions, of course. How could Phillips understand the challenges of managing a multi-million dollar for-profit research laboratory, where the bottom line mattered above all else? Certainly nothing like being a neurosurgeon.

Last thing we need is a bloody bunch of doctors gumming up the works!

George was irritated. He wished Dida were still rubbing his chest.

Phillips continued, "From my perspective, this would be an excellent way to groom a resident for a high-profile academic career. And for you, George, such a physician-scientist would become a living, breathing advertisement for Angion. Handsome dividends for both of us, I'd say!"

"Our experiments are at a very sensitive stage. I don't think this is the time …"

But Phillips interjected crisply, "My friend, this is an *excellent* time. Your work is at a cusp. You should plan on one or two residents from Saints in your laboratory – *always!* Remember, these doctors will be our ambassadors."

MacGregor thought about Phillips's Swiss banker buddies with their millions, not to mention Phillips's doctor friends scattered around the globe, all of them operating on brain tumors, prescribing drugs, talking to *their* friends …

"Marion, of course you're right. You have someone in mind?"

"Young chap by the name of Steve August. Sharp as a whip. Interesting background. Bit of an athlete – champion high-diver at Harvard College, nearly went to the Olympics. Smart, though – studied religious philosophy on a scholarship. Routinely quotes Milton, the Bible, Confucius – entertaining in small measures, though bit stale at larger doses. Still, he's competent – placed third in his class at Harvard Med. As a resident, the boy works like a madman. And he's pleasant. You'll like him."

MacGregor betrayed no emotion. "Fine. We'll find him a front-row project with Angiotox."

"Excellent, George, excellent. This will be a win-win all around. Cheerio!"

MacGregor cradled the phone, his eyes turning up to a framed poster hanging on the far wall: a Porsche Carrera GT, the quarter-of-a-million dollar toy that was one of his life ambitions. He was searching for comfort.

Dida spoke, "So, you've got yourself a new apprentice? How sweet. Is this a problem, George?"

He stared at the poster. "Yes, Dida. The timing couldn't be worse. I'm going to have to think about this."

Dida leaned over the desk, her shirt falling loosely forward.

"Well, tiger, think about this," she growled, grabbing him by the hair, pulling him across the desk.

That night Steve came home carrying flowers. Phillips's suggestion that he work with MacGregor had sounded ideal, and he wanted to share his excitement with Morgan.

He unlocked the door and stepped inside the apartment. The furnishings were leftovers from med school – worn couch, TV, stereo with two speakers in the corners of the room. He walked into the kitchen.

The attack was unexpected. A mass of muscle slammed into his back. He started to spin on his right foot, but not fast enough. Expert feet shifted against his leg, his body twisted off balance, and he fell flat.

Giggling, Morgan threw herself on top of him. "Ah, Inspector Clouseau, you are no match for the mighty Cato!"

Helpless, Steve was laughing.

∾

Some time later the bouquet was lying in the hallway, clothes were scattered across the kitchen floor, and the two lovers were nestled naked on the bed, glistening with sweat, satisfied.

"Hey, where are my flowers?" she cried, and ran into the hall.

His eyes followed her. He had met Morgan a year ago at a *bagua* class at Harvard. They were both black belts – but she was better, strong yet graceful, almost poetic. The moment he had first seen her in class, rolling an instructor onto the ground, knee flattening the chest against the mat, palm below the chin baring the exposed throat – Steve had fallen in love with this dangerous, beautiful woman. Her intense hazel eyes radiated both intelligence and mystery, while her raven black hair, strong chin, and sculpted form completed a stunning picture, even if slightly threatening.

Having saved the flowers, Morgan returned, pizza box in one hand, two longnecks in the other. She plopped down on the bed, handed him a beer, and opened the box revealing four slices of day-old pepperoni pizza. She laughed, "I slaved for hours" – and bit into a slice, "So, how was your day?"

Steve grinned broadly. "Excellent. Had two solid cases in the OR this morning. Drained a hematoma in a 24-year-old biker who got lucky after he crashed his Harley without a helmet. Then helped Phillips fix an aneurysm in some corporate lawyer who they say is one of the meanest bad-asses in Boston. Guy by the name of Joseph Myers. Know him?"

Morgan nearly choked. "Joe Myers? Sure, he's famous, or maybe should say, infamous. He once filed a class-action lawsuit against MacDonalds because they cut back on the number of pickle slices in a Big Mac. Won millions in fees without the public collecting a dime. Yeah, a real piranha. He survive the operation?"

"Good as new. I'm glad I didn't know more about him."

"Yeah, I bet. While you were in there maybe you could have hooked up an extra blood vessel to his altruism center. Make him more of a *mensch*."

This was a recurring theme: Morgan often encouraged Steve to improve his patients' wiring.

"I'm glad I don't know how. What if I did? You'd *never* leave me alone. Thought we agreed that changing people's personalities is wrong?"

"You're such a prude. Just imagine … You could eliminate *sin*. Take away the impulse to beat one's wife, or, …" she leaned her hands against his shoulders, pushing him back on the mattress, " …one's husband. You could make the rich more generous, the warrior more gentle, the meek more confident, and the lover more … more … hungry!"

Her hazel eyes flared.

"Well, when you put it like that, it seems like a wonderful idea."

Still holding him down, she started nuzzling his ear.

"So tell me, what else happened today?"

Steve was having some trouble concentrating.

"Phillips talked to me about a research project. He wants to set me up in an angiogenesis laboratory run by a biotech guru, George MacGregor."

"Hmm. Angiogenesis. That means growth of blood vessels, doesn't it? I think that's very sexy."

Kicking the pizza box onto the floor, Steve rolled over on top of her, determined not to be distracted.

"MacGregor's the international king of angiogenesis. He's a boy genius. He trained in England, but by twenty-five he had his own laboratory at MIT. By thirty-five he was a full professor, bringing in millions a year in commercial grants. But he wasn't satisfied, left MIT, and started this private biotech company Angion. His own boss."

Morgan reached up. "I can't take this anymore," she breathed.

And she pulled him close.

～

Half an hour later, propped up on an elbow, Morgan was looking at him, "So, go on."

"Morgan! Again?"

"Silly – your research on MacGregor."

"Oh, right. He's typical for the 21st century scientist running a major research lab. He develops ideas, brings in the money, and hires the talent. It's tough work!"

Her voice dropped an octave, "Recognizing your talents is easy."

Steve shook his head, smiling, "I'm serious. He knows nothing about my purported talents. He's taking me on as a favor to Phillips. From his point of view I bet he'd rather not waste time on some resident. From my point of view it's the chance of a lifetime, that is, next to working at Saints."

"Mmm. And spending quality time with me."

Steve gave an appreciative laugh. "Babe, not even in the same category. I just meant work."

She wrinkled her nose, "I know."

"MacGregor's lab Angion has exclusive use of a special lab test called SAGA, whose details are super, super secret. With it he can circumvent months, even years, of conventional laboratory testing."

"The test's that good?"

"The test's that good. They say it's one hundred percent right for spotting winners, though it misses some on the side. MacGregor's picks have been sucked up by Wall Street, delivering big pay-offs."

"Steve, you like the idea of working for MacGregor? He sounds more like a businessman than a scientist."

Steve rolled close next to her.

"Morgan, I'll work in the lab and learn all I can. Doctors are needed to make the science work for people. MacGregor's research team is one of the world's best – and thanks to SAGA, very rich. And Phillips suggested I do it, so it's the right thing even from the hospital's point of view. Should be a guaranteed winner."

Morgan's eyes grew serious. "But Steve, science is about the unknown. There can be no guarantees. You never know what you might learn."

Steve snuggled against her, "Yes, sweetheart. You're absolutely right."

3.

TUESDAY, DECEMBER 14

Late the next morning Steve was walking up the icy steps of the Angion laboratory.

The former textile factory embodied the utilitarian ugliness of the worst of the 1930s' Depression-era architecture, its walls solid brick with but a handful of windows, less designed for shelter than for isolation of the inmates from the outside world.

He surveyed the neighborhood. The other buildings were similar, old red brick stained with soot and weathered paint, anonymous except for one just across the street that sported a sign, "Winston Vision Systems." Steve laughed silently, admiring its spunk. Legible from a hundred yards away, it announced itself boldly to all passersby, even though the street was utterly desolate, the only motion a plastic bag flopping down the road like a crumpled, urban tumbleweed. But other than its sign, the Winston building gave no hint to its contents.

Steve pressed on the cold steel handle. A buzz sounded, the lock clicked, and the thick metal door swung open.

With two steps across Angion's doorstep he was inside a world radically different from the outside brick façade. He was standing in a small area lined with glass walls and glass ceiling, the entire space encompassed inside a much larger room. All was still. A video camera with a red blinking light was pointed directly at him. Another buzzer sounded, and a glass door slid open, admitting him to the surrounding space.

This larger antechamber was antiseptic white, lit by recessed bulbs overhead. He scanned down the long directory on the far wall until he found the entry:

George MacGregor, Ph.D., Director
Laboratory 105, first floor

Wide enough for four people to walk abreast, the hallway invited him into the building's depths. His footsteps echoed in the silence. Recessed lights cast occasional spots of light. After about fifty yards, he came to two opposing doors to his left and right, labeled "101" and "102." Fifty more yards and the hallway ended with a large unmarked door and two smaller side corridors angling off to the left and right. He paused, looked around the silent hallways, and slid the door open.

He was looking into an immense hexagonal room, at its center a raised dais, suggesting a theater-in-the-round with a large central stage. Around its circumference giant potted palms towered more than fifty feet high, yet the space continued upwards much further, ringed by five concentric balconies. High above was a huge skylight: triangular panels arranged into the spokes of a giant twelve-sided pinwheel, bright afternoon sunshine pouring through the windows casting sharp lines of shadow and golden light across the green palms, white walls, and recessed balconies.

It was beautiful. Yet the complete absence of people was eerie – the space seemed like such a natural gathering spot, but not a single soul was here.

The door through which he had entered was labeled, "101, 102, Exit." He strolled counter-clockwise around the room, passing "103, 104, Library," then reaching "105, 106, Helipad." Opening that door revealed a dim gray corridor. He turned back to take in a last glimpse of sunshine and then proceeded away from the light. Fifty yards later he reached Room 105, but its door was locked.

He knocked, and a prim secretary with thick glasses answered.

"Good afternoon, Dr. August, we've been expecting you." She smiled sweetly, moved back to a spotless desk, and pushed a button. "Professor, Dr. August has arrived."

Within seconds the inside door opened, revealing a short but corpulent man standing about the height of Steve's shoulder, soft folds of pink flesh spilling over his neck collar. His beefy hands swallowed August's palm in an enthusiastic shake.

"Come on in, mate, come on in. Been looking forward to the visit!" he exclaimed in a thick Australian accent.

As Steve entered the office, his first impression – like that in the atrium – was of wide-open space. Scattered across the vast room were several pieces of black leather furniture along with chrome and glass tables and cabinets and computer monitors, and at the far end a giant black marble desk. On the desk was the room's one spot of color: a dazzlingly bright, golden globe.

Moving closer, with a shock Steve realized that it was not a globe but a perfectly shaped form of the human brain resting on the pointed tip of a small hexagonal base. But even as he stared at the form, it shimmered, almost translucent, for a moment light reflecting off its brilliant golden surface, but then off its very core.

"Magnificent, isn't it?" asked MacGregor, settling his girth in his chair, feet propped up, waving at the brain. "Have a look-see. Of all people, a neurosurgeon should appreciate this."

As he looked closer, Steve realized that what had appeared a solid matte was in actuality a collection of thousands of tiny fibers, emanating from the base of the structure as four larger vessels that quickly branched, divided, and segmented into smaller and smaller threads until they formed the thinnest of spider webs at the surface. The webs seemed to end in thin air, yet there shimmered before Steve the intact human brain, no edge or line defined, the entire structure without substance but perfect in form. It was beautiful.

It's as if a surgeon perfectly dissected out the tissue, but left all the vessels – Shakespeare's "Merchant of Venice" taken to its impossible completion. The pound of flesh has been removed, leaving only the blood.

Steve shook his head, realizing he had been staring at the statuette and ignoring his host. "Sorry, Professor. I'm a bit awestruck."

"Don't worry, Steve, most people react that way."

For a moment Steve thought MacGregor was referring to himself, not the brain.

MacGregor gestured at an armchair, and then back at the figurine. "So, what do you think?"

Steve sat down.

"Incredible! It's perfect. Is it … is it real?"

"Aye, real as you and me, laddie. Remains of a donor human. We make 'em in the lab."

He chuckled at Steve's look. "Here at Angion we study blood vessels. But to study deviations – whether hypertension, tumor growth, Alzheimer's or any other disease – we have to understand that which is normal. So, one of our polymer chemists designed a plastic microsphere complexed with a gold alloy. When injected into the aorta the spheres flow through the branching vessels till they reach the capillaries, but they cannot pass through, and then they polymerize as they cool. You end up with a gold fiber thinner than the eye can see – strong, yet very delicate, best modeling material in the world. We then use optical scanners to input the entire structure into a computer. With more than fifty brains in our database from young, healthy donors – like yourself – we have the world's most accurate, complete three-dimensional digital atlas of normal human brain arterial vascular anatomy."

"But vascular models and atlases already exist," said Steve. "What's gained with this level of detail?"

"Simple, laddie. Once you know what's normal, then you know what's not. With our maps we can categorize any person's brain vasculature. Some day we will be regularly screening people's brains throughout their lifetimes. Ultimately, ours will be the gold standard – so to speak."

He chuckled. "Meanwhile, mate, what counts is everyone *believes* ours is best, because if that's what they think, then that's what they'll buy!"

Steve had imagined the lab would be like the ones he had known in college, led by professors who dressed in shabby patched jackets and smoked pipes in oak-paneled studies. But MacGregor, in a tailored grey Italian suit that draped elegantly off his heavy frame, was different.

Obviously.

Steve tried to laugh. "Professor, I thought science was about discovering the truth. 'You shall know the truth, and the truth shall set you free.' That sort of thing. Freedom, not power."

MacGregor's smile vanished. His tone turned flat. "There's no difference between freedom and power. Power is the freedom to do what you want."

Steve shrugged, "You also might call them opposites. Power is the capacity to bend others to one's own will, while freedom is the capacity to act independently. One man's power equals another man's slavery."

"That's politics – not relevant for science."

"But wasn't that the point of the Enlightenment?" asked Steve, striving to be pleasant, but not wanting to give up.

This seems so important!

He continued, "I think knowledge doesn't derive from divine edict or imperial decree, not from the imposition of our wills upon others or upon reality. Knowledge requires freedom – to test ideas, question assumptions, explore alternatives. Isn't that what research is all about?"

MacGregor stood up, his face folding back into a series of upturned curves. "Blimey, Steve, of course you're right – to a point. Phillips cautioned me you were a philosopher. *Wonderful* cocktail chatter, I'm sure. But the Enlightenment is … so … seventeenth century."

Smiling broadly, he wound around the desk, "Welcome to the twenty-first."

His hand on Steve's shoulder, he steered him towards the door.

"Come with me, mate. I'll show you around the place."

4.

WEDNESDAY, DECEMBER 15

Early the next morning Steve drove Morgan to work before heading to the hospital. Her firm's principal office was in Manhattan, but recently she had been assigned a case at its Boston branch. Steve guessed this was not entirely coincidental, as the senior partners liked her – smart, industrious, attractive, good family – and they had met Steve at office parties and seemed to like him, too.

He parked his old Corolla in front of the dark skyscraper and ran around to Morgan's door. In front of them a black Lincoln Town Car with tinted windows had stopped at the curb, its chauffeur standing at attention.

From the limo's passenger door emerged long tanned legs of a thirty-something woman. Both Steve and Morgan noticed the elegant figure in her tailored jacket and tight skirt as she took the driver's hand and stepped onto the sidewalk.

Steve looked at his rust-encrusted car, then back at the shiny Lincoln. "Guess we could use a spot of paint."

Morgan put her arms around his neck and kissed him thoroughly. "Mmm, but I've got a much nicer driver. Good luck in the OR, sweetie! Save some energy for tonight, OK?"

She kissed him again, laughed, and then ran to the entrance of the building.

As she stepped out of the limo, Dida noticed the handsome young man and the pretty young woman kissing, oblivious of traffic, pedestrians, and surrounding office windows. The man looked like an athlete, shirt and slacks hanging off a lean, angular frame topped with a shock of unruly blond hair. The woman wore pumps and a dark professional suit, discretely hinting at a svelte form, raven-black hair cascading onto her shoulders. A strange emotion touched Dida as she watched them embrace, a feeling she seldom experienced. It took her a moment to recognize its stale taste in her mouth …

Envy.

I bet he's great in bed.

She watched him move around the Toyota and fold his body behind the steering wheel. Her eyes narrowed.

Oh, yes, I bet he'd be fun.

She timed her entry so the young woman had to wait at the revolving door, and she kept the spin slow – just so the girl's day might be brushed with at least a tincture of irritation. Once inside, as they joined a small group waiting for the elevators, Dida noted the girl's eyes were sparkling not quite so brightly, to which Dida's lips turned upwards.

It's the little things in life.

The Boston branch of Edwards, McAvoy, and Garfield, unofficially "Eddie Mac" amongst the firm's younger members, occupied floors 22 through 24 – enough space to accommodate its 200 or so attorneys in reasonable comfort. With some satisfaction Dida watched the pretty young thing get off at the 22nd, where the associates worked.

Associate, clerk, or secretary – she's not important.

She re-focused, putting the girl out of her mind, as she continued to the 24th floor, home to Eddie Mac's top echelon.

When she entered the boardroom, Dida ignored the Oriental rugs, antique lamps, and the men in midnight blue suits sitting at the teak conference table. Instead, she walked to the end of the table, bent down to the outstretched hand, and kissed the proffered jade ring on its old withered finger. He enjoyed such rituals.

"*Bongiorno*, beloved uncle."

Dida straightened, noticing that the suits, to a man, had been focused on the slit of her skirt.

She sat down at his right hand, giving him a sly wink.

"It's a shame, Don Calibri, that men are such pigs."

And the suits blushed – to her further satisfaction.

Antonio Calibri licked his thin lips and grinned at his niece, exposing two rows of tobacco-stained teeth. Withered skin stretched across high cheekbones and bare skull. Deep-set eyes, yellowed from decades of martinis and cigars, flared intently at her.

She smiled back at him.

He blinked slowly, his eyelids without lashes – a permanent reminder of a 1962 car bomb in Palermo – and then he hissed at the suits, "Gentlemen, as always, my niece, she has no manners. But, of course, she is right – all men are pigs. And I am Chief among them all."

He cackled at his own joke, and the suits smiled in response, seemingly relieved.

The eldest one, his silver gray hair pulled back in a ponytail, nodded towards the old man, "Don Calibri, you are an inspiration." He inclined his head towards Dida. "Ms. Medicia, lovely to see you, as always."

Dida smiled prettily back at him. "You must be confusing me with someone else, Mr. Edwards."

Calibri exposed his teeth again, "I'm sure you're right, my sweet – but let us focus on other matters."

She always enjoyed her uncle. The Sicilian countryside of his youth colored his speech even now, though evoking an image not so much of an olive tree warmed under bright Mediterranean sunshine as of a hot, hungry lizard lurking under a rock. His decades as a successful corporate financier had only reinforced this persona.

"What of MacGregor, my dear? Is he going to sign?"

His expressionless face looked out over the suits – eyelids closing and opening, opening and closing.

Dida nodded, "He smells money. And, as you know, he's developed a very, shall we say, personal, even intimate interest in … exploring … the many aspects of his relationship with us. Yes, he will sign."

"*Molto bene*, Dida. It is clear that whatever you do, you do it very, very well."

"Thank you, *Zio*. I am told I exceed expectations."

Calibri touched his tongue to his upper lip, about to speak, but just then the intercom sounded, and his smile vanished.

"He is downstairs. Truly, Dida, have you prepared him for this?"

Her lips again turned up. "Entirely. He knows the extraordinary success of your other top clients. And I've told him you believe that Angion is based on an idea so important, and that he runs it so very well, that it will eclipse all our prior projects. His will be number one! Of course he likes that. And of course I have suggested to him, since he is the very best, that he should negotiate to keep majority control – under the provisions of your contract, of course."

"So he trusts you?"

"A man will always believe he's the best, as long as you tell him when he's naked."

"Indeed, my dear, you are *bellisima*."

Calibri turned to the suits, his eyes luminous yellow. "Gentlemen, the contract?"

"As discussed, Don Calibri. It does meet MacGregor's stipulations."

Edwards handed him a black binder. Calibri leafed through the pages.

"Let's see," said Calibri, the words slipping from between his tongue and teeth. "Let's ssseeeee. ... Ah, here we are ...

"'Antonio Calibri or his designee will be named to the Board of Directors ... The Executive Committee will be expanded to include a permanent position for Antonio Calibri or his designee ...'

"And ... *si, molto importante* ...

"'All decisions regarding the employment and termination of senior management shall be made with the expressed, written approval of Antonio Calibri or his designee, acting on behalf of the Calibri Fund.'"

Calibri looked at Dida. "Perhaps he thought I meant you."

"Perhaps," she purred.

Calibri looked up at the suits. "He will be here in a moment." His voice deepened, "Mr. Edwards – with this, we will have him?"

Edwards leaned forward. "Yes, Don Calibri. As always. The contract promises privileged intelligence derived from your networks within the international biotech community. Of course, just like your other conquests, over time he will grow reliant on these information sources. So, on paper he will own a majority of Angion, but in truth he will have no real control, neither in terms of legal management, nor in terms of daily decision-making. His wealth will be yours to grant or destroy. Our usual trap."

Nodding, Don Calibri touched his tongue to his upper lip.

There was a rap on the door. With the agility of a man half-a-century younger Calibri was out of his chair and across the room.

Calm and erect, baring all of his brown-stained teeth, he ushered in George MacGregor. "Professor, professor," he hissed, "We are honored. Let me present the founding partner of Edwards, McAvoy, and Garfield – Tom Edwards."

MacGregor shook Edwards's hand and smiled at Dida as he sat down, surveying the suits complacently.

"An impressive array of hired guns, Mr. Calibri, but hardly necessary at this juncture. I've reviewed the contract, and it is acceptable."

Calibri gave a loud sigh of relief. "Professor, I was concerned you might have residual concerns."

"No, no, not at all," said MacGregor. "Your lovely niece and I have discussed the material in great detail. I'm very comfortable with the mutual benefits. To be crass – it will make me and you very rich."

Calibri's tongue flicked out, moistening his thin reptilian lips. "I like crass, Professor. It makes me feel honest."

MacGregor laughed, though he seemed a bit nervous despite his bravado, "Right-o. Say, Tony, assuming Angion is successful, what is your personal long-term plan?"

Calibri showed no hesitation. "Once Angion is fully established, I will retire from the Board and name another designee for the Fund. Maybe that will be Dida, to exercise continuing control of the company, carrying on our family traditions. And then we will name another CEO."

MacGregor's eyebrows shot up. "Excuse me, but that's not the contract? Dida's management style is valuable. I don't want to be switching midstream, and I want to be able to work with whoever ..."

His voice trailed off as Calibri's gaze focused upon him.

"The Calibri Fund, either through myself or another designee," said Calibri, "will have veto control over senior staffing decisions, Professor. You know that."

"Well, aye. But I and the Board should have *some* say, particularly regarding its CEO – subject to the Fund's review, of course."

Calibri's eyes closed halfway, his voice softening into butter, "But, Professor, of course you're correct. Your Board will have every discretion. We never dictate, only suggest. Of course, if the Board cannot name a

CEO who passes our muster, then the Calibri Fund would be free to *withdraw* its support. But majority ownership would remain yours – unless, of course, you chose to sell your stock at some point, *for some reason.*"

MacGregor stared at the thick contract. Dida thought his eyes seemed slightly glazed, though just seconds earlier they had shone with enthusiasm.

Better step in!

She leaned over, letting her cleavage cast a shadow above the neckline of her blouse, and gave him a direct look, "George, you know we all want what's best for your … firm." Her voice lowered in timbre. She said softly, "You know that I'll do *anything* to make this a success. Angion will be very, very *big* indeed."

The suits were quiet, like fishermen watching a fat bass confronting a wriggling worm, its fishhook nearly hidden, the only sound Calibri's sibilant hiss as he exhaled, then inhaled, inhaled then exhaled. Dida kept her upturned eyes on MacGregor, her lips parted – in anticipation, in hunger, in triumph.

The moment passed.

Nodding, MacGregor picked up the pen. "Of course I'll sign. It's the deal of a lifetime."

And she let her lips smile, ever so slightly. *Oh how right you are!*

5.

TUESDAY, JANUARY 4

Steve arrived at the appointed time on his first day – nine o'clock – only to find the meeting already in progress.

Later he learned about the others in the group. Sanjay Jain was a graduate student finishing his second Ph.D., his first in statistics, this one in biochemistry. Alison Harris was a post-doc expert in mouse genetics. Mai Sachamachi had joined the lab at the ripe age of twenty-three after finishing a doctorate in brain tumor physiology from Tokyo University. The group's leader, Pieter Igoranovich, had been on the pharmacology faculty at Brown, but then had realized he could "do better" and had gone back to Moscow, started a drug company, and four years later sold it for more than ten million dollars. Upon meeting Pieter, MacGregor had convinced him to come to Boston to head product development at Angion. The sixth was George MacGregor.

The table was at the center of a hexagonal room, its dimensions like those of the giant atrium Steve had seen on his first visit to Angion, although here the ceiling was modestly only fifteen feet high. Six counters littered with lab equipment stretched out from the central area to the back walls, like spokes on a wheel, along which sat a score of young women and men performing experiments. But the attention of the other five at the table was focused inwards on the papers strewn in front of MacGregor, who was stabbing a finger at a colorful graph.

"Pieter – bloody exciting! Angiotox works just as expected. Here's clear evidence. Just a few more weeks, and then … show time!"

He turned back to the group. "Thoughts?"

Alison responded cautiously, "Tell him, Mai."

"The numbers still show variability," said Mai. "The average values look like there is a benefit, but the variances wash this out." Mai laid several glossies on the table. "These are photos of five different mice treated with Angiotox. Here are the brain blood vessels branching into capillaries, changing as they grow into tumor tissue. And here are five control mice without Angiotox."

MacGregor studied the pictures. "With the drug treatment, in some there is little change from the controls, while in others the difference is dramatic. A mystery. Hmm … Alison, you've looked at this. What do you think?"

She shrugged. "With more numbers the variances will tighten up."

MacGregor nodded. "Exactly. Here we have an exciting new demonstration that Angiotox will cure brain cancer, and for this I congratulate all of you. Soon we'll be celebrating, drinking champagne on a yacht in Boston Harbor! But meanwhile we need more data to reduce these variances."

MacGregor turned to August. "Steve, what do you think? It's very important work, but also very simple. The experiment's already designed, and we already know the expected outcome. Yet, if you're successful, your name will be tied to Angiotox's development into a clinical wonder drug." He laughed. "And then you become a world-famous professor! Fame and fortune await. So?"

Steve was taken aback but tried not to show it. "Sure. Slam dunk."

MacGregor spluttered enthusiastically, "Wonderful!" His gaze swept the table. "Anything else?"

Alison spoke up, "Chief, you think it's a good idea handing this project to a neophyte? No offense, August, but a lot's riding on this."

Pieter interceded, "Steve comes with strong recommendation." He glanced at MacGregor, who inclined his head. "The work must be proven. Dr. August has every interest that this is great success. This is good decision. *Da!*"

Alison's blue eyes flashed. "Sure. Whatever."

MacGregor grinned wide. "I thought this would work out just fine. Alison, why don't you show Steve around the lab? In fact, you're in charge of him. Make sure he puts out!"

MacGregor laughed. "Got that doc? She's your boss."

He turned back to Pieter. "If we're otherwise set, please join me in my office. Great work, everyone. Keep it up!"

He heaved himself out of the chair, Pieter in tow.

~

For a moment the table was still.

Alison looked over at Steve. "Well, August, welcome to the circus. Ever been in a lab before?"

"In medical school I worked two years on a project in brain pharmacology. But this seems a bit different – more results oriented."

"OK. Like I said, welcome to the Big Top. Mai, Sanjay, why don't you get back to work? I'll show Steve the ropes."

Alison stood up. "Come on, I'll introduce you to the techs. They're the *best*."

"What exactly will I be doing?"

"You heard the man. We already have data on about eighty mice – half treated with Angiotox, and the other half controls. All you have to do is repeat the experiment till we have enough numbers so the statistics are airtight. Don't worry. I'll be with you every step of the way."

"Thanks, Alison. This should be an exciting project."

"Yes, *very* exciting! You may be surprised."

As they walked along a long row of laboratory countertop littered with glassware, solutions, and petri dishes, cabinets stocked with pipettes, beakers, test tubes, and electronics, Alison introduced Steve to each lab tech. For the most part, however, they stayed focused on their tasks, muttering simply "Hello" or "Greetings" before returning to their labors. They neared the end of the row.

"This is Shiu-Wei Chen," said Alison. "She will be your assistant."

Shiu-Wei looked up from suturing the leg of a small, furry white mouse. "Hello, Dr. August. I know I work with you. We make many mice."

She turned back to the anesthetized animal, her hands fluttering over the tiny mouse with forceps and suture needle, as delicate as a fairy spinning gossamer spider webs across the leaves of an oak tree.

Alison and Steve moved on.

"Not much time for small talk," Alison explained, as they reached the end of the aisle. Here the countertop and sink were devoid of equipment.

"This is your space," she said.

"Why are the techs so quiet?" Steve asked. "Vow of silence?"

"We're one of the world's top laboratories in angiogenesis. Maybe you think science thrives on the free exchange of ideas – but ours is a highly competitive environment. Within these walls are trade secrets, special techniques, unique compounds, all of which are ours and ours alone. Other commercial labs, drug companies, even university researchers, would love to steal the methods we've painstakingly developed. But we won't let them. Secrecy rules."

"So the techs don't talk," he said.

"No one does. When you were hired you signed several papers, including a confidentiality agreement. Outside these walls you speak with no one about what you see and do in here: *no one* – not your lover, or boyfriend, or pet cat, or inner child, or whoever. No one! And inside the lab, all conversations are on an exclusively need-to-know basis. It's all monitored."

She gestured at the ceiling. "You noticed the security camera when you entered? They're everywhere. No privacy here. The techs do exactly what they're told, nothing else; work hard; ask no questions. More paranoia equals better security."

Steve looked around again: no cameras that he could see.

"We think they're in the smoke detectors," Alison whispered. She laughed, slightly nervous: "Kind of makes sense, don't you think? Smoke detectors ... you know." She leaned forward, her eyes glistening. "Nothing official, you understand. You ever see anything like this?"

Steve shook his head. "No. Never." But he couldn't help thinking of the ubiquitous smoke detectors at All Saints Memorial.

Alison shrugged. "Probably just a story made up to scare stupid lab techs into behaving themselves." Her face turned serious. "More to the point, you are now my responsibility, and as far as I'm concerned, you know nothing. You will learn these assays immediately, and you will complete the experiments quickly. We know what the results should be, so generating the needed data will be the measure of your competence."

Steve nodded slowly.

"Angiotox," Alison declared, "is the most potent treatment for brain cancer known to man. Remember that, Steve. That's a fact."

"Sure, no problem."

"Any issues, you come to me. Pieter's in charge, but he works with George on the big-picture. In terms of the nitty-gritty, I'm your man. Got it?"

Steve nodded again.

"To get you going," she continued, "you'll need more background. Here's a file for you to read on Angiotox, some of it's published, but some of it's *highly* confidential." She handed him a sheaf of papers. "The published papers you may take home, but everything stamped 'Confidential' stays here."

"Keep them here? Where?"

"When you're finished for the day, not even a scrap remains. All materials, papers, random notes, must be either locked in your safe or destroyed. Several paper shredders around."

She pointed to a small black steel cabinet mounted below the countertop. "That's your safe. Key in your combo, and it only opens when you key it in again. Fire-proof, bullet-proof, steel-framed, the building could crash down, and the safe would remain."

A bullet-proof safe? Totally paranoid!

"You've got your reading assignment," she continued. "Tomorrow I'll set you up with training sessions to learn the assays. Any problems, you come to me. Don't forget: anything confidential goes in the safe. And, from now on, *everything* is confidential."

Steve nearly smiled. "Okay. Loose lips sink ships."

But Alison remained stern. "One more thing. The lab's closed all of Sunday, as of midnight Saturday, and re-opens Monday at four in the morning. Security and maintenance go over the entire lab, so here's a hot tip. Make *sure* your work area is spic-and-span when you leave Saturdays. No loose papers, no random notes, no extra chemicals – nothing! Security breaches are *big* trouble. By Saturday at midnight you must be out of the building, or else you'll be fired. No questions asked. Fired."

Steve wanted to look upwards for support, but feared making eye contact with a smoke detector. Instead, he muttered, "You bet, Alison. Great project."

"Welcome aboard."

6.

SATURDAY, MARCH 26

Three months later, hunched over a microscope at his lab desk, Steve had reached four conclusions.

He tallied them as he carefully opened a mouse skull. First, he liked doing surgery on living people more than on dead animals. Second, surprisingly, laboratory science demanded a level of surgical skill that rivaled his most challenging OR cases: mouse blood vessels were tiny indeed! Third, you did not *have* to be smart to do bench research; more important was a willingness to work hard for months with no prospect of success, in the hope of a lucky break.

These three conclusions were not all that controversial. Almost everyone in biomedical science would agree with them. However, the fourth no one else would have agreed with – so he kept it quiet.

As far as Steve could tell, Angiotox did not work.

Alison had told him when he started, "Pieter and I have reviewed the numbers. We need another two hundred-twenty mice within the next three months to cut the variances, so you'll need to average more than twenty mice a week. That'll give you enough time to complete the analysis at the end."

So Steve had put in the hours. By March he was coming in at six and leaving around ten, Monday through Saturday. No matter: even with Shiu Wei's help every week he fell further and further behind, producing only fifteen or eighteen mice instead of the necessary twenty.

But more importantly, the data's variances were not improving. The Monday lab meetings had become dreaded events, at which MacGregor expressed worsening dismay at the worsening variances and the worsening need for more and more data.

The unending workload, grueling hours, and constant criticism reminded him of the last year on his father's farm. As the silent tumor had blossomed ever larger in the old man's head, he had grown weaker, leaning on the ten-year-old boy as they walked into the barn to milk the two dozen cows in the pre-dawn darkness, muttering quiet, sick criticisms, of Steve, of the cattle, and of the world in general: "You'll 'mount to nuttin', boy, if you don't work harder. Life ain't no easy walk, never no easy walk."

And it hadn't been for the old man, up until the day he collapsed hammering a fence, and the ambulance took him to the hospital, and he died.

As the weeks crawled on, Steve's frustration mounted. Although he had tried to believe that what he had been told was true, that Angiotox was the universal cure for brain tumors, and therefore that any shortcoming in the experimental outcomes was his, in truth he couldn't believe he was at fault.

Not at all.

Meanwhile, Morgan's situation was no comfort. She had returned to Manhattan, her work demanding all her time including weekends, so they had had to make do with bedtime phone calls and the promise of an upcoming Memorial Day weekend at her family's cabin on Lake Winnipesauke.

But tonight would be boy's night out – a rare event, and for that reason so much the sweeter.

∾

They were sitting at a bruised wooden table in a South Boston Irish pub – four neurosurgical residents who'd become friends through common suffering. Joe and Charlie were in their fifth residency years, Scott and Steve a year behind.

"Hey, Steve, any hot babes you working with? Pickings sure are slim at the hospital. They don't call it All Saints for nothing!" laughed Joe.

Slurping his beer, Charlie still managed to sputter, "Joe, you'll chase anything wearing a skirt. You should lower your standards – you might get lucky."

Joe grimaced, "They're low enough. I'm drinking with you, ain't I?"

Steve broke in, "Boys, that sounds like a Brain Drain to me!"

Scott chimed in, "Yessiree, that's a Brain Drain."

Charlie laughed, "What must be ..."

They all lifted their mugs, and chanted in unison:

There once was a surgeon whose brain
Did shrink with each drink he did drain;
Yet he soused and caroused
Till none him would house,
Save the Brain Trust, the world's greatest bane!

Together they delivered the last line with force, and then to the man downed their beers in a collective gasp, slammed the mugs onto the table, and broke out laughing.

A waitress made the mistake of walking by.

Scott called out, "Fair maiden, have mercy on us weary travelers. Our throats are parched; our lips dry. Please bring us more ale, that sweet brew, that nectar of the gods!"

She was in her fifties – leathery skin, hollow cheeks, a glaze of sweat across her forehead. She looked at them without blinking. "Four Guinness?"

"Aye bonny lass. Guinness."

She retreated to the kitchen.

With the female gone, Joe turned to Steve. "Come on, buddy. You can share. Listen, with a babe like Morgan, your motor's all tuned up. How's the lab? I sure could use a mechanic."

"Not much," said Steve, "but there might be an available candidate. Her name's Alison, smart and cute; but she eats nails for breakfast and spits them out during the day. On the other hand, my lab tech, Shiu Wei, is about thirty, married I think, and only talks about dissecting mouse brains – nothing else."

"Slim pickin's," grumbled Joe.

"The lab's not like anything I've ever seen," said Steve. "All info is need-to-know – for your eyes only – burn before reading – that sort of thing. Labbooks, notes, papers – everything gets locked in safes. No one talks with anyone. Feels like I'm at the CIA."

"Sounds exciting," Charlie said drily. "Must be some kick-ass stuff, if it's all so hush-hush."

"That's what they think, or what they want us to think, or what they want us to think that's what they think, or something like that – full of equal parts greed, ambition, and paranoia. Everyone has a clear idea of what my results should look like, even *before* they're in. The whole lab seems designed to ensure the preferred conclusion. Not too sure what happened to the open exchange of ideas, or to research as exploration."

"Steve, your problem is you're a romantic," said Charlie. He was the oldest of the group, having served in the marines for four years before entering residency. "You're hung up on the notion that science is about truth."

"It's about something else?"

"Yeah, it all goes back to Einstein."

Scott broke in, "Einstein! Charlie, give me a break. What d'you know about Einstein?"

"Hold on!" exclaimed Charlie. "Enough that Einstein's theories are based on the idea that all knowledge is a product of observation. That's why it's called 'the theory of relativity.' Our most fundamental science – including the greatest destructive power our world has ever known – comes from the idea that reality is nothing beyond our capacity to perceive reality."

Steve thought for a moment. "Einstein also said, 'God does not play dice.' If our world is only a function of perception, then reality would be nothing more than a roll of the dice – who saw what, when, where … That sounds like playing dice to me."

"Maybe … but if no one knows otherwise, then it doesn't matter what the dice showed," said Charlie. "Maybe your buddy MacGregor is more than just a control-freak." His voice dropped to a conspiratorial whisper. "Maybe he thinks he can control reality by controlling perceptions, our knowledge about that reality. If he has a monopoly on the knowledge, and on the scientific techniques that generate the knowledge, then he has a monopoly on our perceptions, hence on our beliefs, and hence on reality itself."

Steve slurped his beer. "You can't be serious. And even if you were, or even if MacGregor was, that's just crazy. No one can control knowledge."

But Charlie kept a straight face. "Why not? You can, anyone can, at least for a while, since some perceptions are ours no one else can share."

Steve's grin broadened. "There's a word for that: lying. That's where God comes in. OK, so maybe all truth is perceived. But maybe God's the Ultimate Perceiver – the umpire who calls 'em balls or strikes."

Joe broke in, "You guys are cramping my karma. There's only one solution – a fine solution – beer!"

He yelled out, "Brain Drain!"

The four looked at each other, laughed, bleary-eyed, and broke into song:

> *There once was a surgeon whose brain*
> *Did shrink with each drink he did drain …*

$\sim$

Slightly after midnight the four staggered onto the sidewalk, small piles of snow left over from winter still lining the street, their breaths steaming in the cold night air. Together they walked, giggling, happy, drunk on beer and friendship and thoughts of bright futures. Scott and Joe sat down at the bus stop, while Charlie and Steve kept moving towards the T, Boston's proud old subway.

Steve gently punched Charlie's arm.

"Hey, you really think science is only about perception?"

Charlie gave him a serious look. "No, *I* don't think that. But MacGregor might. Maybe you and I think we're good, but our egos are nothing compared to the beasts at the top of the food chain. These guys are sure they hold the keys to truth. I'll bet you George MacGregor answers to *nobody*. He doesn't believe in Jesus, or Jehovah, or Allah, or Buddha … he believes in George. You told me about his $5,000 Italian suits – that gives him away. The guy thinks he's royalty. Steve, be careful. To answer your question, MacGregor's reality is your reality, and that's all that counts for you right now."

They were at the entrance to the T.

Steve replied, "Man, that's so cynical. MacGregor's a world-famous scientist. He must feel accountable."

Charlie spoke slowly, "What you're telling me about the lab makes me think MacGregor's a very brilliant guy. He's figured out the System, and he's controlling a piece of it."

"Holy mother of God, Charlie, you're scaring me. I'm not sure I want to go back to work Monday."

A train pulled into the station. "Gotta go, Steve. Don't worry. Just keep your head down. Do what you're told, and you'll be OK. See ya!"

Charlie stepped onto the train, its doors closing behind him.

Standing on the platform, feeling very alone, Steve pondered the conversation.

No way! That's why institutions like All Saints exist. They screen their people, so they can be trusted. Their reputations are everything to them. If MacGregor's tied to Saints, then he's got to be on the up-and-up. But what makes me think he's not honest – just because he's a control freak? Just because I'm not getting the results he wants? Just because he keeps pushing the lab about money? That's not bad … it's simply practical. After all, he's running a lab that needs money to survive. And in this hyper-competitive environment he has to worry about security.

With a start Steve realized he was not alone. A short way down the platform was an old man with shoulder-length gray hair. His clothes bagged around his thin frame, a black T-shirt folding over frayed olive pants that revealed torn tennis shoes. His misshapen leathery hands were warped with thick outlines of crisscrossed veins. In one hand he held a plastic Filene's bag, and in the other a beaten leather attaché case, as though he were just coming home from shopping after a day at the office.

A train pulled into the station. Steve sat next to the window. He sensed the man settled into a seat behind him, maybe later to sleep the night away hidden under a bench.

How thin the space that separates us, yet how great the distance.

Fifteen minutes later, they arrived at Charles Street. As Steve stood to exit, he looked over at the bum. The grizzled old face looked back with intense blue eyes …

And an electric shock slammed through Steve. In that second he felt naked, exposed, examined. Then, as if searchlights had passed, the penetrating intelligence was looking out the window, and Steve found himself wondering whether there was something wrong with his imagination.

The subway doors were open.

Strangely, he felt he had made a friend, though the two obviously had nothing in common.

"Take it easy," Steve said, as he stepped off the subway car.

The bum grunted.

Back outside, standing on the cold empty platform, Steve watched as the train pulled away with its mysterious occupant.

7.

FRIDAY, APRIL 1

Almost a week later, Morgan was looking over the skyline from the 87th floor of the midtown offices of Edwards, McAvoy, and Garfield. Tall skyscrapers cast long blue-black shadows across the burnt orange sunlight, as though a giant tiger pelt had been draped across Manhattan.

"Hey Morgan, you ready?"

Morgan turned to the blond ticket in a short cocktail dress.

"Laurel, I just can't believe you. Couldn't you show just a little *more* skin? Every guy will be waiting for that button to pop."

Laurel looked down at two tanned mounds, her cream jacket ending strategically at bosom's edge.

"Morgan, you're repressed. These boys love to be *titillated*. And if a fat wallet gets interested, promising Caribbean adventures and diamond necklaces, well hell, then I don't mind a good time."

Her eyes turned wicked. "More fun than your boy-toy."

Morgan tried to smile convincingly. "As you well know, my boy-toy is busy saving the world from brain cancer – so Morgan's alone, pining, with this goddamn romantic Manhattan skyline all to herself."

Laurel grinned, "Honey, all you've got to do is give in to temptation! Tonight Eddie Mac has invited M-and-A boys from three of our investment houses to encourage cross-fertilization. Sweetheart, you know me. I just *love* mergers, especially when they include acquisitions."

"Laurel, you're a tramp."

"Sure, but a successful one." Laurel eyed her friend's skirt. "Morgan, you really have *got* to show more leg. Ankles don't promise enough."

Morgan tried to smile, "You know I'm off the market. But don't worry; I'll watch your back. In my eyes you're still an angel."

"If I'm an angel, then the Pope's Jewish."

Smiling, Morgan grabbed her jacket, and they were out the door. A quick elevator ride took them to the 92nd floor, the law firm's penthouse.

The elevator doors opened onto a giant room with floor-to-ceiling windows revealing the wonders of the Big Apple, the East and Hudson Rivers, Brooklyn, and the wide world beyond. Young men and women filled the room, majestic and beautiful, dressed in suits from Brooks Brothers and Ermengildo Zegna and dresses from Ann Taylor and Armani, as well as older men and (a very few) older women – cunning and powerful, watching the younger with a complex mix of lust, pride, and regret.

"Oh, baby, I smell money," breathed Laurel.

The two descended into the melee of suits and skirts. Within moments a waiter was at Morgan's elbow, presenting a tray. "Champagne?"

Laurel took a glass, "To decadence."

Morgan lifted one in response, but Laurel interrupted, laughing, "Hey, wait a minute … yours is fuller. I refuse to start at a disadvantage!"

Morgan shook her head – "Evil creature, you're incorrigible" – and handed Laurel her flute. They traded, clinked glasses, and sipped the champagne.

Shortly thereafter Laurel disappeared into a group of handsome men who were debating the relative merits of the Mercedes and Jaguar suspension systems. Morgan moved on, drifting from conversation to conversation, a fresh champagne flute magically appearing at her elbow from time to time.

The next two hours went by in a gradually worsening blur. Following the Mercedes-Jaguar debate, Morgan joined some women arguing about diamond settings for wedding rings. This made her uncomfortable, so she quickly left this circle and entered another, this one discussing Americans' lack of sexual prowess versus those of the Far East. She moved to the next circle, which was reviewing wool textures in the latest fashions of designer suits. One discussant's comments were particularly engaging, as he was pointing out the merits of his own dark blue finery in contrast to the shortcomings of his opponent's "less than eloquent" tailoring.

The preceding night Morgan had been reading *The Inferno* at bedtime. Dizzy from champagne, Dante's words from the first Canto came to her unbidden – his introduction to hell:

> *… This beast, at which thou criest still,*
> *Suffereth none to go upon her path,*
> *But hindereth and entangleth till she kill,*
>
> *And hath a nature so perverse in wrath,*
> *Her craving maw never is satiated*
> *But after food the fiercer hunger hath.*

A cold chill ran out to Morgan's fingertips. She felt lonely, and also very light-headed. She looked at the near-empty champagne glass in her hand: her third – enough to give her a light buzz, but …

Not like this.

Maybe I'm catching a cold.

Nearby was a plush red divan. She shuffled towards it, her feet numb, her ankles wobbling in her high heels.

Is this how a faint feels?

Her brain seemed to speed up as her body slowed down.

Please God, don't let me fall down; just let me get to … Just let me sit. OK. Sit.

No one's noticed. Stay cool, Morgan, stay cool … I can do this.

Keep your head up … Focus! Look at that plant. Count the flowers.

Focus, God damn it …

Oh, hello … Wait. This is …? I know him!

No, thank you, I'm fine … Yes, air would be good … Some fresh air … OK …

Morgan, don't fall down.

Please. Oh God.

∼

She found herself on a cold stone bench. Light was streaming from the penthouse windows, soundless views of well-dressed women and men drinking, eating, talking, flirting. Maybe she'd throw up?

She gulped at the cool evening air, trying to make out the figures, but they kept floating before her – blurred, clear, blurred, clear …

"Morgan! I say, are you alright?"

The voice crashed inside her head.

She looked up at the windows – not those people. She looked to the left – a distant couple was necking, lips pressed together. Oh, how she wished …

She looked to her right. Three inches away was an aged face, silver gray hair in a ponytail: Thomas Edwards, Esq., her employer and mentor.

What's he doing here?

As she watched, Edwards licked his lips, but his eyes seemed sympathetic. He draped his jacket across her shoulders.

"Young lady, you gave me quite a scare. You were pale as a ghost. I thought you might faint, or worse. My God, you're so unsteady on your legs …" And he glanced down at the folds of her skirt, " …normally so strong! Too much to drink? Happens to us all occasionally. A touch of excess from time to time …"

He started kneading the back of her neck, rubbery fingers slipping across her skin. "You're looking good now."

A fleck of spittle was forming at the corner of his mouth.

Did he just say that?

Two days before her graduation from Harvard Law School, in her mailbox she had found a hand-written note from Thomas Edwards, Esq., congratulating her, personally welcoming her to the firm. Over the ensuing three years Tom had taken her to lunch periodically at his private Wall Street club. He had grown to know her quite well, including stories about her family, Morgan's father a federal judge, her mother a professor at Yale Medical School, much of her childhood in private boarding schools. He knew her current personal life – including Steve – and her professional aspirations.

She had treasured him as her mentor. Rumor had it that Edwards looked after his own throughout their careers. And his appearance now seemed fortuitous. Yet …

"Thanks, Tom. I'm feeling better."

But in truth she wasn't. There was a taste in her mouth reminiscent of house paint. Nausea and vertigo were playing ping-pong between her ears, while her hands had turned into lumps buried in tapioca. She inched away from him as best she could, but his hand was still touching her neck.

"Great party," she murmured thickly.

Edwards nodded, "Many otherwise respectable people having a very good time." His eyes swept over her face. "Your color's coming back. I truly thought you might be sick. You were leaning on me heavily as we walked out here – not that I minded. I thought the evening air might do you good."

"You're right. I remember nothing from the last few minutes. Whew! I've never fainted in my life."

"Too much to drink, not enough to eat." His voice turned harder – the boss. "Really, Morgan, I hope you don't make a habit of this. Everyone knows I'm mentoring you. How you act reflects on me."

She found herself coming to her senses – with several questions. "Is that why you're here?"

His voice had an edge. "Frankly, yes. I wanted to get you away from inquiring eyes, not to mention groping hands. A young fellow had approached you who did not seem discrete. These M&A boys are hungry, and I'm not referring to their interest in new business." He gestured towards the windows.

Light blazed from the penthouse, unveiling hints of untold stories. Smiling men and women were raising glasses to their lips, their faces, hips, hands, and mouths, all in an unconscious rhythmic dance. A flash of deep cleavage caught her attention.

A tanned chest with long blond hair was leaning against a thin tall man, diamond cufflinks glittering at the edges of a tailored charcoal suit. The suit held Chip Spader, the only child of the founder of Mitchum and Spader, one of the top private investment firms on Wall Street. His father was worth a billion and change.

Laurel, on the other hand, was definitely *not* looking a billion, not even a million. She seemed off-balance on her high heels, ready to topple if given a well-calculated nudge, her cream jacket unbuttoned and her slinky cocktail dress hanging low. Indeed, she had one hand strategically nestled under Spader's lapel, steadying herself as if, should a well-calculating foe nudge her, she might take down the billionaire-to-be in a tangle of designer arms and legs. Her other hand cradled his chin, holding his ear to her lips, guaranteeing optimal position for the secrets in her mouth.

Morgan was unsure whether Laurel was whispering conspiracies or tasting her dessert, but Spader's expression suggested he did not mind, whatever it was.

Indeed, Spader was smiling *very* broadly. In one smooth motion he slipped his arm around Laurel's waist and half-led, half-carried her towards the door as she laughed, her feet slipping on the polished cedar floor. Moments later they were out of sight behind an ornate column.

Edwards cleared his throat. "Laurel looks rather happy about the goings-on, wouldn't you say?"

His hand gave her neck a friendly pat.

Morgan shook her head. "Looks like she doesn't know much at all about what's going on."

"The firm of Spader and Mitchum is a very big client."

She looked over at him.

He can't mean …?

She again shook her head. "We have rules. We came together; so we leave together. Looks like she's even drunker than I was, till you pulled me out here and sobered me up. Truly, thanks for that, Tom …"

She looked directly at his lumpy, hungry face. " …But I've got to go!"

She staggered to her feet and walked back inside with determined steps, though still feeling groggy. Thankfully, she heard no footsteps behind her.

She surveyed the party, but Laurel and Chip were gone. She guessed they were leaving the building. Chip had not looked like he wanted a tour of Eddie Mac's offices.

She almost did not notice the man leaning by the elevator, as still as the adjacent marble carving – two statues surround by the madding, shuffling crowd. And when she did notice him, she did not know him. He was tall and gaunt with close-cropped hair accenting sharp facial features, a thin dark scar across his cheek. The face registered to her gaze only a second before the door closed.

In the elevator she wondered how long it had been since Chip had carried Laurel out the door. A minute? The elevator ticked off the 92 floors to the ground, its door finally opening with a soft "ding."

A security guard sat at the lobby's front desk.

"Joe, you see a couple leave just now, a drunk blonde and a tall fellow in a charcoal suit?"

The old man's face was a study in secrets.

"Just a bit ago, Ms. Najar. South on 5th. They couldn't be walkin' far, not the way Ms. Farthington was."

Morgan felt her face flush. She had hoped he wouldn't recognize Laurel.

"Thanks, Joe."

She flew down the sidewalk past random couples and singles and groups.

There – up ahead! That guy entering the taxi.

He was just closing the door when Morgan reached it and yanked it back open, swinging around to look into the backseat. There was Laurel, her head lolling back against the cushion, eyes half-closed, mouth half-open. Chip's right hand was on the door handle, his left on Laurel's knee – lust, surprise, and hatred simultaneously dancing across his face.

Morgan gave him no heed. "Laurel! Goddamn it, Laurel! Wake up!!"

Laurel's eyelids drooped open.

"Morgan, honey! It's so good. Oh, it's so good," she cooed. And then she giggled, closed her eyes, and put her head on Spader's leg.

Spader kept pulling at the door, but Morgan refused to budge. He looked up at her, his eyes wicked.

"Morgan Najar … I've heard about you, you and your absentee boyfriend. Why don't you take a holiday … you, me, and your honeysuckle friend?"

He squeezed Laurel's leg appreciatively. "I'm sure she'll do for me, and even for you, anything we want. We could have some real fun …"

He raised his hand to Laurel's cheek. Eyes closed, breathing heavily, she opened her mouth and started gently licking each finger in turn, like a dog greeting its master.

"Laurel!!!" screamed Morgan.

But Laurel only giggled and started sucking Chip's thumb. Her left hand moved under her dress, rubbing between her legs.

"Goddamn you, Spader! Laurel, get out!!"

And she let go of the cab door to reach for her.

But then she realized she'd made a mistake.

"Bitch!" Chip wrenched the door closed, slamming it into Morgan's shoulder. She slipped on her heels and landed hard on the street, her knees in the gutter.

∿

Gasping for air, she could only watch as the cab's lights receded into the Manhattan traffic. Then the nausea returned, and this time she couldn't hold back. She retched – one, two, three times.

And then there was quiet.

Breathing hard, she cleaned off as best she could. She wiped her mouth with the back of her hand. One heel was broken, and the dress was torn. Her scraped knee was bleeding.

And likely her friend was being raped in a cab that very minute.

Eventually, struggling against ever-increasing gravity, she looked up. Traffic was streaming by – bright lights, dull metal.

An approaching cab flashed its headlamps. She feebly flapped her hand, nestled against the curb, cradling her knees in her arms. Her head was in an anvil against which some bastard was swinging a hammer.

"Hey lady, you OK?"

He had stepped from the cab. His gray hair was tied back in a pony-tail, just like Edwards, but this man had a round silver peace sign hanging from his neck on a thin leather strap. He was wearing a thin lime-green T-shirt, but the night air seemed not to bother him.

She couldn't inspect his pants, because by now he had picked her up in his arms, and she could only see his shoulder and profile. His leathery brown neck looked old – maybe seventy? – but he was strong, strong enough to carry her and then lower her gently onto the back seat.

"Miss, you've had a long day. I'll take you home. What's the address?"

∿

She woke up when the engine switched off. She felt more than saw him carry her upstairs. Even at the top of the landing he wasn't breathing hard.

"Miss, you'll be OK from here?" he asked in a soft gravel voice.

She steadied herself against the doorframe. She could not make him out in the dark stairwell. Her head was pounding.

"Thanks, I'll be alright. What do I owe you?"

She felt herself bobbing slightly.

In the dark, his face was inscrutable. "Whatcha' owe me?" He scratched his neck, examining the question. "Twelve-fifty."

She fumbled at her purse, handed him cash, and closed the door. She flopped onto the bed without undressing.

In the moments before unconsciousness she realized several things. She did not know how much money she had given the cabbie. She was very worried where Laurel was. She would never again trust Thomas Edwards, Esquire. And she badly, horribly, awfully missed her Steve.

But all these things did not matter – right now all that mattered was sleep. Sleep … to stop the sick feeling in her stomach and the pounding in her head, to take away the shame, and the hurt, and the anger, and the loneliness of the night – complete, total loneliness.

All had betrayed her: Laurel, Edwards, her job, and the whole system that had put her and her friend in harm's way – the system that she had so stupidly trusted.

Never again.

Nothing is safe.

She could trust no one.

She could trust herself, of that she was sure. But no one else.

Maybe not even Steve?

Why did she feel ashamed?

That's not right! It's not my fault.

She needed time to think.

Alone.

She might tell him later. Not now. Later.

Moments before unconsciousness, she remembered a phrase from somewhere …

We're born alone, we live alone, and we die alone.

Was that really true?

And then she slept for a very long time.

8.

SATURDAY, APRIL 2

Sitting at his lab desk Steve too was feeling lonely. It had been a week since he and Morgan had last spoken, though they had traded phone messages several times. This was a result of what they called "The Rule" – their mutual agreement only to call one another at home, to respect each other's time at work. Steve had called Tuesday night, and she had called back Wednesday night, and he had called early Thursday morning – but she had already left for work – and then she had called Thursday night. But each time the one had missed the other. He had left a message last night, and this morning he had called again, but no Morgan.

It was now past five o'clock, and Steve was thinking this was a really stupid rule. Steve picked up the phone.

"Morgan, it's me. Still at the lab. Please call!"

Maybe she had called him at home? He dialed his home number. No messages.

He decided to worry later, but not now. Now he would work.

Hours passed.

~

Steve looked at his watch: *10:34.* He found it bizarre everyone had to be out by midnight Saturdays – with Sundays blocked – thereby cutting into potential research time a full day, more than ten percent of the week. It made no sense.

He turned back to the photos on his desk. He used them to measure the caliber of blood vessels, to count branch points, to calculate the concentration and number of vessels – for each and every mouse. It was slow work. Holding his breath for his phone to ring, he picked up another photograph.

After three more mice he again glanced at his watch: *11:32*. The second-hand swept a steady arc around its dial. The lab was silent. Where was Morgan? His stomach tightened.

Quickly he tidied his desk, wrapped the photos into two bundles, one set completed, one set to be reviewed, and packed them along with lab book and calculator into his safe. The electronic lock beeped when the door closed.

He glanced at the wall clock: *11:35*.

He hefted the phone in his hand, thought about dialing her number, but did not – he had already left so many messages. Then he thought about calling her office, but did not – that would be a breach of the Rule, and anyway it seemed pointless at midnight on a Saturday. Then he thought about throwing the phone against the wall, but did not – though that did promise the most satisfaction of the three options.

"Damn it to hell," he muttered.

He closed his eyes, centered his weight in the chair, and focused attention on his fear and anger. He would calm himself.

There was silence.

Kan, the 29th gua of the *I Ching*, the words of Confucius, drifted into his mind:

Darkness is doubled.
Dangers succeed one after another.
Water flows and fills,
Not accumulating but running.
Pass through dangerous places;
Never lose self-confidence.

Kan was Darkness, the pit, the abyss. Why did he think of this now?

Steve's awareness, his *chi*, drifted into himself, floating over his inner terrain, crossing the mountains, plateaus, valleys, opening himself just as Master Huang had taught him over the years.

He swept down into the dark canyon of his fear – narrow floor and high walls with no sunlight – but as he explored the crevice, its slopes softened, the height lessened, the sky widened, and there was light. Here was hope. He did trust Morgan – this was true. He stepped out on faith: MacGregor was merely eccentric, not psychotic; the lab was reputable, world class.

As the meditation deepened, his pulse slowed: 70, then 60, then 50, 40, 35 … 30 … 28 … 26 … 23 … … 17 … … 12 … … … 8 … … … 5 … … … … His breathing grew imperceptible. His body cooled. His metabolism slowed. The trance deepened.

He was at the bottom of the canyon. Here was a River flowing wide and deep. As he plunged his arms into the warm waters, he felt … love. He wanted the River to wash over Morgan, protecting her.

His contact with external reality had neared zero, but Steve's internal world was growing complex. He was surrounded by rainbows – formless, fluid, flowing. The River rolled across his naked skin, its reds, blues, greens, yellows, purples infinitely blending. He breathed in, and the warmth filled his lungs. It spread inside his chest and belly, extending out to the tips of his fingers and the bottoms of his feet. He felt his body dissolve.

He was *chi*.

The River was swirling. Colors split, merged, split, merged, casting shadows, beautiful, dancing. But there … a break in the rhythm. A rock? Eddies, spirals, turbulence, the colors were spinning in confused circles.

A nexus.

Morgan.

His *chi* was beside her. Inside her?

She was struggling against the rock.

He felt fear, and rage, and hurt, and sadness.

The River pinned him against the rock.

He was so alone …

He looked at the telephone, but he couldn't call.

Nothing was solid. No one was trustworthy.

Nothing.

No one.

We are born, and live, and die alone.

~

Steve recoiled.

No! You're not alone … Must we be apart to be together …? Where are you?

The hero Siegfried had bathed in dragon's blood – just so he felt suspended.

Am I drowning?

Water seemed everywhere.

His heart beat, the rush of blood lazy in his ears. *Whoosh …* then after a time, *whoosh …* and then again, *whoosh …*

But as he listened, between the beats, there were more sounds – voices – voices so soft they were muffled even by his heartbeat.

Morgan?

"This one needs help," said one voice. "He needs boost … Hey big boy, you want good boost?"

"Pieter, you are what Americans call 'PITA' – pain in the ass. Stop talking to mouse and do work."

"And you take slow boat to your stink rat hole. It is stupid our mother Russia not crush your little island. Here, hold mouse."

"Yes, honorable Soviets make humble Japan proud. Poor industry grow big. Toyota great – when make cars like Russia. Sony make no more bad TVs. Mitsubishi with great hope. All hail Russia, holy Mother."

"Die on sushi rot. *Boch!* Hold still. No marks!"

Steve opened his eyes. He found himself at the lab bench, just as he had been when he had entered the trance, except for one difference: the lights were out, other than a faint glow from red, green, and blue electronic lab instruments casting faint shadows of midnight black. His body remained motionless.

His heart beat again.

Whoosh …

"That should be enough, you think, Pieter?"

"*Da.* This mouse ready. Ha! Lucky mouse. Next one …"

Whoosh …!!!

His heart was deafening. He wondered why the noise didn't wake the whole neighborhood. Then he realized – he was alone. But where were they?

He felt his *chi* fold itself, like delicate origami paper, back inside his body.

Whoosh …!! Whoosh …! Whoosh …

His heart was speeding up, its sound receding as his consciousness advanced. He took a breath, the air rushing in his ears. Details cleared in the darkened room: the edge of the desk, the bulk of equipment, the clock on the wall, its digits a soft luminescent green – *1:32.*

"Hold still, goddamn you."

But I am still.

Then he recalled, *Not me – mice! They're talking about mice.*

"Ah, it's coming loose. *Babushka* holds still. *Da … da … da.* We fix this."

Steve was now fully awake, but motionless. He held his breath. He could barely hear the voices, mere whispers in the still air. Every time his heart beat, its sound roared over them. But he could still hear them, and now he knew where the voices were coming from.

His eyes focused on the air vent, a dark patch in the paneled ceiling, fifteen feet overhead near the edge of the wall. Below the vent was the clock: *1:36:42.* Steve noticed how slowly the digits were advancing. He guessed he was still within a suspended state of animation, wherein he moved like a glacier relative to the world's machinery. From the outside, he would seem a statue – but from the inside he was telescoping experience.

He pondered his situation, which presented several problems. For one, he should have left the lab two hours ago. Why had no one kicked him out? And now that he was here, how could he get out without trouble? Curfew was midnight, an absolute deadline that Alison and Pieter and MacGregor all had repeatedly stressed – one that must be respected, on pain of being fired.

And then there was the problem of Morgan. What had his vision meant? Steve was never quite sure whether his dreams during meditations were truly real, or whether they only reflected his mind's integration of subconscious impressions with conscious information. No matter. Over the years he had learned to trust these instincts. He was sure that Morgan was in trouble and that she needed his help.

The voices coming from the air vent posed a third problem. These sounded like Mai and Pieter. What were they doing here, so early on a forbidden Sunday?

9.

SUNDAY, APRIL 3

Motionless as a stone in the dark lab, Steve reflected more carefully about problem number one. Why had no one realized he was here? Surely, as Alison had warned, there were surveillance cameras?

After his father had died, he had lived on his grandmother's farm. He remembered an automatic switch on the floodlight outside her garage, which as a teenager he had been excited to learn used infrared motion sensors, like the "night-vision" goggles of Army commandos. The flood would switch on if heat patterns changed fast enough – if a warm object, like a car or a human body, moved across its field of view.

Maybe this explains why no one knows I'm here? The cameras are off, because I haven't moved?

His eyes glanced at the clock, its seconds flashing super-slow: *1:48:22*. He could just get up and leave as if waking from a nap, but then surely security would stop him, and then likely he would lose his job. He suspected MacGregor would be happy to see him leave.

And there's still problem number three: what are Pieter and Mai doing?

His lab space was at the far end of the long counter. To his left was a tall cell incubator set against the wall. Next to it was a giant industrial freezer, where the lab techs kept chemicals for large-scale experiments.

Very, very slowly, his body moving by infinitesimal degrees, Steve slipped down underneath the lab bench. The lights stayed dark.

Five minutes later he was curled under the bench.

His next goal was the space between incubator and freezer. Inch by inch he moved out from under the counter into full view of the smoke detectors, ever so slowly forwards across the four feet of open space until he had reached the wall.

And the lights stayed dark.

Carefully he twisted around until his back was wedged against the giant incubator and his hands and feet were braced against the freezer. Then, with mind and body focused on this one goal, he moved up the side of the freezer – slowly, slowly, his progress akin to that of a flower opening its petals to the morning sun.

But the lights stayed dark.

About forty minutes later he had reached the top of the freezer. Wrists, forearms, biceps, shoulders, calves, thighs, buttocks, even the soles of his feet, burned like the stones of a hot brick oven.

Yet he continued.

Wedged against the incubator he placed both palms on the top of the freezer and then pushed down, slowly raising his waist to the edge of the freezer top. Slowly, very slowly, he lifted his knees over the surface. Pain was everywhere, a blowtorch running over his whole body, but he kept his breathing slow, deep, silent.

And the lights stayed dark.

He pulled himself into a crouch and then onto his feet, and then extended himself until he was standing erect. For a moment he rested in the black silence.

What was it Confucius had said?

Darkness is doubled.
Dangers succeed one after another.

Water flows and fills,
Not accumulating but running.
Pass through dangerous places;
Never lose self-confidence.

Rely on heart and mind.
The firm are in the central places.
Deeds will be honored.

Going forward, there is success.

The voices from the air vent were louder.

"You little mousie, good fortune smiles. How lucky you are ..."

He raised his hands to the ceiling, every inch a slow eternity of savage agony. His hands pressed against the ceiling panel. It shivered, but then gradually edged upwards.

At this first motion a small plaster chip, loosened at the panel's corner, brushed against his cheek and then, warmed with a drop of his sweat, wafted down to the floor below.

Steve froze, the loosened panel in his upstretched hands, the ceiling inches above his head.

There was a quiet *click* from the smoke detector near the center of the room.

And the lights came on.

As slowly as he had crawled, so quickly he now flew. He shifted the panel, reached inside, and felt a support beam's cool metal. In a single, soundless motion he swung his body into the crawlspace, his weight coming to rest on the trestle. A moment later he had replaced the panel.

His eyes adjusted to the light filtering in from the room below, revealing the airshaft winding back towards the center of the building. Large tubes, wire bundles, and pipes interlaced around the shaft, the nerves and vessels that coursed beneath Angion's skin, feeding the beast, monitoring it, sustaining it, all draped across a skeleton of steel girders.

Exhausted, Steve wrapped himself around the trestle. Would anyone come? What next?

Nestled deep in its subbasement, Angion's security center was a plain room with video monitors and computers on two large tables and an electronic map of the five floors of the Angion building covering its far wall. The map displayed diagrams of the entire complex, each room with glowing green lights marking alarms, monitors, and automatic systems.

"Hey, Bobby!"

Rusty McAffee was pointing at the wall. A light had switched from green to yellow and the outline of a room on the map glowed, "105."

But Bobby Erskin had already turned to the video monitors. Three screens had clicked on, revealing fish-eye views of Room 105. From slightly different angles, none of the monitors showed anything abnormal: no intruder, no loose mouse, not even an exploded beaker.

"You see anything?" asked Rusty, a tall, thin man, red hair sticking out in random wisps from under his cap, a thick orange moustache covering his upper lip.

"Nope. Nothing."

As fat as Rusty was thin, Bobby lumbered over to a computer console and started working on the keyboard. The center screen shifted from a fish-eye to a wide-angle lens. In silence the two men watched the camera pan along the first four successive aisles, but these showed no motion, no unusual object, not even a leaky faucet.

At the fifth, Rusty spoke, "Ain't nuttin' here. Third time this month."

The camera continued its surveillance. Finally, it reached the end of the fifth row, then swung back to the center and ran its review of the sixth.

"Damn. Third time this month," repeated Rusty.

Bobby grunted, "It's your turn. I'll log it."

Rusty stood up, checking the gun in his holster and the keys on his belt. "Doors locked?"

Bobby hit a key. "Yup. Since midnight."

Rusty pulled his cap down on his head. "Waste of time! Crazy, checkin' a locked room with nuttin' there."

Bobby showed no sympathy. "I'll be here." He leaned back in his chair, and it creaked in response to his massive corpus. "Don't shoot yerself."

Steve heard the lock click. There was shuffling, the rattle of metal, a cough. Holding tight to the girder, he leaned down, bringing his eyes close to the ceiling panels.

A uniformed security guard was walking down the aisle, jingling his keys, moving to the conference table in the room's center. Back and forth he walked the room, whistling, trying the locks on random cabinets, tapping on safes at various desks.

Steve watched, motionless. The oblivious guard walked past the tiny plaster chip on the floor.

After traversing all six aisles he moved back to the center table and waved upwards. "Nuttin' here, Bobby."

He stepped to the door. There was a click, and everything went dark. A bolt snapped shut.

~

Still wrapped around the girder in the lab's ceiling, Steve leaned his ear against the airshaft, listening for Pieter and Mai.

There!

Carefully but quickly he shimmied forwards. The airshaft split and joined others across the crawlspace. At each division he paused to listen which direction the voices were strongest.

He progressed, and the voices grew louder. Eventually, relieved, he saw faint light ahead.

At the source of the sounds, holding onto the girder, he let his body drape down to the ceiling panels. Through a gap in the tiles he could see two figures, each at a microscope with small surgical tools, between them a sleeping mouse mounted on a small platform.

"Pieter, you are butcher. Hands more like hoofs, like ox. Fat Russian ox."

"Twisted samurai, just do work. Only one mouse in five – that is good."

"Good work for butcher, Russian butcher. Like Stalin."

"We do better if you nap. Sleep, not work. Make no difference."

"Better sleep than slaughter."

"Japanese whore dog! Work faster!"

"Finished."

Mai lifted the mouse by the tail and waived it at Pieter. "There – five. Mice important. Months to grow; seconds to butcher."

"*Da. Da.* Keep work. We must finish soon."

Mai pulled a cage off the rack. He opened it, deposited the sleeping mouse inside, and then returned it to the stack. He studied the cages for a moment, then selected another, and took out its sleeping occupant.

"This one looks good," he said, picking up a syringe. "Ha ha! Number six."

Steve tried to make out the labels. He could see a cage on which was taped a blue card, the color code for the C3H-mouse, a common breed. Stuck to the left side of the card was a piece of tape, striped yellow and red.

Yellow-red tape – the Angiotox experiment. These were his mice.

10.

SUNDAY, APRIL 3

Steve watched Mai tape the mouse to the microscope's plastic stage. Looking into the binocular eyepiece, Mai nicked the scalp open with forceps and scalpel. Meanwhile, Pieter took out what looked like a tiny drill, placed it in a metal frame, and centered the assembly over the mouse's head. Only occasionally did they interrupt the silence to trade insults.

"Here we go, mousie," said Pieter. He flipped a switch. A high-pitched whine arose, and the drill bored into the skull. Then Pieter hit a button, the whine stopped, and a whirring, humming sound began, lasting about a minute.

Mai kept his eyes at his microscope, muttering to himself. Suddenly, he reached over and threw a switch. The whirring stopped. In an instant he was adjusting controls on the drill.

"It is slipping, Pieter."

"Mai, today you dance with Lenin in hell."

"There, needle now in right spot."

"You certain it is in tumor?"

"Of course. My mice do not die."

"Worm, I will crush you."

No reply. Mai turned back to the machine. The whirring began again.

Time to go – I get the gist.

He looked around. Tubes and wires wound around everywhere like giant spaghetti. He guessed the building's towering central Arena to be behind him – the most likely access to the other floors.

He shimmied along the girder, leaving behind the trace light coming from Mai and Pieter's lab. He maneuvered as quickly as he could across the cables, shafts, and pipes obstructing his path in the darkness. The air was warm, thick with dust, and soon his clothes and body were dripping with sweat.

Shortly he encountered an impenetrable tangle. For several minutes he searched for a gap – to one side, then the other, the cables turning slick from blood and sweat. Finally, his hands found a space. He gauged the opening as best he could: a tight squeeze, but he had no better choice.

He stripped off his jacket, tied it into a ball, and shoved it into the gap. Locking his legs against the spaghetti-wire at the top of the girder, he pushed as hard as he could, inching forwards. Massive cables crushed against his chest, making each breath an effort. For a moment he thought he might be trapped, blind in the blackness, unable to move, slowly to suffocate.

And then he found a breath of room.

The cables ripped at his clothes, and blood trickled from new wounds, but then his arms were free in the space ahead, then his face felt air, and then he could bend his head. His cheek felt the tickle of a breeze. He gasped with relief – the air was no longer packed with dirt. And he could see …

The mass of cable wrapped in a gentle concave spiral, curving more tightly inwards to his left – from whence came light along with a gentle breath of air. To the right it wound outwards, giving off smaller strands that supplied rooms above and below – the nerves and blood vessels of this giant animal.

His jacket stung as he put it back on.

No matter. It'll help stem the blood.

He turned left, crawling towards the light, picking his way along the crisscrossing girders. Ahead was the dark mass of the wall surrounding the Arena, but the light seemed brighter, and the airflow stronger, gently hinting at an outside world.

Within minutes he had found the source. From a ten-foot diameter hole in the ceiling the giant monster cable spilled into the crawlspace and then continued down into a similar hole in the floor, but with a collection of offshoots that joined together in another giant tangle and then spiraled out in the mass of wiring that had been his guide. As he approached, he could see a metal ladder running vertically between the openings in floor and ceiling.

Looking down, he could make out almost nothing, a bottomless pool of black ink. Air wafted up that smelled stale and old, like wet leaves rotting on a forest floor.

Looking up, he could see straight up the shaft. Far, far above was a patch of midnight heaven, luminescent blue in the black surrounding it. The ladder's two steel rails were a slick gray in the soft light, converging like a railroad track at their vertical horizon. He hefted himself onto the thin ladder.

Rung by rung, moving quietly, he passed several crawlspaces like the one he had left behind. He counted as he climbed: *two ... three ... four ... five ...*

His legs and arms were heavy as lead. Occasionally, he looked down, but he could see nothing but the monster cable and the ladder, together disappearing into the pool of black ink. Up above midnight blue softened to gray.

At the top of the ladder he stopped, surprised, mesmerized by a new vision ...

Above him was a giant skylight with its hub centered over the Arena – twelve giant triangular glass panels slanting off to the sides of the huge hexagonal space, each anchored in a large steel crossbeam beyond the Arena's edge. Through the window panels he could see the sky turning a lighter gray, the first hint of dawn coloring small, scattered clouds a faint pink, the start of a beautiful spring day.

He looked at his watch: *5:23.*

Someone keeps these windows very clean – and they're getting out there somehow!

Below was the cavernous space of the Arena. At this hour on a Sunday he had expected it empty, but he was wrong. In surprise he pulled back, and then slowly raised his head over the edge to look again.

Three or four dozen people stood scattered across the Arena's floor and first balcony, all wearing long white lab coats.

Perplexed, Steve watched as they arranged themselves in semicircles facing the Arena's central dais, where stood a solitary figure wearing a blood-red robe. Before the figure was a golden orb on a stand, resembling the golden brain he had seen in MacGregor's office.

And then another surprise: from the entire assembly came a low-pitched note, a single "ooommm," that crescendoed, held steady, fell, then rose again in the morning stillness. As the sound's intensity increased, the sun's first rays dripped over the edge of the skylight, splashing a pink tint along the top of the wall.

The chanting grew louder, and the figure standing before the orb raised its arms, as though to take flight. "OOOOMMMMM …"

A motor's whir brought him back to earth. At the center of the glass panes a small mirror mounted on motorized hinges flipped into position.

The sound was deafening. "OOOOOOOMMMMMMM!!!!"

A metal plate rotated back from the mirror, and a split second later the dawn was reflected down onto the golden orb below, which splintered the rose light back in all directions, bathing the entire Arena in hues of yellow, red, pink, and burnt orange.

Instantly, the crowd was silent.

Time to go!

He scaled the ladder. At the top was a door, the old-fashioned kind with a doorknob – no sign of a wire or monitor.

That's no guarantee.

The door opened, he stepped through, and it shut with a soft "click."

He was outside.

In the basement security center, a light on the wall marked, "Rooftop Access" flickered from green to red, and then switched to yellow. The room, however, was empty, as Bobby and Rusty were outside, walking towards the employee lounge.

"Whole thing's crazy, isn't it?" Bobby mumbled, moving down the hallway. "Three hours, every Sunday morning, he takes us out of the Center and puts us under a camera. What for? It's crazy."

"Pretty clear he wants to keep tabs on us," said Rusty. "I bet they're doing somethin' in the Arena. And I say we don't wanna know what."

"Herbie says a guy who stayed in the Center on Sunday mornin' got fired next day. Nobody knows where he went. They say he's dead."

"Yeah, heard that, too."

In silence they walked the rest of the way. Rusty sat at the linoleum table, while Bobby picked a candy bar from the vending machine.

Rusty pointed to the camera on the wall, its red light flashing. "Like we don't know it's there."

Bobby grinned, exposing spots of *Three Musketeers* between his teeth. "I get a kick watching us in playback."

"Yeah, you're a hoot."

After fifteen minutes, unobserved, the amber light on the control panel re-set to green, its automatic response to an electronic spike in the system. Like hundreds of other "low priority" detectors, this switch required no further intervention. The event generated a one-line entry on the night's log.

The hexagonal skylight was in the middle of the roof. Other than the small hutch from which Steve had emerged, there was only one other rooftop structure: a small, squat, glass-paneled building next to a large red square with painted stripes, a helicopter pad.

He scanned the perimeter. Near the southeast corner a curl of brown metal looped onto the rooftop – a gesture to the city's decades-old fire code.

Figuring any cameras most likely would be focused towards the helipad, Steve ran back for the corner, away from the pad and observation room, and rolled flat onto the black asphalt next to the roof's edge.

He glanced over, and grimaced: at least sixty yards straight down.

Now or never!

He swung onto the fire escape's top rung. Rusted metal flaked onto his hands, but the rungs seemed firm. He descended quickly, not pausing too long on any one step.

Soon the roof's edge was a dark line against the brightening blue sky. Oozing blood made his grip slippery on the old metal. He felt like an exposed insect crawling down the blank red brick wall.

Only when he reached the bottom rung did he realize the ladder ended fifteen feet above the ground, but with an extension clipped against the rungs. Exhausted, he considered dropping the extension, but then realized his only hope of remaining undiscovered lay in *not* extending the fire escape.

I won't be able to put it back.

Hanging by his arms, Steve lowered himself to the end of the ladder, and then let go.

It was more of a drop than he had thought. His left knee twisted, knife-like pain digging under the kneecap. No matter. He was outside Angion.

~

The early-morning street was quiet, interrupted only by the far-away rumble of an occasional car on Massachusetts Avenue. Steve looked around– no one – then stood up and ran as best he could. Up the access road, down the side street, at the next building a quick right turn, and he was out of eyeshot of the Angion Corporation.

The dawning sun cast shadows across the pavement. He slowed to a hobble, the injured knee burning hot. His neurosurgeon's hands were caked with grime, rust, and blood. His clothes were layered with the grime from Angion's innards, shredded during his crawl. Had any of his friends seen him, none would have recognized Steve August.

Nevertheless, he smiled when he reached the T-stop. He had reached civilization. Here was a Starbucks opening its doors. Cars drove by. A kiosk displayed stacks of virgin newspapers – freshly folded Sunday editions of the *Boston Globe* and *New York Times*. The world had not stopped. Normal people were leading normal lives, doing normal things like buying coffee and reading newspapers and worrying about their kids and going to church and sleeping late and making love and walking the dog and having breakfast and all the million other things people do on a Sunday morning.

Steve tottered down the steps to the train platform.

If only Angion has the assays that can test Angion's results, then who can prove them wrong? If Angion does not tell the truth, then who can know the truth to tell?

Just asking the question was exhausting. He was spent.

A train stopped; its doors opened; he stepped inside and collapsed on a bench.

Numb.

Minutes later they arrived at Charles Street. As he stepped out, Steve noticed an old man by the window. The man looked familiar, though the beard, clothes, and features did not. Then they made eye contact.

Another electric shock.

It's the same guy – the guy from last week!

Steve turned back towards the doors, but he was too late. They had shut, and the train was rolling away, its metal wheels squealing in protest against the old rails.

11.

SUNDAY, APRIL 3

The phone was ringing.

Steve opened his eyes.

Why do I hurt so much?

He rolled onto his side, but then the bruises reminded him of last night.

He looked at the bedside clock: *2:07.*

Night? No ... there's daylight outside.

The phone rang again. He groaned and rolled to the side table. "Hello?"

"Steve, honey?"

He shook himself awake. "Morgan, my God, you alright?"

"Yes, I'm OK. But I miss you awfully. You sounded so lonely on the machine."

"Morgan, where've you been? I'm going nuts to talk to you! You won't believe what's happened."

"Work, Steve, work. I've been in the office non-stop. Why, what's wrong?"

Her voice confirmed last night's intuition – trouble. The pitch was too high, the words too rushed, the tone too casual. But she seemed not to want to talk about it. He decided to let it go – whatever "it" was. That would come later.

At the moment he had to tell her ...

What? That the lab was a fraud?

Steve loved the truth. Right now, however, he'd have to be careful how much truth he told.

Am I sure?

"It's the most incredible thing," he said. "After I called you last night, I fell asleep at my desk. When I woke up it was after one in the morning."

"Oh, Steve! You're never supposed to be there after midnight on Sundays. What happened? You get escorted out by the police?"

"No. I was scared I'd get in trouble, so I snuck out through a ceiling vent."

"You did *what*?"

"Yeah, I know, seems pretty stupid now. But at the time it seemed the best way to avoid a scene. Now in the daylight it makes less sense."

He had nearly said, "no sense," but then had remembered Pieter and Mai.

Actually, it made a good deal of sense.

"Steve, sweetheart, you're crazy. Why didn't you just call security and apologize?"

"MacGregor and Pieter already say my progress is too slow. I've been told you lose your job if you're found in Angion on Sundays. If they'd learned I'd fallen asleep at my desk – who knows what they'd do …"

He bit his tongue. He couldn't give her a more complete explanation till he was sure.

"Steve, you sound paranoid. You must be very tired – when did you get in?"

"Yeah, I guess I'm overreacting. When I got in this morning I was totally beat."

"Oh my God! You *are* crazy. You get any sleep? I woke you up?"

"Hon, you did me a favor. Otherwise, I won't sleep tonight, and I have a lab meeting in the morning."

"You going to tell them?"

"Are you kidding? If they don't know, I'd just as soon leave it alone."

Like hell I will.

"Hmm. Speaking as a lawyer, the best advice I can give you is to limit your downside risk. What if they find out later? You're better off telling them now."

Steve was fully awake. As he considered the matter, telling *anyone* about his adventure seemed a very bad idea.

"No, I can't tell them. There'd be hell to pay."

"You think they won't know?"

"I don't think I was seen getting out. There were no alarms, no lights, no security – nothing."

"I don't know, Steve. Maybe they're just waiting to see what you do."

"Then they can just keep waiting. They say nothing, and I say nothing. They'll know I feel like an idiot and am just saving face. And they may let it go, because making an issue of it doesn't do anyone any good. Or, on the other hand, they may just not know – which is the theory I prefer."

"Steve, you going to be OK?"

"Sweetie, I'm fine."

"OK, babe. I wish I was there to take care of you."

"Hmm. What did you have in mind?'

And their conversation safely turned to romance. Nothing further was said about Steve's misadventures of the night before, and nothing at all was said about Morgan's weekend.

After hanging up, Morgan stared at the phone, as she had been doing for the last two days. In fact, she had moved very little since Friday night. She was still wearing her favorite flannel pajamas, nestling under her grandmama's homemade quilt, lying on the sofa in her small living room in Greenwich Village.

She had slept like the dead throughout the night and most of Saturday, finally waking around 5 PM with a nasty headache. Chamomile tea had helped, and later that evening she had fixed herself tomato soup and a slice of toast, but since then she had had nothing to eat. By 9 PM she had been back in bed, asleep, not waking till noon Sunday.

Now a constant pain was gnawing at her belly, but it was not hunger. On the contrary, the thought of food made it worse, but if she tucked her knees up under her chin with the quilt wrapped around her, that made the pain a little better. And so for the whole of Sunday she had stayed curled under the covers.

She wanted to talk with Laurel, but also she did *not* want to talk with Laurel.

Was I drugged? Laurel was drugged.

Who did it?

What about Edwards? Did he know? He seemed so very wrong.

If I can't trust Edwards, where does it end? I can't trust anybody.

What about Steve? He sounded so strange on the phone.

Trust no one.

The evening loomed before her, and then tomorrow – work. The thought was lead in her stomach. She was so very tired, but so very wide awake.

She needed a good night's sleep, but what could she do?

She wandered into the bathroom and found the small brown bottle with the little white pills in the medicine cabinet. If she took one, she might feel a bit better. If she took two, she would sleep well. And if she took more? She stared at the bottle. Could these take away all her pain?

Morgan looked into the mirror, studying her tired face.

Who am I? Why should I even be alive?

But then she dropped the bottle into the sink, as though it had burned her hand.

No, I must not think like that.

Then Spader wins.

She felt alone, so very alone.

12.

MONDAY, APRIL 4

Monday morning Morgan found three projects waiting on her office desk, but the first was not due till Wednesday. She glanced at her calendar: no meetings today. She had some breathing room.

But her mind gave her no quarter, without mercy reviewing the weekend over and over and over and over. For several hours, staring at her work, she found concentration impossible, such that by the afternoon she had no choice but to accept defeat.

She pushed herself away from the desk and stepped to the window.

Skyscrapers vanished into a fog draped over Manhattan, a light drizzle speckling the glass. Morgan rubbed her eyes, as though the blur might clear with force of will, but the gray remained when she looked again.

She hit the speed dial on her phone.

A voice answered, "Farthington."

"Hey, Laurel."

"Morgan! I've been thinking about you all weekend. What a great party Friday! So, babe, did you have a good time, or *what*?!"

"Laurel, you mind coming over here?"

"Uh oh. You don't sound so hot."

"I need to talk to you."

"Can't sweetie, not now. Meeting in five minutes. How 'bout tonight?"

Morgan thought of the many nights she and Laurel had laughed, trading stories over drinks. This would not be one of those nights.

"Sure, Laurel. Say seven? Charlie's?"

"Perfect, babe," Laurel purred. "I want *all* the dirty details."

Morgan slowly put the receiver back into its cradle. Seven o'clock would be a long time to wait. Hopeless, she turned back to the contracts on her desk.

~

Shortly before seven Morgan walked into Charlie's Saloon, a joint off Washington Square, a few blocks from her apartment in the Village. Charlie's was a hole-in-the-wall caught in a time warp for the last eighty years, hardly changed since its birth as a speakeasy during Prohibition. The bar's counters were warm burnished mahogany, its bar stools blond from countless years of seated patrons, its dark, high-backed booths ideal for furtive rendezvous. Light came from a window looking onto the street and from three imitation-Tiffany lamps casting rainbow shadows across the two men at the bar. These days no one knew about the place, which was why Morgan and Laurel liked it.

The bartender was at her elbow moments after Morgan had settled in a booth.

"Evening, Miss Morgan. The usual – glass of cab?"

No, tonight was different. "Thanks, Lou. Coffee'd be fine."

Two cups later Laurel showed up. She slid into the seat opposite Morgan's, waved at Lou, and mouthed, "Cosmo."

"OK, Morgan, lay it on me. All of it. Drew take good care of you?" She licked her lips. "He's really delicious, don't you think?"

"Drew? Who's Drew?" Morgan murmured.

"You were with Drew Smythe, one of the fattest new wallets on the Street. You don't recall?"

"Exactly," Morgan snapped.

"But I saw you on the couch. He was nuzzling your neck."

"Laurel, I've lost part of the night. I think I was drugged. And maybe you were, too. Words like 'assault' and 'battery' come to mind. Another might be 'rape.' Do *those* ring a bell for you?"

"Unbelievable."

Laurel sounded like a schoolteacher recognizing an undeniable absurdity – *It is unbelievable the dog ate your homework.*

"Unbelievable? Laurel, where were *you* this weekend?"

Laurel smiled. "I partied with Chip. We just had fun. You know, no strings." She shrugged. "It was – how to put it? – 'mutually gratifying.'"

Was that sarcasm?

Laurel continued, "Now he'll feel warm and fuzzy whenever he thinks of Eddie Mac, so everybody wins." Her eyes narrowed. "But Morgan, you can't use a word like 'rape.' People wouldn't understand."

"What's there to understand? – sexual intercourse without consent. That's a felony. Illegal, right?"

"Morgan, many things are against the law."

Laurel's eyes were turned down, her face in shadow.

Is she joking?

"What do you mean?"

"Oh, babe, I'm just suggesting you be careful what you *say*," said Laurel brightly.

But her eyes were still on the table.

"Laurel, what happened?"

"Miss Laurel, here's your Cosmo." Lou had appeared.

He ceremoniously placed the drink in front of her and turned to Morgan, "More coffee?"

She shook her head. "No thanks, Lou."

Morgan looked back to Laurel, who was eyeing her rose-colored drink.

"So, Laurel, what did he do?"

Laurel's mood seemed less bright. "Everything I wanted him to."

Then she added, very softly, "I think."

Morgan reached across the table and grabbed her wrist. "You think? You don't know? I think you do know. What did he do?"

Laurel looked up, eyes wet but angry. "What do you want me to say? That I can't remember? That he's an ass? Morgan, get a grip. This guy can make or break me. Go along, and get along. Rape? No, not to my knowledge. On the contrary, we had a great weekend!"

Morgan's hand slid from Laurel's wrist to her palm, and she held it tight. "Tell me."

"Morgan, you're nuts. What's the point? Complain? To whom? Eddie Mac won't care. They won't want to know. They sure can't afford to – Spader's a big client. Go to the police? That's crazy. There's no proof, and he can always give them a little sugar, if they have a sweet tooth. So, c'mon Morgan, lighten up. Have a drink."

She pulled away her hand, shaking, and took a drag on the Cosmo.

Softly, Morgan said, "Honey, tell me about it."

Silence.

Then Laurel leaned forward, fixed her eyes on Morgan's coffee cup, and started talking.

"Last I remember we were in the cab – and next thing you know I'm waking up in his bed. It must have been a hell of a night, cause I *never* black out. So, I figure, what the hell, maybe there's potential here, and we spend the weekend under the covers. Sunday afternoon all of a sudden he turns cool; says I've got to go home, but when I get a little mad, he's all business. Rubs my shoulders; tells me that he had a great time, that he'd like to see me again as a 'mutually beneficial experience.' I said something, and then he turns *real* cold. Flips on the TV, and there's a video of me naked screaming with a hand holding a vibrator reaming me from behind. He says if there's any trouble then the video ends up on the Internet: bye, bye, blue-chip legal career. Then the asshole turns it off, thanks me again for a 'mutually beneficial experience,' and next thing you know I'm on the street in the rain."

Her voice caught in her throat.

Morgan took a deep breath. "Horrible! Laurel, I'm so sorry."

Together they were silent, staring at the table.

Laurel finally spoke, "It's not even clear he broke the law. Since I can't remember, maybe I did say yes when I might otherwise have said no. Who knows? Maybe I would have said 'yes' anyway."

"Laurel, this is wrong."

"Yes, dear, I know." Laurel finished her drink. "Damn, that's good … So I say, let's just party, because our lives are worth jack. We live in the palms of rich perverted psychopaths." She waved at Lou behind the bar, "Lou, two more Cosmos."

"I'm not having any."

"Then I'll have both. I need to get drunk."

"C'mon, Laurel, you're not alone here. The same thing nearly happened to me. But this guy Drew didn't close the deal."

Laurel was looking more and more agitated. "This is all mixed up."

"What do you mean?"

"I've had an eye for Drew Smythe. I kept track of him as he played the crowd that night. He moved across the room a couple of times, but I'm *sure* he never got close to you. I would have noticed. It was only when you were on the couch that he approached you. When could he have put something in your drink?"

"Oh God! You think he had help?"

"Why not? Chip or Drew could buy any of those waiters with a wave of the hand."

"Excuse me, ladies." Lou was at the table with the Cosmos. "Stirring up trouble?"

Laurel batted her eyelashes at him. "Why Lou, you looking for some?"

His ancient face folded into a series of wrinkled smiles, "Too hot for me, Miss Laurel." And he took refuge behind the bar.

Together the two were silent for a time.

Eventually, Laurel said, "Chip's an asswipe. So what? Life goes on." Her eyes glistened wet. "I do nothing, and he leaves me alone. Maybe he has good memories of our 'mutually beneficial experience.'"

Morgan's hopes were dwindling. Her friend really seemed to want to walk away. "Laurel, all the wishful thinking in the world won't make that video disappear. For the rest of your life that maggot will have an angle on you, if you do nothing. Is that what *you* want?"

Laurel picked up her Cosmo and drained the glass. She reached over to Morgan's untouched drink, pulled it over to her side of the table, and took another swallow.

"Morgan, I tell you, I've thought this over and over. There's no way out. I'm stuck."

"Maybe. Maybe not. Right now I can think of at least two possible strategies. One is to get something on Chip – so you reach a standoff. You know – like the Cold War – 'Mutually Assured Destruction.' That's better than his 'mutually beneficial experience.' He doesn't press the button, if you don't press the button."

"Yeah, sure. The reason it worked between the Soviets and the West was because there was a balance of power. If I try to start my own Cold War with Chip, then I'll lose. He is very, very, rich, with many powerful friends. And everyone already knows he's a slime ball. It's crazy, but that's what makes him so powerful. He doesn't care if he gets mud on his face, so no one wants to cross him. There's an expression for this, Morgan."

"Yeah?"

"Never mud-wrestle with a pig. You'll get dirty, and the pig will like it."

"Hmm. Better to wrestle with the pig than to sleep with it."

"Damn it, Morgan. I'm not suggesting sleeping with the pig, just leaving it alone."

"Sooner or later it'll roll over and squash you, as long as you're in the pigsty."

Laurel stared at her drink, silent. Then she murmured, "OK, so what's strategy number two?"

"We tell Edwards the story, so he knows Spader is developing potential blackmail on Eddie Mac's employees. It's the kind of thing that the firm should know about a client."

"Yeah, right. They won't do anything. Spader's too big."

Morgan shook her head. "But the potential for this to burn Eddie Mac is very real. Also, if two associates tell them about the problem and they do not respond in some way, they create liability for themselves."

"You think there'd be any danger to our careers, if we confide in Edwards?"

"He's been good to me. I think he'll handle it with discretion."

"Didn't you say he was bothering you at the party?"

"True, but I think he was drunk and feeling lonely. Likely his wife isn't good for much conversation, though she looks great in a bikini even at the age of twenty-eight."

"Morgan, you're wicked."

"Simply honest."

"This Edwards strategy makes me nervous. Don't involve me in the conversation. He'll be more open if it's only you."

"So you're OK with this?"

"It's a good idea, Morgan, but keep it real discrete. My name has to stay out of it; otherwise, it's a given Chip will make his tape public. And give yourself room to walk away."

"Laurel, don't you get it? I can't walk away. It's too late. I'm in. It nearly happened to me. And you can't walk away, either. You can do nothing, if you choose, but no matter what, you're already in the game. And if you do nothing, you lose, guaranteed."

Laurel drained the drink. Fresh tears welled up in her eyes. "OK. Good luck, Morgan, I've gotta go. I love you."

"I love you, too, hon."

Laurel plunked two twenties on the table and slid out of her seat, her coat in hand. Quickly she walked out without glancing up. "Thanks, Lou."

At the conclusion of that morning's lab meeting Steve breathed a sigh of relief. After looking over his records MacGregor had only declared, "This isn't enough. Work harder, mate. We're losing time."

Back at his desk Steve dialed the combo for his safe. The data books were as he had left them. He went to Shiu-Wei's desk.

"I set up next mice under hood, Steve. Professor MacGregor tell me, four mice for you today."

Her face was expressionless.

Or was it? Steve studied her.

Is she more than what she seems?

Steve felt himself sinking into the world of the spy, a world of inscrutable secrets, a world where every person was a potential enemy. For his own sanity he would have to disentangle the weekend's events, soon. The alternative would be paranoia. He'd learned about paranoia in medical school – he did not want to end up a delusional psychotic.

So, what about Shiu-Wei?

Man, I've got to pull myself together.

Her eyes seemed guileless, expecting another week of processing mouse brains. Whatever she was thinking, if anything, it did not show.

Only an innocent can be so simple. This thought made him feel better.

"Sure, Shiu-Wei. He told me: I've got to speed up."

"I help you later, Steve. I still doing project for Alison. When I finish slides, then I help you. Later. Maybe tomorrow."

This was bad news, but she delivered it without malice – of course. From her point of view it didn't matter whose project she worked on; she arrived in the morning and put in her time and then went home at five. And it was Alison's prerogative to prioritize Shiu-Wei's time.

Steve retreated to the mouse cages under the fume hood. Quickly he opened the first cage, holding the squirming little rodent in one hand while with the other he injected anesthetic into its belly with a tiny syringe. Once the mouse was quiet, he laid it on its back and shaved its throat bare, exposing its pink skin. He then set it on the microscope stage, tilting its chin to expose the neck overlying the carotid arteries. He picked up a scalpel to incise the skin, but then stopped, the blade poised over the mouse's neck.

He had had a black thought.

He detached the mouse from the stage and turned it onto its stomach, centering its skull under the lens. He glanced up quickly, but no one was near. He looked into the microscope.

Each individual hair loomed like a giant redwood trunk in the scope's magnified view. With two delicate glass probes he pushed the hairs aside to examine the underlying skin. Slightly to the left, slightly to the right, a bit down to the right – there it was. Three weeks ago he had created a tiny, hair-thin burr hole in the mouse's skull and injected a small inoculum of tumor cells into the animal's frontal lobe. Then after two weeks the mouse had been treated with an IV solution of either Angiotox or sugar water, randomly assigned, with the idea that he should now be able to see a decline in tumor blood vessels in those animals receiving Angiotox – if it worked.

He had injected the tumor cells three weeks ago, so by now the tiny burr hole should have healed. But, there it was: a tiny scab at the site, no more than a few days old.

At that instant he came to several realizations.

First, this was the kind of scar that Pieter and Mai's work would have left behind, confirming that they had been working on *his* experiment.

Second, that meant the sabotage was being performed multiple times. The wound on this mouse was several days old, not inflicted yesterday.

Third, repeated manipulation suggested a coordinated effort. With both Pieter and Mai involved, likely the coordination extended up the food chain. But would MacGregor sabotage his own experiment? Maybe so. The investor meeting was only two weeks away. The lab needed some hot results.

Beads of sweat formed across Steve's forehead.

He flipped the mouse over and proceeded with the planned experiment.

~

Early that evening he finished injecting, fixing, and dissecting the last mouse, yielding four mouse brains ready for processing. They needed to sit in a gentle hydroxide solution for at least two hours, which would melt away the brain tissue and expose the gold-filled blood vessels for analysis. Normally, at this point Steve would have left them to sit in the vat overnight, but he was too curious to wait. Of the four mice he had processed, two had had fresh puncture marks on their skulls. Would their results be different from the other two? He needed to know.

He gently lowered the four brains one by one into the hydroxide solution. Bubbles formed. He left the brains to digest and returned to his reading.

Just after ten he fished out the four golden casts, placed them under a fume hood, and dried them with a small air blower. Once finished, he carried them to the video computer to re-construct their three-dimensional structures as digital images.

Within minutes the monitor displayed the brain images and their statistics. Two brains showed broken, stunted tumor blood vessels, while the other two had intact vasculature. Curious, he pulled out the code-book: all four mice had received Angiotox. He checked the ID numbers of the two mice that had shown the treatment response ... and he felt nauseous. These were the mice that had had the fresh incisions, the ones that had been tampered with.

Steve collected the computer print outs, logged the gold models for storage, locked up his lab book, and walked out of Angion. It was 1:20 AM, and Steve August had a lot to think about.

13.

FRIDAY, APRIL 8

The rest of the week Morgan kept her office door closed, shortened her phone conversations to single sentences, and attended meetings only when necessary. She was not ready to talk with anyone – not colleagues, not Steve, not her parents, and certainly not again Laurel, not until she had reached a decision on how to proceed.

But Friday afternoon James Hazleton, one of the senior partners, stuck his head in the door. "Morgan, we need you at the ArtStart party."

That night was a reception at the Museum of Modern Art, hosted by a group of investors who were forming a cooperative fund to develop promising young artists.

His tone left no option. "Sure, Jim, I'll be there."

"Great! Keep 'em happy, know what I mean?"

She heard him chuckle as he left.

~

So here she was. Drinking nothing stronger than bottled water, she remained cold sober, though she halfheartedly did try to chat up some of Manhattan's hottest new artistic talent. The young egos, fed with promises of money and fame, their tongues loosened with caviar and champagne, were eager to impress the beautiful attorney. But they failed.

"My roots are my influences. When I create, I express my primal urges."

The sculptor Rollo, sporting goatee, diamond earring, and black turtleneck, was standing next to a large round marble sphere, from which extended a gnarled wooden beam.

She was silent.

He continued unabashed, his adolescent tone laying his offering before her altar. "Here there is the old in the new, the organic in the material, the straight in the round."

He took Morgan's elbow in one hand and gestured to the sculpture with the other, "What do you feel, when you take it all in?"

Tempted to say, "Repulsed," Morgan tried to excuse his indiscretions, reminding herself that Rollo was badly inebriated. Instead, she nodded, "It's a statement in contradiction. Very profound – the single in the infinite, life in death, weakness within strength."

"Yes, yes, yes," said Rollo. "You're so right. You *really* see it."

He drew closer. "You and me, we should talk more, in private, just one on one. You'd like that, I know – getting real cozy at my place. I'd roll you a fattie. We'd soar. What d'you think – you want some fun?"

That was it. Following only days after the encounter with Chip and Laurel, Rollo's inquiries, smelling of wine, ego, and desperation, could not have been timed more poorly.

"Frankly, Rollo, your art's more exciting than your offer. I'd rather sit next to a giant granite block than listen to your idiotic repartee. Of course, I could close my eyes – listening would be better than looking at that ridiculous goatee. But as for sharing a joint with you, why that's not such a bad idea. To tolerate your company, I think I'd have to be blind, deaf, drunk, and stoned."

Morgan marched over to the cheese table, leaving the artist gasping for air. With a large cheese knife she started slicing chunks off a Gouda wheel, her knuckles white on the grip.

"My goodness, Morgan, go easy with that thing, or you'll chop off something valuable."

Edwards was standing at her side.

"Oh, hello, Mr. Edwards. Just a little trouble with this cheese block."

"Morgan, let's take a walk."

Edwards took her elbow, steering her away from the crowds in the main gallery, and then guiding her down the hall past a giant Andy

Warhol tomato soup can. They turned left into another gallery, empty except for two misshapen sculptures.

"My dear," said Edwards, " it doesn't take a doctorate in psychology to know something's wrong. This week you've been living a hermit's life, avoiding all human interaction, and some of the partners have noticed. Just now I saw you obliterate that young man. You know what he did when you walked away? He whimpered. You made a grown man cry at a cocktail party. Granted, he struck me as excessively sensitive, yet this isn't like you, Morgan. Normally I wouldn't pry, but this is affecting your professional life."

Edwards leaned towards her, his face radiating empathy.

Morgan wavered. In the past Edwards had always seemed so trustworthy and caring. And this was her opportunity – to advocate for Laurel, and for herself, and for every other female associate. Edwards understood the firm and its dynamics, and he was one who had real power to Make Things Happen. Eddie Mac needed to know that one of its clients was a poisonous rotten apple.

She reached her decision.

Her eyes stung with tears, but she managed to keep her voice steady as she told Edwards about Chip and Laurel leaving the party, and then what Laurel had told her about the ensuing weekend, concluding with Spader's threats about the video.

Edwards's face reflected serious concern. Only at the mention of the video did his expression change, eyebrows slightly arching, though only for an instant. Morgan noticed but continued, "Mr. Edwards, all this about Laurel is in the strictest confidence. Laurel asked me not to use her name, but you do need to know the facts, and you, far better than I, know how to be discrete. No one else may know about her videotape – but it's important that you understand how dangerous Spader is. He's a predator, one who sees his money as a license to act however he likes, crushing anyone he wants, a danger to us all, and thereby a danger to the firm. Maybe more victims exist – now, or in the past, or in the future. I'm sorry to burden you with this, but you should know."

In the silence that followed, Thomas Edwards, Esquire, looked his most wise and judicious, as though centuries of Anglo-American jurisprudence had descended to rest upon his shoulders. He stood erect, and his hands stretched out to take hers.

"Morgan, thank you for telling me. This is very sensitive. Does anyone else know?"

"No, not from me."

"Good girl. Tell no one else, not even friends or family. We need to keep this away from the police and – above all – the press and the public."

He looked at her intently.

Morgan nodded.

Edwards's voice turned sharp. "Morgan, I promise he will never again have the opportunity. We will contain him."

Morgan wanted to feel relief. She looked into his eyes, radiating wisdom towards her and compassion towards Laurel and anger towards their enemy. She reminded herself that this was a man whom she could trust, one who would help her and Laurel reach justice. She wanted to believe him.

"We will get to the bottom of this," he continued. "He may have pulled this stunt before; maybe he's blackmailing other Eddie Mac personnel even now. Indeed, this may have implications with the SEC, since he's a banker with whom we work. Such a conflict of interest! Forewarned is forearmed. You've done well telling me, Morgan."

Edwards pulled her close, for a moment holding her in what may have been intended to be a warm embrace. But his withered arms offered no security, and his fetid, martini-laden breath offered no comfort.

"Thank you, Mr. Edwards," said Morgan, stepping back. "What should I do?"

"Nothing, Morgan. This will require much thought and discretion on my part. Please, tell no one about our conversation – not even Laurel or your friend Steve. I will need the freedom to act without encumbrance."

"Yes, of course, Mr. Edwards. Thank you for hearing me out."

Smiling, Edwards took her arm and steered her towards the hallway. He was holding her close to his side, offering assurance, but her stomach tightened into a knot as they walked back to the party.

14.

FRIDAY, APRIL 8

During the remainder of the week they worked like mad. By Friday evening Steve had processed another twenty mice, and Shiu-Wei had done another twelve – yielding between them a total of thirty-two mice in four days! However, secretly Steve checked each one for a scalp wound, found many, and confirmed that these and only these were showing evidence of a treatment response to Angiotox.

The whole thing's a fraud.

But why involve him in the process? And why go to such efforts to concoct inconclusive data? If they (whoever "they" might be) were going to go to the trouble of creating a fraud, why not make the data convincing? Wouldn't "they" want Angiotox to be a winner? The variances in the numbers were still too wide. At this rate the data wouldn't be ready for the investors' meeting on April 18.

And, who were "they?" Was everyone a part of it? Could he trust no one?

And then there was the matter of Morgan. On Monday she and Steve had exchanged two sentences late at night. Wednesday he had left a message. Thursday he had left another. Finally, on Friday she had called during the day – while he was out, of course – apologizing for the prior two evenings, explaining she had had to work late. And she had said she would be gone on a work-related project for the weekend, but that she would try calling him … maybe Sunday.

She had sounded more like a business partner than a lover and confidante, her message offering no real solace.

He pondered these problems as he sat at the lab hood. Today he had dissected another four brains, and he now was ready to begin the digestion process to check their vasculatures. With a little luck he should be home before midnight.

"Hey Doc August, what'cha doing?"

Out of nowhere, Alison was standing next to him.

"Not too much, Alison. In fact, I'm told I'm doing too little."

He looked at the vat in which he had just placed the four brains. "Puny, aren't they? Eleven hours of work, and only four little morsels left to show for it."

"Yes, but underneath all the layers, what's left is pure gold."

Alison's voice was soft and husky. Steve glanced up.

This was the first time he had seen her without a lab coat. She was wearing tight black jeans that showed off hips and a narrow waist, and a soft purple top that draped off shoulders and a full chest. In her lab coat she had always looked professional, but now she looked – well, she just looked plain sexy.

He caught a whiff of perfume.

"Sure. I wish the results were pure gold. Seems like the data just don't make any sense," he said.

She shrugged, her eyes round, sapphire pools.

"Steve, if your data don't make sense to you, then they won't make sense to anyone else. Hey listen; let's not talk about work. I really need a break. It's Friday night. You want to get a bite?"

Steve couldn't disagree; he needed a break, too. "You've caught me at a good time. These brains won't be ready for at least two hours, and I'm hungry."

Alison walked from the hood to his desk, where she turned around, leaned back, and locked his eyes.

"Yes, a tasty bit of meat sounds good to me. You up for it?"

"Sure. Where to?"

How 'bout the Chopping Block?"

She's a surprise a second.

"That's a ways. You driving?"

"Lazybones. It's worth the trip. Best ribs around."

"But promise we're back by nine. I have to finish these brains tonight, with another five to do tomorrow. I've got to get the numbers up, you know."

"Sure you do, Steve. I'll get my coat. See you in the parking lot – five minutes?"

She sashayed off, undulating to an unheard drumbeat.

The thought came unbidden: *She's hot!*

But then he shook his head, realizing Morgan's absence was posing a problem. He closed his eyes.

Why do I love her? – beauty, charm, brains, loyalty, trust … Oh, right!

Re-armed, he locked the safe and walked outside.

Alison was already there, standing next to a black BMW convertible. A streetlight highlighted her profile, her breath steaming in the cold air. The car's fenders bulged like muscles: sleek lines of dark horsepower.

"Wow, nice ride!"

"You like?"

She stepped next to him.

He touched the glistening ebony. "I didn't know you were into high-end sports cars – very sharp!"

She laughed. "You might be surprised what I'm into. You driving?" And she pressed car keys into his palm. "Intelligence has its rewards, Steve."

He sensed the scent of her perfume, the warmth of her body, the contact of her skin …

Whoa, boy!

He stepped back, holding the keys. "Careful, Alison, I may not give it back."

She laughed again. "No worries. I'm sure you'll follow my lead."

And she got in the passenger side.

Keep cool.

He turned the key. The motor revved, a warm rumble.

"Intelligence sure does have its rewards! How'd you swing a ride like this?"

"On my last project we patented a new molecular marker. George sold it to 21st Century Pharma Exploration, and my share was five percent. Five percent of twelve million dollars makes a nice bonus, right? I paid for this baby in cash, and had lots of change left over."

Steve pulled onto Memorial Drive, the car purring as he touched the pedal.

Alison turned slightly to face him. "Money's nice, isn't it?"

"Great cars, sharp clothes, big houses, elegant yachts, beautiful friends ... it's amazing what money can buy."

She chuckled. "Yes, it's amazing what people will sell. That's just the way the world works."

"Only to a point. Some things aren't for sale."

He turned off Memorial and swung into the Chopping Block parking lot. "Sweet! Thanks for the taste."

"Any time. But just think – you could have your very own."

Steve shook his head. "I have a while to wait. It's another five years before I'm out of training, and even then I'll have a ton of loans to pay off."

As they walked inside, she asked, "Why wait? You don't want to be old and gray before you have a little fun, do you?"

Steve grunted in response, as a waitress led them to a corner booth. Their conversation turned innocuous for a time, but Alison picked up her theme again when the food arrived.

"I think that delayed gratification is for the birds. If we don't enjoy life now, what's the point?"

"Alison, you're a scientist. You chase experiment after experiment until you get results that make sense. That's delayed gratification if I ever saw it."

"But I don't sit around waiting years and years! I work on a timeline of weeks and months, and I get big payouts. Don't you deserve better than what you're getting?"

"Sure, I get frustrated. But that's true for every doctor-in-training. Your college buddies turn into successful lawyers, and bankers, and computer engineers, while you're still checking blood pressures and reading textbooks and writing hospital notes and working long hours for dirt pay. So what? We knew the deal when we signed up."

"But Steve, it doesn't have to be that way ... at least, not for you."

Steve stopped, his hamburger halfway to his mouth. "What do you mean?"

There was no one close by, but Alison still lowered her voice and leaned forward. Under the table her knee pressed against his leg.

"Just imagine, Steve, that your project works out. Some possible investors are meeting in less than two weeks. Your data could prove Angiotox works in living animals, not just on cells in a SAGA petri dish. Your results could convince these guys. George wants to take Angion public with Angiotox as our first homegrown product. If these guys back us and we hit it big, you'll be able to afford a whole fleet of BMWs!"

"Wait a minute, Alison. No one's promised me money."

"Oh, right. I almost forgot."

The pressure of her knee grew stronger.

Her voice dropped lower: "MacGregor wants to issue you options. They're not worth anything unless Angion's stock gets over ten dollars, but then you make out like a bandit. He's prepared to offer you 500,000 options, potentially two percent of the company. If Angion goes public, we're guessing market value should be minimum ten dollars a share – at least five million dollars in your pocket. But with a little luck we might get to thirty or even forty a share, and then you'd be sitting on fifteen or twenty million. Nice, huh?"

To emphasize the point, Alison put her hand under the table and squeezed Steve's thigh. She left it there, nestling his leg against hers.

Steve's pulse accelerated, his breathing deepened. He caught another whiff of perfume. He was having trouble staying focused.

He whispered, "But why would George give me millions of dollars? What's the expectation – the *quid pro quo*?"

"Hmmmm," she purred. "What do you think? Loyalty. You'll be his entry point to clinical medicine – running clinical studies in patients, providing contacts with other doctors, opening doors at hospitals across the country. What a career! Not only will you become fabulously wealthy, but you'll be a shining star on any medical school faculty, internationally popular at a young age. Just imagine – wealth and power beyond your wildest dreams."

Her hand moved slightly higher on his thigh. A warm flush was growing between his legs. He felt dizzy.

"I haven't yet generated successful results – and you're offering me the world on a platter? This is crazy."

"No, honey child. 'Crazy' would be wasting this opportunity. We all know Angiotox works – but just not in every case. So the sooner we get Angiotox available for real people, the sooner we'll figure out which patients really need it, for whom it really works, how to make it work better, how best to administer it – all the practical details we need to start saving lives. All that's standing in the way, Steve, are a few data points in your lab book."

Steve's mouth turned dry. "Alison, you're not making sense. If I changed the data, sooner or later that'd be found out. And it would be even crazier for me to try to get a drug to work in the clinic, if I couldn't get it to work in the lab. That'd be guaranteed failure, and in the process I'd hurt a lot of people, who were hoping for a cancer cure but instead just got shafted."

Alison's eyelids drooped low. "Steve, honey, think about it. No one's talking about changing anything. Your data show that Angiotox works – you've seen it yourself! – *most* treated mice responded beautifully. The problem is that not *all* responded. So your variances are too wide. Now we're running out of time, and it's *your* lab book."

Her one hand on his thigh, the other lightly touched the back of his neck. "So, what do you think?"

It's a total set up – that's what I think.

"Alison, I can't do that."

Her soft voice was smooth as a silk bedspread: "What's 'science?' Facts? Be careful, Steve August. Don't confuse facts with truth. It's not just facts we're about at Angion. It's results. It's perceptions. What's truth, anyway? You do a little experiment and get a little result? That's not truth – that's just an isolated fact. 'Truth' requires lots of facts, facts that are put together and interpreted. Truth is constructed. *That's* real science. So it's your responsibility, as keeper of all these facts, to help people construct them correctly. And the truth is – as we've seen over and over – Angiotox works. That's what SAGA tells us. That's what we've seen in two years of research on the drug. That's what you've seen in your own experiments. You just need to pull your little facts together so that this truth becomes obvious."

Steve remembered Mai and Pieter at their microscopes, and the little marks on the mouse scalps. Those were facts, too.

"Come on, Steve," she cooed, "the issue is not what happens in mice; the issue is what happens in people. Have some faith – in Angiotox, in MacGregor, in the system."

She squeezed his thigh harder.

He tried to slow his breathing.

"Alison, I can't just throw away a bunch of data. That would invalidate the whole experiment."

She straightened up, pulling her hand away.

"Hmmm. All I can do is point you towards a more powerful strategy. *You* have to choose to do the right thing. We are sure Angiotox works. So, we must start testing in patients. We've gotten all we can from the mouse data, don't you think? People don't need to know every detail. The investors wouldn't understand. The FDA wouldn't understand."

"Let me think about it."

At that, her face brightened. Before he could react, she gave him a big smile and planted a soft kiss on his lips.

"Good boy, Steve," she murmured. "Think about it!"

The waiter stopped at the table. "Any dessert for you two?"

Alison smiled, "No I don't think there'll be dessert tonight. Maybe some other time."

She looked back at Steve, excitement dancing in her eyes. He guessed she meant it to be contagious, so he grinned back at her, trying not to reveal what he was thinking.

This is a dangerous game, real high-stakes poker, and there's more than money on the table.

Across the restaurant a thin man sat in a booth. He was leaning an elbow on the table, his head cradled in his hand, delicate fingers nestling an earphone snug in his ear. His other arm lay across the newspaper he was reading, the microphone inside his cuff aimed at August and Alison.

Riker's eyes narrowed, as he listened to the bitch's pitch, and August's response.

The bastard was trouble. They might need a fallback.

Riker disliked people shackled by convention. Weak. The world was a jungle full of beasts that either killed or starved.

He would talk with MacGregor. Maybe he would have to involve Calibri. Motivation was a coin that had two sides – pleasure, or pain.

Yes, he despised Steve August.

Pleasure. Or pain.

For August he would enjoy inflicting the second much more than observing the first.

15.

That same night George MacGregor sat alone at his desk under a reading lamp, the framed poster of the Porsche GT gleaming black in the faint light while the brain glimmered gold on its pedestal, but he ignored these symbols of wealth and glory. Before him were several folders summarizing the development of Angiotox.

Tomorrow he would be reviewing the entire project with Silverstein – and Silverstein could be as ugly as a koala crossed with a kangaroo. In fact, as MacGregor thought back to his childhood outside Melbourne, he had seen koala bears that resembled Silverstein in several respects: the giant paunch, the beady eyes that looked sleepily out onto the world, but with sharp claws that served equally well to climb eucalyptus trees or to tear into the flesh of the unwary. Silverstein looked fat, cute, and dumb, but in reality he was smart, tough, and nasty.

Just like a koala.

It had been six years ago, while still a professor at MIT, that MacGregor had met Silverstein at a scientific conference. By the end of their dinner together MacGregor had decided that Silverstein was a genius – and MacGregor *never* called anyone genius.

Some years earlier, as a graduate student at Harvard, Silverstein had concluded that modern science moved too fast for the stuffy universities. On his own he had developed SAGA, the "Silverstein AngioGenesis Assay," and then had left the world of academia and established his own private testing company. While still doing good science, he had made great money doing it.

Nevertheless, that night during their conversation, MacGregor had also realized that Silverstein was rather lazy. He did not want to work too hard, and he relished the idea of being left alone. As a result, he had made plenty of money with SAGA, but he had never taken the obvious next step of developing a larger organization to exploit SAGA's potential economies of scale. Instead, he simply tested drugs for a fee and left the rest to Big Pharma.

So, after martinis, a couple of bottles of wine, and a long dinner spanning hours, MacGregor had suggested a marriage of their talents – his organizational expertise in exchange for Silverstein's unique product, SAGA, to serve as fuel for an integrated, global biotech firm.

"George, that's a fine suggestion," Silverstein had responded, stuffing a fork-full of flourless fudge cake into his mouth. He swallowed without chewing, and then continued, spewing bits of fudge onto the tablecloth, "Very fine indeed. But let me be honest with you, George. You're right that SAGA has great potential, but even now it's a moneymaking machine. I don't have the patience to deal with the bureaucracy, personnel, and administration needed to 'go global' – as you put it. Even so, I've refused several offers from Big Pharma to buy SAGA. They'd muck up SAGA without me, but there's no way I'll work for some Fortune-500 Big Daddy. So, I just do what I do."

He took another giant bite of cake. After two chews and a swallow he continued, "Your offer's intriguing. Frankly, I'd rather be developing my own ideas than worrying about employing a dozen scientists who are doing SAGA testing, as I must do now. I could come and go and create as I like. It could free me up."

His beady eyes turned thoughtful. "Still, I'm in no particular hurry. SAGA's making plenty of money, so I'll only change for a clearly winning proposition. The way I see it, we can cut a deal – but only if you can bring some important pieces to the table – an organization with solid financial footing and investor contacts, a physical plant capable of large-scale production, and a cadre of employees loaded with brains, energy, and – above all – loyalty. Three things, George: organization, plant, and people."

He stuffed more cake into his mouth while talking, getting excited, waving his fingers in the air. "In exchange – one – I'll sell you SAGA for a bit of cash and a fat percentage of the company, though you'll need me to keep SAGA running. Two – I get loads of free time to play in the lab, no questions asked; if I come up with any good ideas, you'll be the first to know. Three – we leverage each other's talents into a mutually profitable enterprise, and together we become billionaires."

He swallowed the cake. "I tell you this, George." His voice lowered, "You do know, don't you … SAGA's worth it. Cancer, heart disease, stroke, diabetes, aging, wound healing, even weight loss – the applications are endless."

At that time MacGregor had a net worth of around seven million dollars, and he had promised himself he would be satisfied at ten million or so. But deep in his heart of hearts he had sometimes wondered what it would be like to be truly, completely, thoroughly, *filthy* rich. He could have buildings named after him – hell, maybe even the lab at Oxford where he'd been a graduate student – "MacGregor Hall." He would go to the best parties, meet the most fabulous women, sit on the most powerful committees, travel the world! This was his very private fantasy – and Silverstein had managed to nail it with that one word …

Billionaire.

One thousand millions. One million thousands.

"I'll need time. Organization, financing, people – they don't show up overnight."

"One year, George. I'll give you one year."

And so they shook hands: MacGregor would leave his academic post to start the company, while Silverstein would not entertain other offers for SAGA for one full year.

Every time MacGregor recalled that fateful day, he was amazed at Silverstein's genius – a peculiar combination of intelligence and sloth. He had known the formula for their success, he had handed the roadmap to MacGregor, and then he had stepped back to let MacGregor do all the work.

Flash forward one year …

They had sat in MacGregor's office in the newly acquired Angion building, here at this very desk. They had reviewed MacGregor's efforts: the company, its employees, its financial structure, and its burgeoning network of scientific and industrial contacts. At the end of six grueling hours Silverstein had sold SAGA to Angion with the stipulation that he would remain as Senior Scientist running "Product Discovery" – meaning he would continue to rule SAGA. The deal cost MacGregor three million dollars plus twenty-five percent of the company.

And that had been four years ago.

Since then, SAGA had proved itself over and over again. No one else discovered its secrets – identifying angiogenic factors with such speed and accuracy. As a screening assay it was invincible, and therefore very profitable.

He opened the top file – *Angiotox, Year I.*

With the proceeds as seed capital, they had set out to discover and develop a novel anti-angiogenic anti-cancer drug. Brain cancer seemed an excellent initial target: lethal, with largely ineffective treatments and with many tens of thousands of patients the world over. A homerun might be worth hundreds of millions, maybe even billions, in annual revenue.

MacGregor turned to the next set of folders – *Angiotox, Year II.* Once Silverstein had identified and narrowed the list of candidate drugs using SAGA to a final short list, AGA-01 through AGA-28, he turned these over to MacGregor's lab group for further development.

These studies continued into the next year – *Angiotox, Year III.* MacGregor had worked closely with Pieter and the other scientists on the team until he was sure they had a winner – AGA-16.

Then when they verified AGA-16 with tests in living rabbits, the results were perfect. (They liked to use rabbits, because the blood vessels in the rabbit ears were a perfect window to monitor the effects of treatments on the animal's vasculature.)

And at that point MacGregor was convinced Angiotox was their ideal wonder drug. SAGA endorsed it, and the rabbit tests were perfect. All systems were go!

They christened it, "Angiotox."

Unfortunately, the FDA required safety data from two separate animal species before testing in people. To satisfy this FDA requirement, they ran confirmatory tests in mice. By all expectations the results should have been acceptable.

But the results were off – an inconsistency that required rectification. And shortly thereafter he had received the phone call from Marion Phillips suggesting Steve August work in the lab. So, the next logical step was obvious.

He opened the next folder – *Angiotox, Year IV* – thinner than the prior three.

At first he had detested Phillips's pushing August on him, but then he had realized the boy was a gift from the gods. He could use August to solve his little problem, while simultaneously the boy would serve as MacGregor's bridge into the clinical world. All that was needed were the right psychological controls.

And MacGregor had been certain he could set up those controls. He knew human nature. Everyone was corruptible – of this he was certain. And once August compromised himself, he would be MacGregor's in the years ahead. How fun! And how useful.

But August had not followed the playbook. Week after week MacGregor had increased the pressure, demanding more data, better numbers – proof that Angiotox worked – yet Steve was *still* reporting inconclusive results. Tonight Alison had represented a gamble, but a necessary one, because time was running out.

In all of this, MacGregor had been careful that Silverstein only knew what MacGregor chose to tell him, ever since Alison and Shiu-Wei had started getting contradictory results last year. "We're collecting more data. It's working out. Don't worry." But now with time running short, MacGregor had asked Silverstein for tomorrow's meeting, explaining they needed to discuss … "issues."

MacGregor had hoped tonight would bring good news. If August took Alison's bait, then he could keep this under his own personal control, and he could keep Silverstein out of the loop. If not – well, MacGregor did not want to reveal *everything* to Silverstein.

The phone rang.

"We have a problem." Riker's voice was quiet, but it contained violence, as it always did. This made MacGregor uncomfortable, as it always did.

Of course, he had his faults, but MacGregor drew the line at physical intimidation. Such behavior was fit only for mobsters and criminals, not for the civilized and educated such as himself.

He remembered well the day when first he had heard Riker's voice …

∽

It had been the day he had signed the contract with Calibri. Afterwards, MacGregor, Dida, Calibri, and Edwards had gone out for a celebratory luncheon at Radius, one of his favorite restaurants.

Halfway through lunch, Dida had whispered in MacGregor's ear, "Come with me. I want to show you something special."

MacGregor had been lusting for her. He nodded enthusiastically.

"I'm off to the powder room to freshen up," Dida declared to Thomas and Calibri, "and George will escort me."

She stood up, as did MacGregor, and the two of them circled the tables.

Steps along the building's rotunda led down to the wine cellar, where rows of floor-to-ceiling wine bottles stretched into the recesses of the former giant vault, hermetically sealed behind giant glass panels.

Dida bent her head to one side, "Come this way." She took his hand, passed the rows of aging, expensive wines, turned a corner, and then reached the restrooms.

"I'll be out in couple of minutes," she said, patting his cheek.

He felt sheepish standing in the hallway with nothing to do, so he entered the men's room. At the urinal, his pants unzipped, an unexpected voice broke the silence.

"As you're occupied, Mr. MacGregor, there's no need to shake hands."

His flow froze in mid-stream, partly out of surprise, but partly out of fear. The whisper had sounded like death itself. He folded himself back into his pants as quickly as possible, tugging at the zipper, but this stuck. His fly was still open, but his worry for personal safety trumped his sense of personal decency. He turned to face the unknown speaker.

There stood a gray, tall, thin man in a charcoal jacket, white shirt open at the collar, black pants, scar along the left cheek. Ageless. He reminded MacGregor of a mortician – tie off, shirt loose, ready to bury another corpse.

"Mr. MacGregor, good to see you."

MacGregor did his best to pull his dignity together, given that he was standing next to a urinal, pants unzipped, facing a stranger who knew his name.

"I'm sorry. I don't recall us meeting ..." MacGregor's voice trailed away. The man's face showed only a detached, analytical interest, like a scientist studying a rat in an experiment.

"Yes, Mr. MacGregor, you're right. We haven't met, but I know you very well. My name is Michael Riker. I run security for Don Calibri. He asked me to say hello."

MacGregor tried to stay calm.

"Nice to meet you, Mr. Riker."

"No, Mr. MacGregor. It's never 'nice' to meet me," hissed the man, a hiss reminiscent of Calibri's. "My job, Mr. MacGregor, is never, ever, to be nice."

He stepped towards MacGregor. His long body looked relaxed, one hand in his pants pocket. MacGregor imagined the hand fingering a hidden switchblade, debating how best to carve him into a form more to the man's liking.

Riker grinned, showing off pointed teeth like a shark's, and then licked his lips, again reminding MacGregor of Calibri. He wondered if this man was about to attack him – in this posh restroom in this famous restaurant in this most respectable of cities. Maybe he was about to die, the day of his signing with the Calibri Group?

The hand still in his pocket, Riker leaned gently against the bathroom tile. He looked MacGregor up and down, head to foot to head, as though measuring him for a coffin.

"Relax, Mr. MacGregor. I'm just here to say – congratulations. Look at what you've accomplished! You have sired an entire company. I'm here to remind you that you are not alone, that your child has a family. We have adopted your precious newborn, Angion. We will protect it, help your baby grow, provide nurture as it becomes big and strong. What a lovely daddy you are."

Riker turned away, while MacGregor remained frozen to stone, but at the door he stopped, without turning.

"You will not often see me, MacGregor. I'm not much for chitchat. But you should know – we will be watching you carefully, and all aspects of Angion. I have responsibility for its security apparatus. Don't get in my way, and in return I'll help you achieve your dreams. Won't that be nice?"

He pushed the door open and walked out.

But MacGregor remained frozen, standing alone next to the urinal with his fly still open. One part of him had wanted to run after Riker, challenge him, let him know that George MacGregor – world-acclaimed scientist and entrepreneur – was never intimidated by a two-bit hoodlum, even if he was "head of security" for Angion's new number-one investor. But another part had wanted to hide, or maybe just to stay in the bathroom for a very long time. Riker had revealed a dark underbelly of the Calibri Group, whose implications worried MacGregor.

Worried …? The mere hint of violence repulsed him.

But a thought nagged him. If he was willing to compromise the integrity of science, then didn't that imply he accepted violence to achieve his ends? Wasn't science based on fallacy a form of assault on thousands of researchers, students, and patients? Wasn't that *worse* than simply shooting a single man? The one violated the intellectual integrity separating truth and falsehood, while the other violated the physical integrity separating one man's body from another's. He could break down the fences between fact and fancy in the laboratory, or he could stick a knife in another man's chest in a dark alley. Was there no difference, except in terms of global scale? Was he no different from Michael Riker?

No, there is a difference. I know Angiotox works, as does everyone at Angion. And we control the facts. There's a world of difference!

He continued to reflect. A snag during testing had required corrective action. So what? The alternative would have been many months of delay while the FDA regulators created all sorts of interference until Angion could generate the needed animal data. Meanwhile, thousands of people would die, because they had been denied access to George MacGregor's life-saving drug.

Reassured that he was a lifesaver – not a murderer – MacGregor returned to the present, sitting at his desk with the file, *Angiotox, Year IV,* and with the voice on the other end of the telephone.

∼

Riker was saying, "We have a problem."

Best he could, MacGregor swallowed his fear. "Riker! It's about time. I've been waiting for your call."

"They arrived late. I must compliment you on the bait, Mr. MacGregor. The girl has horsepower. She can race an engine. By the end of dinner she had *me* wanting to take her out for a test drive, and she wasn't even near me, let alone feeling up my leg."

"Hmm. She did that? And August?"

"No dice. She walked him right to the edge. Offered him big bucks and big orgasms, but he brushed her off."

"Blimey. How the hell could he?"

MacGregor's heart sank.

"Said he'd think about it. Whole thing's strange. I think he's dangerous. Does he know something we don't know he knows?"

"Impossible. Security's airtight. Riker, you went over the whole system yourself. No ant moves without us knowing."

Riker's words dripped like acid on an open wound. "Given what I just saw, I believe you're wrong. I think we have a security breach."

"Hold on, Riker – tread lightly. Remember, August is tied to Phillips. If Phillips gets wind of any problem with the Angiotox project, then …"

Riker cut in, "Don't lecture me! There're plenty of ways to handle Steve August. He's just a boy who's stumbled into a man's game. Leave that to me."

"What are you proposing?"

"Every human action, Mr. MacGregor, has an underlying cause. There was a reason why August turned the girl down tonight. Yeah, sure, could be some damn loyalty to his lawyer friend in New York – but seems to me there was something else. He's on guard. I'll come in and review the tapes. And my boys will set up a tail. Don't worry, no one escapes me. We'll turn him inside out."

Bullocks, this guy's death itself.

His testicles ice cold, MacGregor tried to keep his voice level, "Realistically speaking, do we have enough time to induce his cooperation?"

"It's tight. By Monday we'll have him under a microscope. By Friday I'll have enough to pull a plan together, maybe sooner. I've a couple of ideas already. You good for a back-up plan, just in case we don't turn him in time?"

MacGregor had already thought this through – but putting it into words made him nauseous. "If we must, we can pick out the points from his data that tell the story the way it should be told. We know the truth – Angiotox works – and we can select the data that will corroborate this fact. The investors will bite. But if we take this route, then at some point we'll have to clean his lab books."

Riker's voice almost sounded gleeful, "I see. You *are* willing to get real, real dirty. Good for you, Mr. MacGregor."

MacGregor was very close to throwing up. "Damn it to hell, Riker, stop calling me *mister*. I'm a professor! It's Professor MacGregor to you! Who are *you*?"

"No … *sir*." The sarcasm was heavy. "To me? To me, it's not Professor MacGregor at all. No sir, no. It's mister … Mister MacGregor."

And the line clicked off.

His heart pounding, MacGregor stared at the golden brain, luminescent from the desk light, its shadow giant on the wall. The shadow obscured the Porsche. He put the dead phone back in its cradle.

16.

SATURDAY, APRIL 9

Even in the sunshine MacGregor needed several minutes to find the gate hidden among the majestic oaks. Silverstein's Brookline estate was discretely tucked away, its driveway winding past rolling green lawns that reached a giant brick colonial with tall white columns.

An elderly butler with an East-European accent ushered him in. They walked past a central marble staircase and along a hallway with several life-size oil portraits of Silverstein in various poses, then into a tall open room with burnished cedar floor, marble fireplace, art deco furnishings, a walnut grand piano, and a floor-to-ceiling picture window looking out on terraced flowerbeds.

"Herr Silverstein will be here shortly. Kaffee?"

Nodding, MacGregor settled into a plush armchair. Moments later the old fellow reappeared with a silver tray coffee setting. He placed it on the side table, poured MacGregor a cup, and then disappeared as silently as he had entered.

MacGregor waited. There was no point rushing matters. Silverstein would appear when he was ready.

Twenty minutes later the Venetian doors at the far end of the drawing room swung open. Silverstein was wearing a silk Japanese bathrobe festooned with Samurai warriors in a variety of poses. His skin was moist, and the silk robe stuck to him in spots. Layers of rubbery fat folded over the drawstring, creating a series of flaps that rolled as he waddled towards MacGregor. In one hand was a giant steaming mug, in the other the remains of a croissant. His surprisingly delicate baby face was nearly lost in the pink mounds of his cheeks and neck. As he settled into the chair next to MacGregor's, puffing slightly, MacGregor noticed bare ankles and feet adorned with slippers: hot pink fluffy rabbit fur, each with a big, yellow, smiley face.

"How the hell am I supposed to take you seriously, when you're dressed like that?"

"Hey, good morning to you, too, George!" Silverstein set his cup down and stuck out a fleshy paw. MacGregor, himself a man of bulk, watched his hand disappear within Silverstein's grip. They shook, Silverstein enthusiastically, his face folding into a grin with a dozen upturned wrinkles, MacGregor reluctantly, never sure what was the cosmic joke that made Silverstein smile so bloody much.

"You want more coffee?" Silverstein picked up the coffeepot, but MacGregor shook his head.

Silverstein shrugged, "Suit yourself," poured himself coffee, stuffed the last of the croissant into his mouth, and grinned happily.

"We've one week to the meeting with the Swiss VC group," said MacGregor, "and we have a problem."

"What's that?"

"There's excess variability in the data."

Silverstein shrugged again, his eyes twinkling. "You told me this months ago. OK, some variability – no problem. More data points resolve that. Enough data narrows the variance, then there's a statistical difference between the groups, and then we go to the investors and the FDA. Easy."

"Right. That's what we thought when we started. Hasn't happened."

Silverstein's shook his head. "Impossible. Before this all the tests were perfect. SAGA demonstrated efficacy. Your follow-up tests in the rabbits demonstrated safety and specificity and confirmed efficacy. This final series should have been simple – a slam dunk."

MacGregor remained silent.

Silverstein shifted in his chair, rolls of flesh moving from side to side uneasily. "You've got something."

"This new guy Steve August is a problem."

"The kid Phillips pushed on us? He screwed up the experiment?"

"He should have been more careful."

"More careful? Are you crazy? George, the meeting's a week away."

MacGregor paused. "I think some of the data are invalid. We've asked him to identify the aberrations in his work."

Silverstein's face turned rosy pink. "Asked him? *Tell* the bastard to get his act together and get it right!"

MacGregor leaned back; he enjoyed watching Silverstein lose his cool. It didn't happen often.

"We're not waiting for anything, except better data. I'd use a heavier hand, except Phillips is part of the equation. August is his golden boy, so we can work on the guy, but we can't push too hard."

Silverstein's face was turning pinker and pinker, nearing a shade of light scarlet, as he bounced up and down in his chair.

"What the HELL are you talking about? You're jeopardizing the entire Angiotox project, for the sake of keeping some senile neurosurgeon happy? Are you goddamn insane?"

"Aye, crazy like a bloody fox. If we're going after August, we must factor in Phillips. He can sway the medical establishment, so we must tread carefully ... not to mention his connection with the Swiss money-men. It's best if August cooperates voluntarily. Then we own him, and Phillips knows nothing."

"Phillips, Shmillips!! I always thought August was risky. So now I'm proved right – as always – and we're stuck with an incompetent who's garbled our data. We've got one week to fix this mess, and you're worried about upsetting Phillips! MacGregor, are you a Grade-A moron?"

"Listen! By the time Phillips's Swiss banker buddies show up, everything will be clean as a whistle. August understands that he must correct the variances. If he has trouble with this, then the backup plan is that Alison and Pieter open his safe, review the data themselves, and make the necessary changes. Of course, in the process Alison and Pieter will find many errors in his lab work and records. Don't worry; he won't dare argue."

Silverstein darkened, as though a thunderstorm had descended over his armchair. A new suspicion showed in his beady koala eyes.

"George, tell me you're not holding back. Angiotox is clean – right? Smooth sailing until now – right? All the tests over the last year, they've all been clean – right? Tell me there's *no* evidence August knows something we don't?"

MacGregor shook his head. "No question – he's wrong."

Silverstein was still staring at MacGregor. He spoke slowly, "George, whatever data we show these Swiss banker boys – ultimately they'll be watching us take it to the FDA. If there's any discrepancy, there'll be hell to pay. And if the data we give the FDA are wrong, and they find out, then there will be hell to pay twice over – once to the Feds, and once to the bankers."

MacGregor grinned. "Relax, David. No lectures. I know the stakes. Don't worry; Angiotox is good. Here are summaries of all our background data. I put them together to reassure you – and me – that we're right."

He pulled two thick folders from his briefcase. "Forgive my handwriting – and the personal visit this morning. Didn't want to use a courier: security's too much an issue. It's all there. The data we get from August will merely put icing on our cake."

Slowly, as Silverstein leafed through the thick folders, his face gradually folded back into an upturned series of smiles. After twenty minutes he closed the folders, nestled them on his lap, and settled into his armchair.

"OK. Convinced," said Silverstein. "It's solid. But I still don't understand why August's tests aren't clear-cut. He must be sloppy."

He started giggling – and his belly started bouncing. MacGregor was sure he felt the vibrations through his feet.

"Damn, George, you went through a helluva lot of work to pull this stuff together. This August guy must've got you worried! Relax."

Silverstein reached over to the coffee pot. "Have some more coffee. Don't worry about August; the whole truth will out."

But somehow MacGregor did not find this reassuring.

That same morning Steve was at his desk, working. Near noon he punched in the combination to his safe. He bent over the door, obscuring its view from the ceiling cameras, and slipped the lab book inside his book bag. Then, more slowly, so the cameras *would* see, he placed some other papers into the bag. He was crossing the line – if anyone discovered he was carrying the lab book, there would be no end to trouble.

A few minutes later he was at the T, and three stations later he was at Downtown Crossing, the epicenter of lunchtime Boston pedestrian bustle. As soon as the train stopped, he was out the doors and up the steps.

He stopped off at his favorite Chinese bookstore and picked up two vintage texts on the *I Ching* – establishing his alibi for the trip. Back outside, he saw nothing unusual. He loped up a side street towards Boston Common and hailed a cab. "Post Office at Fort Point, and hurry."

Shortly they arrived at Boston's main post office. Steve took a number, waited impatiently for his turn, and five minutes later was the proud new renter of a post office box. He paid in cash – untraceable.

Back outside, he jogged across Fort Point channel, found another cab, and within five minutes was back downtown.

Out of the cab, he walked down the block. Nothing. One block later he spied an anonymous print shop.

Perfect!

He moved to a copy machine in the far corner and looked around. The teenage clerk behind the counter was reading a comic book, an old gray-haired man was working another copier, and a mousy-looking woman with thick glasses was studying a display of paper styles.

Steve flipped open the lab book and started copying. He worked as quickly as the machine would let him, but it still took more than a half-hour. Periodically he looked up, but only a couple of people came in, and those that did were quick with their business – nothing odd.

Finished, he collected the four sets of copies, stuffed each in a separate manila envelope, and then sealed the envelopes with packing tape. He set one aside, and for the other three slapped on several stamps being careful to partially cover the tape with the stamps, and then addressed each package to his new post office box address.

Back in the afternoon sunlight he dropped the packages into a mailbox at the street corner, looked around only to see anonymous crowds, and walked to the T-stop. Minutes later he was at his desk, the lab book back in the safe.

My God, I hope I'm doing the right thing.

But he also desperately hoped he was wrong.

Early that Saturday morning Thomas Edwards rolled out of bed, careful not to wake Summer, his twenty-eight year old swimsuit model wife. He took a cab from his 5th Avenue townhouse to his office. Only the guard at the front desk noted his entrance shortly before 7 AM.

Once sheltered in the office, Edwards took a moment to admire the stone mass hanging on his wall. It was a 2500 B.C. large alabaster fragment, stolen from an Egyptian tomb by grave robbers about a century ago. More than 4000 years old, it depicted the judge Thenti sitting at dinner with his family, raised Egyptian hieroglyphics in the background. Edwards loved this relic, reminding him of the expanse of the world outside, eons beyond the very tiny bit that was contemporary New York society. "A sense of perspective," he liked to call it.

He dialed the phone number hidden in his wallet.

"Yesss …" the hiss was too familiar. Edwards shivered.

"Don Calibri, Tom Edwards."

"*Bongiorno*, Tom. So early on a Saturday?"

"Don, we have a security matter."

"Security always matters, Tom."

"Don Calibri, we have reason to believe a competitor of yours – a partner in the firm Spader, Mitchum, and Marshall – has engaged in racketeering. Is this of interest to you?"

"Indeed, yesss …"

"Seems Chip Spader, son of founder Cedric Spader, is collecting leverage on our staff. He's a smart man. If I were to guess, I'd say he wants to break into lawyer-client privilege, perhaps when we represent competition of his."

"Such as the Calibri Group's upcoming acquisition of Mercer Medical Systems?"

"Exactly."

"There's been a leak?"

"Don't know. But he's developing leverage on our firm."

"He's blackmailing Eddie Mac?"

"Not yet. But last week a second-year associate ended up in his apartment, which he now has on video. She was one of our more promising second-years, though her getting mixed up in this reflects bad judgment. Worse, she told another of the associates, who then shared the information with me. She says she was drugged, but …"

"Just get rid of her."

Edwards wondered whom Calibri meant.

"We may have to do just that. But she hinted there might be others in the same boat."

"I see. You think Mr. Spader may have a modus operandi, that he may have compromised several of your little chickies."

"If so, then he could damage the firm. We have several women at the junior and senior associate levels, but we have almost none at partner. It's already embarrassing that the ladies aren't more prominent. This would be a real black eye, if it became known that a valued client was drugging and abusing our female associates, that we knew about the situation, but that we did nothing about it."

Calibri's voice was cold. "We may use the video to remove Spader from the situation and to compromise the reputation of his father's investment house. But, this would require the sacrifice of your young lady."

There was a long silence. Edwards stared at the alabaster for inspiration. He failed to notice the fault lines across Thenti's face – defects in the stone worsening over the years in the poorly humidified air of his office.

He exhaled slowly. "She has proven herself a liability. Making her a public example would be a warning to others. And perhaps in the process we would destroy Spader, minimizing any further threat."

"Yes, I agree with this approach. Leave it to me."

"I was hoping you'd take an interest. Thank you, Don Calibri."

Calibri's breathing was very audible, "But Mr. Edwards, you know I always care for my friends. I much enjoy doing favours."

17.

SUNDAY, APRIL 10

Late that night, or – more accurately – early the following morning, around 4:30 AM Chip Spader was wrestling with his right pants pocket trying to find his keys, while his left hand was fondling Inga Lindquist's ass and his mouth was moving along her neck. Inga was a marketing manager for a Swedish vodka company whom he had met earlier that evening at a cocktail party. She spoke four languages but seemed unable to say "no" in any of them – and for this Chip was grateful to all the gods. A classic Swedish beauty with light blond hair and a complexion as smooth as a bedspread, Inga seemed well-equipped to keep him busy for hours, and Chip was excited to get started. She seemed not to mind his attentions, giggling softly, her hands pulling his shirt out of his pants.

Finally, he managed to get the damn door open. They stumbled inside, and Chip kicked it shut as he turned on the light.

They froze in mid-fondle.

The apartment had been destroyed. The furniture was ripped apart, feathers and fiberfill spilling out onto the floor. Paintings had been torn off the walls, their frames lying in heaps of broken wood and glass. The closet doors were open: clothes and skis and tennis rackets and golf clubs and suitcases flung onto the ground resembling the aftermath of a bomb blast. Beyond the bedroom doorway could be seen tall piles of goose down, the remains of a mattress, an empty bed frame, and scattered heaps of paper.

"Oh my god," he said.

Chip forgot about Inga and sat down on the floor, staring at the ruins.

Inga looked around the apartment without comprehension: "You live here?"

Chip blinked.

He turned to the Swedish playmate in her slinky black cocktail dress, feeling as though he were seeing her for the first time. Then he spoke, slowly, "Yes, I live here. I really need to be alone right now. Please leave."

He stood up and opened the door. She looked around the room, aghast, taking in the demolished contents, then disappeared down the stairs.

Chip walked around the living room, noting the savage precision with which the coffee table had been chopped open so that no hidden door, no hollow wooden leg, might keep a secret.

He walked into the kitchen: broken crystal, shattered plates, scattered utensils.

He moved to the bedroom, its floor thick with white fluffy mattress filler and goose down, broken book bindings and loose pages creating a strange, sterile white landscape of craters, hills, canyons, and valleys.

He moved to the closet. The hangers were empty, clothes in heaps on the floor. He reached up to the top shelf – the shelf where he kept his videos– but he already knew what he would find. Nothing. His palms were sweating. He looked around the closet floor and the bedroom contents, but there were no DVD cases, no VCR cassettes.

He turned to the writing table underneath the bedroom window that looked out on Park Avenue. Pens, stationary, envelopes, files, papers, markers, scissors, everything thrown into one chaotic giant pile. He pawed through it – no computer disks.

The desk was bare except for computer and keyboard. With a shock he realized that his screen saver was bouncing back and forth on the darkened monitor – its one word, "DOMINATE," merely ironic in the ruined apartment. He tripped over the mattress in his haste and fell to his knees, his palm skimming across an open pair of scissors. Blood welled from the cut, but he ignored it, turning to the computer. He hit a button, and the screen lit up …

His own personal e-mail account.

Chip shook his head. Someone had opened his e-mail server? Impossible. But there it was on the screen: "Message sent."

What did this mean? The e-mail read "4:10 AM." He looked at his watch, and his skin crawled. 4:32 AM. Someone had sent this from his computer just moments before their arrival?

He spun around, wide-eyed, drunk, panicked. He lunged across the mattress and found a golf club – his trusty four iron.

Hands shaking, sweat stinging his eyes, with two hands he clutched the club, ready to swing. He returned to the living room but found the front door locked. Methodically he went through every inch – living room, dining room, kitchen – but no sign of the intruder.

No one.

What about that email?

He returned to his desk amongst the bedroom destruction, clicked on the computer display, and a message flashed on the screen:

> *Hey guys,*
>
> *Had one hell of a time last weekend! Don't think I'll see action like this again for a long while. I mean, on a scale of one to ten, this was a definite thirteen.*
>
> *She's hot, she's good, she's willing, and she's very able. This is Manhattan's best talent. She's Laurel Farthington, and you can reach her at Eddie Mac … anytime.*
>
> *Check out the video! What a rush!!!*
>
> *You're Partying Bro,*
> *Chip*

In disbelief he stared at the email. The list of recipients went on … and on … and on … the entire contents of his address folder. Not only did it include his comrades at Spader, Mitchum, and Marshall, but every business contact accumulated over the last three years, and personal friends from college, and business school chums, and …

"Oh, no!" The list included his entire family. Yes: his father's personal e-mail.

The Old Man won't like this.

With faint hope for reprieve, he clicked on the attached video clip.

He watched from painful start to anguished climax. Laurel was clearly recognizable. He had edited the clip to blur his face; but his body was still in focus, and in the context of the e-mail the fact that it was himself was undeniable.

This is all wrong!

Blind rage took over. He swung the golf club – hard – against the video monitor. Sparks flew across the room … shards of glass and plastic everywhere. He swung again. An electric arc blazed like lightning, and then all the lights went out. He didn't care. The moonlight gave him light, and again and again he swung – smashing the monitor, smashing the desk, smashing the chair and mattress and bed frame and computer console and broken divan. Into the living room he kept on with his attack – swinging the four iron against the remains of the sofa and the TV and the love seat and the stereo and the coffee table and …

He stopped. There was banging on the door. He realized he was drenched in sweat, his ripped tuxedo shirt flecked with spots of blood.

But at this point he did not care. Clutching the golf club in one hand, he opened the door, and light streamed in from the hallway.

"Mr. Spader?" Two uniformed policemen were standing there, hands on their unbuttoned gun holsters, necks and arms thick from pumping iron and eating donuts.

He nodded.

Without further invitation they stepped inside, looking around the demolished room with its scattered wood chips and tufts of pillow down and shards of glass, and then they looked at him.

Gasping for air, suddenly realizing how drunk and angry he looked, Chip shook his head. "Sorry. Too much noise? You know, fellas, I'm glad you're here. You won't believe what's happened."

The two officers glanced at each other. The first one said, "Mr. Spader, please put down the weapon."

Chip closed his mouth with a snap. Sympathy and respect should have been forthcoming, but the cop sounded hostile. Chip dropped the golf club.

"Mr. Spader, you're under arrest," said the second one, as his partner stepped quickly behind Chip, grabbing an arm and snapping cuffs on the wrist. He twisted Chip's arm slightly as he did so, forcing him to turn to one side, and the cuffs clicked again behind his back, securing the other hand. That hurt.

"You have the right to remain silent …"

As the one detailed his Miranda rights, the other, gun pulled, walked through the apartment. Soon he was back. "No one else, Mickey."

Pursuant to the officer's initial statement, Chip had remained silent, but this was too much. "Of course there's no one else! Can't you see I've been vandalized? Why are you arresting me? Okay, I was disturbing the peace. But for God's sake, I was upset!"

The two officers looked at him. Chip realized that he appeared less than the model citizen: vodka breath, bloody hand, torn clothes, bent golf club, ruined apartment, etcetera.

Mickey said, "You're under arrest for aggravated assault, Mr. Spader. There's a young blonde at the station. She says you forced yourself on her, offered her drugs in exchange for favors, and when she refused you started smashing furniture, and she ran."

Chip felt dizzy and hot and sick, the room spun in a circle, and he blacked out.

～

He awoke staring up into space with Mickey shaking his shoulders, the cop's thick face filling Chip's vision.

Chip managed, "I'm saying nothing till I speak with my lawyer."

"Sure, Mr. Spader, anything you say. You can call from the station."

They took him downstairs to the waiting patrol car.

Unable to reach his lawyer for several hours, Chip spent the rest of Sunday morning alone in his jail cell. On one level, he did not mind, because he had a lot to think about.

18.

SUNDAY, APRIL 10

Around the time Chip and Inga were nearing Chip's apartment, Dida's alarm was waking George from a sound sleep. Rousing, he remembered last night they had gone out to dinner and returned to her condo for a half hour of scalding sex. As usual she had worn him out, but that made for a great night's sleep.

He shut off the alarm – 4:10 AM – and looked over at her sculpted neck and shoulders. Sometimes on these early Sunday mornings he wished he could stay in bed and further enjoy her pleasures, but he had to get to Angion for the Science Service.

The springs creaked as he rolled out of bed, and she stirred.

"George, this makes no sense. Why not hold your Service at a more reasonable hour – like ten – the way normal churches do."

He grunted in response and moved into the bathroom for his shower. Upon his return he found her leaning back on her elbows, thick raven-black hair tossed behind her shoulders, bare breasts and stomach exposed to the world.

"You're not interested in a little early morning work-out?" She swayed her shoulders.

"You know I've got to be there before sunrise," he snapped.

"You sound like a vampire."

He was putting on his shirt. "Well, I'm not sucking blood, only ideas."

"I'd love to watch. From what you've told me it sounds like an orgy!" She chuckled.

He stopped putting on his socks. "Don't be ridiculous!"

"Several dozen scientists meet pre-dawn, share their most intimate secrets, and two hours later you're all refreshed for a week of experiments. Sounds like an orgy to me ... and it makes me feel *hot*!" She threw off the covers and rolled her naked body to his side of the bed, where he was putting on his pants. "Come on, Georgie Porgie, come to mama and get some sugar!"

He bent to put his shoes on, but her arms encircled him from behind. "Dida, please!"

She flung herself back onto the pillows. "Honestly, George, why won't you let me watch? I bet it'd be awful fun!"

"That's why I *won't* let you watch. Someone merely frivolous would be a guaranteed disruption."

Finished tying his shoes, George started to stand up, but Dida grabbed his belt, and the next thing he knew she was on top of him, her legs wrapped around his waist, her arms locking his wrists.

"What's so frivolous about this?" Her legs squeezed, forcing him to exhale. "Oh, you like being frivolous, Georgie, don't you?"

He moaned – with pleasure, with pain, with exasperation. "Dida, please, I've got to get going."

"Not till you tell me more." She squeezed harder, making him wince.

"Okay, okay, just let go, please!"

∾

Several minutes later, they were still lying on the bed. He had finished the story.

"So let me get this straight." She stretched flat. "You hypnotize your best scientists so they shout out the first idea in their heads. They talk and listen to everyone else all at the same time. If they're not talking, they're humming 'ooomm," depending on how happy they are with the conversation. You ask questions. And – *voila* – this nuthouse gives you an answer?"

"No, not a nuthouse. This has rocketed us forwards, bringing Angiotox to the point of clinical testing!"

"Georgie, be straight with me. Deep down, you're not really thinking about scientific discovery. You set the terms of the SS, right? Tell me the truth – this isn't about science at all. It's about *power!*"

He had been putting on his jacket, but he stopped to look at her. She was curled on her side, naked, her eyes locked on his.

"Dida, you're a smart woman."

`He paused, and then spoke slowly: "You must understand – reality is only a function of perceptions. Control perceptions, and you control reality. Successful science both anticipates and defines what others will find to be real. Angion has assays, tests, procedures, that no other group has, anywhere – so *ours* are the perceptions that define *others'* reality. That is real power. And this power crystallizes in the Science Service, because through the SS we unify our perceptions."

He moved towards the bed, eyes locked with hers, "By controlling the perceptions of the SS, I control reality. Controlling reality means controlling the world. It's that simple."

He bent over her, his face inches from hers.

He whispered, "If we can do what no one else does, if no one can disagree, and if we thus can choose the lens through which all people perceive, then we can create whatever world we choose. Isn't that ultimate power?"

He moved away from the bed. She was breathing fast, her eyes two dark almonds, her nipples erect.

A smile played on his lips, "Ah, you understand. Bye, Dida. Gotta go."

~

George reflected as he drove to Angion. Never before had he discussed details of the Science Service – not with anyone – but for some time now he had wanted to embed Dida within Angion (so to speak), thereby ultimately controlling her fealty, and maybe someday using this loyalty as a counter-lever against Calibri. Revealing the Science Service to her seemed a necessary step.

Meanwhile, there was the sex.

And the power. She loved power maybe even more than he did.

He thought back. As a naïve twenty-two year old he had believed in an underlying objective reality – simple right and wrong, true and false. After all, didn't the success of modern technology *prove* science to be true – achievements like antibiotics, genetic testing, nuclear power, space flight?

But by the time he reached thirty he had come to a more sophisticated realization. While such examples were the conclusions of research spread across decades and thousands of scientists the world over, experimental results at the level of the *individual* were merely subjective assessments of ambiguous data. It was the most *persuasive* researcher who published his work faster in more prestigious journals, acquired more funding, trained more students, and thus created more data confirming his results. And then the system would snowball. Competition between labs often degenerated into intellectual beauty contests, with one or the other "winning" only when the rest of the scientific community agreed with the more persuasive of the two.

He had once shared these thoughts with a colleague, who had responded, "George, you're too cynical to be a scientist."

But he wasn't cynical. He was merely practical.

And as a practical man, he had realized his best protection was to produce results so intricate that no other researcher would care to – would dare to – attempt reproducing the data. If no one else did the experiments, then MacGregor would have a monopoly, a lock on this corner of the scientific world. And then he was the arbiter of this, his own reality.

In the early 1990s angiogenesis research had just been born. In on the ground floor, MacGregor found himself with a wide-open space of possible topics, options, and techniques. Wasting no time, over the next few years he had achieved first-mover advantage, patenting dozens of compounds, tests, and assays, thereby cornering the intellectual market of this particular piece of biomedicine.

But the greater his success, the higher the lab's profile, the worse became the need for secrecy. This need for better security became vivid when he lost one of his post-docs to a rival lab, Vessel Strategies, and within three months Vessel Strategies had patented a new assay, beating out MacGregor's application by forty-eight hours.

That day he had resolved *never* to be burned again. Secrecy became Angion's top priority, so that the loss of a scientist would do no more than minimal damage. This meant that any one person should know as little as possible about what fellow scientists were doing – and the outside world should know even less.

When MacGregor first instituted his secrecy policies, two of his best researchers had quit, both giving the same explanation – that his approach was exactly the opposite of good science, that open discussion reinforced critical thinking, tightened intellectual rigor, and enhanced creativity. One of them had sneered, "George, this is pure poppycock!"

MacGregor had to admit they had a point. Indeed, scientists needed to be able to critique each other's work. But if he could employ their brains *without* them walking away with secrets …? This was the idea that had led him to the hypnosis experiment with Andropov, Mueller, and Richards.

The idea had come to him after watching a rerun of that old movie with Frank Sinatra, *The Manchurian Candidate*, in which a war hero is secretly hypnotized to kill the President.

George chuckled – *such a stroke of genius!*

He had spent months researching the topic. He learned a hypnotized subject might explore ideas in creative ways, processing information with enhanced concentration, imagining beyond the constraints of habit and embarrassment, and – most importantly – forgetting and remembering upon command.

Once ready, MacGregor had approached three of Angion's senior scientists, Mueller, Richards, and Andropov, with an unconventional proposal – undergo hypnosis under his guidance. He explained this might help them tap their underlying creative scientific geniuses.

Flattery rarely fails. Each agreed.

According to the textbooks he read, the suggestibility of intelligent, skeptical subjects was unpredictable at best, so MacGregor prepared a cocktail mixed in ginger ale – a dash of gamma-aminobutyric acid, GABA (the notorious "date rape" drug), a touch of fentanyl (a powerful narcotic), and a pinch of lorazepam (an anti-anxiety sleeper medication). He dubbed the concoction "School-Aid."

The drugs worked. Sleepy and relaxed, within a half-hour they were hypnotized.

MacGregor proceeded to explore their reasoning capabilities. Soon he realized that their uninhibited brains could digest, analyze, and synthesize ideas at lightning speeds, seemingly limited only by how quickly they communicated with each other.

As he experimented further that night, he discovered they could speak and listen *simultaneously* – with all three contributing critiques, rebuttals, and rejoinders nearly at the speed of thought. He could still catch the gist of their conversations, but only if he listened *very* carefully.

And even as he marveled at the three scientists chattering so brilliantly and quickly, MacGregor made his third discovery ...

He could control the conversation.

At the start, he had instructed them, "Listen to every word, integrate this with your own knowledge, and generate further hypotheses. I may make an occasional comment to help move the discussion along." That last sentence – spoken without full understanding of its ramifications – had made all the difference.

The three men were discussing implications of the x-ray crystallography of a chemical compound, when MacGregor lost patience: "For God's sake, the structure doesn't matter. Let's talk about function."

Silence. Then one said, "This conversation is a waste of time. The structure doesn't matter, while *function* is critical: consider the active moiety that mimics the tyrosine kinase receptor ..." And suddenly all three were chattering about the possible functions of their new molecule.

MacGregor listened with only half an ear. Instead, his attention had turned to the implications of what he had just heard.

I can control their reasoning. Blimey – the possibilities!

So, he experimented. Just as they were reaching consensus, he introduced a contradictory premise. Their conversation shifted to incorporate his comments, but then their ideas diverged, and then a new stream of conversation ensued. They did not tire, and MacGregor did not tire listening to them, redirecting them, playing with them. Finally, after about four hours, he called it a day: "You boys are entirely on target. It's wonderful that you have reached some agreement."

The three blinked: "Its wonderful we've reached some agreement."

MacGregor left them with several post-hypnotic suggestions. They would not remember their conversations; but they would feel they had made significant progress; and they would feel happy about the meeting and want to do it again though they would not remember being hypnotized; and they would fall back into their trance at MacGregor's command, "*Ad hominem*."

This was MacGregor's own private joke. "*Ad hominem*" was Latin for "to the man," a phrase used to describe an illegitimate form of argument: if you did not agree with someone's ideas, but if rather than addressing the issues you attacked the person proposing them, then you were guilty of an *ad hominem* attack. By attacking the speaker rather than his argument you demonstrated weakness, hypocrisy, even deceit. For most people that was the meaning of the phrase, "*Ad hominem*."

But MacGregor liked the phrase. He thought it illustrated the nature of science. "To the man" – most people assumed science was some kind of machine floating in a vacuum that magically produced new ideas, innovative products, and revolutionary technologies. But *he* knew that science was a uniquely human enterprise – run by women and men who had the ambitions, troubles, hopes, and fears common to all people. Science – underneath its claims of objectivity, reproducible experiments, falsifiable hypotheses, and logical progression – was merely a human endeavor, subject to all the constraints of any manmade effort. Science, for George MacGregor, was *ad hominem*, nothing more. All of life, as far as he was concerned, was *ad hominem*.

And that was why the Science Service, or "SS" as he liked to call it, was so important. The SS gave him control of that nefarious *ad hominem* element.

19.

MacGregor pulled into his reserved parking space at Angion. There was only a hint of dawn in the night sky. He still had time, and the car was warm. He gave himself another minute to reminisce.

~

The experiment with Andropov, Mueller, and Richards had convinced him the entire lab should be put under hypnotic direction. But the missing key was the scientists' willingness, since one fact was indisputable: hypnosis required a participant's consent.

After his three lieutenants had gone through their session, MacGregor called a meeting of the senior staff. That Sunday night they assembled in a conference room at Angion, about twenty total, and MacGregor outlined for them the issues as logically as if he were solving an algebra problem.

The group listened with increasing discontent. The first to speak was Henri LeBreque, a short Canadian from Montreal: "George, with all due respect, this is crazy. You want to hypnotize us so you can tap into our collective unconsciousness, generate great ideas, and then have us forget unless it suits your purposes? Come on!"

"No, not my purposes," George said smoothly. "*Our* purposes. Each project leader will retain all the ideas, and only those ideas, that are relevant for his or her particular project. The point is that this is for our protection – yours and mine."

He continued, "Think of yourselves as a network of secret agents working in small cells in a foreign country. Members of a cell know only what that individual cell is doing; they do *not* know about the others. So, if the enemy – in our case, a competing lab – penetrates one of the cells, the other cells will not be threatened. In other words, all knowledge is on a "need-to-know" basis. If you do, then fine, you will. If not, well then, why do you care?

"The fundamental issue is this: in our modern information age where knowledge is power, how do we allow science its necessary mutual exchange of ideas, while avoiding the danger of information in too many hands? Mine is the solution!"

Henri looked quizzical. "You think hypnosis is *better* than conventional human interaction? Why would this be any different?"

MacGregor had both hoped and dreaded someone would ask this question. The next five minutes would either prove him right – or prove him a total fool.

He spoke in a formal tone, "Oh, so you want data? Well then. Richards, Mueller, Andropov, gentlemen, please join me."

The three walked to the front of the room with puzzled expressions.

MacGregor looked them over. "John, my good bloke, why'd I ask you up here?"

"Not sure, Chief," said Richards. "Last week you suggested I do a hypnosis experiment – a way for 'exploring untapped creative potential,' as you put it. You want to hypnotize us tonight?"

MacGregor smiled. "Yes. And I had the same conversation with each of you three." The others nodded. "But what you don't remember is that we already did the experiment."

The room turned dead quiet, all eyes riveted on the four scientists standing at the head of the table next to the golden brain on its pedestal.

MacGregor the showman swept his calm gaze over the audience, ensuring their attention, then turned back to the three scientists. "Gentlemen, humor me. Please look at the brain … Focus carefully … Are you ready? … All eyes on the brain? … *AD HOMINEM!*" He declared the Latin words with great force, like an incantation.

The three closed their eyes.

Blimey, this is going to work!

MacGregor tried not to let his excitement show.

While the three stood silent, as though comfortably sleeping erect, MacGregor spoke to his audience: "What you are about to see, my dear friends, is the most novel use of human intelligence in modern history. This may well represent the next stage of human evolution. If we take it public, we will be famous, but then the potential to use this tool will be forever diluted by the fact that others may also employ it. Therefore, this method, in fact, this very evening and all its events, must remain secret. Before we proceed, do you all swear?"

Some looked quizzical, others skeptical, but in response they all nodded, up and down the table.

"Alison, any particular problem been bothering you this past week?" he asked.

"Of course. In our group we've been trying to develop an experiment to test the dependence of the expression of transcription factor XR8 on oxygenation status, but we're stuck because O_2 concentration affects the XR8 assay. We can't do the experiment without altering the measurement."

MacGregor nodded, "You three fellows are aware of the difficulties with the XR8 assay?"

Andropov and Mueller nodded, but Richards shook his head.

"Gentlemen," said MacGregor, "this is what I'd like you to do. First – you two please explain the details of the XR8 problem to Richards. Second – the three of you come up with a solution, the best you can find in the next – shall we say – fifteen minutes. Third – when finished, please explain your solution to the group. John, you can act as spokesman. Fourth – after the first three tasks are complete, you will then awaken upon my command when I speak the word, '*VERITAS*,' but you will remember nothing about this session. Do you understand?"

The three nodded.

"Very well," said MacGregor. "Please begin."

Immediately Mueller and Andropov started chattering so fast that the observers could understand almost nothing – and then Richards joined in. One could catch only isolated snippets – "assay" … "O_2" … "base" … "epitope" … "electrode" – but there did seem to be a pattern, an ebb and flow to the three's "conversation," with the first two dominating, Richards's voice a less frequent contrast. Then, after about three minutes, there was an abrupt lull – for a few seconds' total quiet – and then the three resumed, but with renewed fury, all three chiming in with unintelligible intensity. Information flowed faster than the audience could follow: the three listening, thinking, and chattering simultaneously, a confused cacophony to the outsiders, the three brains functioning nearly as one.

Collective intelligence!

It was awesome.

MacGregor watched his audience's faces go slack with amazement, near disbelief, and yes … an element of fear. Here was the next divide! Men could lose their identities, and in doing so become more than men, more like gods, yet thereby sacrifice themselves. He could see that they were wondering: was MacGregor right; was this the next stage of human evolution?

And then – all of a sudden – there was silence.

Only twelve minutes had elapsed.

Richards spoke, "We have a solution to the XR8 problem," and he proceeded to explain it to the astounded audience.

Over the prior two weeks several of the seated scientists had tried without success to solve the XR8 dilemma. Incredibly, over the next half hour Richards explained the theory and experimental methods for circumventing the problem to the point that, by the time he was finished, every listener understood the proposed solution, and all were convinced it would work. But even more than that, every single one was awestruck that they had just witnessed an extraordinary advance: collective human intelligence, much more powerful than the three brains working separately. The total was greater than the sum of its parts. Much greater.

There was a long silence in the conference room.

Alison spoke first: "OK, chief. Impressive. A good solution for XR8. And that in less than fifteen minutes. Not bad."

MacGregor smiled. "Right, not bad," he said. "Now, watch this."

He turned back to the three hypnotized scientists, "John, Andrew, Sergei, as I instructed you, it is time to awake. VERITAS!"

The three opened their eyes to find themselves staring at the golden brain. Roberts looked up first, his face puzzled.

"OK, we've seen it before. Sure, impressive piece for the visitors. What about it?"

His question broke the tension that had been building in the room over the prior hour, and the entire group of scientists broke out laughing. The three looked even more puzzled, and slightly angry.

"What's so funny?" asked Mueller. "You call us up here and then laugh at us?"

MacGregor smiled broadly, sweeping his hands out in a gesture embracing the three confused men, the awed seated scientists, and even the naïve world outside. "Gentlemen, I apologize. You were unknowing – but willing – participants in a very grand experiment. As you may recall, you did agree to try the hypnosis exercise we discussed last week."

The three nodded, their expressions confused.

"Let me explain …"

As MacGregor spoke, the audience interrupted frequently with questions. They were all worried about the fundamental underlying issues – identity, remembering, forgetting, free will. Alison summarized it best, "How can we be sure we'll keep control of ourselves? I mean, George, you're a sweetheart and all, but I don't want to wake up some morning pregnant without any idea how it happened!"

MacGregor tried to look stern, "There's no question of anything like that. Even when hypnotized, the subject will never do something that he – or she – really doesn't want to do. So, no worries, Alison, you can't be turned into a mindless sex toy." He grinned at her.

Alison's blue eyes were emotionless dark pools. "No worries there."

Henri spoke up, "With all due respect, Chief, you're asking us to trust you with an enormous amount of power over our personal lives."

Several nodded.

MacGregor felt frustrated. He had hoped for more enthusiasm. Didn't they see the possibilities? Didn't they trust him?

But he maintained composure. "I'm a man of my word. Nevertheless, as a further guarantee that I won't implant you with any nefarious suggestions, like blowing up Congress or assassinating the Pope, I propose we do the hypnosis session in two parts. I will hypnotize half of you, while the other half watch. Once that's done, we'll wake up the first group, and then they can watch while I hypnotize the second. That way you can all be sure I haven't done anything besides install the mental machinery you need to participate in this new form of human intelligence – the power of the collective mind! Consider it a software upgrade for your brain."

They looked at each other around the table. No one spoke, the only sound a faint buzz from old fluorescent bulbs overhead, casting their faces with a slight green tinge.

Pieter was the first to nod. "The demonstration, it is convincing. The lab wins; and we all win – greater knowledge, and greater power, and greater security, and so more money. It is genius."

Alison chimed in, "I like the fact that we will witness each others' hypnoses. This gives us a guarantee that this'll be on the up and up."

And one by one, all assented. Last was Henri.

"Chief, I've already put three loyal years into Angion. I won't be the only holdout, but I must be honest: the whole thing makes me nervous. I don't think we understand all the consequences."

MacGregor bowed towards him. "Yes. It's reasonable to be nervous. But ..." and he turned his beaming face onto the entire group at the table, "every great advance is made with some degree of risk. Of course! We are stepping into a great, grand, unknown world!"

Inside, he was exultant – he had won.

And so that night they proceeded with the hypnotic induction. They split into two groups, as MacGregor had suggested, and the one watched the other, and then the second group watched the first. And that had all gone off without a hitch.

And so was born the Science Service – the SS.

The problems with Angiotox had come later.

～

Oh, the challenges of genius!

MacGregor shook his head, took a deep breath, shut off the car engine, and walked into Angion to prepare for the morning's Science Service.

20.

SUNDAY, APRIL 10

Shortly after 8 AM that morning Riker arrived at Angion with four of his security gorillas – hulks in jeans, turtlenecks, and blue blazers that bulged under left armpits. One stayed in the van, while the others followed him inside.

Riker had reviewed Angion's security system the day MacGregor signed the contract. He had toured the facility with the retiring security chief, Jay Tungsten, and had admired the state-of-the-art surveillance already in place. Motion detectors, closed-circuit video, and microphones in every room stored every conversation in the security center's computer databank for later retrieval, as needed. A charged metal lattice inside the walls prevented wireless communication with the outside world.

The place was sealed tight except for one bizarre defect. For three hours on Sundays – 5 till 8 AM – the surveillance shut down. At that time the external doors locked automatically, denying access to the building except by key card and thumbprint scan, but all internal monitoring systems turned off.

"Sorry, Mr. Riker, but I don't know why," Tungsten had said. "MacGregor told me every Sunday morning, from five till eight, he wanted everything shut down – video off, microphones dead. Even the guards have to leave the security center and move to a separate monitored room. Whole thing's screwy."

"He give you a reason?"

Tungsten shrugged, "Nope. He just said, 'Do it.' He pays the bills."

But the bedroom conversation he had taped this morning between

Dida and MacGregor provided some explanation – MacGregor wanted *no* record of his precious Science Service, even within his own security system.

Yet … this explanation bothered Riker. Why trust his security staff with the lab's every intimate detail – but not with the SS? Was there something about the SS that he wanted *no one* else to know?

Well, that was about to change.

They entered MacGregor's office without knocking.

MacGregor's jaw dropped.

Who does this guy think he is?

"Riker! What the hell! You know on Sundays Angion's off-limits for …"

But Riker was leafing through the papers on MacGregor's desk, ignoring him. His three aides wandered around the room, looking behind the paintings, picking up pillows on the couch, opening file cabinets.

Without looking up, Riker said, "I talked with Don Calibri this morning, MacGregor. At this point *nothing's* off-limits. He's concerned about his investment."

MacGregor decided he hated this man. "We went over this Friday night. You're supposed to be bugging August, not barging into my office!"

"Indeed. We need to review Angion's security tapes of August, so I brought along some extra help." He smiled, baring his pointy canines. "However, there's more."

MacGregor arched his eyebrows, meaning to reflect surprise, but his mind was back at the urinal at Radius – his testicles freezing into ice cubes.

"More?"

"Don Calibri wants to know about your Sunday mornings. And we're very interested in plugging that three-hour hole in Angion's otherwise excellent system."

Of course, MacGregor had an answer ready, as Tungsten long ago had warned him about Riker's questions: "The senior staff come in for a brainstorming session early Sundays. It's our fundamental strategy session. It *must* be confidential so the scientists feel secure with *no* risk of records getting into the wrong hands!"

"Offline conversations are a vulnerability," said Riker. "But we'll talk about that later. Right now we want to review your tapes of August. You better pray there's nothing wrong."

He waved at his companions. "Gentlemen ... the Security Center."

Once they were gone, MacGregor exhaled audibly. Had Dida said something? Surely she realized Angion's success relied on the complete confidentiality of the SS? Could she have told Calibri, or Riker – and that only hours after their conversation?

No, not possible, he thought, recalling her legs wrapped around him. *She's mine.*

Riker hated being wrong.

At the Security Center, Riker's three crew shortly were seated at monitors, one with DVDs from January, another with February, and the third with March, Rusty and Bobby showing them details of the equipment. Once they were settled, Riker looked around. He was kicking himself for not following through back when he had visited Tungsten in January, but the mistake had been understandable – the place had seemed airtight.

Throughout his career, he had enjoyed being *always* right.

In 1972, at the age of 23 he had left the Johannesburg police force, recruited to work as a "technical adviser" for the CIA's Phoenix project in the Vietnam Delta. For about a year he had organized the local Vietnamese into "provincial reconnaissance units" to raid contested areas in the South, eliminating key members of the Vietcong infrastructure. But, after the 1973 Paris peace accords, the Phoenix directorate in Saigon had been turned over to the South Vietnamese, his CIA contacts had disappeared, and Riker had become a free agent.

Flying solo, running intel against the Vietcong, he had made it his business never to be wrong. The Americans paid well for good info, and soon they learned Riker furnished the best. Several Vietnamese boys with slit throats had paid the price for giving him less than accurate numbers. Once *that* was known around Saigon, the quality of his intel became A-1. As a result, Riker enjoyed the good life – lots of money, plenty of contracts, popularity with the locals, and access to young girls and boys for his private pleasures.

Over time, besides the U.S. Army a variety of other agencies found his intelligence of value – the French, the Brits, the South Vietnamese, his former CIA employers, and even the Mossad (though he was unsure why the Israelis cared). The Chinese and Soviets also paid well, though trading with both sides required delicacy. Gunrunning soon became a lucrative side business – what was the use of knowing where your enemies were, if you didn't have munitions? By the time Saigon collapsed in 1975 he had built a network of contacts that spanned the globe, virtually guaranteeing his success as a purveyor of boutique paramilitary services at global flashpoints.

But here was a situation where he seemed proven wrong – wrong to have thought Angion secure. Twice – first with that pup August likely pulling some stunt, and second with MacGregor creating a damn-fool weekly three-hour hole. Riker kicked himself.

Idiot!

He should have stopped it the day Tungsten told him.

He noticed Rusty and Bobby fidgeting at their respective consoles. He nodded at them – sending ripples of terror across their faces.

Monkeys!

He stepped outside, for the next hour wandering Angion's desolate hallways. Sundays the building was empty – other than MacGregor's office and the Security Center. As he moved through the building, Riker observed everything: row upon row of clean desks, carefully stored supplies, methodically arranged equipment. Sometimes he leaned against a doorframe, his heel gently tapping against the wall.

A careful observer would have realized Riker's journey took him through each floor's conference room, and an even more careful observer would have realized Riker spent considerable time studying each of these rooms. But not even the most astute observer would have noticed the series of tiny metal needles that extended from Riker's shoe, tapped gently into the wall each time he paused.

These were not commercially available, although useful for those in the surveillance community with good connections and deep pockets. Riker had several buddies from his 'Nam days who were still in Army Intel, buddies who had access to high-tech toys others couldn't get. This was why Riker ran IPI, and why IPI ran security for Calibri: the Don knew that Riker's bag of tricks could do things others could not.

The needles were a triumph of miniaturization. Each was a hollow tube with a shell of microscopic photocells that generated electricity from incident light. Folded inside the tube were a tiny microphone and video camera. The entire assembly was mounted on a base with rotors and wings – a tiny helicopter less than 5 millimeters long. Powered by ambient light the microphone could run virtually indefinitely, and with a fully loaded battery the helicopter assembly could tour a room for an hour, no more noticeable than a mosquito. This was one of Riker's favorite gadgets. He called it, "the barfly."

Riker had brought a total of eight, four loaded in the heel of each shoe. He deposited one in MacGregor's office, one in the Security Center, and five in each of the conference rooms, one on each floor. The last he planted in the central arena.

His tour completed, the eight barflies set, Riker returned to the Security Center. At first glance he figured his men had hit pay dirt. Rusty and Bobby were no longer at their consoles but instead were cuffed back-to-back in the middle of the room.

Bravo was seated next to the two-man pretzel, his 9-millimeter Glock dangling loosely in his hand. Alpha and Charlie meanwhile were clicking through Angion's security archives. Both had their coats open, holsters unbuttoned, Glocks at the ready.

Riker betrayed no surprise. "Status?"

Bravo answered, "Under control. Our friends here got nervous when we started asking questions, so we shut'em down."

Rusty glared at him, "We ain't done nuthin'!"

Without hesitation Bravo drilled a punch into Rusty's jaw, spattering flecks of blood against the wall.

"Don't talk unless you're talked to, asshole," growled Bravo. "Your mother teach you no manners?"

Rusty didn't answer, blood oozing from his mouth.

Riker ignored the interchange. "What've you found?"

Alpha said, "Sir, I was going through March and April, following August through each day. He came in early, worked late, nose to the grindstone except for an occasional call to his girlfriend in New York – squeaky clean, until …" He punched a couple of buttons. "Until … last Saturday. Look at this."

Alpha hit more buttons. Video flashed onto the screen – date, time, and location in the lower left corner.

"Here is Angion's one entrance. Entry's by keycard and thumbprint scan, or can be overridden manually from the Security Center. Exit requires no key. Last Saturday's monitor shows 142 entrances and 141 exits. The one missing is ... Steve August. Where'd he go? We can trace his path through the building. Here ... he enters ... 6:38 AM. For the day he's at his lab bench ... except for a total of five bathroom breaks, and one lunch break at fourteen-fifteen. By the evening he's obviously tired. He nods off a couple of times. He keeps calling his girlfriend, but no success."

"Get on with it," snarled Riker.

"Here it is, after twenty-three-hundred hours ... curfew's midnight. He packs his bag, closes the safe, puts on his jacket. He tries to phone Morgan one more time ..."

"Who?"

"Morgan. Morgan Najar. The girlfriend."

"Oh, right. The one in Manhattan," said Riker. The name was too familiar.

Alpha proceeded, "Exactly. The girlfriend. So, end of the night he puts on his jacket, tries to call one more time, puts his head on his desk, and then ... nothing. He snoozes, not a move, and the monitors cut out. After thirty minutes the sensors shut down."

"They shut down with him still in the room?"

"Right. His body temperature was constant. Any flux makes the cameras switch on, so they'll pick up a mouse running across the floor, but not the sweep of the second-hand on a clock. After thirty minutes the system shuts down to conserve memory. It re-boots when there's a change."

"OK, so he falls asleep. When does he wake up?"

"He doesn't."

"What?"

"There's no record of it."

"The cameras didn't switch back on?"

"No."

"So he slept until early morning, and then left between O-five-hundred and O-eight-hundred, when that fool MacGregor had the system shut down. Goddamn!"

"No, Mr. Riker, that's not what happened."

Riker never liked being corrected. He replied sharply, "Very well, Alpha, what *did* happen?"

Alpha tried to keep his voice steady. "We don't know. Later that night, O-two-forty-eight, the monitors kicked in. No clear reason. At that time this bozo …" he gestured at Rusty, "says he follows S.O.P. and marches up there to check it out. It's all on tape."

Alpha hit buttons on the computer, and the screen showed Rusty walking the aisles of Lab 105, but a pan-view showed nothing else.

"You're telling me he vanished into thin air, somewhere between midnight and oh-two-forty-eight? Impossible!"

Alpha said, "The most obvious explanation is that August is doing espionage for a competing lab, and that he paid off these assholes to edit the tapes. But they got mad when we pointed this out, so we cuffed 'em so they'd think harder about their answers."

Riker gave him a withering look. "Doubt it. I've watched him. He's a boy trapped in a man's game, and he doesn't know how to play. But I bet he does know something."

"We've gone over the lab tapes twice. There's nothing else."

"How 'bout the adjoining rooms?"

"No activity anywhere from midnight till oh-five-hundred, when the system shuts down."

Johnny cleared his throat. "That's not quite right. Professor MacGregor has two spaces that he's made into 'clean rooms' – for really sensitive experiments that he doesn't want recorded. There's no surveillance for these two rooms."

Riker felt like he'd been slammed in the stomach. "Why wasn't I told about this?"

"Sorry, Mr. Riker, we thought the Professor told you."

Riker kept his face expressionless; but he was damn angry.

MacGregor's holding out. He will fry for this.

He grinned, but then he noticed the terror that resulted on all five men's faces.

Riker gestured at the two handcuffed guards. "Who do you work for – George MacGregor, or Michael Riker?"

Their retorts were instant, "Michael Riker!"

"Fine. You're here routinely on the Saturday night-Sunday morning shift? You and no one else?"

"Yes, Mr. Riker," Rusty answered, his mouth sticky with blood. "The Professor special-picks who works weekends. There's one other guy, Larry, but he only works back-up when one of us's out."

Riker nodded at Alpha. "Take off the cuffs."

He looked at Rusty and Bobby. "You work for me now. Sundays, four-teen-hundred hours, Alpha will meet you both here at the Center. Give him a copy of the compiled videodisc. He'll have two thousand in cash for each of you. That's two thousand a week, tax-free, for as long as you're here. You stay square with me, then you're safe. You don't, then you're not. Got it?"

They both nodded, rubbing their wrists.

"And don't tell Larry," added Riker. "This is just between me and you two."

They nodded again, more vigorously.

Riker gestured to his three henchmen. "Bravo and Charlie, keep going over the tapes. You find anything, call me. Alpha, let's pay the fool another visit."

Alpha grinned, "You bet."

"Hey, chief – wait a minute!" exclaimed Charlie. "Take a look."

His computer screen showed August asleep, head cradled in his arms. "That's Camera Number Three in Room 105, at oh-oh-fifteen, shortly before the circuits cut off. Now, look at this …"

He hit another button. The view on the screen split: the left with August asleep, the right with the same view but with the chair empty, as though August's body had vaporized.

"That's the view at oh-two-forty-eight, exact same angle, when the video clicked back on. Notice anything?"

Riker studied the two images carefully. "Zoom in."

"Roger that."

Charlie hit a series of buttons, and the two images enlarged synchro-nously, then shifting down and to the left, focusing on the floor behind Steve's chair.

"What's that?" asked Alpha.

They could all see it now: a little chip on the floor in the 02:48:14 image, but not on the 00:15:00 image.

The zoom enlarged the object.

Riker exhaled slowly. "Looks like tile. The bastard went up through the ceiling?"

Bravo chimed in, "Makes some sense, Chief. Two other alarms went off that night. System's so sensitive there're false alarms virtually all the time. That Sunday one occurred on the third floor in an unrelated area. We've gone over those tapes – nothing. But you'll never guess where the second alarm was."

"Go on."

Bravo hit another button. "Here's the event log."

The video image was replaced with a computer list, three entries highlighted:

Sunday, 3 April 2005, 05:43:52. Rooftop Door B2. Circuit opened.
Sunday, 3 April 2005, 05:43:54. Rooftop Door B2. Circuit closed.
Sunday, 3 April 2005, 06:03:54. Rooftop Door B2. Alarm reset.

Riker turned to Rusty and Bobby, "If he went out on the roof, how'd he get off?"

Rusty spoke, "Fire escape. We'd have a record of elevator activity."

Riker's eyes narrowed to slits. "How'd he get there? We have blueprints – tunnels, shafts, security sensors?"

Bobby chimed in. "Yep, everything's here on the computer."

Riker pointed at Alpha and Bobby, "You two check out the roof. Bravo, keep going over the tapes. Charlie and Rusty, come with me; let's check out Room 105."

21.

MacGregor was surprised to see Riker return so quickly to his office, though with only one henchman in tow. He was even more surprised that Rusty was with them. Riker said merely nothing, but beckoned with his finger. With a sick feeling in his stomach, MacGregor followed them to the lab.

At August's desk Riker sat down and pulled at the safe door. Locked. He spun around in the chair and looked at the floor where the plaster chip had been on the video. He then looked up and pointed.

"There!"

They all studied the ceiling. Just over the refrigerator was a defect in a corner of one of the ceiling tiles: a small patch of missing plaster.

Rusty shook his head. "How the hell he do that?"

Riker pointed at the refrigerator and incubator, standing near each other against the wall.

"Climbed up."

He studied the two pieces of heavy equipment. "No good handholds. Likely he wedged himself up."

"Why didn't the cameras kick in?" asked Charlie.

"That's what I don't understand," said Riker. "Seems professional, like he was prepared to break through the system."

August is a spy?

"You mean he might be an agent for another firm?" spluttered MacGregor.

"I'm beginning to wonder," snapped Riker. "Charlie, get up there and take a look!"

Charlie tried to shimmy up the side of the refrigerator, but the edges were slippery. After several attempts, he backed off, studied the arrangement of the refrigerator and incubator, and then wedged himself between the two. With much grunting and straining he reached the top.

He pushed on the ceiling tile, which gave way easily, and looked into the crawlspace.

He called down to the men below, "Paydirt! The dust's all stirred up. And there are scrape marks along the piping. Looks like dried blood ..."

Riker grinned, exposing his ugly, even teeth. "MacGregor, you've made the list of the world's top ten dumbest bastards. From now on Angion's survival depends on damage control. Tune in Georgie: only I can save you. You belong to me."

George couldn't decide whom he hated more: Riker, or August. "What the bloody hell was he doing up there? You can't be serious!"

"Damn straight I'm serious. He was spying on you. So, what's up there – dead bodies?"

MacGregor shook his head. "Several hundred miles of cable, plumbing, vent shafts, and wires. I don't see how August could have found his way anywhere up there."

"Seems he did," said Riker, dryly.

He called up to Charlie, "You need equipment. Get the climbing gear and IR goggles from the van. You and Delta do a complete map of his movements."

"Roger that!" Charlie dropped from ceiling to floor and left the room.

Riker stepped in close to MacGregor. "Georgie, I know you've not been straight with me – but now's your chance to come clean. Come on, sweetie, tell me about Sundays. I'm betting this kid got himself a good look at your Science Service – that's what you call it, right? And if your hot little secret had its security breached, well then ..." He leaned forward, their noses nearly touching, " ...well then ... you're safer if you tell me every little thing."

How does he know its name?

MacGregor was trying to think fast. He could say nothing, but it was obvious Riker knew more about the Science Service than he was letting on.

If he started talking, where could he draw the line? If August had seen the SS in action, then the secret was out! If so, then better Riker know the truth.

So, over the next hour he told Riker about the Science Service. But as he explained the SS, its capacities for creative thinking, for critical reasoning, for complete security through secrecy, even for manipulation of memory, there were two matters that he did *not* mention.

He did not explain his ability to direct the Service's deliberations.

Nor did he explain the falsified experiments with Angiotox. He did not see why Riker, Calibri, or even Dida, should know about those.

These dangerous facts he carefully kept to himself. After all, there was no way anyone else could know.

Morgan's weekend in the Hamptons had consisted of a series of pleasant parties entertaining a potential client firm, the Spanish banking concern Alhambra Holdings. Several of Alhambra's younger members, not to mention a couple of the older ones, had made passes at her – offering dinners, wild nights, weekends, polo ponies, even vacations on yachts – but Morgan had turned them all down with a smile. Nevertheless, by Sunday afternoon the Spaniards were convinced Eddie Mac was the ideal Wall Street law firm to negotiate their upcoming U.S. acquisitions. Conversely, senior partners Gerald Hamilton and Pamela Moulton were pleased with Morgan, as they realized the presence of the beautiful raven-haired lawyer had fueled the Spaniards' enthusiasm.

Morgan was feeling better by the time she arrived home. She was back on her game: the senior partners liked her; powerful attractive men found her desirable; and that little worm Chip Spader was about to be crushed under the boot of her trusted mentor Tom Edwards. Hadn't he said as much on Friday? The only piece missing was Steve. She was thinking about him as she unlocked the door to her apartment.

A ring sounded, and she rushed to the phone on the end table.

"Morgan, it's me." His voice was flat.

"Steve, honey! How are you? I've had such a nice weekend! But it's still no fun without you ..."

"Morgan, we've got to talk."

Uh oh. Steve didn't so right. In fact, she couldn't remember his voice ever sounding like this.

"Steve, what's wrong? You miss me?" She tried to hit a light note.

"Morgan, we've got to talk. Not on the phone. Face to face."

Why's he so tense? We've been out of touch, but …

She felt a bit guilty. Preoccupied – appropriately, of course – over the last two weeks with her own concerns about Laurel, Spader, Edwards, the firm, and life in general, she'd been out of touch. She vowed to repair the damage. After all, she was the stronger one. But why his insistence, his urgency? Was this the first hint of a disaster in the making? She'd have to fix it.

"Yes, Steve, you're right. We need some time together. I can take off a couple of days … a family emergency … or maybe I'm sick. Hell, I don't know – I'll think of something. I'll be there tomorrow afternoon. That work? Can you swing it?"

"Yes. Screw the lab."

""Honey, please hold tight."

"I will. Let's talk tomorrow – really talk, not on the phone. Call me from JFK. I'll meet you at Logan."

"OK." Weird, but he seemed insistent – no more conversation. "Good-bye, Steve. I love you."

"And I love you so very much, Morgan. See you tomorrow."

The phone clicked off, leaving her alone, her foreboding worsening.

22.

MONDAY, APRIL 11

Following a sleepless night, Morgan knocked on Edwards's office door. As was typical, he was at his desk before dawn.

"Mr. Edwards, may I speak with you?"

He waved at a leather chair. She glanced at the 3000-year-old stone carving mounted on the wall, the figure of a famed Egyptian judge, stolen from a Pharoah's tomb.

How ironic: a stolen symbol of justice.

His smile was magnanimous, "My dear, what's the matter?"

His eyes made her nervous. It was the look when he was cross-examining a hostile witness.

"I'd like to take off a couple of days. An urgent family matter ..."

"Morgan, my dear, I'm *sure* it's an urgent family matter. Take off as much time as you want. Of *course*, we can manage without you. This business about Laurel bothering you?""

He spun the computer monitor on his desk so that it faced Morgan. The screen showed Laurel naked on her hands and knees, Chip Spader behind her, her mouth open in a scream of pain, or was it delight?

Thomas's voice was inquisitorial: "Early this morning someone e-mailed this to every senior member of our firm. Laurel's career at Thomas, McEvoy, and Garfield, is effectively over. Meanwhile, the reputation of our blue-chip law firm has been tainted. Frankly, Morgan, I'm embarrassed for us to be talking about this, but we must. You know anything about this video's release?"

Where was the kind mentor in whom she had confided just three days ago – the man so eager to help her, so willing to take up the cause against Spader? She felt like Alice, her world flipped in the looking glass.

"No, Mr. Edwards. You were the only person I told about Laurel and Chip, and about their video. No one else."

"I hope so, Morgan, for your sake. Laurel is being shown the door as we speak. As for you, it would be prudent to disappear while we investigate. The video is Spader's. We have trouble believing he released it, though there's email evidence to that effect. We suspect someone else may have done it. Frankly, I don't think it was you, but we need to clear that up."

"Me? Are you kidding?!"

"After you spoke with me about your suspicions regarding Spader, I reviewed these with several senior partners. The release of this video complicates matters. Until cleared of any wrongdoing – such as launching a personal vendetta against one of our prime clients – you should be keeping a low profile."

"I see."

"Take the next two weeks off. I'll make sure you're covered here at the firm. Personally speaking, I don't believe you are involved directly. Once this is clear, it will be a simple matter for you to return."

"But ..."

"No buts, Morgan. See you in two weeks."

"Very well, Mr. Edwards. Thank you."

She shut the door. Only then did she notice her palms were drenched with sweat.

∼

Morgan hailed a cab, arriving back at in Greenwich Village just shy of ten o'clock. She was running late. In her rush she nearly tripped over the large manila envelope under her door.

It was flat, legal-sized, eleven by seventeen inches. She could feel cardboard backing inside. On the cover was a note in large block letters:

THOUGHT YOU SHOULD KNOW ABOUT THIS.
IT'S BEEN GOING ON FOR A WHILE.
A FRIEND

Oh hell! What now?
She sat by the window and ripped open the seal.
Inside were several glossy black-and-white photos. They had an amateur look, grainy, blurred, as though someone had paid a seedy detective a seedy amount of money to catch a seedy business.
They were pictures of Steve with Alison. She had never met Alison, yet she had heard enough from Steve to guess it was her. The first showed Alison leaning against a black BMW, her body highlighted by tight clothes, her breasts casting shadows, Steve standing close to her, her putting something in his hand, him smiling at her and looking into her eyes, his lips parted. The second showed the two of them at a table in intimate conversation, her left hand between his legs, her right arm encircling his shoulders. The third showed him in the car's passenger seat, Alison leaning over from the driver's side, her head barely visible near his lap, her left hand hanging onto the car door, Steve's face registering surprise and pleasure. The fourth showed them in the restaurant, Alison's arms around Steve, kissing him on the lips.
Morgan gasped, the air knocked out of her like a fist had slammed into her gut. But she tried to stay cool. Maybe the photos were pre-planned? Yet their quality was poor, making them seem genuine. And who would send her such pictures? Maybe she really did have a guardian angel, someone who'd warn her against a philanderer like Steve August?
She shook her head, still breathing hard.
No fairy tales! Facts. I believe in facts.
Steve loved her. That was a fact. He was as dependable as the morning sunrise. But then, what about these photos?
Which story is the fairy tale?
As she thought about everything – Spader, Laurel, Edwards, her uncertain future, and now Steve and this wench Alison – Morgan despaired. The photos were too much, the last straw. Maybe it would be best to separate from him? How could she trust him?

Through the window she noticed a tree across the street, its green leaves just emerging from winter slumber. She squeezed her eyes shut.

My life. every life, is a sequence of priorities. What is important?

She opened her eyes.

She had packed last night. She phoned for a cab, grabbed her coat and bag, and walked downstairs. Within three hours she would be at Steve's doorstep. She'd wait, then she would decide.

Shouldn't I be free, a woman who depends on no one, no man?

She shook her head.

Every relationship is a two-way street.

She shook her head again.

And I do love him.

The April air was brisk, her breath coming out in short, tired puffs. Anxiety and anger were wearing on her, but the cold helped, stinging her cheeks, reminding her she was alive.

Inside the warm taxi Morgan laid back her head, and to the cabby's question she answered only, "JFK." She was tired of it all – of pleasantries, of performances, and of people. In fact, she really did not care for the world at all.

Why should I? Why, when it hurts too much?

23.

MONDAY, APRIL 11

That same morning, at August's arrival George looked up from the lab group. He had wondered if August would have the temerity to show, given his data's certain failure.

"Ah, the man of the hour. Anything for me?"

August spread out some papers on the table. "Here, take a look."

Over the next twenty minutes the boy walked the group through his results. He showed them the whole data set – a total of 312 mice between his and Shiu-Wei's efforts. He summarized the analyses by various parameters – including mouse characteristics like weight, age, and gender, tumor characteristics like size, growth rate, and brain location, and blood vessel characteristics like density, diameter, branching pattern, and even fractal geometry. But it seemed no matter how he sliced the data, the results were the same: he could find no significant differences between the mice that had received Angiotox and those that had not.

MacGregor chuckled to himself.

After Steve finished, Alison spoke first. "Wow, Steve, you're such a tease. Some mice really responded to Angiotox, but there just aren't enough of them. And this is true for the whole group as well as for every subgroup you've analyzed. How frustrating! It's almost like someone is playing a massive practical joke: giving you just enough of a positive result to keep you going …"

She smiled playfully.

Steve looked up from his papers. MacGregor saw the glance – shrewd, analytical, intelligent, skeptical. It lasted only a nanosecond. But it was real.

Who is this guy?

MacGregor shook his head. He could not get around the facts. One – August had evaded Angion's security system early on a Sunday morning. Two – August had crawled through the bowels of Angion. Three – August may have witnessed MacGregor's greatest secret: his ability to control the SS.

Witnessed it? Hell! Maybe he's recorded it!

The thought made his testicles freeze – even worse than with Riker. If August ever showed such tapes to Angion's scientists, then they would crucify him. They had not signed up for mind control. His dream would be ruined.

One thing was clear: the guy was *not* the naïve innocent MacGregor had thought back in January when he'd hired him on Phillips's recommendation. He was more than that …

Phillips? Bullocks!

Is this his doing?

Maybe Phillips had planted August at Angion? Wasn't August his protégé? And weren't the Swiss bankers Phillips's friends? Was August feeding Phillips information about Angiotox?

Always plan for the worst: Steve August – spy for Marion Phillips.

Meanwhile, MacGregor still was listening with half an ear.

"…If we put all these different subgroups together," August was saying, "maximally powering the dataset to detect *any* effect at all, the fundamental result remains unchanged: no statistically significant difference between mice with Angiotox treatment versus those without."

Around the table the faces varied from incredulous to enraged – as they should be.

Mai stared at Steve: "How can you even *think* that? Of course Angiotox works! Angiotox is the most potent treatment for brain cancer known to man!!" He was half out of his lab chair, his face twisting with rage.

MacGregor looked around – the natives were growing restless. "Now, now, now," he interjected, "we all know Angiotox is the most potent treatment for brain cancer known to man. Steve's just mistaken, that's all." He let his gaze turn onto August: "Aren't you, bloke?"

MacGregor saw August's jaw tighten, but the others visibly cooled, their shoulders relaxing, teeth unclenching. He was invariably amazed how his words could guide their post-hypnotic states, a symphony orchestra under the conductor's baton.

Alison smiled. "Steve, why don't you relax a little? Over and over again, in many dozens of experiments exploring all the facets, we've seen Angiotox work as predicted. So, what's the problem? Why doesn't your experiment work?"

August's expression remained blank. "Alison, you're absolutely right. It's a puzzle."

She continued, "How can I say this gently? Steve, we've all discussed your results – after all, we've already seen them in rough form. And we have concluded what must be obvious to *anyone* who looks at your data: that you must've made mistakes. Come on, Steve, get with the program!"

MacGregor was intent on August's face – *He's really not willing. Best if he just died – a lab rat of no further use.*

But instead he said, "So sorry, mate, but you're slow on the learning curve. Time to kick it up a notch. The situation today is no different than it was last week, or the week before that, or last month. If your data don't show a significant benefit with Angiotox, then the only solution is that you must generate more data. Of course, Alison makes a good point. We know Angiotox works, yet you're not seeing an effect. Therefore, *you* must be making mistakes. If you rectify these mistakes, then you'll be left with a slam-dunk conclusion! That's one strategy. The other is for you to keep making the same mistakes, slogging away, generating more screwed-up results, and maybe some day, some year, finally pulling together enough data proving that Angiotox is– as we all know already – the most potent treatment for brain cancer known to man."

At that moment something clicked in August's head. Until then he had not understood *why* his results were always inconclusive. If Mai and Pieter were "fixing" his experiment, then why had they not fixed *all* of the Angiotox mice and thereby generated a definitive result that everyone would buy into? Why just string him along?

He now had the answer, but he did not like it.

He looked around the table. The scientists' faces were focused, excited, angry, alert – yet none of them looked *intelligent*; none had that spark of individuality, criticism, and creativity. August sensed that these men and women had somehow given away a bit of their own minds. They were not themselves; they were the tribe.

He understood. What MacGregor wanted from him was not data – hell, MacGregor could get Dai and Pieter to generate whatever crazy data they wanted. They didn't care about data; they cared about *him*. MacGregor wanted Steve to capitulate, to compromise, to doctor his data into something "acceptable." They were trying to force him to surrender his integrity in exchange for – what had Alison offered? – sex … money … power …

The usual seeds of human corruption?

He understood. Steve looked around the table. Every face held defeat: each with its own needs and wants, each broken, each trying to pursue science but without a solid commitment to its underlying truth. Science for hire. Intellectual prostitution.

All had been bought. And now they wanted to buy him. For the past month, they had been trying to buy him.

He understood.

If I give in, they will own me, and that is what they want.

If I give in, I will be their puppet, a marionette.

If I give in, my words will no longer be mine, no longer able to speak what I know is truth.

If I give in, I will no longer be who I am.

And then, even while the group was waiting for his response, from nowhere came a quote of Winston Churchill's. Back in 1941, during the darkest days of the battle against the Nazis, Churchill had given a speech to a group of schoolboys at Harrow. From nowhere, the words rang loud in August's ears:

> *Never give in – never, never, never, never, in nothing great or small, large or petty, never give in except to convictions of honour and good sense. Never yield to force; never yield to the apparently overwhelming might of the enemy.*

Frustrated, MacGregor saw the flicker of a smile dance briefly across August's face.

Why is this bloody idiot smiling – now?

August said, "George, you're absolutely right. What was I thinking? I need to be more meticulous. I'll go over my old data again, and I'll toss out the questionable ones. And I'll be more careful and collect *more* data, if I need to. This'll work, I'm sure."

"Steve, my boy, that's the spirit!"

But MacGregor didn't know what to think.

Is he really giving in? Even if he's Phillips's now, maybe he can still be bought? But we'll have to watch his every move!

He continued, "Make this work, and you'll be part of this team's core. You'll be our medical star, the Man who carries Angiotox to the clinic. Imagine the possibilities!"

"I'm sure I can pull something together. You're absolutely right!"

MacGregor beamed, "I thought you'd see reason."

He put his hand on Alison's neck, "Why don't you and Alison go over your data more carefully? I'm sure there's much she could teach you." He rubbed her neck, "What do you think, Alison?"

"I think you're a letch, Chief," replied Alison, but she put her hand over MacGregor's, nestling it against her bare skin.

The entire lab group laughed, as though Alison had said something especially witty.

Steve laughed, too, but he started putting the papers back into his notebook, shrugging apologetically, "Can't right now."

Is this arse playing ball, or not?

"Very sorry, Chief. I have family in town. I'll be in early tomorrow. I promise I'll pack in the hours!" He turned to Alison. "Let's talk then. You can show me how to clean this up!"

"That's fine," said MacGregor.

"I'll look forward to it," said Alison softly.

"Sounds good," said Steve August.

And he left the room.

24.

Early that same morning Riker had parked his rented gray '94 Honda down the street from August's apartment. The boy had emerged at 4:26 AM. He had watched as August drove off, but kept waiting till his cellphone rang.

Alpha said, "He's here, chief. Just sat down at his desk. He's sorting through a bunch of papers from his safe. Looks like he's going to be here a while."

"Roger that. Call me if anything changes."

Smiling, Riker flipped the phone closed.

His breath steamed in the early dawn. He took off his leather gloves, the dry cold biting his hands, and from his jacket pocket pulled out two thin rubber gloves. They clung to his skin as he put them on.

His long fingers wrapped around the doorknob. Locked.

No matter. From another pocket he took out a tiny metal box and held it against the door, his other hand adjusting the earphone in his ear. A tiny bulb on the box flickered red, then glowed green. He inserted a small pick into the lock, carefully moving it from side to side, listening intently. Moments later he pushed the door open.

Riker quickly moved through the apartment. Oil-stained pizza box on the living room couch, portable TV, futon in the bedroom, cramped kitchen sink with dirty dishes – the rooms of a man with little means.

His survey complete, Riker walked back through each room slowly, opening every closet and cupboard, reviewing contents of dressers, drawers, shoeboxes, paper stacks, and piles of clothes. His hyper-acute mind catalogued it all.

As he worked through the place, Riker nailed Barflies into the baseboards: one in the kitchen, one in the living room, one in the bedroom, and one in the hall. He had brought four, a market value in surveillance more than $100,000; but the value of Steve August, or more exactly his net potential cost, could not be overestimated. August could cost Angion – and therefore Calibri – many, many millions.

In the bedroom he found August's checkbook and bank statements and photographed each page. He also found a stack of photos in the bottom dresser drawer featuring scenes of Morgan and Steve: dinners with friends, a weekend in the Berkshires, a vacation skiing in Vermont, Steve visiting Morgan's parents ...

The search turned up nothing interesting: no drugs, no booze, no porn, no vice of any sort. *Positively goddamn boring!* Even more bothersome were the many books with a spiritual bent spanning a range of topics: Catholic theology, Jewish philosophy, French existentialism, even the Chinese *I Ching*.

This guy could be a goddamn saint, thought Riker. But then he opened a bedside drawer – condoms! He grinned.

Except for the sex.

Riker did one more tour. Nothing else.

With a shake of his head at the poverty, Riker was glad he had never considered medical school. "Pathetic," he murmured.

He glanced at his watch: eight o'clock.

About time to find the landlord.

∼

After waiting two hours back in the Honda, Riker was relieved his cell phone finally squawked.

"Yes?"

Alpha said, "He's left the building. MacGregor roasted him. Told him to take his pansy ass back to his desk and work harder."

"What'd August say?"

"Claimed Angiotox didn't work. But the other lab guys thought he was full of crap."

This was getting interesting.

"Angiotox doesn't work? He say why?"

Riker's mind was racing.

What the hell does August know? The boy's too dangerous.

MacGregor must be hiding something.

I must talk to Calibri.

Alpha's voice brought him back to earth: "They didn't believe him. MacGregor said it was his work, and then August backed off. By the end they were singing Kumbaya with that wench Alison ready to tear off his clothes."

"Screw him."

"Yeah, she wants to. But then he says he's got family in town and takes off. I catch his face on one of Angion's monitors as he walks out, and man, he's pissed!"

"Any ideas?"

"He played MacGregor."

Looking out the car window, Riker saw August pull into the driveway. "Yeah. He's going to roast before this is over. Signing out – he's here."

Riker watched August walk into the apartment, then arranged the four monitors on the car seat: living room, kitchen, hall, bedroom.

Riker listened as August banged drawers, opened the refrigerator, pulled plates out of a cabinet, and heated his lunch in the microwave. He moved to the hallway.

BEEP!

"You have one unplayed message," said the answering machine; and then came the landlord's recording – power would be cut off for an hour while an electrician worked on the wiring.

Riker kept listening as August cleaned his apartment, folding up the pizza box into the garbage can, picking up dirty laundry, arranging the bathroom countertop.

But then his phone rang, its jangle over the speakers filling the Honda like the front row at a rock concert. Riker jumped and swore, spilling coffee over his electrician's overalls.

The clanging stopped mid-ring. August's voice echoed in the Honda, "Morgan?"

Riker hit the mute on the Barfly kitchen monitor and turned to a speaker on his dashboard. This was a wiretap on August's phone – a simple project accomplished with the assistance of the landlord, who had thought he was helping a repairman from Boston Edison. Riker had attached a switchbox that gave him complete control over Steve's telephone and computer cable access. When it came to Steve August, he was determined: Riker would know him, control him, and – once Calibri gave the word – destroy him.

The speaker buzzed as Riker dialed up the volume.

"Steve, it's me." Riker recognized Morgan Najar's voice.

What good luck for Riker that August was dating an Eddie Mac attorney – but what bad luck for Najar! He shook his head.

She's crazy, telling Edwards about Spader. Loose cannon.

"Morgan! You already at Kennedy?"

"No … better. I'm here at Logan. I'm grabbing a cab. Sit tight."

"Wow! That's great!! I love you, hon."

"And I love you. I'll be there soon."

The line clicked off. This was just *too* sweet. Riker felt nauseous.

But then he smiled: *At least they're getting a taste of reality. Maybe the world's nastier than they thought.*

He listened as August cleaned the apartment with renewed enthusiasm. Eventually, he stepped outside to drop two full trash bags into the garbage cans in the side alley.

Riker had to give the guy credit: in his white T shirt and blue jeans August looked *cut*, chiseled muscles rippling across his back as he tossed the bags into the cans. He seemed strong for such a stupid, Ivy-league candy-ass.

His eyes on August, Riker hit the phone's speed dial. A voice answered, "Chief?"

"Delta, get moving. He's already here."

"We're on the way. Should be ten minutes, tops."

"Be careful. His girlfriend's showing – likely in a cab."

"No worries. Won't see us."

"Any word on an apartment?"

"Bravo's working on it. Maybe one down the block."

"Good enough."

"Not quite. Occupancy not till Monday."

"That means a week in the van, Delta. The longer you're in the van, the more likely you'll get made."

"We could go remote."

"No. Too much data in the air. Risky. I want you on-site."

"Don't worry, Chief, we'll get a room. We'll do what we gotta do."

"Right. Hey! Here she is."

Riker watched Morgan get out of the taxi. She ran up the steps quickly, an overnight bag under her arm.

"For Chrissake, Delta, get over here! I'm not set up for this."

"We're moving, Chief! Five minutes …"

The line clicked off.

Exasperated, Riker flipped the phone shut. He wished he could get this recorded, but he needed the systems in the van. Meanwhile, he would just have to pay attention.

Their voices filled the car, speaker volumes at maximum.

"Morgan!"

"Steve, you bastard, I missed you!"

There was a "bang," Morgan's case hitting the floor, then the sounds of clothing falling, mouths kissing, feet scuffling, bed creaking, lovers moaning. The passion mounted fast, hot, loud, and long, ending with a finale of shouts.

Riker smiled another twisted grin: *Yeah, enjoy it while you can, asshole.*

He listened carefully, but the only sound remaining was an occasional squeak of a mattress spring.

Three blocks up a gray unmarked van turned the corner. The driver waved as he drove by, and Riker kept watching in the rearview mirror as the van turned right into an alley between two apartment buildings halfway down the block. He flipped his phone open.

"Delta. You parked?"

"This neighborhood's like a sardine can. Yeah, I'm in one now. 'Resident parking only.' We'll have to move if a cop shows."

"No, just duck and sit tight. If you get a ticket, we'll fix it later. Wait for me."

Riker paused to listen to the speakers, but nothing stirred.

"OK, I'm coming. Get the doors open."

Riker pulled out around the parked cars and drove to the end of the block, turned down the alley, and found the van parked against the blank brick wall of an old apartment building. As he drove up, its back door rolled open, revealing Charlie and Delta.

They wasted no time, collecting the speakers, moving everything into the van.

Riker pointed at Charlie, then at the Honda. "Ditch it, and get back here pronto."

"Roger that." Charlie slipped behind the wheel, and in seconds he had pulled down the street. Delta lowered the van's door closed.

In the cabin's dim light the two men connected the Barfly monitors into USB ports on the van's computer. Within seconds monitor lights were glowing green, and then the three video screens along the van's wall clicked on. Delta settled himself at the computer console, his fingertips moving across the controls.

"OK, Chief, let's check out the show."

It was like watching a video game, except the game was real.

The Barfly's fish-eye lens revealed a mouse-level view of Steve's bedroom. The bed loomed before them, the sheer face of a precipice, folds in the heaped-up sheets like a massive mountain range.

Delta's hands moved lightly across the controls. Had August been watching very, very carefully, he might have noticed a tiny silver bar emerge from the baseboard near the bedroom door. Moments later, only the most careful of observers armed with a magnifying glass would have been able to see a tiny set of filaments extend out of the end of the metal bar. These started spinning, faster than any eye could have made out, and the bar slowly pulled out of the wall: a helicopter thinner than a human hair.

Riker watched the monitor as the folds of linens and blankets grew ever more mountainous, the Barfly's fish-eye lens exaggerating the tiny into the gigantic, a Lilliputian's view of the world. There was a brief blurring as the Barfly went airborne, but then all three video screens displayed different views, one a fish-eye view looking up, another a fish-eye view looking down, and the third a stream of digital data monitoring the Barfly's position relative to its home base along with time, velocity, acceleration, and battery life.

The Barfly had re-oriented to a vertical position, hovering in the giant open space over the jumble that was August's bedroom. Flung off the bed, the covers had hit a lamp stand, which had crashed to the floor scattering glass shards across the carpet. In turn, the falling lamp had knocked over the potted palm next to the door, spilling wet earth onto the scattered sheets. In the middle of this chaos sat Morgan's travel bag. Layered over the bag, sheets, and soil were articles of clothing – jeans, shoes, T-shirt, blouse, bra, panties, boxers – recklessly tossed in spasms of starved passion.

Lying on the bed were the naked bodies of Steve August and Morgan Najar, their eyes closed, seeming asleep: Najar on her side, nestled against August's shoulder, August on his back, arms encircling her neck and chest, both breathing slowly – deep, solid, trusting.

Riker did feel nauseous.

And the Barfly hovered above the bed.

25.

MONDAY, APRIL 11

Riker waited.

After an eternity, Najar stirred, nuzzling August's shoulder. He rolled onto his side and pulled her close. "Hmm, hot stuff, you trying to get my attention?"

"Just making sure you're still breathing."

After that? I'm not too sure!" He kissed her.

The Barfly hovered overhead, its rotor spinning, its fisheye watching. Najar locked eyes with him.

"Steve, it's been a horrible week."

"You've always had a talent for understatement."

"Steve, I have to ask you something."

"Sure. But let me guess … Yes, I'll support you, whatever you do. You're leaving Eddie Mac to become a novelist?"

"No, Steve, that wasn't my question."

Gently she pushed him away, her hands on his shoulders, examining him intently.

"Honey," she whispered, "this morning I found an envelope under my apartment door, an envelope with a bunch of pictures. Is there something you want to tell me?"

August's face registered surprise. He blinked several times, his eyes narrowing.

"Morgan, what are you talking about?"

But for a time she said nothing, studying his face.

Finally, she said, "Stephen Leland August, I love you. But the photos in that packet are of you with a sexy woman at dinner, and also together in a sexy BMW – obviously on personal terms. If I hadn't witnessed Laurel's disaster, I'd be tearing you limb from limb, sure that you're a bastard. Even now, I'm having a hard time not believing my own eyes. Steve, tell me you haven't been cheating!"

Her voice was breaking.

Riker's jaw dropped. *What the hell!*

"Delta – you know about this?"

Delta shook his head.

August's expression betrayed no emotion. He stared at Najar, but then in a split-second rolled out of bed and crouched like a panther on the floor, staring at the wall.

His naked muscles defined the lines of his arched back, bent neck, curled arms, angled legs. Like a naked statue, motionless he stared, expectantly, at the blank wall in front of him.

"Steve!"

But that instant the coiled body sprang into a whirlwind of fury, fists pummeling the wall.

Plaster chips flew around the room, faster and faster, as the attack continued. Cracks formed in the wall, then deepened, the onslaught accelerating, spots of blood spraying as his knuckles turned raw.

A drop of blood arched high in the air, nearly hitting the little Barfly, coming so close that the men in the van flinched.

"Steve!!"

His blows softened to a rhythmic *thwack, thwack, thwack.*

"Steve!!! Stop!!"

Eyes wet with tears, she was shivering, kneeling on the bed.

His hands dropped to his sides, knuckles bloody, and he leaned his forehead against the wall, closing his eyes. He began to sob – deep, wracking shudders, tears dripping from his chin. His body glistened with sweat.

Najar threw her arms around him. "Steve, Steve, talk to me! Just tell me it's okay. Tell me ..."

They were both crying. Morgan pushed her face into his back, but Steve's head and arms remained pressed against the torn plaster, his body heaving with sobs.

"Listen to me, Steve August. I need you. Stop it! Damn it, look at me!"

With expert ease she spun him around, turning his back against the wall, shoulders pinned by her arms, her face inches from his.

"Look at me, damn it!"

He spoke as if from very far away, "Another set-up! That was Alison, Morgan. She came on to me, but nothing happened. You should know that."

She pressed her cheek against his chest, sticky with blood, sweat, and tears. "Oh, sweetie! I just needed you to tell me." She swallowed. "Oh my God, Steve, what's happening to us? Who's doing this?"

And she started crying again.

August stretched his arms around her, his bloodied hands at the small of her back, and pulled her close.

And so they stood, giving and taking solace as best they could.

Meanwhile, the Barfly floated overhead.

Riker let out a low whistle. "This is going to be goddamn beautiful. I can taste real pain ..."

Gently, Morgan picked up Steve's hands, held his outstretched fingers, and looked at the torn knuckles, blood oozing from broken skin and exposed nail beds.

"Oh, Steve, your hands! Your fine, beautiful surgeon's hands!" She pulled them up to her lips, kissing them, holding them against her face.

"They're OK, Morgan."

"Come with me, you idiot," she said, leading him towards the bathroom.

Riker allowed himself a broad smile.

"Yesss," he hissed, unconsciously mimicking Calibri. "Yesss ... this is going to be very, very beautiful."

And he licked his lips.

Najar opened the faucet in the sink, tested the water, and put Steve's hands under the stream.

He winced.

"There, stay quiet, and let them rinse. Oh, sweetheart ..." She choked on her words.

She opened the old spigots, and steaming hot water gushed into the bathtub. From under the sink she pulled out a box of Epsom salts and poured handfuls into the churning water.

Delta glanced at his boss.

Riker nodded, "Follow them."

"Roger that."

Delta shifted the Barfly's rotor, and the mechanical mosquito buzzed through the open bathroom door. As August rinsed his wounds and Najar ran the tub, Delta found the Barfly an unobstructed view near the far corner of the bathroom ceiling.

It was then, after Najar had dumped the salts into the tub, that she pushed the bathroom door shut.

Delta glanced at Riker. "Chief, you know this might be trouble."

Riker's eyes were glued to the video. "How much time on the battery?"

Delta gestured at the adjacent screen. "Around thirty-five minutes."

Riker nodded.

There was a knock, a key rattled, and Charlie entered, bright sunlight streaming through the open van door.

Riker waved. "Damn it, close the door! Sit up front. Keep a lookout!"

"Roger that," said Charlie, and pulled the door shut.

All was dark except the monitors.

Following Morgan's lead, Steve had been holding his hands under the sink, gingerly patting his fingers, cleaning off blood clots and plaster bits. His eyes were fixed on the task before him, but his face held a distant look.

"I wonder who took the photos?" he asked, of no one in particular.

Najar nodded slowly. "I think I have a good idea. Steve, I'm so very sorry. I haven't told you about what's been happening. The last week has been so … complicated …"

And she proceeded to tell him about the party, and her blackout, and Laurel and Chip and Edwards and the video and Laurel's firing and her own mandatory leave-of-absence. She concluded, "So, maybe Chip's after me. Likely he figures I put two-and-two together and ratted him out."

"There's only one solution," said August softly.

Morgan looked up from the tub. "What's that?"

"Spader must be stopped. We go to the police."

"But we have no proof."

"Sure we do. There's the video of Laurel he crazily emailed to everybody's cousin, and then there are the photos you found under your doorstep. Anyone who sees them would know it's a set-up! I'm sure the police would believe us."

"Well, they *might* believe us, but that wouldn't *prove* anything. And some people might think that you *really* were messing around with Alison and that I'm being gullible. And I'm sure Eddie Mac would hate having the police involved, and without the firm's cooperation we'd be nowhere. It's not that simple, Steve."

He was silent, pondering, as he rinsed his hands.

She continued, "You're right, I'm sure. He must have hired someone to follow you. But ..." Morgan's voice took on a hard edge. "Hey, what the hell *were* you doing in her car anyway? And *why* were you ...?"

The tub was full. She gave the spigots a couple of savage twists, and the water stopped. On the monitor Riker saw several emotions dance across her face: hope, doubt, anger, fear, sorrow, love. The internal battle was fierce but brief. She grabbed a large washcloth, dipped it into the tub, and with warm water flowing from between her palms she carried it to the sink and wrapped August's hands in the terrycloth.

Even the light contact must have stung, as his face twisted. "Morgan, I just have to say ..."

"Shhh! Don't talk. Not yet."

She guided him to lie back in the warm water. She softly lowered his hands into the bath, and then unwrapped them. The water stained a light pink, but the active bleeding had stopped.

"There, how does that feel?" she whispered.

He closed his eyes. "Very, very good. God, I've missed you, Morgan."

She pressed the washcloth against his brow. His head yielded to the gentle pressure and dropped beneath the surface – strangely reminding Riker of ... a faint memory ... from his early youth ...

Riker grimaced and shook his head to dislodge the thought.

Steve emerged, gasped for air, and looked at her.

Morgan's face registered relief. "You're back."

He smiled, but his voice was serious. "I'm sorry. I lost it when you told me about the photos. All I could see was that someone was trying to destroy us, that we were being set up. I didn't think about *you*, what you must be feeling!"

She shook her head, "No, Steve, no ..."

But he kept going, "Please, let me. The whole thing with Alison was innocent. It was Friday – seems like an eternity, but it was only three days ago. She invited me out to dinner, just in a 'friends' kind of way. But then she really came on to me: offered a ton of money from the lab if my data improved and I joined the lab group; and then afterwards in the car she made another pass. But I didn't take her up on it – not on any of it!"

"Really?"

"Really."

"Steve, move over. That water looks too comfortable. I'm getting in."

During this conversation Delta and Riker had been watching the monitor with worsening concern. At start their view had been crystal-clear, and they had appreciated Najar's slender, muscular curves illuminated to full advantage. But as the seconds ticked by, the colors had softened, gradually turning gray, the edges blurring like an impressionist painting. The two men found themselves leaning forward, more and more, straining to make out details.

Riker nodded, "Condensation on the lens. It's the steam. Any ideas?"

"Not much to do, sir. The Barfly's circuits can handle the humidity, and the battery's got enough juice to keep her flying another twenty minutes. We've got sound, but no video with the lens clouded. She has a lens at each end, but we can't see anything if both are fogged up."

"How about infra-red?"

Delta hit a switch. By now the video screen had progressed to a uniform gray. For a second the screen went blank, and then it was dark. Very faint orange and pink and red shadows moved across it, their outlines indistinct.

"IR's no good either. Show's over," said Riker. "How can we navigate?"

"Not good. The rotor acts like a gyroscope and helps us orient. And we have positional info relative to the docking unit in the baseboard. But we can't go anywhere without risking smashing into something. Strange, I don't understand why the IR isn't working."

"Think!" snapped Riker. "IR uses heat waves. The steam's near body temperature. All we can see are the clouds of hot steam drafting around the room. But keep it on IR. The bedroom's cooler. With luck we'll see the way out if they open the door. But we won't be able to watch these two for the time being."

"Damn shame. She's hot."

"Can it! Listen."

There was splashing as Najar stepped into the tub. "Oh, that feels good."

Then she said, "OK, let me see those hands again ... Steve August, you're insane, but you're also lucky. Nothing's deep; it's just torn skin."

"They're clean now. I'll just let them air dry."

"Wait, don't get out yet. Rest them on my knees ... Steve, why'd he send out his video on the Web? It makes him an asshole in front of the whole world!"

"Yeah, seems more likely someone else did it, but, then again, maybe he did it on his own. Morgan, the guy's insane. Maybe he was high. Maybe his ego was bruised, so he wanted to inflict pain in response. Maybe he figures everyone knows he's a dog already, so he doesn't care throwing some dirt around – won't make him look any worse! Anyway, Chip's from real money."

"But Steve, that's the point! He *can't* afford the negative press – he's a Spader!"

"Hmmm. Maybe. Maybe not. Wasn't it F. Scott Fitzgerald said the rich are different from you and me? Maybe he *can* afford it. Maybe *that's* the point!"

"OK, back to your photos. Let's say you're right. So he's angry and wants me to bleed, has somebody follow you around, and frames the pictures to make you look as bad as possible. Let's say that's all true. Why'd he give me the photos *now*? They're not incriminating enough."

August's voice betrayed annoyance: "Because he knew he couldn't get anything better! Come on, Morgan. Nothing's going on!"

"You've got to admit; they're good: grainy, gritty, real *film noir* material. They *smell* like cheating."

"OK. Enough. That's as good as he's got, and as good as he's going to get. So he makes the play, since you're coming to Boston to see me. He figures now's the best time ..."

His voice trailed off.

"What's the matter?"

"Morgan, good God! Don't you see?"

"What are you talking about?"

"Don't you see? He's *here*! He's watching me, us, here – in Boston, in the lab, maybe here at home."

"Oh my God! You're right! Someone must have followed you to get the photos in the restaurant. Steve, do you remember anyone coming in after you, maybe sitting close to you and Alison?"

"No, I don't. It was pretty late, and I don't think anyone came in behind us. But then again it could have happened, and I just didn't notice."

"Yeah, I bet. Your mind was otherwise occupied."

"For Pete's sake, Morgan."

"Hmph! OK, I'll let it go. I'll grant she's got sex appeal … Try this on for size: maybe Chip put her up to it?"

"You mean he somehow offered her inducements to seduce me? Morgan, that's getting really paranoid!"

"Steve, it's not paranoid if people are after you. Take a step back for a second. It's clear someone's attacking us. Spader is rich, powerful, and totally whacked. He has both opportunity and motive. Why *wouldn't* he contact Alison?"

"The way Alison put it, she was trying to get me to sell out to MacGregor."

"Maybe Chip set the whole thing up? He gets some great photos – they would have been even better if you'd said 'yes.'"

"But if I'd said 'yes' – meaning not to the sex, but to the stock options – then she'd have been lost. On Monday I'd have talked to MacGregor, and the game would've been up. No, that offer had to be genuine."

"Hmm. Good point. OK, if Chip *didn't* set up the Alison deal, how did he know where you were having dinner?"

"Somebody must've followed us, Morgan. That's the only theory that makes sense."

"Fine, I'll buy it." She paused. "So, why'd he drop the photos under my door this morning?"

"He must've known you were coming here."

"How?"

August's voice sounded tense. "He has a gripe with you. Likely he's watching you like a hawk. Maybe the phone's tapped, or maybe even your apartment's bugged."

Riker and Delta could hear splashing, but the steamed lens made vision impossible. The splashing quieted, Morgan saying, "OK, Steve, that's not necessary. Focus with me."

"Sorry. I've never felt so attacked!"

"Come on … close your eyes."

After several seconds of silence there was an inexplicable hum over the speakers – "mmmm" – a pleasant harmonious sound from the two lovers nestled in the hot water.

Delta mumbled under his breath, "These guys are just way too weird."

26.

MONDAY, APRIL 11

For several minutes, Riker and Delta listened to the couple's humming, the only break in the monotony an occasional "plink" from a faucet drip hitting the water.

Morgan finally spoke, "So, what's our strategy?"

"Well, I think it'd be better if you were out of the picture."

"*What?!*"

"Morgan, hold on. I don't have a full-fledged plan ... yet. But a couple of issues are clear. Obviously, Chip wants you to suffer. You'll be safest with your folks. And that'll give me more freedom to move. Chip sent you those photos to make you break up with me. Fine. Let's pretend we did. Have you spoken with them yet?"

"No. I wanted to talk with you first. Steve, I don't want to leave you alone here."

"Morgan, we have to keep you safe. I love you, but I can't protect you. For the next couple of weeks you should be with your folks."

"What do I tell them?"

"Keep the cover. Be vague. Tell them we're having trouble, so we're taking a break to re-evaluate the relationship."

"I don't like it."

"We can fix it later. Meanwhile, no phone calls – but you and I know the reality. Don't worry – I promise I'll be true to you."

Kissing sounds and more splashing. "Steve, let me see your hands! Okay, good. Let's get out; the water's getting cold."

Delta and Riker were staring at the video monitor, vainly straining to see any patterns in the white noise. Delta tapped on the adjacent screen.

"That's our battery time," he said. "Five minutes, thirty-five seconds."

"We've got to get this thing back to base," growled Riker. "Of course, the silver lining is – if it drops and they find it – they'll blame Spader."

"You don't care if it drops?"

"Hell, yes! Damn thing's worth more than twenty G's!" Riker's jaw tightened. "We are *not* losing this Barfly! Delta, move it to the door."

"It's a risk, boss. Can't see where we're going."

"When that door opens we've got to be ready!"

"OK ..." Delta's hands hovered over the controls. "The gyros say we're facing the base."

The screen remained a white blur, though numbers on the adjacent video kept changing as the Barfly inched towards the door.

Riker dialed his cell phone.

Delta grinned, "Smart!"

Suddenly, the screen darkened to black, then turned white again.

Morgan's voice sounded loud on the speaker, "Steve, you really think I should go back to Connecticut? Now? With all the trouble you have here?"

Her voice bellowed in the van. Numbers were flashing across the monitor like lightning – the Barfly tumbling out of control!

"Goddamn fix this goddamn flying goddamn insect!!!" snarled Riker, hitting the "send" button on his phone.

"We lost altitude," said Delta, "weighed down by the steam. We were by her face."

"And where now?"

"Don't know." Delta's hands hovered over the controls, his eyes on the monitor, trying to make sense of the vacillating numbers.

Over the speaker the bedroom phone rang.

"Hell, who's that?" said Steve.

The screen flashed, and a dark shadow appeared. The sound was clear: a door opening.

"Of course I don't want you to go, Morgan. But it's the safest thing to do."

Footsteps slapped on the bathroom tile, then a board creaked as Steve stepped into the bedroom.

"Go for it!" yelled Riker.

"Roger that!" Delta pushed on the toggle, and the dark space loomed larger, filling the screen.

"Steve, close the door. It's cold."

"OH Hell! The door hinges right. Aim left!" cried Riker.

"Roger that."

The dark space was shifting to the screen's left.

"Sorry, babe!" said Steve.

Delta and Riker watched in horror as the dark vertical band started narrowing, the bright edge on the right rapidly enlarging, closing towards the middle, threatening to meet its growing twin on the left.

"Go, man go!" yelled Riker.

"Damn it!!" gasped Delta.

The two vertical edges of light were closing in the middle of the monitor. Delta's right hand held one toggle pushed far forward, while his left jiggled the other, trying to keep the dark area centered, but the space was closing fast.

"Go baby go," prayed Riker.

For a second he thought the two light edges would meet, but at the very last instant the entire screen went dark. They heard the door close.

Riker hit a button, breaking the phone connection. The two stared at the dark screen. Across the adjacent monitor numbers ticked off the Barfly's position.

"Airborne?" murmured Riker.

"Yep."

"Time?"

"Three minutes, twenty seconds."

"Homing beacon."

Delta flipped a switch. A small red "x" appeared on the screen's lower right.

"Bring her in," said a relieved Riker.

"There's no visual. Could hit the furniture."

"Alright. Give it a minute."

Over the speaker they heard Steve pick up the phone, swear, and then return to the bathroom. They waited in silence. Air from the Barfly's beating rotor fanned the lens … and … the view was clearing.

They could see outlines of the unmade bed, strewn covers, piles of clothes.

"Time?" barked Riker.

"Two minutes, fifteen seconds."

"Move it!"

Delta's hands flew across the controls. The Barfly dipped, skirting the foot of the bed, quickly returning to the little spike in the baseboard near the bedroom floor.

"Land it!"

Delta hit a button on the console. The view on the screen spun as the Barfly reoriented horizontally, and then constricted as the unit retracted into the spike. Seconds later the video was dark.

"Time left?"

Delta hit a switch. "Thirty-four seconds. Too close for comfort."

"Audio?"

Delta hit another switch. Muffled voices sounded behind the bathroom door, unintelligible.

"Record it anyway," said Riker. "Maybe we can reconstruct it later. God knows what they're talking about."

"Sex, probably," sighed Delta.

"Battery charging?"

"Roger that," said Delta. "The pod absorbs ambient light and re-powers. We're good for video, too, as long as we don't try flying around. You want to kick in a Barfly from the living room?"

"No thanks. Let's stay grounded. It's the audio we need. But open the lens."

Delta turned the monitor back on, showing the mouse-level perspective from the bedroom baseboard.

~

After about a half hour the door finally opened and the two lovers emerged, wrapped in fluffy white towels.

Steve sounded edgy, "There's no other option! I can take him down, and I will, but you can't be here! It'd be dangerous – and a mistake."

Morgan stamped over to her overnight bag. In one quick motion she dropped her towel and picked out panties from the case.

"Fine. Whatever you want. But I think you're crazy – jeopardizing us, our relationship, our future, all in the name of … What? Revenge? Justice? Goodness? How 'bout me? Where does that leave me?"

As she threw on her top and jeans, her voice stayed level, but her jaw was set: "Stephen Leland August, you want me to walk away so that you can get into a pissing match with Chip Spader? Come on, what's the point?"

Wrapped only in a towel, August answered slowly.

"You, Morgan, are the most important person in my life. I don't want to lose you, but I don't want you to lose, either. Chip must be forced into the open. I think I can make that happen, but … honey … to be safe you've got to be out of the picture!"

"Steve, if I walk out that door, I can't promise I'll ever be back. There are so many unknowns!!"

"Yes, the stakes are high, but we can win. We will win."

"Steve, are you sure?"

"Yes." He pulled her close.

Morgan took a deep breath. "OK. As far as the world knows, we're broken up. No visits, no phone calls, no contact. That's what you want?"

"Not what I want, but what's got to be. They have to think we've split up. I want to get Chip to focus on me, not you. I bet he didn't release that video of him and Laurel. Somebody else did, and he really wants to know who it was. Most likely I'm one of his suspects, and I can use that. Give me a month, Morgan. But remember, during that time I'll always be true. That's my solemn word."

They kissed – long and hard. Finally, she pushed him away.

Her voice nearly broke. "Good bye, sweet thing!"

She grabbed her bag and coat, touched his cheek, and then ran down the hall and out the door.

As he closed the door, Steve again glanced down at the little piece of twine on the landing, still lying unobtrusively at the spot where he had found it when he had returned earlier that morning. Before leaving for the day, he had carefully wedged it in the doorjamb. Obviously, since then someone had been inside his apartment. He would have to check with the landlord Miller whether he had let the electrician inside, but he was sure he already knew the answer. Miller was too conscientious. He would have left a note, or a message.

He sat down on the living room couch, still only wearing his towel, and stared at the wall. Of course, Morgan's idea was perfectly reasonable: Chip might be the one responsible. But Steve had not told her about what he had seen at Angion.

So, he had other ideas about who might be behind the photos of him and Alison.

Steve shook his head. Nothing was what it seemed. Maybe Chip was after him to get to Morgan – or maybe, just maybe, someone was after Morgan only to get to him?

He looked around the room. Someone had been here. The photos of Alison had spurred his imagination. Were there bugs in the apartment? Was it possible that he was right, that even now he was being watched, that his conversation with Morgan had been recorded, that his life no longer belonged to him?

He glanced at the phone. If he called his landlord and asked about the electrician, then anyone listening would know he was suspicious about a break-in.

He smiled, a twisted smile of hope.

I know I'm being watched, but they don't know I know.

He needed to check with Miller.

He glanced at the clock: just after two. Miller walked his Schnauzer every day at two o'clock. It was a sacrosanct ritual – Steve had once kidded him about it, in near-blizzard conditions in midwinter when no sane human would have ventured outside. Miller had answered in his heavy Ukrainian accent, "Vhat? Cold no problem. We no stop till Chloe's piss freezes!"

Steve rushed into the bedroom. He dropped the towel and threw on T-shirt, shorts, sweat pants, socks, sneakers. Seconds later he was out the door.

Sure enough, Miller and Chloe were at the end of the block. Steve ran up to them, just as the dog was inspecting the fire hydrant at the crosswalk.

"Mr. Miller, how're you?"

"Ah, Stephen, good to see you … You are jogging?"

"Yeah, you bet! Say, that electrician finish up?"

"Yes, my boy. He not take long."

"What'd he do?"

"Worked on fuses in basement. That's why we shut off power."

"You didn't let him in the apartment?"

"No, no, Steve! This is America! We have privacy … not like Soviets! You know I tell you if we do that!! No one in your place. No, I took him to basement. He worked, thirty, maybe forty minutes. I saw him drive away. He not go into any apartment … or only mine, when he first showed up. We talked. I invite him."

"What was he like?"

"Sort of nervous. But maybe he not like dogs. Chloe growled. Strange. Chloe never growls, do you Chloe?"

Hearing her name, finished studying the hydrant, she came back to Miller, wagging her tail, and then turned to Steve to inspect his shoes.

Steve scratched her head, and she panted hello.

"Gotta go. Take it easy, Mr. Miller!"

"Always, busy, always moving … Don't work so hard, Steve!"

Steve waved and jogged up the street. At the next corner he turned left, and then sped along the bike path following the Charles River.

His feet pounded the pavement as his mind reviewed the day. So, he *had* been the object of what police called a "B and E" – breaking and entering. Who was behind it? And why?

Thud, thud, thud, thud – his feet flying forward, Steve pictured different scenarios. Angion and MacGregor seemed likely culprits. But it *could* be Spader, or even Edwards – if Morgan, not Steve, was the primary target.

Steve spiraled deeper into darkness.

Can I go to Phillips? But I'm there at his suggestion. What if Phillips has bought into Angion? What if he's part of the set up?

Whoever it is … these pictures of Alison and me are a declaration of war. Someone is after me, or after Morgan, or after us both.

And that person, whoever it is, wants me to know it.

His feet thudded faster down the road.

This is personal.

27.

THURSDAY, APRIL 14

Thursday, three nights later, the butler ushered Riker into Calibri's oak-paneled study. Don Calibri and Dida Medicia were already seated, uncle and niece, the room's air a fog of cigar smoke. Shadows flickered on the dark walls from thin ivory-colored candles set here and there like castaway bits of bone.

Calibri's gnarled body slumped in an over-stuffed red leather chair, a twisted lizard propped on its back, his spine a series of uncomfortable curves against the straight upholstery. In contrast, Dida was draped lengthwise across a scarlet velvet divan, her chest pushed up on one elbow. Riker studied her figure through the brown fog, not in a lustful way, but as a connoisseur appreciating the lines of a prize thoroughbred.

"Mr. Riker, how good to see you," murmured Calibri. "Come in, sit down."

Riker settled into a deep chair, checking that he had their attention. They looked back expectantly, smoke rising from their cigars.

"The Science Service meets every Sunday at dawn," he began. "MacGregor uses the SS – as he likes to call it – to review the week's work at Angion, and to outline the week ahead. My men went through every tape, transcript, and file, but – incredibly – no records of it. Nothing. I now have a couple of his security guards on my payroll – but they swear up and down they know nothing about it. On Sunday mornings MacGregor cloisters them under surveillance to guarantee they aren't watching the SS."

"He's fanatical about security," said Dida. "You mean the SS isn't monitored at all?"

"The entire system shut downs for exactly three hours around daybreak while they meet."

"He is not straight with us," hissed the Don.

Dida glanced at her uncle, but said nothing.

"Yes, he's hiding something," agreed Riker.

"Angiotox?" growled Calibri.

"We've copied his Angiotox files, and we've reviewed the lab meetings. Every Monday at 7:00 AM he meets first with his senior henchman, the Russian Ogoranovich, and then with the other two Angiotox group leaders, Goldfarb and Sachamachi. He meets with the remainder of the group, including August, starting at 8:00 AM, usually finishing by 11:00 AM. But they only talk technical details – *incredibly* there's never an allusion to the SS, which met just the day before, and which supposedly masterminded plans for the week."

"You are right. This makes no sense. Dida, any ideas?"

"No. If they're doing strategic planning at the Science Service, then that discussion must be grist for the Monday meetings."

"Right," continued Riker. "It's almost as though discussion of the Service is off-limits. When MacGregor meets with Ogoranovich, for instance, much seems unsaid."

"Did you tell MacGregor you wanted the monitors activated Sundays?" asked Calibri.

"Yes, but he refuses. Said that the group needed uninhibited creativity."

"How delicious," sighed Dida. "They must be having a massive orgy. I keep offering, but he refuses to let me attend."

"Well, we'll find out soon enough," said Riker. "I've planted Barflies throughout the building. We'll get a good look Sunday."

"*Bene,*" said Calibri. "So, what is he hiding?"

"There's another glaring issue," continued Riker. "Two rooms have no monitoring at all. None. They sit directly off the atrium. Suggests MacGregor is concerned the security of his own monitoring system might get breached, and he wants a way around it. This guy is paranoid in spades."

"*Il bastardo's* most endearing character flaw," murmured Calibri, chewing on his cigar.

"George has not told me much," said Dida. "He says the SS is some kind of group hypnosis. He says an outside observer could interfere with the induced trance, so he won't let me watch. When he talks about it he gets very excited – it's clear he likes it, makes him feel powerful. He gets an erection."

"You do not think he is hiding something about Angiotox?" asked Riker.

"No, I don't," she said. "He's convinced Angiotox is the cure for brain cancer."

"The hypnosis, again this makes no sense," grumbled Calibri. "If he wants the scientists to discuss ideas, then why nothing the rest of the week?"

"Maybe they don't need to," said Dida sarcastically. "Maybe they all remember everything perfectly."

How could I have been so blind, thought Riker.

He looked over at the other two. Yes, they had all shared the same thought.

Dida's eyes were round.

Calibri's lashless lids drooped.

"Or ..." spat Calibri, " ...or ... they remember nothing."

He puffed violently on his cigar.

"O my God!" whispered Dida.

"Hypnosis!" exclaimed Riker. "Maybe MacGregor makes them forget the sessions."

"But if MacGregor's leading the group," said Dida, "then *he* must remember from week to week."

"Yes, they'll need continuity," agreed Riker. "No wonder he gets his jollies from leading the group – he's controlling their memories."

For a while the three chewed on this idea, smoke rising from their cigars, its thickening excrescence shading the candlelight into dark rust.

Dida broke the silence, "What does that imply about Angiotox?"

"Nothing," answered Calibri. "He loses if Angiotox does not work – a mistake he cannot afford. Remember ... it was Silverstein, not MacGregor, who discovered Angiotox. Silverstein – Silverstein and his SAGA test."

"Is Silverstein part of the SS?" asked Riker.

"No, I don't think so," said Dida. "MacGregor doesn't like him one bit – considers him a threat. I think he thinks Silverstein is smarter than he is."

"I suspect he's right," grinned Riker.

Calibri nodded. "Yesss ..."

Silence filled the room for a time.

Then Calibri said, "Maybe this SS is nonsense, a nothing, or ... maybe he is holding back."

"We'll find out Sunday," said Riker.

Calibri nodded again.

He pulled the cigar from his mouth, studied its stubby end, took another from the box, and clipped the tip. With the leftover Cuban between his brown-stained fingers he lit the new one, puffing steadily until its tip glowed red, forming fresh plumes of smoke.

Granting the conversation's intimacy, he gestured towards the cigar box.

Hmmm. Not every day. Calibri could be surprising.

Riker inclined his head, and Calibri handed him a virgin Cohiba.

Riker smiled thinly. "Steve August, however, is another matter."

"Yes, tell us," growled Calibri.

Feeling uncharacteristically tense, Riker clipped the cigar tip. "This guy is everywhere he shouldn't be."

"Go on."

Riker lit his cigar, focusing to keep his hands steady. "My men followed his trail into the ceiling. He must have wandered around for hours – the route gets confused – but eventually he reached the rooftop access door. There he tripped an alarm, but no one noticed because no one was monitoring the system – because of MacGregor. He then clawed his way down a fire escape. Monday morning he says nothing about the whole affair, and we don't figure it out for a week."

Calibri gave Riker a sharp glance. "We look like idiots."

Riker ignored the barb. "Meanwhile, there's a complication: his girlfriend Morgan Najar."

Calibri's eyelids blinked. "More?"

"Pictures of August showed up at Najar's doorstep on Monday

– incriminating photos of August with Alison Goldfarb, his supervisor at Angion – pictures that might make a girlfriend quite jealous."

Calibri's eyes flickered, "Imbecile. Why would you do that? Puts him on guard!"

"That's exactly it. They are *not* our photos. We have our own. *We didn't do it!*"

Silence. Then, "Who else was at the restaurant?" hissed Calibri, tongue flicking across his lips.

"The only people who entered after August and Goldfarb were an elderly couple. Locals. Blended better than I did."

Calibri spat out a torn edge of tobacco leaf.

For the first time, in a very long time, Riker felt truly nervous.

"Who did it?" snarled Calibri.

"Chip Spader, we think – the young punk investment banker. Likely he concluded Najar had something to do with the release of the sex tape of him with that other lawyer at Eddie Mac's, and he decided to get even."

"What sex tape? Who's Chip Spader?" asked Dida.

"Two weeks ago Eddie Mac had a party with three of its client investment houses," explained Riker. "A friend of Najar, one of Edwards's lawyer wenches, Laurel Farthington, ended up in bed with Spader, son of a founder of the house of Mitchum and Spader. Turns out the young Spader likes to videotape his conquests, and he showed the video to Farthington, likely to establish leverage. But then Farthington tells her tale to Najar, claiming she was drugged against her will. Najar then tells Edwards."

Calibri interrupted, "And Mr. Edwards told me. As damage control, I suggested we cut the firm's losses, so Mr. Riker engineered the release of the tape on the Internet. That framed Spader and obliterated Farthington."

Riker continued, "Thank you, Don Calibri. Exactly. So, likely that explains the photos of August. Spader must have concluded Najar and August were at least partly responsible for his troubles, so here's payback."

Calibri's voice dropped to a hoarse whisper, "It is critical he *never* connect us to that videotape. Mr. Riker, everything you now do in this regard – be sure you work through a third party. No direct contact between you and Spader, or between you and August. Make sure nothing is traceable to you … or to me. By the way, what about the Swedish vodka queen?"

"Actress from Stockholm," said Riker. "We flew her in for the event. All cash on the barrel, including the airline. She's untraceable."

"From now on, only work through a third party. No loose ends."

"Yes, Mr. Calibri. It should all be secure."

"Not 'should.' Must. It must *all* be secure!" Calibri's voice was almost shrill. "Find Spader's PI firm. Destroy that contact. Spader must be controlled!"

"Right. I'll take care of it."

"Now, let us get back to this Steve August," said Calibri, more calmly.

He looked at Riker and then at his niece, his face twisting into a nasty wrinkled smile: "Mr. Riker, you're running security for me, yet at the moment I do not feel completely secure. This man August knows too much. Please make me feel secure. But make sure it happens so no one is suspicious, especially this surgeon Phillips."

He looked back at his niece. "Shall we keep this interesting? My dear Dida, MacGregor has been trying to win August over, but he has failed. Likely your charms will appeal more to the boy's taste, and perhaps that will remind MacGregor that your affections are, shall we say, contigent upon positive performance. Certainly, the President of Angion must promote her company's principal product!"

"So, Michael, Dida," he continued, "We will have a friendly contest. Michael, if you win, I will get you a – shall we say – 'comfortable' contact within the Russian government. I know you have been looking for such a lucrative opportunity."

Riker portrayed no emotion, letting this sink in. *Michael?* Calibri had called him by his first name. This was a new level.

But Calibri was continuing, "And, dear niece, if you win, you may choose an item – *one* piece of jewelry – from my collection." He gestured at the wall, where a glass case displayed an assembly of glistening antiques. "You might find the emerald brooch, 17th century, from the court of Louis the XIV, particularly to your liking."

He cackled, "A friendly competition never hurt anyone – anyone, of course, except Steve August! Let's get him, by hook …" – and he flashed his brown teeth at Dida – " …or by crook." – and he nodded at Riker.

Looking pleased, Calibri settled back in his chair and puffed hard on his Cohiba, blowing billows of smoke into the room.

Riker nodded towards Dida, "If you don't turn him, I'll trash him. May the best man win."

But Dida ignored him, turning to Calibri. "Thank you, Tio, but the Swiss investors are meeting with MacGregor and me on Monday to discuss further financing, including a possible larger private offering if the FDA gives us approval. We're supposed to present results on Angiotox, yet MacGregor says we're not ready."

"Because …?"

"He says August is producing inconclusive results."

"Since Monday, since Najar left, what has he been doing, this boy August?" asked the Don.

Riker shrugged. "Nothing but working. We've been all over him, every minute of every day."

"What is he thinking?"

"Regarding the photos? Per his last conversation with Najar, they suspect Spader. I don't think he knows his midnight escapade's been found out."

Calibri grunted. "I'm finished underestimating this *brutto bastardo*."

He turned to Dida. "As for the Swiss, either MacGregor gets August to deliver the goods – maybe with the help of your persuasive arts – or you delay somehow. Silverstein is always convincing; have him talk with them."

"Why are these data so important?" asked Riker, but then regretted it, as he already knew the answer.

"We need animal data to meet FDA requirements to start testing in humans," lectured Dida. "No data, no FDA approval. No FDA approval, no IPO plan. No IPO plan, then no chance for investor financing. Got it? We need the data to prove we can pass the FDA to get to market. And it's the IPO that can make people like MacGregor and his employees, and his various investors – including most importantly Don Calibri – very rich, very fast."

"What if the data are wrong and August's right?" continued Riker, playing devil's advocate.

"It doesn't matter," said Dida. "We'll already have the money. I've gone over this with MacGregor. Once we're in clinical trials, Angiotox *will* find an application to human disease, even if the original animal data were off. That's what the human testing is all about. Mice don't matter. All species are different!"

"What makes you think Angiotox is any good at all, if the animal data are off?" pressed Riker.

"SAGA," said Dida. "If it weren't for SAGA's incredible track-record, I'd be nervous right about now."

"According to Silverstein's conversations," said Riker, "with bad animal data SAGA is not so convincing. Bad intel is worse than no intel."

His words hung in the air, as impenetrable as the clouds of thickening black tobacco smoke.

Calibri spoke slowly, "Bad intel. Yes. Bad intel is worse than no intel ... much worse. Thank you for that, Mr. Riker. Nervous? Yes. We all should be nervous."

28.

FRIDAY, APRIL 15

The next morning Riker was reviewing a list of Boston private investigators. He stopped on the second page.

Nathan Spear.

Riker had heard of him. A one-man show, Spear knew his way around town, he knew the right people to get the wrong things done, and he had no employees, no leaky faucets. Riker, as the head of IPI, "International Plumbing, Incorporated," especially appreciated this last point. If matters turned further south, Spear's flying solo might prove doubly valuable.

No loose ends.

Nathan Spear glanced down at his desk, then back at the speaker.

"It's all a matter of security," Smith was saying.

Whole thing smelled bad. Of course, any gumshoe's sometimes gotta handle a whiff of rotten fruit, but he lived by a few simple rules, and Number One was staying on this side of the law, if only barely. Around town he had a rap as a straight shooter: with the cops, the D.A., even the Irish and Italian joes. He liked to tell the boys at Mickey's, "The hands're dirty, but the shorts're clean." Good for business, such as it was.

This guy in pinstripes had called himself "Smith," but with a curl in his lip. The guy reminded him of a greyhound: high-octane, just like the dogs at the track, ready to race anytime. Over the years he'd lost a lot of money at the Wonderland track, trying to pick winners – but this guy Smith, he was a winner *for sure*. You could tell the guy was deadly.

But only a minute after Smith had stepped into the office Spear knew it would be going nowhere. After a while he started scratching the desk with a fingernail, picking at his worn tweed jacket, even looking at his Timex, but the guy wasn't getting it.

"Sorry, Mr. Smith, this ain't my thing. Why don't you check one of the bigger firms? I do the usual – snapping pix of hubby and his secretary, running backgrounds, staking out a hustle for worker's comp. But this is out of my league."

He pushed away from the oak desk with its stains of coffee and whiskey, stood up, held out his hand: "Sorry. Not your guy."

In his frayed jacket and faded jeans Spear felt as shabby as Smith looked sharp. The guy's bald skull was all angles, tanned brown with creases across forehead and high cheeks, but the deep-set eyes were gray ice. A thin scar ran from left eye to lip. Beyond starched cuffs were long fingers with manicured nails.

Smith studied Spear's hand. "But I must disagree, Mr. Spear. You are exactly what is needed for this delicate assignment."

Spear dropped his hand and leaned across the desk. "Listen. This is *not* my style. It goes over the edge."

Smith's voice was like a diamond cutting glass: "We need your experience, your street smarts, and your absolute discretion. In return, we will make it worth your while – five thousand a day ..."

He paused, letting it sink in.

"...Plus expenses. We provide all the details. You will not be required to do anything truly illegal. You merely are a bridge for us."

Spear stopped mid-breath. Five thousand clams – that was five times his top rate.

So, he eased back into his chair. Maybe he'd spoken too fast. Maybe, like the guy said, there weren't nothing really *illegal*. Maybe, he might even be doing some good. But on another level ...

On another level, it almost sounded like murder.

Over the week MacGregor had carefully reviewed August's findings, eventually reaching the conclusion that he could *not* show the Swiss boys August's current data – that would be a *certain* disaster.

The presentation to the investor group was scheduled for next Monday.

In retrospect, on one level MacGregor wished that Pieter and Mai had fixed *all* the mice; then August would have had a guaranteed positive outcome. But he really had wanted, needed, August to compromise himself – to prove his loyalty, and to give him leverage for the future.

That Friday afternoon he called Silverstein.

"David, August isn't playing ball."

"I warned you, George. His involvement was an unnecessary risk." With more than a trace of sarcasm, he added, "Let me guess, you want more data?"

MacGregor ignored his tone, "For now the best strategy is to present a detailed analysis of what we have from the Westessen rabbits, and to tell the Swiss that we're getting data from a second species, and that we'll be ready for the FDA by June."

"No." Silverstein's voice sounded flat, final.

"No?" MacGregor was incredulous.

"No. Since our conversation Sunday, I've re-tested Angiotox with SAGA, but using more human endothelial cell lines as well as more species."

Something in Silverstein's voice made MacGregor uncomfortable. "And?"

"And … we're not finished yet. But, the preliminary data suggest Angiotox is even *more* potent than what we first thought."

"But if it's more potent, then why aren't we seeing clear effects?"

"When I say more potent, I mean that Angiotox has effects in a wide variety of tissues in *some* species. For example, Angiotox inhibits angio genesis in a wide variety of *human* endothelial cell lines: kidney, liver, uterus, lung, heart."

"Why didn't we know this earlier?"

"You never asked." Silverstein's voice was growing pedantic, as though lecturing a slow student. "Remember? When we did the AGA screenings, we wanted to find a super-selective agent that would only interact with brain endothelium. The cell lines from the Westessen rabbit are our most complete species-specific panel, so that's what we used. As soon as we found AGA-16, Angiotox, you switched to *in vivo* models. We never ran complete *in vitro* SAGA screens across species until now."

MacGregor was astonished. How could they have missed such a fundamental point?

"Silverstein, you do understand what this might mean?"

"Of course," answered Silverstein, annoyed. "Angiotox may not be a slam-dunk in human brains. That's why I'm telling you."

"But then why aren't we seeing effects in the C3H mice?"

"Don't know. I suspect the receptor for Angiotox is hyper-selective only in some species."

But MacGregor then realized, "Blimey!! This doesn't matter. We need only demonstrate *safety* in two species, along with *possible* efficacy. Anything more is gravy. For God's sake, SAGA's only a laboratory assay. It does *not* demonstrate how the whole organism will respond."

"SAGA has never yet been wrong."

"That's OK. We'll work out the details once we're testing in living people," said MacGregor, feeling better.

"SAGA suggests this is a very potent, but maybe *not* selective, agent in humans. Be careful!"

"So what do *you* suggest we do on Monday?"

"Tell them Angiotox has high species-specific activity. We *know* that's true."

"They'll walk."

"Maybe for a bit, but I doubt it," said Silverstein. "They'll see we're playing straight. We need time to figure out what's going on with this drug. Forget the money; remember the science! These are effects we've never seen before. We may have unearthed a truly fundamental discovery."

"We can't afford to wait. I've heard rumors of other firms identifying an agent similar to Angiotox."

"What do *you* suggest?"

"Squelch the SAGA data. Let me work on August. If he agrees his numbers are off, then we can go straight to our Swiss bank, and then to the FDA!"

"This is a mistake, George!"

MacGregor's voice turned cold. "Blimey, David, you know better! This isn't science … This is business."

Disgusted, he hung up.

~

In the silence that followed MacGregor found himself thinking about Dida. He had been hoping for a rendezvous that night, but earlier she had called that she was meeting friends for dinner, and they would be out late, and she would be happy to see him … maybe for lunch … maybe Sunday?

Lunch? Sunday?

Not what he had planned.

The prospect of a weekend of unrequited hunger put him in a foul mood. And the conversation with Silverstein made it worse. Even the Porsche on the wall gave him no cheer.

Then the phone rang.

Dida!

MacGregor's mood lifted.

"Hullo, Professor?" boomed a voice.

"Marion!" MacGregor's heart sank – not the time nor place for a conversation with *him*. Too many unknowns …

"George, I'm so glad I caught you!"

What did *that* mean?

Phillips continued, "I just got off the phone with Hans Stia, our Swiss friend. He's tied up in Kiev at the moment, and can't be here Monday. He asked whether we'd mind delaying the whole business a week?"

MacGregor's world flipped. With all the issues around August, and the mouse data, and the SAGA results, a bit of breathing room was his fondest wish.

But he tried to sound sour, "Marion, what a disappointment! Every day lost is another opportunity for another lab to discover our drug. We must not be scooped. We need the money for more development, FDA approval, and then large-scale production."

"I say, George, your vision for Angion is very ambitious. You intend to internalize manufacturing as well?"

"Yes, we will take Angiotox from soup to nuts."

"Big risk."

"And big reward. But the sooner we line up our backers, the sooner we can take this to the next level."

"Well, Stia's tied up in the Ukraine. That would be bad news, except that his group is closing a deal selling an oil operation in the Urals. Soon he'll be here with more than 230 million Euros in his pocket, looking for a high-yield American investment for some of that cash. Give them a top-flight presentation, and you may seal the deal with a handshake. No, George, this is good news!"

"Perhaps, Marion ... perhaps ... but I am truly disappointed. We were all set for Monday."

"Don't worry, George. I know Stia. This will be worth it ... Say, I have an idea."

MacGregor's heart sank further.

"Tell me, old man, how's our boy August? Quite the character, eh what?"

MacGregor swallowed. "Singular. He's pulled together mountains of data."

"Excellent. With another week at your disposal, why not polish the talks and have August do the presentation? He tells me he's been working on three-D models of the mouse brain vessels – real blood-and-guts to focus Stia's financial mind."

MacGregor groaned inwardly. August talking to those bloody bankers was a recipe for disaster, and them with more than two hundred million in pocket money!

He said, "Steve's presenting is problematic. There are others in the lab who've spent years developing Angiotox, loyal scientists who might resent his getting the limelight."

"O God, George, don't be a limp noodle! August is presenting only a small bit of the picture. But if anyone objects, blame me. I've already mentioned August to Stia. Giving August some visibility will sow the seed – good for business."

No choice but to agree, and it *was* more than a week away. Much could be done in a week.

"Not a problem, Marion. I just need to be fair to my loyal employees."

"Of course. But as Chair of Neurosurgery I'm interested in August's active participation as part of our long-term collaboration."

Although MacGregor did *not* like being pushed around, he felt reassured. Phillips had shown no hint of suspicion about trouble at Angion.

After all, why should he doubt? Angiotox is the most effective treatment for brain cancer known to man.

And even as he thought this thought, a thought he had thought many, many times before, for the first time MacGregor felt a twinge of doubt. He shook his head to clear it.

All life is perception. And if I am convinced, and all are convinced, and no one can contradict me, then that is the truth. Perception … perception is reality.

But Phillips was still speaking, "My Swiss friends hope for a significant return on their investment. Please reassure them!"

MacGregor bounced back to the present.

"Yes, Marion, I'm with you. We'll have Steve present his results. When's the new date?"

"Stia suggested exactly one week's delay, if all works out in Kiev. That puts us on for Monday, the 24th."

"Fine. The dog-and-pony show will be ready. Will you be there?"

"Stia is staying with Margaret and me during his Boston visit. I'll be with him."

"Perfect. We'll be ready."

After he hung up the phone, George pondered – *Phillips is so enthusiastic about his Swiss friends. Does he have a personal interest?*

But then he remembered the note he had written for Dida, and he stopped worrying about the bankers. She had said she would be talking with August. He wondered whether she was making progress.

Late that Friday afternoon Dida Medicia made an unannounced visit to the laboratory.

She disliked walking through Angion. Always had. The labs smelled like antiseptic and dog chow, the rooms were Spartan without any sense of style, and the furniture was a tacky vinyl.

But worst of all, the whole place made her feel stupid.

At least she had some consolation in the nature of her visit. She did enjoy seduction, an art in which she was a true expert, and the conquest of a supposedly unassailable man like Steve August was always a special pleasure. She would enjoy cutting this notch on her bedpost.

And there were other benefits. She was getting tired of George. And in the process she would mark one up against Riker. And also, of course, that 17th century antique emerald brooch would look good against her favorite Valentino gown.

This morning she had picked her outfit with special care, to be professional yet provocative, looking younger than her thirty-eight years: a low-cut, cream bustier, a light pink skirt hugging her hips, white pumps accenting her legs, an unbuttoned silk jacket, and a white silk sash around her thin waist.

With satisfaction she inspected the final result in her bedroom mirror. "Hotter than any stupid college bimbo!" she murmured. Authoritative, feminine, steamy – she liked the package. She was sure the twenty-nine year old August would as well.

Upon her arrival at Angion she stepped into a washroom. She checked the mirror, pulled the jacket open to reveal sufficient skin, and tugged the sash to hold the ensemble in place. Then she entered Room 105.

The lab techs looked up at the sound of high heels on linoleum, and more than one registered surprise. Dida walked up to a girl who was dispensing drops from a syringe into a beaker. Speechless, the tech stopped, the President of Angion standing in front of her.

"Hello. My name is Dida Medicia. Would you please tell me where I might find Steve August?"

Dida pitched her voice to reflect her mood: the growling purr of a lioness at the sight of fresh raw meat.

"Yes, of course, Ms. Medicia," she said. "He's over there, at the end of the counter." She gestured with her head, her hands full.

"Thank you. Carry on."

Dida walked up to the unsuspecting boy, who was staring at the computer on his desk. The screen showed an image of a mouse brain, rotating slowly. A tangled clump of blood vessels was colored red, the remainder gold. Dida heard a printer stir to life, as he copied equations from the screen into his lab book.

"Dr. August?"

He swiveled in his chair.

She was standing arms akimbo, shoulders back, one leg slightly forward, a stretch of thigh exposed along the slit of her skirt. She held the pose long enough to make full impact; and then she extended her hand. "Dr. August, I'm Dida Medicia. I've wanted to meet you for some time."

He stood up, his face registering surprise. "Ms. Medicia! Very nice to meet you."

She kept her voice low and mellifluous, "I was curious what you're working on. Just so that you know it's permissible for us to speak …" – she assumed a half-mocking, half-serious expression – " …I had George MacGregor write me a permission slip!"

Reminiscent of a schoolgirl caught by the hall monitor, she handed Steve a sheet of Angion letterhead with MacGregor's handwriting:

Steve –

Dida Medicia is the President of Angion. She wishes to review the results of your work. You are to do whatever she asks.

Regards,
Prof. G. MacGregor

"Would you show me what you're doing?"

August took this in stride. "Sure." He sat back down. "You probably know that we're trying to find what effects Angiotox has on tumor blood vessels. Up to this point the results have been equivocal at best. Now we're trying a more sophisticated mathematical analysis based on work out of Moscow …"

Her mouth close to his ear, Dida murmured, "Thanks, Doctor, but I don't have time for details. Maybe later. You have dinner plans tonight?"

She gave his chair a playful little push, spinning him away from the computer.

She was almost over him, his eyes the level of her chest. Perfume arose from the warm skin between the open flaps of her jacket.

Yet his face remained passive, blank with no expression.

"I was planning on working late …"

She cut him off. "Dr. August – I want to discuss your experiences here at Angion, your potential long-term relationship with the company, and your most intimate hopes for the future, which we plan to turn into reality. That's an extended conversation, one best held over dinner. Tonight would be good for me."

At the word "intimate" Dida leaned forward slightly, her dark almond eyes inviting him to say yes.

Steve leaned back slightly. "Sure, Ms. Medicia. I'd enjoy dinner. But as for …"

Again, she cut him off. "Wonderful! Then that's settled. Here's my card. By the way, it's Dida."

She touched her fingers to his cheek.

Softly, she whispered, "We have so much to offer you."

And with that she walked out of the lab.

She imagined him sitting at his desk, holding the calling card. It was simple enough:

Dida Medicia
The Ritz Carlton
Suite 4-D
Boston Commons

On the reverse she had written, "8 PM. Be there! Dida."

29.

FRIDAY, APRIL 15

Eight o'clock that evening found Steve on the 28th floor of the Ritz Carlton.

When the door to suite 4-D opened, Steve thought he had been cast in an old Hollywood movie. In the doorway stood Dida, as carnal and beautiful as any femme fatale from the 1930s' Silver Screen. Still in the outfit from that afternoon, minus sash and jacket, she held herself as if on display, her chin high, one hand on the open door, the other on her hip, every curve accented.

Man, she could give Anne Bancroft lessons.

"Steve August. I've been waiting …" She held the door open.

Is this a good idea? – but I need to know what she knows.

He stepped inside.

Dida led him into a spacious room with floor-to-ceiling two-story windows looking out on the Boston Common. The city lights twinkled in the darkening twilight: skyscrapers, brownstones, street lamps, traffic. The room's recessed lights cast dim shadows. Dida gestured at the couch.

"Please, Steve, have a seat."

She stepped to the sideboard. There was the crash of poured ice, the rattle of a shaker, then the splash of liquor in glasses.

A martini glass in each hand, Dida sat on the couch, allowing a bit of space between them. She put the two glasses on the coffee table, as though offering him a choice.

"I'm quite partial to a good dry vodka martini. How 'bout you, Steve? You strike me as a 'shaken, not stirred' kind of guy."

Sounds like James Bond. She thinks I'm a spy?

Since his adventures two weeks ago, till now there had been no hint that anyone knew about his exit through Angion's ceiling.

He had already decided he *must* solve the riddles from that Saturday night. Dida's having him to dinner might represent an invitation to move inside their circle ... though more likely it seemed a trap, especially if they knew what he had seen.

He decided. He would play, he would survive, and he – and Morgan – would win.

The martini would make clear thinking more difficult, but he did have his years of physical and mental discipline within the *I Ching* to help guide his instincts.

He picked up the martini and smiled at Dida. "Quite. 'Shaken, not stirred.'"

She extended her glass. He held up his. The "clink" sounded loud.

"*Carpe diem.*" She smiled and sipped her drink.

Steve tasted the martini. "*Carpe diem.*"

Dida leaned back. "So, Steve, George tells me you've been spending many, many hours in the lab. You ever get any time to *relax*?" She luxuriated in the word as it flowed from her mouth.

"Many things worth doing are tedious. But you're right; I don't have much time away from the lab."

"Mmm, what a shame," purred Dida. "All work and no play makes ..."

Her voice drifted into silence.

Then she said, "So, does Jack have a girlfriend? Doesn't sound like you have time."

Steve smiled, even as his heart ached. "No, no girlfriend. We split up a little while ago."

"Oh, what a *shame!*" But her eyes sparkled, and the corners of her mouth lifted, and she leaned forward, ever so slightly. "So, you're available. Why, Steve, how exciting for you! The world is your oyster. All you have to do is open it right up!"

A buzzer sounded in the kitchen.

"I threw together a veal roast. I should have asked first. You do eat red meat, don't you?"

Without waiting for a response, she put her hand on Steve's knee, pushed herself up off the couch, and stepped towards the kitchen.

Steve watched her, the pink skirt and white top accenting her tanned skin. He shook his head.

Oh boy, be careful.

He picked up his martini and followed. "Anything I can do to help?"

"Sure. Sit down; drink up; put on some music." She pointed at the stereo and disappeared into the kitchen.

There were only a few disks in the CD tower: a bit of rock, some R&B and jazz. He picked out a set with Stan Getz and Antonio Jobim playing Brazilian sambas, and shortly the soft pulse of bass, guitar, and piano emerged from hidden speakers. As soon as he heard it, he regretted the choice.

Damn, too sexy.

But he couldn't very well change it, now that it had started.

Out of nowhere, he recalled Julius Caesar. As he crossed the Rubicon marching on Rome, Caesar had said, "*Iacta alea est.*"

The die is cast.

Steve looked out the window, admired the view, sipped the martini, listened to the music, and practiced staying calm.

The dining table nestled in an alcove that was an extension of the vaulted living room, the table's length along the large window next to the kitchen door. Dida re-emerged and set a serving platter on the table.

"Have a seat, Steve. One of my favorite dishes. Hope you enjoy the spread!"

She poured the wine.

Throughout the dinner Dida was charming, funny, engaging. She showed interest in his past: how his mother and then his father had died, how his grandmother had raised her only grandchild, how he had evolved from college athlete into neurosurgeon, how he had ended up at All Saints Memorial – virtually everything about him, except his work at Angion. That she never touched on.

The veal was tender; the asparagus sweet; the hollandaise creamy. The meal complete, the second wine bottle half empty, Dida interrupted a particularly amusing story of his about Phillips: how the famous surgeon had sewn up a little girl's torn teddy bear while explaining the surgery he had done for her two days earlier. Teddy had done fine, the girl had been cured, and years later she had entered medical school intent on becoming a neurosurgeon.

But Dida broke his train of thought.

"Steve," she said, her cleavage a shadow under the dim lights overhead, "I've whipped up the most decadent, sweet dessert. You want some?"

"An amazing meal. Don't see how anything could be better!"

"Oh, Steve, thank you, but it can be *so* much better," she purred.

Within seconds she was gone, carrying the serving tray into the kitchen.

Shortly she re-emerged, a plate in each hand. "Let's take these on the couch," she said. "It's so much easier to enjoy the view."

She walked into the living room and put the plates on the coffee table. Tossing her hair back, she smiled at him over her shoulder. "Give me a minute."

And she disappeared up the steps of a spiral staircase at the corner of the room.

Steve left the dining table. He sat on the couch studying his dessert plate – a flourless, dark chocolate cake lathered with fresh whipped cream, a light green liquid poured on top: crème de menthe.

From the top of the staircase came a soft laugh. "Don't worry; it won't hurt you."

Dida was coming down the steps, now wearing what appeared to be a ruby red dress. At first glance she seemed more discrete, since shoulders and legs were covered, but then he realized that it was not a dress but a single-piece thin silk wrap – a kimono held in place by the sash draped long around her waist. The ruby silk was smooth against her body, no hint of bra or panty-line beneath its seamless sheen.

"Forgive me, Steve, but I really did want to put on something more comfortable. With that skirt I do have to be so careful, especially when I sit down. There's always a risk that I might flash my guests." She chuckled again.

"No, Dida, you're perfectly discrete."

She walked to the sideboard. "After dinner cordial, Steve? I know … just the thing – a white Russian. The flavor will go nicely with the chocolate and mint."

Glasses tinkled as she mixed the drinks.

Steve said nothing. He took a bite of cake, which was like chewy chocolate velvet, its slight bitter taste sweetened by the mint liqueur. He debated one last time.

Man, you can still walk!

But Caesar had said: *Iacta alea est.*

She handed him the drink and sat on the couch, the Boston skyline at their feet. He took a sip and looked towards her. He half-sensed the erect nipples prominent beneath the thin silk sheen, but he refused to let his gaze drop from her face. He knew she was watching.

Focus, man, focus!

"So, Steve," she reached over and brushed the hair along his ear, "tell me, please, what *is* going on in that over-heated brain of yours?"

She scooted over on the couch, close beside him. Her warmth was inches away.

He took another bite. "What do you mean?" he mumbled through his full mouth. He swallowed the chocolate.

She picked up her drink. She let her other hand drift behind his neck, her fingers hovering lightly against his skin. "Come now, Steve, use your imagination!"

He looked out the window. "Oh, you mean, what do I think about Angion? That's very complicated, Dida!"

"Do you think that's why I asked you over here, tonight?"

She let her hand drape around his neck, and she scooted closer to him. Her hip brushed against his leg.

"Hmmm. Honestly, I think you have a couple of reasons for inviting me."

"Yes, my dear boy, that's true. Are none of them to your liking?"

She leaned slightly closer. He felt her breast softly nuzzle against his arm through the kimono's thin silk. A soft Brazilian samba was pulsing in the background.

Iacta alea est!

"Yes, I do like." He turned and pulled her to him.

They kissed, their breathing deep and heavy, their mouths pressed together.

"You want to know about Angiotox?" he murmured.

"Not now, Steve, for all gods' sakes, not now," she gasped, as she loosened the sash, the smooth kimono sliding off her flawless shoulders.

30.

SATURDAY, APRIL 16

When she awoke, Dida felt *really* good.

She thought back over the night. Not often did she lose control – not like *that*! When had been the last time?

But now she needed to be in control. After last night, he would surely trust her. The boy would think he had conquered her.

Such is the male ego.

She smiled. Thinking he was the conqueror, he would be the conquered.

Leaving him asleep, softly she padded into the bathroom to survey her aching muscles in the mirror. He had made her feel so … so … so young! George certainly could use some lessons. In fact, so could every one of her lovers of the last ten years. At some point sex had become a means to an end, merely a tool for getting what she wanted.

And that takes away most of the fun.

She looked in the mirror.

Whore!

But then she chuckled: *Right, but an expensive one!*

She threw on her black silk teddy and returned to the bedroom. Now she was draped, and he was naked. That set the stage better.

She sat next to his sleeping form, her teddy only half-exposing her breasts, and reached down to stroke his chest.

"Steve August, you sweet thing, you awake?"

He stirred, his torso rippling beneath her touch, and his steel blue eyes opened. "Hey, Dida. Good morning."

"Good morning, baby." She kissed his forehead, then folded her legs up onto the bed and cuddled her chin against his neck. Her hand continued to caress his chest and abs. "That was quite the performance last night."

He lay relaxed, his eyes on the ceiling. "Yes, quite a night. You were incredible!"

"You released my inner animal, Steve. I do like being let out of my cage!"

"Anytime."

"Hmm. I'm counting on it."

"Dida, sex can't have been the reason you invited me here."

"Why not? But you're right. I want to make you a proposition. There are certain things I can offer you, and there are certain things you can offer me."

"What do you mean?"

"As you may know, Steve, I've been seeing George MacGregor for a little while. But it's time for me to trade him in for a better model. You would fit my needs …" she chuckled, " …perfectly. Purrrfectly!"

"You're brutal, Dida."

"That, sweetie, is the key to a successful partnership. Brutal honesty. That's one reason George is no longer of value to me."

"One reason?"

"Oh, baby. Don't get me wrong. Of course, last night was good, but … there's more to life than good sex."

"Yes?"

"The list is simple: sex, money, power. In ascending order. You can give me great sex, but much more than that, you can get me power."

"Me? Sorry, I don't see it. I'm only a neurosurgical resident. George is a world-famous scientist, and the principal owner of Angion, not to mention my boss."

"Steve, he's the past, while you're the future. You hold the keys to Angiotox."

"The keys to Angiotox?"

"Sweetie, don't play coy. You're the one who's done the experiments needed for FDA approval. Once we get that, you'll be *the* link between Angion and the medical community. International fame and fortune await! But at the moment your skepticism is your mojo: your ability either to veto or to approve puts you in control, much more so than George MacGregor! But to *really* have power, to have total control, you need me."

"Why's that?"

"You may have the Angiotox data at your fingertips, but *I* understand how the money works. Financial incentives are the levers that control people – including investors and corporations. Stick with me, kid, and we can turn Angion, and George MacGregor, and the whole lot of them, in any direction we choose."

"You're saying that science plus finance equals power."

"Yes, baby. You catch on fast." She nibbled his earlobe.

"Hmm. Sounds like a plan," he said, and slipped his hand up to cradle her breast.

"Mmm. Now, Steve, don't get me started. We've got some work to do."

"What do you mean? It's Saturday morning. We've got lots of time."

And as he pulled her to him, she pretended to yield.

An hour later, Dida lay spent, her shaken body glistening with fresh sweat. She wanted a cigarette, though she'd given up smoking years ago. Steve was in the shower. She listened to the splashing in the other room, then the soft rubbing of a towel against his taut frame.

Wow. This is going to be fun! Too bad it's only temporary.

He stepped into the bedroom, and she pointed at the closet.

"Robe's in there."

He grinned, 'You're not kicking me out?"

"Not yet. Just getting started." She glanced at the bedside clock. "Hmm. Nine o'clock. Good timing. There's fresh coffee in the kitchen."

He blinked. "How'd you do that?"

Boy needs training.

"I set it last night. I like having coffee ready when I get up."

"I see. Enough for two?"

"Of course. I made extra."

"You plan ahead."

"Always. You mind bringing me a cup?"

"How do you take it?"

Her gaze roamed over him. "Hot, white, and very sweet."

While he was downstairs she rinsed in the shower.

Incredible! I feel like a schoolgirl.

When she stepped into the bedroom, she found Steve back with two steaming mugs.

"Thank you, sweetie." She took a sip. "Perfect."

The condo was a split-level, the bedroom above the living room, recessed for a clear view of the giant windows from both upstairs and downstairs. She pointed at the twenty-foot-long scarlet drapes. "Let's see the day, shall we?"

She touched a button, and an unseen motor parted the fabric, revealing a sweeping view of the city. The morning was clear with a brilliant blue sky and bright yellow sunshine. From the loft the entire city was luminescent gold at their feet.

"Dramatic," said Steve, standing at the railing. "You should play Wagner when you do that."

"Good idea. I'll have the maid set it up Monday."

"Dida, my turn to be brutally honest?"

"Of course, Steve. The key to every successful partnership."

She gestured to two over-stuffed armchairs near the loft's rail, and they both sat.

"Dida, I don't see how I can meet my end of this partnership. All you've said is very abstract. In the concrete, I'm not sure what I would do other than what I'm already doing – so from your point of view, why bother?"

"You've already alluded to one reason: honesty."

"You mean . . ."

She felt good, being so in control. "I told you. George is no longer in favor, not with me, not with my uncle, not with anybody. We think he isn't straight with us at all."

"Your uncle?"

She felt *so* wickedly delicious.

"Yes, Steve. My Zio. Don Tony. Don Antonio Calibri. Although George has majority ownership of Angion, my uncle has actual control through a very neat contract drawn up by our excellent law firm: Thomas, McEvoy, and Garfield. You've heard of them?"

"Well, yes, that's where my former girlfriend worked."

"Sounds like you dumped her at just the right time."

She detected no reaction, which was good.

"Yeah, guess I did. But as for MacGregor, how can he be majority owner, yet not have control?"

"Don Calibri gives him key information about investors, other companies, juicy gossip. If he breaks with Calibri, George flies blind – and crashes."

Steve paused, digesting this. Then he said, "So, if your intelligence is so reliable, why do you need me to understand Angiotox?"

She felt *so* good. "We think George has been using the Science Service to confuse the Angiotox picture. We believe you have insight that would be valuable as we approach taking Angion public. And we suspect George is trying to stifle your perspective."

Dida knew she was taking a gamble, but her instinct was that her frankness might take his youth by surprise, so he might reveal what he knew, especially about the Science Service. And she very much wanted Steve on the inside, so to speak. If he did not open up now, then he'd be Riker's – but she wanted him for herself.

"The 'Science Service?' I'm sorry, Dida, you're going too fast for me."

"You've *never* heard of the Science Service?"

"No."

"Do you know what goes on Sunday mornings at Angion?"

"Brutal honesty?" he responded. "Let me answer your question with a question. Do you know what happened to me two weekends ago?"

Dida leaned back in her chair.

Ah, now we're getting somewhere.

"No. What happened?"

Steve took a sip from his coffee mug.

"I'd been working late Saturday night, and fell asleep. Next thing I knew it was two in the morning. MacGregor's very strict about being out by midnight on Saturday, and I'd already been in some trouble with him. So, I tried to leave without being noticed."

"How did you do that?"

"This may sound crazy. To avoid triggering the alarm, I crawled out through the ceiling."

"That *is* insane! Why didn't you just acknowledge you'd fallen asleep?"

"Panicked. Lots on my mind; I was having trouble with my girlfriend;

lab work was going badly. I didn't want MacGregor going to Phillips with a complaint."

Wow, he's spilling his guts. Sex makes men so stupid!

"OK, so you crawl into the ceiling ..."

"I crawl into the ceiling and get lost among all the airshafts and plumbing and wiring. Eventually, I find a ladder leading to the roof and then get down via the fire escape."

Feels like he's holding back.

"Quite an adventure! And during the course of your travels you saw nothing?"

"It was dawn when I reached the top of the ladder. From there I could look down onto the whole atrium, where people in white coats were congregating on the lower levels, all facing a central figure in a red robe. That's when I decided I should get the hell out while I still could. Let me guess: that's the Science Service?"

"Yes, that was the Science Service, Steve. What did you think?"

"Very little. I only caught a glimpse. I was more interested in escaping."

He's holding back.

"Do you have any idea what they were doing?"

"No."

"Well, my dear, then we share the same problem. It's not clear to me, either. By the way, George did figure out that you left via the roof, although how you eluded the lab's security system is still a mystery. How *did* you?"

"I assumed it was an infrared motion sensor, like an automatic light switch, so I moved very, very slowly."

Incredible.

"That's some fine motor control. If I hadn't seen your performance in bed, I'm not sure I'd believe you. How do you do it?"

"*Bagua.*"

"Is that like kung fu?"

"Sort of. Not really. It's more like Chinese modern dance. And a way of life."

"Right, makes sense to me."

She was feeling a little lost.

He's very sexy – but also very weird.

From nowhere, she remembered a would-be poet she had dated during college.

Why did we break up? Oh, yeah, right – something about "values." Goddamn bohemian.

Steve said nothing, so she filled the silence. "Steve, let's cut to the most important issue. MacGregor tells me you think Angiotox is crap. Why's that?"

"Not crap. Just doesn't work as billed. It seems to work in some mice, but not in all."

"You know why?"

"Right now I'm analyzing all my results again, still looking for underlying patterns that may show an effect for Angiotox, one that may be hidden in the data."

"What do you think the chances are you'll find something?"

"Don't know. Maybe fifty-fifty."

"I'll guess they're lower than that."

"Why do you say that?"

"Steve, did it ever occur to you someone might have altered your experiment?"

"You're kidding, right?"

"'Brutal honesty,' right? Everyone I've talked to – and that includes Silverstein, MacGregor, and all the senior members of his lab group – are all convinced Angiotox is the best thing since oral sex. And then you come along and announce Angiotox doesn't work 'as billed.' This puts you at odds with a group of world-class scientists. One possibility is you've been sloppy in your lab work and are too stupid to know it, but you don't strike me as the kind of guy who's sloppy and stupid." She gave him a sly smile. "So, another possibility is that your experiment's been tampered with."

"Go on."

"From Angion's point of view, Angiotox is a given, a known commodity. The unknown commodity is *you.* To show us you're trustworthy, you must give Angion something – show that you're part of the team, come inside the circle."

"I'm not quite clear …"

"MacGregor needs you, but he has to know he can trust you. Understand: I don't *know* what he did with your experiment, but my guess would be someone undermined part of your data, to test your willingness to be a team player. I'll bet part of your experiment didn't work because they made sure it didn't."

"So you're saying that Angiotox failed in some of the mice ..."

"Likely because it wasn't Angiotox that those mice received: probably just sugar water."

"So it's the faulty mice that are the ones that showed no effect for Angiotox. If I drop those mice, then I'll be a team player, and we can move forward."

"Exactly. You'll be doing the right thing in the process, by removing the tampered mice from the results."

"I never thought of that. You really think the mice that showed no effect were tampered with?"

"Makes sense to me. It would explain everything, including MacGregor's overwhelming confidence in Angiotox, even in the face of your data."

Steve was silent, while Dida waited for him to reach the obvious conclusion.

"OK. I guess that does make sense. How do you suggest we proceed? There's a presentation to these Swiss investors on Monday. I could try to re-do the analysis by tomorrow."

"Mmm. Now you're talking, baby," and she stretched out her legs, letting her thighs show between the folds of her robe. "But there's no need to rush. George learned yesterday that the Swiss moneymen are held up in Kiev, and the meeting's postponed for a week. You can talk to him on Monday."

"Really? That takes some of the pressure off."

"Yes, it sure does. So I was thinking today we might go over the analyses you've done and look for reasons to exclude some mice. I'll guess it won't take too many, as long as they're well chosen, for your work to reach statistical significance. And then we can go to the bank ... the Swiss bank!"

"Hell of a way to do science."

"Steve, this isn't science; this is business. You see, this way Angion has something on you, and you have something on Angion. Then you're tied to the company. That makes for mutual trust, and that's what keeps a partnership solid. Our financial and professional interests are united, not to mention ..." and she licked her lips, "...our personal interests. Deal?"

"You've put this in a new light."

"Great! You bring your analyses with you?"

"Yes. I'm supposed to leave this stuff at work, but you'd said you wanted to take a look. It's all in my book bag."

"Good boy!" She stood up. "I'm going to throw some clothes on. Why don't you get out your papers. We can go over them downstairs."

"Sure. I'll do the same ..."

"No, please don't bother. I like you in a bathrobe."

It was later that day when Riker shut off the video.

For a long while Calibri sat silent, the only sound an occasional hiss as he exhaled through his teeth.

Eventually, Riker spoke: "Don Calibri, this is a very dangerous situation."

"Yesss, Mr. Riker, on several levels. I am disappointed in my niece."

"She should not have mentioned your name."

"Yesss, she made mistakes, serious mistakesss ..."

"What do you think of her theory, that MacGregor tampered with the mice to get a leg up on August?"

"It's only a guess on her part, Mr. Riker – one designed to persuade him to capitulate. Still, it has merit. The secret to power is *leverage*. If he capitulates, then MacGregor has the leverage he needs."

"Don Calibri, we should not waste time on subtleties. We must take full control of MacGregor, and we must exterminate August. Let me act. The time for subtleties has passed."

"Very well. But you must not touch my niece. Leave her to me. She knows nothing about the Barflies in her apartment?"

"Of course not. But I do want to tell MacGregor about her little affair with August. His jealousy will be useful."

"It is not necessary. Do not give away intelligence unnecessarily."

"Yes, sir. Never unnecessarily."

"Leave Dida and the Professor to me," said Calibri. "But as for August, remove him. Be sure to discredit him with Phillips. He is a liability, and he must have no capacity to speak. He knows too much."

"Yes, Mr. Calibri. Gladly." Riker felt pleased.

"You are prepared to monitor MacGregor's Science Service tomorrow?"

"Yes, Mr. Calibri."

"MacGregor knows nothing about your surveillance?"

"Nothing. But he knows we've gone over his security tapes at Angion. He may suspect."

"Unavoidable, under the circumstances. What about Silverstein?"

"We've been watching his laboratory, but he seems straight. He's worried Angiotox may only work in some animals but not others: rabbits for sure, but not mice or humans."

"And this test he has – SAGA. Any chance that's the problem?"

"All say it's the best in the world."

"Very well. Watch him closely."

"Yes, Don Calibri."

Pause.

"Your 'barflies' are remarkable, Mr. Riker."

"Thank you, sir."

There was a long silence.

Finally, Calibri said, "But you are still here, Mr. Riker? Please go do your work."

31.

SUNDAY, APRIL 17

As was his usual habit, early Sunday morning MacGregor entered the Angion building. He had missed Dida the prior night, but nothing could be done about that. Dida had her work, and he his. He dropped off coat and briefcase in the office and glanced at the clock.

5:07.

Plenty of time. He moved down a side corridor to what he called the Green Room, whose other door led to the atrium, and changed into his scarlet robe.

At 5:25 he opened the door. He carried out the large golden brain on its pedestal and solemnly set it in its place, the small raised nubs on the floor fitting into the recesses of the stand. Then he remained motionless, his eyes focused on the pedestal, waiting for the dawn, aware of the quiet rustling of scientists moving into position above and around him.

He loved this moment. The lives of thousands, maybe millions, rested in his hands, in his command of this assembly. He controlled what they believed – and what they believed the world had no choice but to accept. And in the years ahead no one would be so foolish as to risk the massive resources required for a serious challenge! Beneath his hood, he smiled. At least in this lifetime George MacGregor would be god. He would manipulate; he would control; he would create. He was the source.

A green light flashed on the pedestal: daybreak in sixty seconds. The system was guaranteed to work precisely, even on the stormiest of New England winter mornings – if clouds hid the sun, there was a flood lamp at the eastern corner that could pour 5000 watts focused onto the skylight's parabolic mirror, a substitute for Boston's fickle morning light. But today the sky was clear of clouds, and looking up MacGregor could see shades of brightening pink. He raised his arms, and the assembled scientists began their chant, preparing themselves. "Ooommm …"

Waiting, staring up towards the heavens, MacGregor blinked. For a split-second he'd thought a tiny silver shadow had flashed across the sky. *Something on my contact?*

The humming grew louder. He could feel his acolytes' energy, anxious to enter their trances. Often the scientists told him they left the S.S. sessions relaxed and stimulated – almost in a sexual way – their intellectual batteries recharged. This was no surprise to MacGregor, since this was what he told them to feel at the end of each session. It was important to keep them coming back for more.

Sunlight flooded down upon the golden brain. "OOOOMMMM …" The chant swelled as the light splintered into a thousand pieces across floor, walls, walkways, and back to the sky.

"AD HOMINEM!!" he cried.

The chant suddenly turned silent, a soft "ooommm …" in the background of the spacious, echoing Arena. MacGregor dropped his arms.

He let out a satisfied sigh. He felt good.

Parked in a van three blocks away, Michael Riker and Antonio Calibri simultaneously let out a collective breath.

"Son of a bitch!" exclaimed Riker.

Calibri did nothing but stare at the screen, watching MacGregor as he proceeded with the work of the Science Service.

The S.S. session proved uneventful for MacGregor – productive, full of good ideas. He was relieved that the scientists expressed no doubts about Angiotox, about his leadership, or about the overall direction of Angion. (One of the side-benefits of the S.S. was that he could learn what his employees thought about *him*.) But no problems arose. The group did not believe August. They thought him incompetent, or worse. How could he possibly challenge Angiotox – which they knew to be the most potent treatment for brain cancer known to man?

Likewise, the rest of the day went smoothly. For four hours he made notes on that morning's session: tearing apart the discussions and honing their conclusions. Then he went over the reports from the various scientific teams, using insights from the S.S. to make further research plans. By three o'clock he had finished. Following a walk from Angion to Harvard Square, he enjoyed an early dinner at one of his favorite little cafes near the College. He was not seeing Dida, so he treated himself to two martinis and a half-bottle of wine – he would not have to muster a performance later.

George arrived home just after ten, slightly drunk, happy with his day, reveling in the weeklong reprieve from Phillips and his banker chums. Last Thursday he had been considering a showdown with August – scrubbing his data with or without his consent – but now he had the luxury of several days to press the boy. And it seemed success was within reach. August had called yesterday, saying he might be mistaken, that Angiotox might work after all, and that he was re-doing the analysis.

August, he concluded, was an *inferior* opponent. Ultimately, *he*, George MacGregor, would pick the data; *he* would control the presentations; *he* would become filthy rich in the process. It was all *his*.

~

But when the pounding on his condo door woke him after only two hours of slumber, his head hurt, his eyes felt puffy, and his one wish was not infinite wealth but merely sleep.

He staggered to the door and looked through the peephole, hoping it might be Dida. But it was the person he *least* wanted to see, even less than August.

Riker!

Sleepy, irritated, and hung over, George decided to ignore the bastard. He turned back towards his comfortable warm bed.

One heartbeat later there was a mechanical whirring sound; and he turned to watch in disbelief as the door handle turned.

"Hey, what do you think …?" but he had no time to finish.

The door slammed open a few inches but then was caught by the security chain. Instantly, metal cutters appeared and crushed down on the chain, scattering broken links across the floor.

MacGregor was backing up hoping for an exit, but he found none, only empty space till his legs hit the edge of the coffee table and he sat down with a "thump" on a pile of National Geographic and Architectural Digest magazines.

Standing in the doorway was Michael Riker. Hands in his pockets, he stepped nonchalantly across the threshold, as though a break-in was a typical pastime for a Sunday night.

Three shadows followed, faces covered with charcoal ski masks, one of them holding the metal cutters. Nevertheless, MacGregor recognized the outlines of Riker's alphabet soup from *last* Sunday—Alpha, Bravo, and Charlie.

"Don Calibri wants to talk with you, a conversation he finds sufficiently urgent to warrant waking you," said Riker.

"He wants me *now?*" squeaked MacGregor.

"Yes. Now."

Riker stood in front of him, a human razor cutting through the weak and inept. MacGregor imagined his own body slashed in two, blood spreading in a widening pool across the living room floor.

He felt faint.

And then there was only black.

32.

Later that night MacGregor was sitting in Antonio Calibri's oak-paneled study, surrounded by priceless historical objects. He could not appreciate them fully, even had he wanted to, their outlines hazy in the thick cigar smoke and dim candlelight. The heavy acrid air turned his stomach, adding to the misery of his pounding headache.

Calibri's tongue flicked across his lips. "Professor! *Buona sera.* Thank you for joining me at such an inconvenient hour." He waved at the humidor at his elbow. "Cigar? They're aged Cohibas – quite exquisite!"

He grinned, exposing his brown teeth.

MacGregor's jaw tightened. "No thanks."

"Pity. Any idea why I asked you here so urgently, tonight?"

"No." MacGregor was not in the mood to talk.

"I did not think so."

Calibri took a long drag, then released a plume of smoke into the dead air. The nausea worsened.

After a long silence Calibri said, "There are two matters about which we must come to agreement. The first has to do with your tremendous achievement, which I am just beginning to understand."

"You mean, Angiotox."

"No, Professor, of course not. I am referring to your Science Service."

There was a long silence, other than Calibri's *puff, puff, puff.*

Shocked and dismayed into silence, MacGregor could only stare at him.

What does this viper know? Why does he look so smug?

"George, George, George!" Calibri was shaking his head. "How can you – of all people – be so naïve? You think Michael would tell me about your S.S., all the interesting things you told him, and then we would not want to see for ourselves? I must say – impressive!"

"You … watched … us …?" MacGregor's voice surged out between clenched teeth.

"Yes, my friend, we did. With great interest."

"You … you … fool! Do you have *any* idea what might happen? You, your stooges, no one, must ever, *ever,* observe us! Our capacity to control perception depends on avoiding outside interference. All must believe the truth, no matter how that belief is achieved! Do you want to destroy Angion? Are you *mad?*"

Calibri studied MacGregor through the cigar smoke. "Professor, though I think your S.S. is extraordinary, I do not believe your … how does one say … your metaphysics."

He paused to study his cigar, then continued: "Let me tell you what I saw this morning. After entering a trance, your scientists gave you a room full of ideas. But what we found most remarkable was not what they did, but what *you* did. *You made comments.* And every time you did, the discussion followed your lead. You had the final say."

MacGregor grunted.

"So, Professor, I am left with admiration, but with questions. You mind?"

Feeling ever sicker, George shook his head.

"It is true you can tell your scientists what to think?"

MacGregor's voice came out in a hoarse whisper, "Well, up to the point of a logical impossibility. Hypnosis cannot make anyone truly believe up is down, true is false, black is white. But every experimental result *always* involves interpretation – a human element."

Calibri's eyes were yellow globes shrouded in smoke, eyelids opening, closing, studying him. MacGregor felt like an insect under the eye of a collector.

"Indeed, my friend, indeed," said Calibri, sarcasm growing heavy. "The human element. That is your motto, is it not: '*Ad hominem.*' And your scientists have *no* idea you control their ability to reason, to be objective, … to … to … *think?*"

"If they ever suspected," said MacGregor through clenched teeth, "then they would not, they could not, participate – and then the S.S. would collapse."

Calibri's eyes bored down. "One more question, Professor," he hissed. "Do you believe, that if all believe exactly what you think, then you control the truth?"

MacGregor returned his gaze, his voice firm, "If all agree, and if no one can prove otherwise, then that is what we call truth."

"To the point of affecting what other laboratories discover?"

MacGregor held his gaze, "Yes."

The word hung dead in the air.

Then he continued, " …Yes, as long as others believe us. As it stands, we have exclusive control of too much data, too many assays, including SAGA, for any other lab to directly challenge us. And that which they *can* test they must interpret in light of all that we have done before. Angion dominates this corner of the scientific universe. To disagree with us is to risk excommunication from the accepted scientific enterprise."

Calibri's tone was almost respectful, "Professor, I fear no man, but what you have just said … what you are doing … this concerns me."

He muttered, as he puffed on his cigar, "I wonder if you are mad. I wonder if you are a genius. I wonder …"

He shook his head and puffed some more. "I have another question: if *you* don't believe what you tell your S.S., then haven't *you* already broken the spell?"

MacGregor's voice was an even softer whisper, "I tell them what *I* believe, so we all agree."

"And if you don't?"

"I think it doesn't matter what *I* think, as long as no one else knows."

Calibri considered this for a long time.

Finally he spoke, "We will keep your secret safe, Mr. Riker and I. We will leave it at that. No more needs be said."

Inwardly, MacGregor sighed with relief, though he wondered what the implications might be of outside observers, even if they spoke with no one.

"There is only one more little thing …" said Calibri.

MacGregor's sigh stopped short.

"It is a waste not to take full advantage of your discovery," continued

Calibri. "I think, Professor, that you are an ambitious man, so I am surprised."

MacGregor was unsure where this was going, but he was sure Calibri only made proposals that served Calibri.

"You can help?"

"Indeed! Imagine what we could do if every Calibri laboratory had its own Science Service! Just think – what we could sell to investors, to regulators, to the public. No one would suspect results confirmed by three, or five, or eight rival labs! We, but no one else, would know the secret – that all our scientists' ideas were unified.

"We could target competing laboratories one by one, forcing them to lose value as they dropped behind, buying them up at discount, building the empire. In five years imagine the power we would command!"

MacGregor looked pasty white. "You want to give away the S.S.? The secret will out, and then all will be lost!!"

"My friend, relax …" Calibri's soft hiss made him think of a cobra lulling a mouse into a trance. "You have created the prototype. All we must do is re-create it."

"But this depends on Angion's security. I can monitor every *breath* that happens in that building."

Calibri just looked at him, his steady gaze only interrupted by lash-less lids momentarily shuttering liquid yellow eyes.

Finally, MacGregor spoke, "You mean your security systems are secure at all these labs? As tight as Angion's?"

Calibri's hiss was almost silent, "The best."

MacGregor was silent.

Then he murmured, "I understand. And you have the same control arrangements at those other firms, as you do with mine."

Calibri nodded again. "Yesss. Absolutely."

It was MacGregor's turn to nod. "I understand," he said. "The same contract?"

"Yesss. Absolutely," came Calibri's hiss, with an undertone of delight.

"I understand."

MacGregor stared at the wall. More clearly he could see the labeled cases through the smoke: a gold crown from fifteenth century Bohemia, glittering diamonds from Czarist Russia, an emerald necklace from the

Crusades, gold jewelry from an Egyptian pyramid, jade from an ancient Chinese dynasty.

He understood. Antonio Calibri was a man of fabulous wealth. And this man – this incredibly powerful man – wanted to partner with him, George MacGregor, to seize control of a chunk of American science. And given Calibri's wealth, and his security network, and MacGregor's unique tool for manipulating the scientific mind … well, the possibilities seemed endless.

"Mr. Calibri," he said with respect, "You're right. I hadn't recognized the potential of the S.S."

"Yesss," whispered Calibri.

"You want me to educate the leaders of your other companies."

"Yesssss," breathed Calibri.

"Your security systems are tight, tight as Angion's. We will have total control. Every leak will be eliminated."

"Yessssss."

MacGregor was again silent.

Finally, he spoke, "When do we start?"

Calibri grinned, brown teeth luminescent in the candlelight.

"Professor," he said, "This will be a truly lovely, lucrative relationship. Tomorrow, we will meet privately with Dr. Reggie Carver, head of GeneBiotics. We will start there."

MacGregor nodded.

He wondered if he might enjoy a cigar. Calibri seemed to like them.

Calibri exhaled a plume of brown air. "By the way, Professor, there is one other matter … the matter of Steve August."

MacGregor had started relaxing, relishing the idea of vast wealth and power, but at the mention of August his gut tightened.

What now?

Calibri leaned forward, extending a thin hand. He placed it on MacGregor's knee at the edge of the bathrobe, curling his wrinkled, crooked fingers around MacGregor's pale thigh – the hand like frozen ice against his bare skin.

"George, I must apologize for what I must show you. My niece is too full of primitive energy. She is fickle. She is a child in such affairs of the heart. But you should see for yourself …"

With his other hand Calibri pulled out a thin stack of three-by-five prints. Though dim, the candlelight was enough to show their naked bodies to full advantage. The variety of positions demonstrated considerable prowess.

That bastard!!

He choked out, "How long has this been going on?"

Calibri took back the photos. "This weekend was the first, but there will be more. My niece is thirsty, and August satisfies her thirst."

MacGregor felt his face flushing. "How dare you ..."

But Calibri interrupted with a hiss – harsh, savage, sinister. "I dare ... I, Antonio Calibri. I dare. There is no substitute for truth. Surely, Professor, you of all people know that!"

George felt his face burning.

Calibri continued, "May I suggest, my dear friend, that we re-evaluate your priorities. My niece ... well ... you always knew she was not a permanent arrangement. Take comfort in your more important tasks. But as for this man August ..."

George's vision had turned dark. "That puny fresh-faced arse! I swear he dies!!"

Calibri again squeezed MacGregor's knee with his claw-like hand. "Relax, Professor, relax!" he hissed. "Yes, August must die, but not because he slept with my niece – who enjoys him, and I deny her nothing – but because he knows too much. He knows too much, and he is not trustworthy. There is only one solution."

"We'll kill him."

"Not so fast, my friend. By now he is suspicious, and he may have arranged precautionary measures: letters, papers, photocopies ... who knows? No, we cannot simply *kill* him. We must *destroy* him – intellectually, psychologically, socially – to the point where no one will believe him. Then it will not matter what he says or does. *Ad hominem*, Professor, *ad hominem*."

"What are you proposing?"

"Steve August is *your* problem. So, if I eradicate him, my hand will have washed yours. But if you help develop the S.S. in my other companies, then your hand will have washed mine. One hand washes the other."

"Yes?"

"From now on, Professor, fully cooperate with Mr. Riker. He acts with my authority. Mr. Riker is quite good at what he does."

He took a puff from his cigar. "Follow *my* instructions, and you will have wealth beyond your wildest dreams."

Calibri stuck out one wrinkled hand, the other still on MacGregor's knee.

Wanting for sleep, nauseated from cigars, hungry for power, and despairing for his life, MacGregor took hold of Calibri's hand.

They shook.

Calibri let go first.

"Good," croaked Calibri.

33.

MONDAY, APRIL 18

Steve's sex-packed weekend ended early Monday when Dida's hands woke him from a troubled sleep.

"Hey, big guy, big week ahead!"

But he pushed her away, "Dida, I've got to save some energy. It's going to be a nasty day at the lab."

In the shower, water streaming off his back, he considered the weekend. By helping construct the fraud Dida had made his life easier, in a twisted sort of way. He almost felt grateful.

A cheat is the best way for an honest man to learn the ropes.

She had him call MacGregor Saturday morning to try to make amends, but only voicemail answered. They then proceeded to spend all Saturday and Sunday having sex and analyzing data. First they had reviewed the lab books page-by-page, double-checking them against spreadsheets to be sure every number was correct. Then they set up Dida's computer to systematically run through the twenty or so recorded variables using a variety of statistical models, trying to find combinations that might be confounding the results, hiding Angiotox's "true" effect. Mouse age and gender, tumor size and location, experimental details – they included everything they could document.

This had not been simple, as the possible combinations numbered into the millions. But this dark cloud had a silver lining: with so many possibilities, it was virtually guaranteed they would find several that might work.

By the close of Sunday night they had found two promising

combinations that eliminated only a modest percentage of mice while making Angiotox treatment appear effective in the remainder. The plan was for Steve to review these more closely on Monday.

Later, lying next to Dida in the dark, his body aching from another marathon performance, he felt dirty, just plain dirty.

So this is what a whore feels like. No – worse than a whore. A whore only sells her body. But this, this is selling my soul.

～

And then he awoke. Pitch black. He was lying in her bed, his naked body drenched in sweat. A nightmare – something about a vampiress sucking her victim dry, but then being eaten by her fellow vampires.

Silently he stepped into the bathroom and toweled off.

Who are you?

He studied the eyes in the mirror.

*I know who I am. Steve August. They cannot change that. Acting …
Acting is only acting.*

He splashed water on his face and felt a bit better, and then went back to bed, careful under the sheets not to touch Dida's sleeping body – long and firm, beautiful and filthy.

～

Later that morning Steve was sitting with the lab group at their conference table.

MacGregor cleared his throat. "I have good news, and bad news," he said. "The bad news is that our meeting with the Swiss venture capitalists has been held back a week – an additional delay getting cash from these boys! But it's also good news, because we have more time to polish our talks."

He glared at Steve, making Steve wonder.

He knows about the weekend?

MacGregor gestured at him, "Our surgeon here will be presenting to the Swiss. Dr. Marion Phillips is very keen on a neurosurgeon being featured for our banker friends, as they are anxious to build bridges between lab and clinic. Dr. August will be our very first bridge. It is imperative, Steve, that you present the data – perfectly."

Acid dripped from MacGregor's tongue. "I am so gratified you called Saturday to apologize for your inadequate analyses. We need something to make these moneybags sit up! I'm glad you are aware the material you presented to us last week is worse than useless. Angiotox is ..." – and he paused for emphasis – " *...the most potent treatment for brain cancer known to man."*

The heads all bobbed in unison.

"Yes, Professor, I'm re-working the analysis."

Beneath red eyebrows MacGregor's blue eyes flashed. "Well, Steve, that's just bloody fine. But to assure this turns out to be a happy ending, for the next week every evening at six o'clock you'll report your progress to Alison, to be sure you're making *fast* headway. Alison, you then will be at my office at seven to review Steve's output. If by Friday we aren't seeing a satisfactory outcome, then – young bloke – I will take you under my wing for the entire weekend. And then we'll work, nonstop, until you have the *correct* result. *Do I make myself bloody well clear!?"*

He was nearly shouting.

Steve stayed calm. "Crystal clear, Professor."

MacGregor waved his hand dismissively and turned to face the others at the table. "Be off, boy, and get us a good story to tell."

Unbidden, a verse from the *I Ching* came to mind –

Water flows and fills,
Not accumulating but running.
Pass through dangerous places;
Never lose self-confidence.

He nodded, "Right, Chief."

But MacGregor had already turned his attention to some equipment Mai was showing the group.

Mai was saying, " ...and the tip delivers a focused 20 kV photon beam ideal for treating small tumors in our mouse-model systems ..."

Steve realized, *It's the same damn thing he was using on my mice!*

Steve wanted to hear more to better understand what Mai had been doing, but MacGregor looked up. His face darkened: "Bloody cheek, August! I don't want to see you again till you've fixed your problem!"

So Steve left.

～

At his desk he returned to the weekend's analyses. Of course, these efforts were in vain – but he'd play along.

So, he spent the morning searching the scientific literature but found nothing that might justify excluding the mouse subsets he and Dida had identified.

That afternoon he called MacGregor.

"Professor, you have a minute?"

The tone was sarcastic. "Why Dr. August! For you, anything. Any breakthroughs?"

"Nothing solid. From the entire weekend re-hashing data, only two analyses showed hope of passing muster. However, neither is supported in the literature. Since we know Angiotox works, the only remaining sensible explanation is that errors in a few experimental set ups muddied the true positive results."

"Yes. Very obvious."

Bile rose in Steve's throat.

"The difficulty will be identifying the mice in which the errors were made."

His ear to the phone, George smiled. August was turning south.

So bloody predictable. No matter how smart or good or strong they pretend to be, at the end of the day they're all the same: weak, corrupt, all part of the universal stench.

"Steve, incredibly I find myself agreeing with you twice in one day! Finding the exact mice in which the errors were made may be just impossible."

His gaze fixed on his Porsche, MacGregor continued, "But even if impossible, still we must move on. You're new to the lab, Steve. Of course you've made mistakes. You were sloppy: some unknown factor – maybe how you anesthetized the mice, or how you injected the gold coagulant, or how you dissected the brains – *something* you did must have gone wrong. The problem was your technique. And now we have no way of identifying which mice were affected. Bloody hell! Am I right, Steve?"

MacGregor was enjoying this.

"Yes, Professor, you're absolutely right."

MacGregor's voice dropped an octave, "Well then, mate, how do you propose to clean up your mess? We don't have time to re-do the experiments."

Eventually, Steve answered, "Over the weekend I looked over and over again for some plausible set of variables that might eliminate an aberrant subgroup, but without success."

I bet! – thought MacGregor – *though you had considerable success in other areas, you bastard.*

Steve continued, "At this point I don't believe there is a defined subset that shows a benefit for Angiotox."

"So, the solution is …"

Steve was again silent. Then he said, "I pick out mice at random that were treated with Angiotox but showed no positive benefit until a sufficient number are eliminated. We will then have a statistically significant result."

MacGregor waited, allowing the full import of August's words to sink in.

Finally, his voice nearly a whisper over the phone line, MacGregor said, "Once in a while, August, I like the way you think."

Steve's voice was soft: "Professor, this means my lab book will not reflect the data used in the analysis."

Stupid bugger!

MacGregor's voice came out in a whispered hiss, almost like Calibri's: "Don't bother me with details. If anyone asks, I won't know bloody hell. Understand? Just do what has to be done."

Late that afternoon, the phone rang at Steve's desk, as he had expected.

"Dr. August," she cooed, "it's your sex slave."

"Hi, Dida."

"Steve, I just spoke with George. I've cleared you to spend the rest of the week away from the lab, working here at my apartment under my supervision. Lots of good food and naked fun! By Friday you'll be humming like a top, as will I, and we'll have a beautiful, ready-to-wear set of lab books to convince even the most skeptical of investors. And then it's all money in the bank, baby!"

A week spent satisfying Dida's appetites while fabricating lab data was not Steve's idea of a good time. The alternative of a Tibetan monastery crossed his mind.

"Dida, I don't think I'll be able to keep up with you twenty-four seven. Maybe it'd be best if I spent nights at my place. I sleep better alone. But I can be at your apartment first thing in the morning. We can always mix in a few study-breaks while working through the lab books."

"Oh," she pouted, "I was hoping for more action! Fine, that'll do. But by Wednesday you'll be begging for more. I'm very addictive, you know."

34.

MONDAY, APRIL 18

That night walking home over Longfellow Bridge, Steve felt uncomfortable. All seemed familiar – the dark Charles River below, the cold gray stone of the bridge, cars racing by, headlights casting shadows, taillights glowing red. But there was something else.

There was a *smell* – rancid, rotten.

He looked down at the Charles. He turned back towards the street. Nothing.

The smell again. It seemed … it seemed to be from him! He checked the back of his legs, then the bottoms of his shoes. Nothing. He dropped the backpack and inspected his jacket. Nothing.

Imagination?

But when he swung the pack over his shoulder, there it was again.

He dropped the pack and zipped it open, and the stench slapped him in the face – like a mix of foul excrement and rotting flesh. He pulled notebooks and papers out of the bag, their edges stained brown. At the bottom was the explanation.

A dead rat. The bloated body looked like it had been dead many hours. The stench came from the fluids squeezed from the carcass, a dark sludge reeking worse than any outhouse.

Someone had put the dead rat in his pack, intending him to find it.

Someone able to open his safe?

Keeping the pack at arm's length, Steve walked to the side of the bridge, held it over the edge, and let go. The pack dropped, hit a ledge, and bounced away. There was a *plotch*, another *plotch*, and then another *plotch*, as the rat, and the bag, and the sludge, hit the black waters of the Charles.

Think, damn it!

What does this mean?

Breathing hard, he sat down in the shadows, his back against the bridge wall. If the pictures of him with Alison had been a sniper's assault, then this was a full-scale blitzkrieg. Someone had put a rotting carcass in his pack in his lab safe.

A violent threat.

Who?

He was breathing in short gasps, his heart slamming against his chest.

Water flows and fills,
Not accumulating but running.
Pass through dangerous places;
Never lose self-confidence.

He turned his gaze inward, focusing on his fear. His breathing slowed. He stepped away from himself, observing the events from a far-distant place – "the view from nowhere" Master Lao Huang had called it.

Steve smiled at the irony: the dead rat was helpful. Ever since he had seen the photos of him with Alison, and he had found the twine on the landing, Steve had been a bit unsure whether the culprit was MacGregor, or Spader, or maybe even someone else. But a dead rat in his locked safe *had* to be Angion's doing.

The message was simple: play by Angion's rules, or be the rat. The dead rat.

He wondered if Dida knew about this.

He blinked, realizing he had been sitting for several minutes. But the traffic didn't care. He stared at the papers in front of him.

He did not regret the stains on the lab books – under the circumstances these seemed appropriate. Tomorrow morning he and Dida were to begin the arduous task of copying all the records into new books, but with the data altered to Angion's advantage: plain, old-fashioned forgery. The goal was a finished product by Friday to keep MacGregor happy.

The whole thing stunk worse than the rat.

Steve collected the dirtied papers into a pile, took off his windbreaker, and wrapped the stack inside the jacket, leaving him wearing only a shirt. He shivered, partly from the cold, partly from disgust, and turned towards his Back Bay apartment.

But he found his way blocked. Obstructing the sidewalk was an old bum, whose pungent aroma, though not as bad as the rat's, spoke of weeks spent on grates, in tents, under bushes, and at store entries, all without benefit of shower or bath. He had a thick gray beard, mounds of ragged cloth, a mop of dirty white hair, and a maze of shadows across his face.

The bum stepped up close, his nose inches from Steve's, his stale breath reeking of garlic. A passing car's headlights reflected in the bum's eyes – wild, bleary, vaguely focused on Steve.

He cackled, "They're everywhere. They're here ..." and he tapped on his head. " ...And they're here ..." and he grabbed Steve's collar. " ...And they're here ..." and he pointed at Steve's feet. ". ... And they're here," and he tapped on Steve's belt. By this time he was nearly embracing Steve, his mouth an inch from Steve's ear, yet speaking loudly, distinctly.

Steve's first instinct had been to disable the attacker, but he did not.

He had recognized the eyes.

This was the same fellow he had seen on the subway twice: when he had been out with his Brain Trust buddies, and then the early morning following that fateful night inside Angion.

He was sure.

The bum's mouth was close to Steve's ear, but he articulated loudly, like a Shakespearean actor performing King Lear, "If you want to go free, you must go naked."

What the hell?

The bum had one hand on Steve's belt, the other on his lapel, pulling Steve's face into the locks of mud-speckled hair draped over the bum's shoulders.

"If you want to go free, you must go naked," grumbled the bum again loudly. The old man's hand pushed something into Steve's waistband, and then pulled him closer.

Very, very quietly, the bum breathed into his ear, "For emergencies."

But an instant later he had pushed Steve away, cackling loudly, "They're here … and here, and there … and …"

He pointed wildly, at Steve, the river, the traffic, the moon, his head. He laughed again and staggered away, leaving Steve alone on the sidewalk in the middle of the Longfellow Bridge.

The whole event had lasted only seconds.

Steve looked around, but there was no one except the bum's receding figure. He was still laughing loudly as he swooped along, pointing at any object in view – moon, lamppost, buildings, traffic lights, garbage cans, trees, shrubbery. He stepped into the intersection and weaved through the traffic, several drivers honking disapproval.

What was in his waistband? In the bridge shadows Steve pulled out a small plastic bag. *My God, he's planted drugs!* He nearly threw it into the river unopened, but then thought better of it.

Held in place by a rubber band, a piece of scrap was wrapped around a thick bundle of twenty-dollar bills. On the paper were written block letters: "STEVE – FOR EMERGENCIES."

A wad of cash handed over during a hug on the Longfellow Bridge on a cold Boston night: what the *hell* did that mean?

He's not really a bum? Then who is he?

And he seemed to be following him, and he knew his name.

That was disturbing.

Steve folded the cash in half, wrapped the rubber band around the wad, stuffed it into his pants, and turned around.

No one.

He jogged briskly towards home, carrying the jacket bundle. His path along the Charles remained empty. No one stopped him. No blue lights flashed.

Breathing hard, Steve paused at his apartment door. The dead rat had convinced him MacGregor was monitoring him. He wondered if they had video as well as audio.

Likely, since I don't talk much at home by myself.

Clearly the "bum" had wanted to give him a message. He had chosen the bridge as a venue, one that was very public, but one that would excite minimal suspicion from an observer, and one where there was much ambient traffic noise, making monitoring conversation difficult.

If you want to go free, you must go naked.

Seemed more like a "free-love" motif from a 1960s commune than sound advice.

The one thing clear to Steve was the money. This was real. And the note: "Steve, for emergencies." And the bum had also whispered that in his ear.

For emergencies.

What sort of emergencies?

He dropped the bundle of stained papers onto his doorstep and ran back down the street. He made several turns, winding his way into the convoluted backstreets of the Back Bay. After several minutes he stopped under a streetlight.

He looked around – no people, no movement, no signs of life – only parked cars and condos, some with lighted windows.

He unwrapped the cash. Fifty twenty-dollar bills – a thousand dollars even. No marks that he could see. The serial numbers seemed unrelated, no sequences. Certainly they *felt* real.

He looked at the slip again: "Steve, for emergencies" – simple lined paper, like what one might find at any supermarket. The block lettering was so precise it looked stenciled. He was sure the paper hid no finger-prints – someone had been careful to make the source unidentifiable.

But why would anyone give me a thousand dollars?

Maybe to win my trust?

This was not the same party who had put the dead rat in his back-pack. The one wanted to seem a friend, the other an enemy. Maybe the "bum" had intervened to let Steve know he had a friend?

This is one sick game. This must mean there's more than one group watching me – McGregor's boys, but also this "bum," keeping tabs on me, too. Like Morgan said: it's not paranoia to think people are after you, if indeed they are.

Several days ago Steve had formulated a plan, and the bum's advice seemed to echo his strategy. He was already planning on "going naked," figuratively speaking. Some might call it suicidal, but Steve saw it as the only way he could pursue the truth about Angion while keeping his in-tegrity. Maybe that was what the bum had meant?

But what about the cash?

Steve had more than $2000 set aside in the bank for a rainy day, but the $1000 cash in hand was not "on the books," and no surveillance would be able to find this money, unless he deposited it – or revealed it to a micro-camera at home.

The best solution seemed the simplest: he would keep the money on his person. With a bit of care he should be able to keep it a secret, though tomorrow morning he would have to be cautious to keep the money away from Dida's prying eyes and hands.

As he ran home, the questions remained.

Who was he? What sort of emergency? Why the money? Go free? Go naked? What about the rat? What the hell?

&

Late that night he awoke to a noise. He waited, holding his breath. Silence. He started drifting back to sleep.

Again. Tapping. Hard tapping. He sat up in bed, looked at the bedside clock: 2:14 am. He had been sleeping less than three hours. He got up, walked around the apartment – nothing. He drank a glass of water in the kitchen, went to the bathroom, then went back to bed. He dozed.

But then … Loud tapping. Directly behind his head – inside the wall behind the bed. He looked at the clock: *3:05 AM.*

Maybe there were mice? The wind was strong outside. He lay back down and closed his eyes. He felt anxious. He breathed deeply, restored calm, began to drift into …

Tapping again. Loud. Right behind his head. He sat up. There was a wind outside. Rain was hitting the windows.

Must be the storm?

3:32 AM. He lay back down.

He awoke. *Tap, tap, tap, tap.* The clock read, *3:55 AM.*

He turned onto his other side. He wanted to sleep.

Will the tapping start again?

He drifted, dreading the sound …

Then it returned, and he woke up.

And so it went.

&

His clock radio clicked on: *6:30 AM*.

But he was already awake.

The tapping had awakened him twelve times during the last seven hours.

But now he had to go to work. He was supposed to be at Dida's by eight o'clock, and she would be expecting a physical performance as well as an intellectual one.

He was very tired. His head throbbed.

Nothing made sense.

35.

THURSDAY, APRIL 21

Two days later, Steve was already dressed when the phone rang at seven.

He had been awake all night – now for three nights running.

Only three?

He paused.

Monday, Tuesday, Wednesday – yes, three nights.

He had wanted to recuperate evenings at home alone, since Dida's appetites for sex and liquor seemed insatiable. But a nightmare of taps, rattles, knocks, scratches, and other noises had made it impossible to sleep more than a few minutes at a time. Over the last three nights he had slept at best two hours or so – total.

At this point he was a jangle of nerves. His hands shook. His imagination was playing tricks on him. Concentrating for more than a minute was merely impossible.

Steve jumped at the phone's first ring, spilling cereal on the floor. He swore, brushing milk and Cheerios off his lap, but stepped to the kitchen counter quickly, not wanting the ringing to hurt his ears a second time.

"Hello?"

"Good morning, Steven!" hailed Marion Phillips's patrician voice. "My boy, how are you?"

An honest answer seemed inappropriate. "Fine, thank you, sir. How are you?"

"Oh, just splendid, good man. Sorry to disturb you at home, but been unable to find you at the lab. George advised me yesterday you were sequestering yourself, working pell-mell on your Angiotox presentation. Getting much accomplished?"

"I think so. Rough draft's almost finished. Preparing for the investors on Monday."

"Well, that's grand, Steve, just grand. That's what George told me, too. So, listen, I was thinking, perhaps you might give us a quick run-through of your data. I was scheduled for neurosurgical grand rounds tomorrow, but George suggested it might be a good exercise that you present. I could give you a half-hour for a down-and-dirty of your results. Wonderful opportunity! Of course, if you're not ready ...?"

Steve's heart sank – disaster in the making.

"Sure, Dr. Phillips, I'd love to."

"Grand! That'll be at eight o'clock. There's one more thing. George just received FDA approval for an implant device that delivers pharmaceuticals time-released into brain arterial vasculature. He told me about it yesterday, and as chance would have it there's a patient on tomorrow's OR schedule who would qualify. I talked with her, and she's consented, so we'll do the implant tomorrow. I'd like you to scrub in."

Steve's heart pounded. The risk of disaster was increasing exponentially.

"That's incredible, Dr. Phillips."

"Wonderful! It's the second case of the day: Mrs. Ernestine Miller, fifty-two. Bad tumor – glioblastoma. No need to pre-round. Just show up ten thirty at OR-27. I'll take care of the rest."

Phillips clicked off.

Steve stared at the phone, willing his hand to be steady, but it shook as he put the receiver in the cradle.

Back as a medical student, he had not expected *this* when he signed up for residency at Saints Memorial.

What went wrong?

He sat at the table and stared at the spilled cereal. So very tired.

I must clean up the cereal and milk.

This he could do. He tried to focus on the kitchen counter, found a dishrag, wiped the table, and then rinsed it in the sink.

All better; table clear.

He leaned over the sink, more tired than he could ever remember.

Tomorrow morning –give talk, then OR. Today – prepare data, then make slides. Tonight – sleep. Sleep. SLEEP!

The first two thoughts made him anxious, but the third held hope. All he needed was one good night.

The kitchen clock read: *7:18.*

He was supposed to be at Dida's around eight. He had some time. He knelt on the floor and folded his legs. His hands on his knees, his back erect, his eyes closed, Steve began focusing what was left of his exhausted mind.

Silence.

Anxiety eased. Calm descended.

And then the knocking started – right behind him – and his focus broke.

He whirled to stare at the wall, but no sooner had the sound started than it stopped. He pressed his ear against the plaster. He could hear a slight scratching inside. He imagined a mouse building a nest, collecting hair and lint and chips of wood and plaster.

But there was another possibility.

Angion's surveillance people are trying to keep me awake?

Yeah, sure. Come on, Steve. Paranoia is a result of extreme sleep loss – right?

Every surgical resident experienced sleep deprivation. At times the work demanded a thirty- or forty-hour shift before one could leave the hospital for the safety of one's own bed, beeper off, by the second day functioning at a far-inferior level from the first. That was bad enough.

But *several days* of lost sleep were another matter – leading to potentially devastating psychological effects. Somewhere he had read that sleep deprivation had been a favorite tool for torturing U.S. POWs during the Korean and Vietnam Wars. After some days the prisoner's judgment became unreliable, and eventually fantasy and reality became indistinguishable. In short, the prisoner became psychotic. His mental barriers broken, he was then vulnerable to interrogation and manipulation.

Now in his fourth day of sleep loss, August knew he was on dangerous turf. His imagination had started playing tricks. Shadows were becoming real: out of the corner of his eye he kept thinking he saw chairs and vases and plants where in truth there were none. Conversely, he had trouble focusing on objects that *were* there: even reading the side of the cereal box had been almost impossible.

But other events were also contributing to his angst. The rat in the backpack Monday night had been bad enough, but that had been only the beginning.

Tuesday morning there had been three giant piles of dog stool on his front porch when he left for work.

Then, as he walked into the elevator at the Ritz, a man had slammed into his shoulder and snarled, "Nice shirt, asshole!"

That evening he had tried to start his car, parked next to Dida's condo, but the motor refused to kick over. It had taken two hours to get the car towed to a garage, after which he took the subway home.

Back at his apartment he had found a message on his voicemail: "Hello. My name's Lex Maximillian. I'm an attorney representing Joyce Archer in a lawsuit involving a spine operation Dr. Steve Leland August performed three years ago that left my client paralyzed. You will be receiving a registered letter detailing the issues in the next few days. Feel free to contact me. 617-603-5555." Click.

Steve could not remember any patient named Joyce Archer, nor any spine case warranting a lawsuit.

A half hour later the lights in the apartment flicked off. He called Miller, who said, "Sorry, Steve, power's out for the whole block. I've called Boston Edison. Hopefully won't be long."

By the time he went to bed, power had not yet returned. Then followed another night without sleep, the sounds in the walls constant.

Wednesday the nastiness grew worse. He arose at 6:30 to prepare for work at Dida's apartment, only to smell gas. He opened all the windows and again called Miller, who dutifully came downstairs, but they couldn't find the leak. Eventually Steve left with Miller's encouragement, "Don't worry, Steve. The gas company is coming soon. Say, my boy, you look tired. You should be getting more sleep."

That Wednesday had been a tough day at Dida's. He tried to keep up, copying page after page from his old lab book into the new one, but he found himself nodding off. Dida noticed it, too, not to mention that his horizontal performance was less than ideal.

"Steve, what's wrong?" she had said after their afternoon sex break, "I thought you worked best under pressure?"

Wednesday evening the power was back on in his apartment; but right before bedtime – which in his fevered exhaustion he had half-anticipated, half-dreaded – the toilet overflowed, pouring sullied water onto the bathroom tiles. Exhausted, he debated ignoring the problem; but then reason took hold, and he found a mop and bucket and cleaned up the mess.

He did not make it to bed till after eleven. He slipped under the covers with a sigh of regret – less than eight hours before he had to be up again. Still, sleep would be so welcome!

The lights were out less than five minutes when the noises started. And again they kept him awake all night.

So now, Thursday morning, three nights without sleep, he could still function, but only barely.

If I don't sleep tonight, then I'm doomed tomorrow. I'll be incoherent presenting the Angiotox data. Worse, in the operating room I'll be a danger.

It's imperative that I sleep.

But today he and Dida still had to finish their awful project.

And meanwhile he would have to decide *what* to present tomorrow. His original plan – the plan to "go naked" – had been to show the original data to the Swiss, forcing a showdown with MacGregor. But he had counted on the weekend to prepare the slides that *he* wanted to present to the Swiss. Now he had no time …

He would have to consider this, once he had a moment to spare, once he could think a bit more clearly.

Coat. Cap. Backpack. Ready.

He stepped outside and locked the door, only to find the mailbox full of coal dust – maybe a childish neighborhood prank, maybe not. He went back inside, grabbed a trash bag and scoop, and emptied the coal into the bag. It took him just a couple of minutes, but the inside of the box was black. He had no time to rinse it – his letters would end up dirty today.

He walked to the subway, since his car was in the shop.

~

Dida opened the condo door wearing a black negligee.

She pulled him inside, shut the door, and put her arms around his neck. "Steve, I've been waiting for you *all night long.* You better be ready for some valuable output!"

Steve shook his head. "Sorry Dida. Phillips called. He wants me presenting to the neurosurgeons tomorrow, and then scrubbing in on a case. So, we *have to* finish the lab books and analyses today. And tonight I really need to get a good night's sleep. We can't waste time now."

"Waste time? Don't be silly! C'mon, baby, just a quickie! Then we'll be charged for a long day of hard work!"

She scrabbled at his shirt.

"Dida, really, I won't be any better than a corpse."

The shirt was unbuttoned. "Steve August, as long as you're a *stiff* corpse, that's all I ask."

And she dragged him to the couch.

～

Afterwards, Steve laid back, eyes closed, muscles aching with exhaustion. "Maybe it'd be best if I stayed here tonight, rather than go back to my place. I'm not getting good sleep there."

Dida was bustling in the kitchen making coffee. "You do seem tired. What's the matter?"

"Noises keep waking me up."

"Hmm. Worried about our project? You shouldn't be. It's under control."

"Still, you mind if I stay here?"

"Can't baby, not tonight. George called yesterday. Said we needed to 'talk.' Fine by me. He wants closure? He gets closure. He'll be here around eight, and by then you need to be gone – know what I mean?"

Steve groaned. The harassment, then Phillips's phone call, and now the loss of this last refuge – all seemed covered with MacGregor's fingerprints. Likely he wanted two things: revised lab books in Steve's handwriting to serve as insurance should anyone start asking questions, but also public evidence of Steve functioning badly to undercut his reputability should he ever be tempted to talk.

"OK, Dida, I'll be out by seven. But that means we've got to move!"

"Of course, baby. You want sugar in your coffee?"

And they went to work, Steve's mind and spirit in a very bad way. Over the next several hours he repeated silently, so many times the words nearly lost their meaning:

The highest good is like water.
Water benefits ten thousand beings,
Yet it does not contend.
Nothing under Heaven is as soft and yielding as water.
Yet in attacking the firm and strong,
Nothing is better than water.

~

Shortly before five o'clock Steve put down his pen and pushed over the last two books – original and revised – to Dida's side of the table.

She looked up from her computer. "Steve August, you're done?"

She pulled the lab books over, checking the charts in the revised book against the original, in which she had crossed out data and written in new numbers in various places. Her review took only a few minutes.

"Steve, this looks good. And we've finished with two hours to spare!"

He put his head down on the table. "I'm beat!"

"Hey baby, not so fast. We still have to go over your talk for tomorrow. I've put together slides for you: with sharp pictures and graphs. You'll be a hit."

Steve moved to look over her shoulder, leaning on her chair for support. He was afraid he might fall down.

"Here, you start with a quick introduction," and she flashed the first slide on the screen. He squinted, the words swimming. Dida walked him through the slide show, but concentration was impossible.

Just after 6:00 pm she popped out the computer disk and handed it to him. "OK, you're ready for tomorrow. Don't worry about George. He's putty in my hands."

"Fine, Dida. Good luck to you, too."

Steve put on his jacket, picked up his stack of papers along with the disk, and threw them into the pack.

"I'm leaving you the old lab books, Dida. They're dangerous. I'll take the new ones and give them to George tomorrow."

"Fine, Steve. I'll lock up the old ones in a safe place."

"Thanks."

Steve zipped up his pack. He walked to the door, Dida right behind him.

"Why don't you come over for dinner Saturday, Steve? We'll have a really sweet night and Sunday brunch?"

"Sure, Dida, sounds great!"

He kissed her on the lips. "Thanks for the help."

"Anytime, handsome."

~

With a sense of foreboding Steve stepped onto the sidewalk in front of the Ritz. He guessed another night of terrors awaited him. Then tomorrow he truly would be non-functional: incoherent in his presentation and incompetent in the OR. He held out his hand in the late afternoon sunlight: the tremors in his fingers and wrist were obvious. He shuddered at the idea of operating in his current state.

He desperately needed time to think. He decided to take a walk through the Boston Common, its tree-lined walkways a sanctuary from insanity.

His original plan seemed unworkable. If he followed the current roadmap, as apparently laid out for him by MacGregor, then his reputation, his hopes, and his career, were shot to hell.

In the twilight a park bench beckoned.

He stared out across the green expanse of trees, paths, and flowerbeds, their shadows lengthening in the ebbing twilight. Slowly they darkened: light purple ... dark blue ... flat black.

Still Steve sat on the bench. It was cold; but no sounds disturbed him.

~

Hours later, after nine o'clock, he arose. His body ached. His legs were stiff, and his face nearly frozen. No matter. He had a new plan.

Steve worried as he shuffled unsteadily towards Park Street. The next few hours would demand a high caliber physical performance. In a more normal state he would have felt sure of success, but in his current condition he ran the real risk of failure, and failure might mean death. No matter. He could think of no better option.

He assumed he was being watched. No matter. They'd have no time to respond.

The bum's words kept coming back – *If you want to go free, you must go naked.*

He laughed, because he doubted the bum had intended his current interpretation.

He staggered across the Boston downtown, finding along the way an open Seven-Eleven. He bought a box of plastic kitchen trash bags, a ball of twine, a penknife, and a quart of milk. He glanced around as he entered, and again as he exited, but he saw no one following him.

He staggered through Boston's West End neighborhood towards the southern foot of the Zakim Bridge, which spanned the entrance of the Charles into the Inner Harbor. As he walked through the shadows, he tore off the box cover, pulled out four bags, and opened each, one inside the next.

A layer of four bags should be watertight.

He dug through his pack until he found the original lab book he had lifted from Dida's apartment. With any luck it would take her days to realize he had taken it and left a new one instead – by accident or on purpose, she might never know. He dropped the book into the quadruple-layer of bags.

Then he pulled out the $1000, stuffed the wad into the layered bags as well, and knotted the bundle tight.

Still walking, he pulled out another half-dozen bags, puffed them out with air, and tied them closed.

During this exercise he kept walking and drank some of the milk. The best he could figure was that MacGregor's boys had a tracking device planted somewhere on his person, so stopping would likely invite scrutiny. Even then, any passing car might be watching.

Just for a second, he paused in the shadows behind a dumpster and tossed away the box of remaining bags as well as the last of the milk.

Working quickly, he then pulled out a bit of twine and tied several knots around the bags. He pushed this bundle back into the pack. Quickly he measured out six arm lengths of twine, cut the end, opened his shirt, and stuffed the twine's end down the left shirtsleeve till it reached his wrist.

He started walking again.

All was quiet on the street. As he walked, he tied off the end of the twine around his wrist. Then he took his key ring from his pocket and removed two keys: one to his post office box, the other to Morgan's family's cabin on Lake Winnipesaukee.

The keys might tear the plastic.

He took a deep breath, put the one key in his mouth, swallowed, and then did the same with the second.

Ahead he heard the interstate: hundreds, thousands, of commuters speeding to their homes and families. Tonight, he was not one of them – maybe never again.

He had reached Commercial Street. To his left was the giant Boston Garden sports arena. Straight ahead he could see the Zakim Bridge, emerging from its tunnel under the city. A white van drove by, turned onto Commercial Street, and double-parked.

Maybe that's them. Maybe they know …

It was now or never. He ran across Commercial, dodging traffic. His perception kept blurring, then focusing, on the traffic on the bridge ahead. Color vision gone, peripheral vision gone, he was running down a narrow black-and-white tunnel. Only moving his legs mattered. All his muscles ached. Then he was on the dirt path next to the Bridge. His lungs were gravel against his chest. He kept running.

A fence with girders and a railing ran along the side of the freeway, meant to keep pedestrians off the bridge. He hefted himself onto a large empty barrel, and then he was up on the railing. He moved fast, spinning around the girders, pulled himself up, and then he was over, on the bridge.

Cars raced by, honking. He ignored them, running hard, breathing in gasps. He thought he heard shouts far behind. He kept running.

His vision narrowed. All he could see were the lights ahead, a path into the night. His lungs were screaming, unable to keep up with his oxygen-starved body.

Yes, there was shouting behind him.

Too late!

He laughed inside: *Too late!!*

His sprint had taken him to the middle of the bridge.

Now.

He looked back. He thought he could see figures coming.

Now.

His vision was nearly black.

Now!

He pulled himself up. He was standing on the railing: a fifty-foot drop.

NOW!

He opened his backpack in full view. Papers, notes, pens, the precious lab books – all floated into the night air. But he was careful not to let the trash bags out.

NOW!!

A yacht sat in the locks, pointing towards the harbor. He zipped the bag closed.

NOW!!!!

And he jumped, pack in hand.

On the way down Steve filled his starving lungs with air.

He straightened out before his feet hit the water.

He wondered if he would die.

36.

THURSDAY, APRIL 21

But he did not die.

Underwater, Steve tore off his clothes. Everything. He tugged the bags out of the pack, held them close on the twine around his wrist, and swam hard with the tide towards the ocean.

After about a minute, his lungs screaming, his body growing colder, he cupped a corner of a puffy bag into his mouth and ground his teeth till a hole opened. Carefully he squeezed the bag, inhaled the life-giving air, and then started swimming again.

It was only about a hundred yards to the locks, but it felt like a hundred miles. Just ahead was the yacht he'd seen from the bridge, but the iron gates were closing. He was behind one of them, then with a kick he was next to it. He grabbed the edge, the door yanking him forwards, tearing at his shoulders.

The two gates were nearly closed.

His arms pulled, his legs pumped, and then he was inside. Behind him the massive metal doors clanged shut.

Seconds later water was rushing out of the lock, soon to expel him with the boat out to the Harbor and the open sea beyond. He grabbed the boat's hull, staying below the waterline, occasionally breathing from the bags to feed his oxygen-starved body, waiting, shivering.

Time was his enemy.

Standing beside the Zakim Bridge, Riker and Delta looked out on the dark waters. They could see no body, no bubbles, no signs of life – only dozens of papers, notebooks, binders, and miscellaneous rubbish, scattered across the surface of the Charles River.

For a moment Riker was not sure whether to be pleased, or disgusted. Personally speaking, he hoped the bastard was dead. But from Angion's point of view, the lab books were critical, and getting them back might not be easy.

"This is not good," he said.

Delta nodded. "Houston, we have a problem."

But Dida was in an especially fine mood.

"George! Sit down."

She kissed him on the cheek, then moved to the sideboard and poured two glasses of merlot. "Don't worry about dinner; I've ordered Chinese. We're celebrating. Steve's notebooks are finished. They're beautiful – very convincing."

MacGregor settled on the divan in front of the Boston skyline. "Dida, I was wondering what became of you. You dump me for your new boy toy?"

She had anticipated this, and she knew what to do. She sat at his side and let her fingertips dance lightly across the back of his neck.

"Georgie-Porgie, I'm sorry Dida's been a bad girl – but I needed Steve's cooperation. How can I make it up to you?"

She stepped away from the couch. In one quick motion she had pulled her dress up over her head, revealing black leather bra and panties.

"You want to spank bad, nasty Dida?"

MacGregor looked at her lustfully.

"Georgie-Porgie has some good news, too," he cackled, "but first let's have a good, hard spanking!"

Dida giggled and ran up the steps to her bedroom, MacGregor in hot pursuit.

≈

Afterwards, Dida lay with her back to him, staring at the wall. He had not reached orgasm easily, and she not at all.

"So, George, tell me your news."

"Mmm," he purred. "Well Dida, while you've been entertaining August, I've been meeting with your Uncle Tony – and also, unfortunately, with Michael Riker."

"Go on," she said, her mouth suddenly dry as cotton.

"Don Calibri thinks August knows too much, and he wants him out, despite your recruiting him to the dark side."

Dida sighed. "Too bad ... Tio changed his mind. Steve would have been a tasty recruit."

"Hardly," grumbled MacGregor. "The boy's stupid, arrogant, and incompetent."

"What are you going to do?"

"Crush him. He's being subjected to severe psychological destabilization even as we speak. By tomorrow he will have collapsed, never again to waste our time. Good riddance, I say!"

Her mouth turned drier. "Georgie, you really think it's necessary to be so aggressive? After all, we have the revised lab books – in August's own handwriting."

MacGregor's face was stone. "There's no way, Dida. Don Calibri, Riker, and I all agree – he knows too much. We have to eliminate him as a player."

"Shame. Seems such a waste." She shook her head. "Well, I suppose my efforts still were useful. At least we now have improved lab books on hand."

MacGregor frowned. "Dida, where did you say the new ones are?"

"Don't worry, Georgie. He has them, but he knows nothing. He's giving them to you tomorrow. Best would be if someone were around to witness him handing them over. That way both you and I are protected."

"You have the originals?"

"Right here." Dida pointed at the stack on the table.

MacGregor stepped over and leafed through the pages of the first notebook.

"It's obvious you've been editing this," he said. "You realize how implicating these would be if the wrong person got hold of them?"

"I'm not stupid, George. That's why I kept them here. These are the real data. We'll destroy them once he gives you the new ones."

George glanced through the stack, but at the bottom a puzzled expression crossed his face. He picked up the next-to-last notebook, opened it, and studied its contents. Within seconds she saw the look of puzzlement vanish, replaced by rage ... and maybe an element of fear.

"Dida," he whispered, "This is one of the revised books."

"He left it behind? No surprise – he was so tired! I'll call him tonight. He can pick it up tomorrow morning before meeting with you. Or you just take it and pretend he gave it to you when you meet. No big deal."

"Dida, this is the revised lab book for the original – number five. But number five isn't here."

"What?"

He spoke very slowly, "Lab book number five, the original, the one with all your changes, is not here. Gone. He must have it."

Oh my God!!!! By now her mouth was as dry as the Sahara.

He slammed the notebook shut and walked to the window.

"Dida ..." he squeaked, but the phone interrupted.

She tried to keep her voice level: "Hello."

Riker. She listened, and as she did so, her stomach twisted.

"Right. I see." She hung up.

"George, that was Riker. He witnessed Steve August jump off the Zakim Bridge an hour ago. Suicide. The police are searching for the body."

But MacGregor's calm demeanor shocked her even more.

His voice was cold, "Where are the notebooks?"

"Riker said August emptied his backpack into the Charles. Papers are scattered all over Boston Harbor."

"We've got to get them back. Especially original Book Five."

"Riker's men are collecting what they can. But he said you should go to the precinct and sign out whatever the police recover that belongs to Angion."

"Why didn't he call me directly?"

"He said he knew you were here."

MacGregor grunted. "That man is scary. August have any family?"

"I don't think so. He's an orphan, no siblings. Raised by his grand-mother. She died last year."

"You know a lot about him."

"What do you expect? We spent most of the past week together."

Too late she realized her voice held a hint of regret.

"That's fine, Dida. I don't care." But his tone was sharp. "Do you have a copy of the revised data?"

"It's all on my computer. I pulled together a slide presentation for him."

"The police will be investigating. We *must* get rid of the old books. Dida, did anyone see him entering or leaving your place?"

"Maybe. The concierge would probably recognize him. There's also the doorman."

"That means the police will be here. Show them the one revised book. Tell them he left it behind by accident. Tell them you worked with him on his talk. You'll have the computer presentation as evidence. Deny any romantic involvement, of course. Good that he went home each night."

"Yes."

"I'll burn the original notebooks in Angion's incinerator. Won't be a cinder left. I'm sure Riker's going through his apartment right now, to be sure there's nothing incriminating left behind. Twenty-four hour surveillance, you know."

"You mean Riker's been watching *my* apartment?"

"August was a grade A-1 security risk. The only possible solution was to keep him under lock-and-key – twenty-four hours a day."

Dida's eyebrows shot up. "There are cameras *here*, in my *home*?"

"No, no, no, Dida, of course not. When I say 'twenty-four hour,' I don't mean it *literally*."

"Better not! A woman's entitled to her privacy."

"Yes. Yes, of course. But Riker did have cameras set up at August's place. He couldn't yawn without us knowing!" MacGregor chuckled. "The guy was dead meat from the word 'go.'"

Dida's brow furrowed, "I didn't realize the effort you boys were putting out."

"Riker doesn't play softball. I'm growing to appreciate him."

Dida looked at MacGregor, her gaze steady as a surgeon's hand: "One doesn't have to *grow* to appreciate Riker."

"Hmm. To his credit, he does what is necessary. The plan was for August to implode, to collapse from within. I never dreamed we'd succeed so well."

She spoke softly, "Yes, I never would've dreamed. You boys must have really done a number on him."

"Right-o. Too bad. But now we need to recover the revised books. Bloody hell! They're probably all over the Harbor."

"Riker said they collected as much as they could before the police showed."

"The man has ice in his veins. But the key is whether he found the missing original. You sure August took it?'

"Must have, by accident. He left the revised copy here. Just took the wrong one. He did look exhausted, strung out. He must have snapped – too much pressure."

"Yes," he said. "I hope Riker found it. That's damning evidence."

He flipped open his cell phone and punched a number, his voice turning conspiratorial. "Hello, Riker? Say, bloke, strong work! ... Right-o. No, I totally agree. ... Listen, it's important you know – August had one of the original books. Total of six, but one of them – Number Five – was an original. ... Right, with all the edits. ... Exactly."

He closed the phone. "Now he knows what to look for."

Dida nodded. "George, you should leave before the police get here. This may be the last place he was seen alive."

"On my way!" He picked up the lab books. "Any questions about why he was here, then just show them the slides and talk about data analysis. They'll back off. Police and reporters hate looking stupid."

"I hope Riker finds the other one! George, any chance that August staged this, that he's still alive holding that notebook?"

MacGregor shook his head. "It's a fifty-foot drop to the Charles. How could he possibly survive a jump like that ... into freezing water? If the impact didn't kill him, then the cold would."

Dida nodded, but said nothing further.

Riker flipped his phone closed and looked over the railing at the black harbor water.

"I swear the asshole planned this," he said. "He's alive; I can feel it."

A Boston Police patrol boat puttered passed their mooring, its searchlight sweeping the dark river. Several frogmen were visible below the bridge at the shoreline, their headlamps tiny specks of light. Police cruisers along the harbor's access road peppered the night with blue and red sparks.

Riker looked at his men. "MacGregor said August was carrying one of his original lab books – 'Number Five' – along with the copies. You guys see a 'Number Five?'"

Still in his wetsuit, Bravo pointed at the deck, piles of soggy papers at their feet. "The skiff's pretty quick – up and down the River in nothing flat. That's everything we skimmed off before the cops showed."

Alpha shook his head. "These are the books we found: One, Two, Three, Four, Six."

"Let me see."

Riker leafed through the stack and then straightened, his face expressionless.

"These are the revisions. Incredible – you got them all! We're missing only the one … but that would be an original."

He turned to stare at the police boats with their searchlights.

"I swear, the asshole is alive – and he's got the goddamn book."

Half a mile away Steve was hanging onto a rubber tire.

For twenty minutes he had swum out of the Inner Harbor towards Charlestown, but at the final stage his legs had ceased to obey, instead screaming protests with painful spasms that left him breathless. Desperately, gratefully, bobbing in the water, gasping at the air, he wrapped his arms around the tire hanging from the pier.

Tied to his left wrist was the twine running to the plastic bags floating in the waters below – now empty except for the money and the lab book.

Get out of the cold!

Steve held on with one hand, and with the other grabbed his leg, the thigh cramping.

First the one, then the other.

Finally, he was out of the water, standing on the tire. He pulled himself up, and forwards, and then the pier was under him.

For a while he lay naked under the moonlight; but then the twine tugged against his wrist, reminding him. Carefully he pulled it up, until he held its precious cargo against his chest.

He took a deep breath, staggered into the shadow of a warehouse, and in its dark embrace limped around the edge of the Navy Yard. Quietly, he crossed the empty four-lane highway separating the Yard's entrance from the remainder of Charlestown, and then moved into the maze of Charlestown's old brick houses at the foot of Bunker Hill.

Behind a wooden fence he spied a clothesline with laundry flopping in the soft night breeze. Shivering, he climbed into the yard and pulled a T-shirt, sweatshirt, and jeans off the line. The clothes were slightly loose, but nearly fit. He folded up his plastic bag and its contents, stuffed them into his crotch, and put four twenties on the back porch, weighted down by a flowerpot.

Fair trade.

Still shivering he moved north into the crowded housing projects on the far side of Bunker Hill – the tough streets. He was desperate for sleep, but he had to find a warm, safe place.

After several blocks he was looking down at the Boston Autoport, a sixty-five acre lot of newly minted cars unloaded off freighters from around the globe, awaiting distribution to dealerships across New England. Steve hid in the shadows, waiting, but he saw no activity.

Too cold. Watchman must be in the warehouse.

He slid past the empty sentry post at the closed gate. Avoiding patches of light from scattered streetlamps, he moved along aisle after aisle of new cars – Ford, Lexus, Audi, Toyota, Hyundai, Cadillac …

At the lot's far corner he found a comfortable-looking Lincoln. No one around.

He tried the driver's door.

Unlocked!

His luck held. Above the visor he found a key ring.

His shaking, frozen hand dropped the keys onto the mat. He swore softly, groped under the seat, but finally found them. Struggling to stay steady, he tried one key, then the other – there, a fit.

The massive V-8 lumbered to life. He opened the door, listening, but the new engine sounded only a whisper. The warehouse was a football field distant. The breeze, blowing from Massachusetts Bay, carried the sound away onto the open fields at the far end of the lot. If the wind held steady, no one would hear.

He turned the car's heater to 85, moved to the backseat, and fell asleep – finally, gratefully, deeply asleep.

37.

THURSDAY, APRIL 21

Nathan Spear had spent Thursday preparing for August's return from Dida's.

Nothing truly illegal?

Well, that was debatable. He thought back to last Friday's conversation.

"You will not be required to do anything truly illegal. You merely are our bridge."

And he had answered, "At five grand a day, those limits are pretty broad."

"Yes, we thought you'd be interested. Let me explain."

"Yeah?"

"Steve August was a talented young surgeon, but he's buckled under the pressure. We think he's had a psychotic break."

"What'd you mean?"

"He's made many errors in the lab, and rather than just dealing with his incompetence, he's constructed a fantasy world in which his boss, George MacGregor, an internationally respected professor, is lying about the company's revolutionary product – the drug Angiotox. August has become a danger to himself, to his coworkers, and to the public. We just need to prove it."

"What are you planning?"

"Of course, if we wait, some day his psychosis will become public. But we want to accelerate the process."

"Yeah?"

"That's where you come in. The primary tool will be sleep deprivation. Assuming he's unstable, after about four days he will break down – physically, mentally, psychologically – he will be hospitalized, and he will no longer be free to hurt the people of the Commonwealth."

"And if you're wrong? What if he's as sane as the next guy?"

"Then he'll laugh off the stress. This will be our own little test to nail the bastard."

"You talk like a cop."

"I run security for several high-level corporations. I'm tougher than any cop."

Spear nodded. "You're telling me this guy's a loony evil genius, he's dangerous to normal folk, and you want me to take him down."

"You'll be doing the world a service. Meanwhile, you'll be making a very large amount of money."

~

Later that same afternoon Smith had returned. Spear was not surprised to see him, though the paper bag seemed out-of-place in his manicured hand.

"Hey, Mr. Smith. Glad you're back!"

Smith nodded wordlessly and reached inside his coat pocket. For a split-second Spear's hand itched towards the Smith & Wesson under his desktop, but he held back. If Smith wanted him dead, for sure he wouldn't be that messy.

Smith pulled out an envelope and tossed it on the desk. "There, ten thousand dollars, retainer for the weekend – pure gravy. You start work on Monday: five thousand a day. But from now on you'll have to work for it. No sitting on your hands."

"You got that right. I'm all yours!"

"Fine. You ever hear of a Wall-Walker?"

"What?"

"Here, look."

Smith dumped the paper bag's contents onto the desk. Out spilled a half-dozen small rubber balls covered with short, thin, sharp metal points. The balls quickly rolled to a stop, their tiny sharp spikes digging into the wooden desktop. Smith pulled out a small handheld unit like a TV-remote. He hit a couple of buttons.

Amazed, Spear watched as one of the little balls quivered. It rolled to the edge of the desk, then rolled off and with a soft *thud* hit the floor. It bumped into a pile of old *Hustler* magazines, rolled to the side, bumped into the wall, and then, defying gravity, slowly rolled up the doorstop. Smith hit another button, and the ball stopped moving, its position on the wall, five feet above the floor, held in place as if by magic.

"Thousands of tiny metal spikes make these beauties stick to wood and plaster like glue," said Smith. "If it hits metal, the spikes can bend slightly and roll over it."

"Son of a gun," said Spear. "How does it know up is up?"

"Tiny gyroscopes inside keep it oriented."

"What's it good for?"

"Each has its own microphone and speaker. The Walkers are small enough to mount inside a wall – August's apartment, for example – so you can listen to any conversation, track his movements, and so on. It's easy to re-position the Walker, just by activating the motion control. But for our purposes there's even a better feature."

"Yeah?"

Riker hit a button – and a soft rustling came from the unit. He hit another button, and a sharp *knock* sounded. With a satisfied look Smith pulled the unit off the wall and set it back on the desk.

Spear blinked. "Why'd you want them to make noise? Thought the idea was to keep 'em hidden?"

"They are hidden – inside the walls. He'll think they're mice or rats, keeping him awake. After several days, his stress level will be in the stratosphere. He'll break."

Spear chuckled, "Nasty stuff, Smith."

"Steve August is a nasty man, Mr. Spear. He deserves nothing more."

"What if he gets close to finding one?"

"Each has an auto-destruct feature. If there's a risk, then you dial in the code 666 and that Walker's ID, and the unit melts down into a small pile of ash and rubber. Watch."

Smith hit some buttons, and the walker on Spear's desk shook slightly, and then folded in on itself, quickly dissolving into a tiny pile of black muck.

Nathan picked up the control unit.

"Wow. OK, how do you work this thing?"

"Here. I'll show you."

~

Per Smith's plan the first assault had been the rat on Monday. Wearing a lab coat, glasses, and a fake ID reading "Nate Koplinski, Maintenance Division," Spear had loitered outside Room 107 until August emerged for lunch. Spear slipped into the lab, found no one near August's desk, opened the safe, and deposited the rat. Less than a minute later he was out the door.

A rat for a rat!

Spear grinned.

That evening he had tailed August on foot. When August stopped on the bridge and found the dead rat, Spear walked right by him, but he hadn't noticed the fat bald guy in an old Army-surplus jacket. At the far end of the bridge Spear slipped behind a tree, but it was his turn to be surprised when that crazy bum showed up and started yelling in August's face.

What was it he'd said? "If you want to go free, you must go naked!" Weird! Spear could think of a couple of lady friends he wished would take that advice.

That night Spear had started Plan Rattrap in earnest. He parked his old Buick half-a-block from August's place and worked the Walkers. He had fifteen inside the apartment, eight in the bedroom walls, the other seven scattered around the other rooms. With the remote he could shift a particular unit wherever he wanted.

Next to him was a carton of Marlboros and a half-gallon of Dunkin' Donuts coffee. The night was freezing cold; he only opened the window when the smoke got so thick he couldn't read the remote.

Throughout the night Spear listened to August's breathing as he lay in bed. Whenever it slowed, he triggered one of the Walkers and woke him up. He varied the sounds: a quiet rustle, then soft knocking, a pause, then a light pitter-patter, then silence, then noises from another spot. Eventually, all he had to do was start a light whisking in any wall, and August would stir and toss to the other side of the bed.

By the time dawn colored the sky, Spear was beat. The coffee was empty, and he'd finished two packs of cigarettes. His eyes were bright red in the Buick's rearview mirror, a headache pressed hard against his temples, and he *really* wanted to go to sleep.

But August's gotta be in worse shape than me. All that stress, workin' all day, and then no sleep.

He smiled.

But if he's hurtin' now, he'll be a basket case by the weekend. Serves him right – messin' with a cure for brain cancer!

August was dirt. He thought of his sister Nancy, who'd died of a brain tumor.

Steve August – asswipe!

Nate smashed his cigarette into the over-full ashtray. It was time to get some sleep. He'd already scattered the dog crap on the porch. In the afternoon he'd set up more fun for the bastard. He was dead tired, but he was smiling.

~

Now three days later, Spear still was smiling. It *had* been fun.

Asswipe's twisting in the breeze.

That afternoon he'd installed another dozen Wall Walkers (courtesy of Smith) and checked each one for sound and volume. Spear wanted to be sure he'd have no place to turn.

He settled back in his car, broke open a fresh pack of Marlboros, and poured himself coffee.

Come on, asswipe, I'm ready!

~

His cell rang just after 6 PM.

"Spear, it's Smith. He's sitting on a park bench in Boston Common, muttering. He's on the edge. If his clothes were dirtier, you'd think he was a homeless bum."

Spear chuckled. "He's toast! We're on schedule?"

"Like clockwork. I'll call you when he's moving."

"Hey Mr. Smith, I've been wondering, how're you guys tracking him?"

"RF-emittters in the heels of his shoes, stitched into all his jackets and coats, and also hidden in his back pack."

Spear whistled. "You think he knows?"

"We *want* him looking over his shoulder. The more paranoid he is, the more psychotic he'll look when he breaks tomorrow. Best thing would be for him to rant, accusing people of spying on him."

"Sweet."

"We'll call you when he gets close. Tonight we push this idiot over the edge!"

"Don't worry, I'm ready. We'll close the deal."

"Good."

The line clicked dead.

Spear tapped the pack and pulled a cigarette out with his mouth. He lit it, staring at the silent apartment steps down the block. There were no signs of life.

~

Two coffees and five cigarettes later, his phone buzzed. 9:42 P.M.

Smith's voice: "August just took a dive from the Zakim Bridge into the Harbor. Likely dead. No body yet."

"You're kidding!"

"'Fraid not. Cops'll be there soon. Kill the Walkers. I'm sending Bravo to do a run-through of the apartment. Wait till he gets there."

Click.

Spear shook his head in disbelief.

The kid snuffed himself? Jesus!

So now he had work to do, fast. He picked up the code list and started dialing the destruct sequences.

~

Fifteen minutes later an unmarked van pulled up at the end of the street, from which emerged a man in black turtleneck and jeans. He ran up the steps and disappeared into August's apartment. Watching from the safety of his car, Spear wondered what was so important about Bravo's visit.

Must be looking for something.

His phone buzzed.

"Spear, Bravo. All the Walkers dead?"

"You bet."

"You made tapes, right?"

"Sure. Just like Smith said."

"You got 'em?"

"In my trunk."

"Roger that. Anyone outside? Cops?"

"No one."

"Roger that. I'm outta here. Meet me at the Shell Station on Memorial Drive. Fifteen minutes. Smith wants the tapes. In exchange you're getting fifty thousand clams – not bad, eh, for one week of work."

"I'll be there."

Seconds later the door opened. Bravo emerged carrying a small cloth sack. Then he was in the van, driving away down the narrow street.

Spear turned the ignition, pulled out, and followed him.

About ten minutes later, two police cruisers and a brown Ford sedan pulled up in front of August's apartment. They searched for a half hour, but found nothing noteworthy.

Still wearing his brown trench coat, Inspector Brogan stepped into the living room. He nearly stumbled over Steve's sneakers in the middle of the worn rug.

He pointed at the kitchen floor. "Spilled cereal and milk. In a hurry this morning?"

His partner, Mike Thatcher, emerged from the bedroom.

"No, he's just a slob. Dirty laundry's piled up in the bedroom. Kinda weird – it's all pushed against the walls, like he was trying to pad them."

Brogan smiled grimly. "Must've known he should've been put away."

"Relatives?" asked Thatcher.

"Hospital has his boss, Dr. Marion Phillips, listed as emergency contact. Both parents dead. No brothers or sisters."

"You talk to Phillips?"

"Yep. The usual –no idea there was a problem. Thought August was bright, hard-working, positive attitude – real boy scout, though kind of a loner. Said there was a girlfriend."

"Yep. Photos on the bedroom dresser. Pretty. Also found his address book. Her name's Morgan Najar, lawyer, lives in Manhattan. Here's her number. Not a whole lot of names in the book. Phillips mention any?"

"Couple of guys in his training program. Tell ya Mike, the guy's working a million hours a week – not exactly a good racket for a social butterfly. He's doing OK keeping a girlfriend."

"Yeah. She's a hot number!"

"Keep it in your pants, Thatcher."

"You gonna call her?"

"Now's good a time as any."

Standing in the middle of the mess that had been Steve August's home, Brogan flipped open his cell phone.

"Ms. Najar? This is Inspector Patrick Brogan, Boston Police."

38.

The car's clock read 5.23 AM.

The few hours' sleep had helped. Now he felt like he could think again – more or less.

Steve studied his new clothes: the blue jeans bagging, the shirt falling in folds over the pants. He needed something better. Socks and shoes might be nice, too.

He checked the bag: the twenties were dry, as was the notebook.

Outside, nothing moved across the giant parking lot.

Quickly he left the car, jumped the fence, and jogged toward the Bunker Hill T-stop. As he ran, he relished the deep breaths of crisp air, the dawn above the harbor, the sidewalk cool under his bare feet. He was glad to be alive.

At the T's entrance he slapped a twenty on the counter in front of the bleary-eyed attendant.

"One; and I'll need some quarters, please."

On the station platform he bought a *Classified Advertiser*, listing thousands of items for sale.

A half-hour later Steve stepped off the T at Central Square. He bought a bagel, coffee, and a pack of cigarettes, and then plunked down on a bench next to a gray-haired lady with a shopping cart loaded with cloth bundles and green trash bags. He offered her a cigarette, and together they sat on the bench, smoking silently. Steve figured no officer of the law would recognize the decrepit smoking bum as the missing neurosurgeon, Dr. Steve August.

Shortly after 9 AM Steve stood up. His new friend had fallen asleep, her head leaning against her shopping cart.

Once inside the Salvation Army store he was done in short order. Fifteen minutes and thirty-five dollars later he was almost presentable: pants, jacket, shirt, socks, and boots.

He checked the address again in the *Advertiser.*

Three blocks north, on the driveway of a small duplex was an old motorcycle with a "For Sale" sign hanging off the handlebars. Lights were on inside. He rang the doorbell.

The door opened, framing a thin, fortyish woman in a shabby green housecoat. Her wrinkled face told of tough times and long hours. Her free hand held a lit cigarette.

"Yeah, what'cha want?"

"Hi. You selling the bike?" Steve pointed at the Honda.

"It's my boy Davie's. He's in Iraq. He said I should sell it. Why?"

Wow, everyone has a war to fight!

Out loud he answered, "Ma'am, the ad said four hundred dollars. It runs OK?"

"Should. We've had it twenty years, ever since Max turned sixteen. He was real proud of that bike. It's a Honda 450 Nighthawk. Max died five years ago. The guys kept it tuned real sharp, but no one's ridden it in a while, not since Davie's gone."

Too much info.

He had planned on haggling, but now he did not want to.

"If it runs OK, I'll take it. Come with a helmet?"

The woman blinked, surprised.

"Sure, you want to try it?"

Five minutes and four hundred dollars later, Steve August was the proud owner of a 1986 Honda CB450SC Nighthawk motorcycle.

He zipped up his jacket, adjusted helmet and goggles, waved at the woman, "Tell Davie good luck," gunned the engine, and roared north from Central Square.

Never give up! Never give up!

He kept repeating it, as he zipped onto the on-ramp, sped onto the Interstate, and then flew northwards away from Boston, his old life, and everything he had held dear.

~

Morgan's family had a cottage on Lake Winnipesaukee. The Najar family liked to spend time there – not just her parents, but sometimes aunts, uncles, and several cousins. He shuddered at the thought someone might be at the cabin, but then he shook his head and gunned the motor, pulling around the Subaru ahead of him.

No one will be there – not at this time of year, not in the early spring cold.

The miles flew by. Beyond the I-93 tollbooth the traffic thinned, and so did the highway, until he was on a two-lane road that ran upwards into the foothills of New Hampshire's Presidential range. Spruce and pine colored the hills green, along with birch, maple, and ash showing the first signs of life following the cold of winter. How sweet the arrival of spring!

He smiled grimly: *Just what's needed after a suicide.*

Around noon he turned from the highway onto the road along the lakeshore, passing scattered gas stations, diners, and shops, until he had made his way into the quiet forest to the north. Spattered with golden drops of sunlight, green budding trees cast soft gray shadows as the road curled along the shoreline, the lake sparkling blue beyond them.

He knew the way, as he and Morgan had stayed there a couple of times for romantic retreats. He recalled they had been planning a long weekend here in May.

But then he banished the thought – too painful.

The road wound up along a hillside. He passed several driveways, then a long wooden fence, then a break in the trees where a creek flowed towards the water. At the next small drive he turned in, killed the engine, and coasted along the path between the trees, finally emerging in a clearing at the lakeshore.

The old wooden cabin looked out on an expanse of lawn sloping down to the water. There was no car, no sound, no sign of life, only the soft lapping of water against the shoreline. He wheeled the cycle into the shed at the edge of the clearing and moved to the cabin door.

The key fit. He locked the door behind him and did a quick walkthrough. Dust covered the windows, and spider webs draped across the door hinges. No one had been here for a long while.

At the top of the stairs was a bedroom with a giant bed sporting mattress and pillows and blankets, though no linens. He did not care. He stripped down, crawled into the old four-poster, nestled under the wool blankets, and fell dead asleep.

39.

FRIDAY, APRIL 22

Dawn that same day Morgan's eyes were open. She had not been able to sleep, yet being awake was no different from dreaming.

She closed her eyes. What were those lines of Confucius Steve had always liked?

The good is like water ...

Pain burned in her belly. She moaned, curled under the blanket.

God, how I miss him!

She scrunched her eyes tight and willed the world to go away.

A weight settled on the bed next to her.

"Morgan, honey."

Steve?

She started crying softly.

"Oh, honey!" Laurel pulled Morgan close.

"Laurel, what am I going to do? He was hurting. He had weird ideas about the lab; he thought we were being spied on. He wanted me to pretend we'd separated – he said, to protect me. Too strange! Now I can see he was breaking down. I should've known."

She pushed her face into the pillow.

Laurel held her close. "Steve was sick. He had a psychotic break. How could you help that?"

They were quiet for a while.

"Morgan, sweetie, I have to go," whispered Laurel. "You going to be OK?"

"Yes, yes, yes. Thanks for being here last night. Don't worry about me. I just need some time alone."

"What do you mean?"

""My family has a cabin on Lake Winnipesauke. I'll head up there for a few days. You don't need me here, do you?"

"No, babe. I found this sharpshooter Joe Meyers. He thinks I have a good angle on a wrongful termination lawsuit, maybe a Civil Rights Title IX sexual discrimination case to boot. I never liked working at Eddie Mac – might as well get a chunk of change out of it. But maybe you should stay with me? I'm not sure you should be alone right now."

"Laurel, it's *exactly* what I need."

"Honey, once you're up there, and you want to talk, anytime, you call me right away."

Laurel hugged her, then stepped to the door. "Call me when you get there, OK?"

Morgan wanly smiled back. "OK."

Laurel blew her a kiss as she left the apartment.

⁓

Hours later, Morgan awoke. She rolled onto her back and stared at the ceiling.

I never dreamed he was crazy!

She stifled her tears, rolled out of bed, and opened the top drawer of her desk.

The letter had arrived in yesterday's mail, but she hadn't seen it until last night, only minutes before the policeman had called informing her of Steve's death. Had she read it sooner, maybe she could have stopped Steve, contacted someone, done something.

As she read it again, she thought her heart might break:

Tuesday, April 19

My love,

Last week was an eye-opener. I must warn you.

The key to what is happening is the relationship be-
tween MacGregor and a very powerful financier Antonio
Calibri. Eddie Mac is also involved. Most importantly,
they know we are an item.

I've seen Angion use extreme violence to achieve its ends.
And I have evidence that will bring them down.

You are not safe alone in Manhattan. You must leave New
York. Likely you're best off with your parents in Phillie.

Be careful, Morgan. You must *assume every action is*
watched. When you move, ditch your credit cards and
clothes. Instead, use cash and public transportation. Get
off the grid.

Be careful. Give nothing away in what you say or in what
you do. Share this letter with no one.

I miss you with all my heart and soul.

Morgan, dearest, I know how crazy this all sounds.
Forgive me. It is real.

I love you,
Steve

Her eyes brimmed with tears: obviously, a psychotic break.

Silent woods, beautiful mountains, quiet lake, all with good memories – these might help. She so desperately needed a safe place to heal.
There is too much pain in the world.

～

Delayed by thunderstorms, her plane touched down after midnight. It
was too late to go farther, so she checked into a hotel by the Manchester
airport, exhausted.

Finally in her hotel bed with the lights out, Morgan felt hopelessly lonely. Maybe she should have gone to her parents in Phillie instead? She kept doubting herself.

Maybe I should call Laurel?

Laurel would make her feel better.

"Morgan? What's the matter?" The voice sounded bleary.

"Nothing, Laurel. I'm here in Manchester. The plane was delayed. Just wanted to say hi."

"Honey, I can't really talk right now."

"What's the matter?" Morgan laughed sheepishly. "Hot date?"

"Ummmm, well, umm, yes. He's this really cute broker. Don Johnson look-alike! Really can't talk *right now*."

"Sure, Laurel, sure. I'll call tomorrow. Have a great time."

Morgan hung up. She lay in bed, tears on the pillow.

Hours passed.

That same night Steve awoke famished; the morning's bagel and coffee were the only food he had eaten since noon yesterday. He remembered there was a roadhouse about ten minutes down the highway off Weir's Beach – rough crowd, mostly bikers, but solid food.

In the closet he found flannel shirts and a pair of overalls. These fit pretty well. He glanced in the mirror – rough, unshaven, hair disheveled, but his eyes were bright. The nap had helped.

Am I crazy?

Actions cannot be understood without their motivations, he reminded himself.

He threw on his jacket and stepped outside. The evening air was crisp. He kicked the bike's starter and rode back to the highway.

The roadhouse was a ramshackle wood building a stone's throw from the lake. He parked his Honda next to four bruiser Harleys, each gleaming as though straight from the showroom. Inside, the old wood furniture was blond, worn light over the years from heels scuffing the floor, leather chaps rubbing the seats, and whiskey glasses crossing the bar. Steve waved at the bartender and crossed to an empty corner booth.

Three older guys with beards and beer bellies sat at the bar, sporting big belt buckles and biker boots and chaps and leather jackets with giant American Eagles across their backs.

Maybe vets.

In the booth against the far wall was a younger man with close-cropped hair, also in a leather jacket, but this one with a skull and crossed-swords stitched across the vest pocket, his face hidden in shadow. Opposite him was a woman with blond hair and dark roots that fell loose below her shoulders, her back towards Steve. There was no one else.

The bartender came over, and Steve ordered beer and ribs. He stared into space for five minutes till the food appeared.

The ribs were spicy and chewy, and the beer was fresh and cool. He savored the tastes, closing his eyes.

"Doc August!"

A hand descended upon his right shoulder. His eyelids jerked open as his left hand started to swing toward the attacker's arm and his shoulder dropped away from the hand. In another moment he would have seized the man's wrist, but then he recognized the voice. He stopped his hand in mid-reflex, deflected it, and scratched his ear instead.

He turned and smiled.

"Doc August," repeated the guy, "this is incredible! Here's my woman, Betty. We just got engaged. Hey, it's bitchin' you're here!"

Steve kicked himself for not having recognized him before: Jake Murdoch, the biker who'd taken a tumble off his Harley without a helmet, the guy whose subdural hematoma Steve had fixed back in December. And now here he was! Steve should have remembered Murdoch lived near Laconia. He should have stayed away from public watering holes. He should have …

But Jake was speaking. "Hey, Betty. Come meet Doc August! Remember when I mashed my head? This is the guy who fixed me up."

As she approached, Steve could see the woman had intricate purple and green ivy vines tattooed along the side of her neck and right shoulder. Betty was staring at him as though she were seeing a ghost. She sat down opposite him, her eyes never leaving his face. She reached over to Jake, took his arm, and pulled him down next to her.

"Jake, shhh! Quit being an asshole!"

Steve wished he'd stayed at the cabin.

Jake sat next to Betty. His chiseled face, partly obscured by a goatee, radiated enthusiasm and gratitude. Steve noticed that the craniotomy scar over the right ear had healed nicely. More prominent was a gold skull-and-bones earring dangling from the earlobe.

Jake turned to his girlfriend with a puzzled look. "Come on, Betty, what gives? This guy saved my life. Nothing secret about it!"

He turned back to Steve, "Doc, this is great! Been thinking about you a lot." He took in Steve's unshaven beard and worn clothes. "Hey, you on vacation? Roughin' it, huh?"

Betty grabbed his jaw and firmly turned Jake to face her. "Jake, shut up!" She turned him back to Steve. "Look at him, Jake! That's *not* a doctor on vacation."

She leaned forwards, eyes fixed on Steve's. "OK, mister," she whispered. "I don't know *what's* going on, but I smell trouble. I was down in Manchester this mornin', and I saw a *Boston Globe* that had your picture – Steve August, MD – no mistakin' it."

She threw her arm around Jake's neck, "Hon, I was gonna tell ya, but there wasn't a good time, and now …"

She glared at Steve. "The article said you jumped off a bridge. Big mystery. They're calling it suicide, but no one knows why. No note. They're dragging the River. They can't find a body, obviously." Her eyes narrowed, staring at him.

Jake's eyes were as round as Harley headlamps, his expression a mix of a dozen emotions.

"No way," he whispered. "This true, doc?"

Steve looked at his former patient. "Jake, good to see you. Glad you're OK." He bent his head towards the door. "The three of us should go outside. I'll explain. But not in here."

Betty opened her mouth, but Jake cut her off.

"Yeah. Sure, doc," he said.

Steve paid his tab at the bar, and they stepped outside. The sky was lit with a thousand stars. Their breaths steamed in the cold night air. Steve walked over to the bikes at the corner of the lot, Betty and Jake beside him. No one else was around.

"Betty, you're right. I'm in trouble. Yes, I jumped off that bridge. The reasons are complicated, but they have to do with a lab I was working in.

A crazy scientist named MacGregor set me up, and faking suicide was the only way I could see out. So that's what I did."

"Doc, that sounds crazy," said Jake.

"Yeah, I know. But it's the truth."

"Why didn't you just go to the cops?" asked Betty.

Jake gave her a withering look. "Why d'ya think?"

Steve nodded. "Right. They wouldn't have believed me. I needed proof."

"Proof of what?" asked Betty, skeptically.

"Fraud," said Steve. "I'm working on it. But the one thing I need right now is an ironclad promise that you both will tell *no one* about tonight. You never saw me! Remember – I'm dead."

"You picked a funny place to be dead," said Betty. "Why here? You chasing Jake?" She put one arm protectively around her fiancée, the other one flexing at the shoulder.

"No. No, I'm not. Laconia? Has to do with my girlfriend – that's another story, a long one. Believe me, I'd forgotten about Jake being here. I never dreamed of involving you!"

Betty looked mollified. "Oh. Apology accepted."

Abruptly she turned back to Jake, her words tumbling out in a rush.

"OK, I buy it. He's in trouble. He's got a girl to take care of, and some assholes chasing him, and he saved your life. Jake, he's *alright*! It's like my cousin Richie when the cops were after him ..."

Jake cut her off by kissing her on the lips – "That's what I love about this girl. She don't mess around!"

He turned back to Steve. "Doc, what can we do? Need a place to crash?"

Steve shook his head. "No, thanks, I'm all set. Like I said: just forget you saw me."

Jake's face grew serious. "Look, Doc, I owe you. You're all alone up here, and everybody think's you're dead, but your picture's in the papers. You need *somebody*. This bastard who's givin' you a hard time ... we can rough'm up for ya."

He grinned dangerously.

Steve shook his head. "No thanks, Jake. Already have a plan."

Betty was staring at Steve. "What're you goin' to do? No friends, no family, no money, no ID … Man, you're *dead*! Doc, you need money? We can get you some cash, or an ID. Jake's got a guy who can set you up with a fake license …"

Steve touched his hand to his forehead in a gentle salute.

"Jake, you're right, that's a very special lady you got there. Thanks for the offer, Betty, but I've got a bit of cash. Should be enough."

"So what're you going to do, Doc?" asked Jake.

"Tomorrow I'm calling the fellow who was my boss at the hospital. I'm sure he'll back me on this. I've got evidence that will put MacGregor away."

Betty's voice took on an edge, "What if you're wrong and he doesn't bite? They can trace your call."

Jake nodded. "She's right, doc. Betty, you thinkin' what I'm thinkin'?"

Betty nodded, "You bet!"

Jake walked over to his Harley, a giant monster with wide handlebars, bright silver chrome engine, and gleaming black pearl lacquer. "HELLLRAISERS," was painted in bright yellow letters along the gas tank, along with a skull and crossed swords.

"Doc, if you're gonna mess with crooks, then you gotta think like one."

Jake undid the saddlebag on the bike, pulled out a plastic Macy's shopping bag, and handed it to Steve.

In the bag were several cell phones in a variety of sizes and shapes. None looked new.

"What's this?" asked Steve.

"You wouldn't believe what people lose in bars and restaurants, 'specially strip joints. My sister works at the Puss'n Boots down south near the border, and she sometimes collects half a dozen phones a night. Not sure how, but she does. They're good for making untraceable calls."

Steve digested this in silence.

"Make only one call," continued Jake. "Once they know the number, they can trace the location to the service tower where the phone connected. So ditch the phone after you've used it. And don't turn the phone on till you need it."

Steve nodded again. "Thanks. I'd planned on using a pay phone."

Betty shook her head. "Most're around gas stations, convenience stores – all got tons of security video. If they lock down a call to a payphone at a particular time, then they can ID you on the tape."

Steve was wondering whether Betty and Jake might be involved in activities of questionable legality, but he thought it best not to ask. "Thanks for the tips."

"Don't mention it." Jake grinned again. "Doc, let me do you a favor – makes me feel good. Take the phones. After a couple of days they get disconnected, so use 'em!"

Steve considered this, then nodded. "That'll be a real help. Thank you!" And he stuffed the bag into the compartment under his Honda's seat.

"That's your bike?" Betty nearly snickered.

"Yeah. Just took the training wheels off this morning."

"Leave him be, Betty," said Jake. "The bike's alright. Doc, one more thing. You may find yourself in a spot where you need some real muscle."

Jake reached under his jacket and pulled out a dark-blue pistol with a walnut grip.

Steve knew nothing about guns. His experience with human violence was limited to the martial arts. His skin went clammy as he looked at the shiny handgun, Jake holding it, extending the grip towards him.

"Go ahead, Doc. Don't worry; it's legal. It's registered to me. You can borrow it. Return it when you don't need it no more."

Steve's hand inched forwards, but he did not take the weapon.

Jake continued, "That's a nine-millimeter Beretta, 84-F Cheetah, semi-automatic, a real sweet piece. Flip off the safety, and it's ready to fire. Works on what's called 'blow-back:' pull the trigger, the shot kicks back the slide, and that ejects the casing, re-cocks the hammer, and slams a new cartridge into the chamber. You're ready to shoot again before you've blinked. Holds a thirteen-round mag. Loads through the grip. When you're out, just hit the release with your thumb, and the empty drops out. Pop in another one, pull back the slide, and you're good to go. Here, let me show you."

Jake demonstrated in one lightning motion – dropping the cartridge, slapping another in place.

"Long-range she's not perfect, but short-range she'll do the job. Oh yeah – keep the safety on. You flip it with your thumb. Here."

Expertly he spun the pistol around and slapped the grip into Steve's palm.

Steve stared at the gun in his hand.

"Betty, you wanna get him a couple of extra mags?"

She rummaged through the saddlebag and pulled out three magazines, which she then put in the container under Steve's bike seat. "There you go, Doc," she said. "Fully loaded, thirteen rounds each."

Steve studied the pistol, flipped on the safety, checked the trigger, then stuffed the weapon into the small of his back under his belt, concealed under his jacket.

He nodded, "OK. Thanks."

"Hey doc," said Betty, "one other thing about those phones. If you use one around here, and somebody traces the call, they'll know where you were calling from. If you really want to go to ground, then you've gotta ride somewhere else before you turn it on."

Steve took a breath. "Got it."

"You *sure* you don't want to crash with us?" asked Jake.

"Thanks. I'm already set up. But if I get into trouble, maybe I'll call you. You alright with that?"

Jake grinned again. "Yeah, but its unlisted. You got a good memory?"

"Try me."

"603-747-2535."

"Check."

Betty's eyes were wet. "Boy, I don't know what you're doin', but … Doc, you've got me real worried. You call us if we can do anything. Anything! You hear me?"

She reached up and kissed his cheek.

Jake pointed to the inscription on the Harley: "Hellraisers raise hell!" And then he patted Steve's shoulder. "Man, you've got friends. Don't forget!"

"Thanks. I'll call if I have to. And you'll be getting the gun back unfired, unless there's a real disaster."

Steve gave them a smile and mounted his bike.

Once on the road he looked over his shoulder. The two were still standing by their Harleys, holding hands. He gave them a thumbs-up, and they waved.

He turned back to face the dark road ahead.

40.

That same evening MacGregor was surveying Calibri's study. The unholy Trinity had reunited.

Trying not to cough, MacGregor took a deep drag on his Cohiba. Cigars were an acquired taste – but why not acquire it? He was tired of waiting. He wanted every part of the "good life." He thought of Dida in his bed.

But I want it all.

He studied the other two. Lacking a cigar, Riker was on the edge of his seat, a hawk ready to swoop off its perch. In contrast, Calibri was folded deep into his easy chair, a lizard tucked between rocks, eyes glowering a dull yellow behind the cloud of smoke rising from between his gnarled fingers.

Unblinking, Calibri was looking at MacGregor. "So, Professor, are we ready to proceed?"

MacGregor nodded. "Yes. August's out of the way, and we have his fixed lab books. The Swiss will love the data, as will the FDA."

Calibri shook his head and waved at Riker. "Michael tells me there is a new wrinkle. This fat pig, Silverstein, is worried Angiotox is not working right, because his test, SAGA, is raising doubts. It almost seems he may be backing away from Angiotox. What do you say to this?"

MacGregor tried to keep his voice calm. "Bloody nonsense. We all know Angiotox is the perfect anti-cancer drug in brains. The 'new wrinkle,' as you put it, is that some of its effects are different in mice than in rabbits. This means the response possibly, *possibly*, may also be different in humans. The only way to know is to test people, but we were going to do that anyway. This doesn't change anything."

"What about the Swiss?" hissed Calibri savagely. "Their enthusiasm will be dampened if they learn the results are … are …" – he searched for a word – " …are … *inconsistent*?"

MacGregor proclaimed, "There is every indication the drug will act *perfectly* in the human brain. According to SAGA, it works on brain blood vessels in rabbits, and in mice, *and* in humans."

"What then is the difference across these species?"

"It's not the effects in the brain that are different. It's the effects in *other* organs."

Riker interjected, "So it's the toxicity we can't predict!"

MacGregor took a deep breath.

Blimey, these buggers are slow.

But he responded, "The only way to know what this will do to human beings is to try it. We know it'll stop the blood vessels in their brain tumors, but we can't say about the effects on other organs – whether based on SAGA, mouse, or rabbit data."

"And that's because …?" asked Riker.

"Because," said MacGregor very slowly, "we don't know what the *relative* effect will be in normal tissues. SAGA showed Angiotox to have highly selective effects in rabbit brain tumor cell lines as compared to normals, and this was confirmed in the living rabbit experiments. But the more recent SAGA tests show less *selective* effects in mice cell lines. Even so, August's data show the drug to be *safe* in living mice. That's the key point. So, we should just move ahead."

Calibri's face was expressionless.

MacGregor continued, "We'll do fine in people, as long as we dose the drug to the right level: enough for the appropriate response in the brain, but not so much that it damages other organs."

"What kinds of damage?" asked Calibri.

Bullocks, how stupid!

But he said, "Pretty much anything you can imagine – internal bleeding, strokes, vomiting blood, bruising so bad the whole body turns purple, that sort of thing."

The room was silent.

Calibri's eyelids drooped low, his voice pure acid: "Perhaps we should sell Angiotox before it collapses on us. There is too much risk."

"What?" spluttered MacGregor. "Wait a minute. We don't *know* these side effects will happen. Maybe they'll *never* happen! All we have to do is get the dosing right. For God's sake, these are *cancer patients*! They'll accept a few deaths in exchange for eradicating their disease!!"

"How do you choose the right dose?" asked Riker.

"That's based on the animal tests. We just extrapolate to humans."

"But what if the drug doesn't work in people?"

"That's the beauty of it!" exclaimed MacGregor. "We don't have to show efficacy – merely *safety*. For that we don't need brain tumor patients. Anybody can take the drug. We just need to assure it's not *toxic*. That's called Phase I testing. Once we've established a tolerable dose, then we start testing efficacy. Within six months we'll be testing Angiotox on human brain tumors. Within a year we'll have enough data to make a case for full-scale clinical trials involving hundreds of patients. And all the testing will be done here in *our* facilities at Angion. We'll have total control! Don't you see?"

But Calibri still sounded skeptical, "You say Angiotox works perfectly in the brain – that *other* tissues are inconsistent. Then why weren't August's brain experiments consistent?"

"He botched them. But even so, his results were consistent in as much as they showed no *toxicity* in the mice. This will make *no* difference when we test in people."

MacGregor wondered whether the other two might have heard the small catch in his voice, but they seemed not to have noticed.

Sometimes the mirage is real. It is mine to choose.

He felt himself stiffening between his legs. A flashback to Dida in bed this morning made him even harder.

I am all-powerful!

But Calibri was talking: "Very well. If we control the clinical testing, that will guarantee success."

"Exactly," said MacGregor. He took a deep drag on the Cohiba, let the smoke luxuriate in his mouth, then blew it out slowly. He no longer coughed.

Riker asked, "Silverstein will back this up with the Swiss?"

"All he really cares about is SAGA," said MacGregor. "And SAGA conclusively predicts that Angiotox is powerfully effective: in mice, in rabbits, and in people."

"Silverstein will help sell Angiotox to the Swiss?" hissed Calibri, with emphasis.

"In short, yes," said MacGregor.

"You know what would clinch the deal?" murmured Riker, his face emotionless, but his voice wicked.

"What are you thinking?" asked MacGregor.

"The Swiss will buy it if *they're* convinced *we're* convinced Angiotox is safe as well as effective. Silverstein will speak to its efficacy. Our confidence in its safety, however, is the issue."

"So?"

"If you're so sure it's safe, Georgie," said Riker, grinning, "Why don't you take it yourself?"

The words hung in the air, as heavy as the thick smoke rising from their cigars.

MacGregor recalled he hated Michael Riker.

Calibri nodded slowly, "Yes – yes – Professor," he said. "That's not a bad idea."

MacGregor felt blood flushing his face.

How dare they even think about risking MY life?

But then he had an idea – and he looked at Antonio Calibri with a glimmer of new insight.

"That's a fine idea, Michael," said MacGregor smoothly. "But obviously there's a risk to my taking Angiotox, in as much as the best scientific experiments in the world, run in animals, cannot predict with certainty the reaction in any one human being. But I'm too valuable. There's a better solution."

Calibri glared at him. "Yes …?"

"Dida," said MacGregor.

For a moment, the only sound was the sizzle of hot wax dripping from the candles.

Calibri's eyes flashed yellow fire. "You are suggesting that my *nipote* …?"

MacGregor felt no emotion: "Let's be clear, Don Calibri. She slept with him, yet we're trusting her. What she and August put together we're submitting to the Swiss, to the FDA, and to the world at large. We must be sure she stands behind the data that she transcribed with August in the conspiratorial secrecy of her bedroom. So, to do that, we'll use the data from the lab books to set the initial dosing level, and then we'll check it with Dida as our first subject."

Anger contorted Calibri's face. "But you, Professor – *you* are the source of the numbers she gave to August. *You* are responsible!"

"I gave her the right numbers – the numbers that we want and that will work. But whatever she did with those numbers is her doing, not mine. We need to check that she stands behind the books."

Calibri's eyelids drooped low, hooding his gaze. "Go on."

"Dida wants to be part of the S.S.," said MacGregor. "But she's no scientist, so how can she contribute? Her knowledge base will be of no practical value unless ..."

Riker completed the thought, his voice flat, " ...unless she contributes her personal experiences as a subject."

Calibri blinked: "My niece could give me entry to your S.S.?"

MacGregor waited.

Calibri nodded, "There is a poetry here. She will take your drug, and she will be part of your S.S., and she will give me access. So there is a balance."

He licked his lips.

Riker smiled, bloodlust in his eyes, but pure sugar dripping from his lips. "With Angion's president testifying to the drug's safety from personal experience, we'll be home free with the Swiss! Screw August. She'll be perfect as Angion's figurehead."

"Yes," said MacGregor.

But in his heart he hoped she might suffer just a little – because she had slept with the bastard.

Calibri leaned back, exhaling cigar smoke, exuding satisfaction.

"Yesss ..." he sneered. "Perfect."

He glared at MacGregor. "You will set this up, Professor. This will be the guarantee for her future as president of Angion. I'm sure you're fond of my niece, but *I'm* fond of insurance."

Riker grinned, "Yes, Georgie, and you better be carrying some insurance, too, because if Dida gets into trouble, your ass is mine. Right, Don Calibri?"

Calibri blinked slowly, looked directly at MacGregor, back at Riker, and then gradually inclined his head.

"So be it."

There was sweat under his armpits, but MacGregor kept his voice steady: "Right-o. Angiotox is gold in the bank."

41.

The next morning Steve awoke to the sounds of birds chirping. He rolled out of bed and stepped to the open window.

A light gray mist arose from the lake, thinning under the sun's warm yellow light. The sky was cloudless, its pale blue promising another beautiful spring day.

Tucked under the eves of the cabin roof, hardly three feet away, was a nest with four chicks chirping many times louder than their tiny size. Then Steve noticed a robin glaring at him belligerently from a nearby tree. He remembered a time years ago when he had seen two little robins attack a hawk that dared encroach on their young. He decided to play it safe and close the window.

Downstairs he fixed himself black coffee, since there was nothing else. Mug in hand he stepped onto the porch and surveyed the beautiful early spring morning, enjoying deep breaths of the clean crisp air – but he had an open road ahead, and a phone call to make. He downed the coffee and moved to the bike.

Two hours later he was in Kennebunkport, a sleepy resort town on the Maine seacoast. Only a couple of pedestrians were scattered across the town square. He and Morgan had vacationed here last summer with friends, so triangulation of his phone call would likely lead away from his hiding place on Lake Winnipesauke.

He rode east out of town nearing the ocean, then turned down an access road to the beach. He pulled out the Macy's bag: reserve cash, lab book, cellphones. He picked out a phone and returned the rest under the seat. Then he checked the Beretta nestled behind his back.

Insurance.

The morning sun cast the beach in pastel hues: luminescent blue sky, splashing green waves, sparkling turquoise ocean stretching out to infinity. Steve filled his lungs with the salty air, but his agitation remained.

All beauty holds tragedy. Our lives hang in a balance.

Steve looked around. Far down the beach was a kid tossing a Frisbee to a dog – no one else.

Crossing his fingers he called Boston directory assistance. He was in luck: Marion Phillips had a listed number. The phone rang three times before Phillips' patrician voice answered, "Hello?"

"Dr. Phillips?" murmured Steve.

Steve heard a sharp intake of breath, but the voice was steady, "Steve?"

"Yes, Dr. Phillips, I'm alive, but I need your help."

Phillips' voice revealed an edge, "Thank God – Steve! – we thought you were dead. There have been many newspaper reporters …"

"Yes, I'm sorry, Dr. Phillips. I had no choice. I staged the suicide."

The edge became more noticeable. "Steve, that doesn't sound very good. I'm concerned for you. Where are you? We must speak in person."

Steve ignored the question. He tried to keep his tone calm, his voice measured. "Dr. Phillips, please, let me explain. This all has to do with Angiotox. George MacGregor has been faking the laboratory results to make the drug look good, to get FDA approval and investor financing. They were trying to strong-arm me, to generate bad data. I staged the suicide to get out."

There was silence.

Then Phillips spoke slowly, "My boy. You must know how off-balance you are sounding: conspiracy, fraud, fake suicide – hardly the norm at All Saints. Where are you, Steve? I can drive out and pick you up. You need help."

"Dr. Phillips, I have proof."

Phillips sounded almost gruff. "'Proof?' What do you mean?"

Steve breathed deep. "I saved one of the original lab books. It shows changes, edits, and entries made in Dida Medicia's handwriting."

"The president of Angion fabricated lab data?"

"Yes."

"Steve, you're not making sense. You've been under a great deal of stress. My boy, where are you? Let me help you."

"Dr. Phillips, do you believe me?"

"Yes, of course, Steve. I believe you're very upset and confused, trying to make sense of a very complicated world."

Steve's heart sank.

"Dr. Phillips, these are very dangerous people. They've been following me. Over the last few days they were keeping me awake, torturing me without sleep, trying to force me to such a point of exhaustion that I'd break down. I think they wanted me dead!"

"Steve, you're sounding insane. Why would Dida Medicia want that?"

Steve heard Phillips' incredulity, but he had no choice.

Iacta alea est.

"A 'preemptive strike.' MacGregor's intent was to make my credibility the issue."

But as he said it, Steve realized MacGregor had succeeded. His credibility *was* the issue.

Then Phillips spoke, his voice grave. "If I understand you correctly – and I'm hoping I'm not –you are saying that you staged a fake suicide, that you believe an eminent, respected member of the world's scientific community is persecuting you to the point of trying to destroy your career and your life, that you believe this scientist is perpetrating fraud, and that you're now playing private detective trying to prove your theory. Doctor, that's insane."

Steve tried to maintain calm, "I know it sounds insane. I can't help that. The fact is that it's true."

"Steve, I will be frank with you. Last night, I received calls from several people – the police, reporters from the *Herald*, the *Globe*, even the *New York Times*, not to mention the FBI. But the *first* phone call was from George MacGregor. He was distraught at the news of your death. *Distraught!* He told me the police had called him, informing him of what had happened. He explained everything: how hard you had been working in the lab, how you were putting yourself under such pressure to perform, how you were the model fledgling researcher. He had only good things to say about you, virtually singing your praises. You want me to believe that this same man is an evil criminal, hell-bent on your destruction?"

"Yes."

Phillips cleared his throat.

"Steve, please tell me where you are. You're a good man, but troubled. Let all of us help you: me, your friends, even George MacGregor. We care for you."

He paused. "Steve, are you having girl troubles? You have a girl-friend … Megan, right? Have you talked with her?"

Steve flipped off the phone. He hefted it in his hand, then hurled it out over the water. It arced high into the air and plopped down in the ocean, a small splash in the cold Atlantic. He ran back to the motorcycle, kicked the starter, and rode away.

Ten minutes later a dark blue sedan pulled up to the stretch of beach. One dark-suited passenger studied the dirt on the roadside for fresh tire marks, while the other walked oceanside and found the boy with the frisbee. But he remembered nothing.

A half-hour south of Kennebunkport Steve stopped at a small mom-and-pop and bought groceries, a trowel, and a backpack. He saw no video cameras.

When he hit the Maine-New Hampshire border, at the sign marking the boundary, he pulled off the road, killed the engine, and dropped the bike behind some bushes. No traffic. No houses. Not a soul in sight.

Carrying the lab book still wrapped in the plastic bag, he found a tall birch, fresh green leaves springing out on branches far overhead. He studied the tree relative to its neighbors, to the road, and to the sign marking the state border. Comfortable he could find the spot again, he dug into the soil with the trowel. Then he carefully nestled the wrapped notebook in the hole and covered it with earth.

42.

When Steve got back to the cabin it was nearly noon. He parked the bike at the porch.

In the kitchen he dropped the pack on the counter, opened his groceries, and fixed himself a sandwich, carving off slices of cheese and roast turkey and layering them onto two slabs of fresh farm bread. He poured himself a glass of milk, set up the coffee machine, and stepped onto the front porch. The sandwich was salty, the milk was sweet, and Steve was hungry.

Sitting on the porch steps, he stared out at the bright blue water, mulling over the conversation. He had thought Phillips would believe him, given their relationship forged inside the OR over the last four years. But – obviously – MacGregor had gotten to him first. Once labeled clinically paranoid, the more Steve told Phillips his unbelievable story, the more Phillips would think him psychotic. As counter-argument, would the one lab book be enough? Maybe Phillips would think Steve had created it himself, in some kind of delusional fit?

"Steve August!"

The voice came from around the corner.

Adrenaline shot through him like lightning. He dropped the sandwich and rose to a crouch, center of gravity low. His left hand dropped behind his back and pulled out the Beretta, clicking the safety off.

How did they find me? What was my mistake?

The unseen voice spoke again. "Steve, don't panic. I mean you no harm. I'm stepping forward. Please stay calm. I am unarmed."

Steve did not move, his feet planted on the porch steps, gun at the ready.

Around the corner of the cabin came a short, round, elderly man. He had a shining bald pate but a full white beard, as though all the hairs on his head had decided to slide down his face to take up residence along chin and jaw, it being more comfortable to grow downwards than push upwards. His orbits were set deep with prominent brow and strong cheekbones casting them in shadow. He wore a light gray linen suit. His shirt was faded white cotton, but set off by a bright green silk bow tie that mirrored the emerald intensity of his eyes.

He walked slowly, as though he were measuring each step, weighing the consequences of going forwards rather than turning back. He looked up at Steve as he neared the porch, and the corners of his mouth turned ever so slightly upwards.

Steve watched, every muscle tense, his hand pointing the Beretta without a quiver.

The old man walked up to the porch, his eyes as focused on Steve as Steve's were on him. At the steps he gestured next to Steve, "May I?"

Steve nodded.

The man sat down but said nothing.

Steve folded himself into a coiled spring next to the old man, maintaining the gun leveled at his chest.

"Hello, Steve," said the man. "Finally, finally – glad to meet you."

The man extended his hand.

"Sure. Steve August," said Steve. But he did not extend his hand.

"Winston Schmidt. Pleasure," said the old man with a slight German accent.

"Never heard of you," said Steve.

"But I've heard of you."

"You have? Well, forget about it!"

"Cute, August, but no, I won't."

"I wish you would. Who the hell are you?"

Schmidt said nothing, his intense eyes focused on Steve's.

"Steve, with that question you are about to enter an entirely different world, one where the rules of every day life do not apply. Are you really ready to walk through the looking glass?"

Schmidt's face betrayed no emotion.

At that moment Steve realized that, for very certain, he was in the middle of a complicated chess game, one with several players at the table.

Steve nodded, "OK. Walk me through."

~

Schmidt looked away to the sunlight sparkling on the lake water.

"Some years ago, before you were born, I founded a laboratory at Cambridge University, the first in the world dedicated to the study of angiogenesis. Over the years we developed an international reputation, and received many prestigious awards, including the Nobel Prize in 1976."

"Nobel Prize? Come on, Mr. Schmidt, then I should have heard of you!"

The old man smiled, his face breaking into a thousand up-turned wrinkles. "'Schmidt' was my mother's maiden name. After carrying my father's name for most of my life, when I made my career change, I switched to my mother's. Seemed only fair."

"Your father's name?"

"Schoenberg."

Steve's eyes widened.

"Winston Schoenberg? As in the 'Schoenberg Transposon' – the discovery that shook the foundations of evolutionary biology? Winner of the Nobel Prize and knighted by the Queen of England – *that* Schoenberg?!"

"Yes, Steve, *that* Schoenberg," said Winston simply.

Steve was silent for a time. "So, why 'Winston Schmidt?'"

"No one's heard of Winston Schmidt – that's helpful in my current line of work. And I was very fond of mum."

"Of course."

"To continue: one of my most promising students was a young research chemist, number-one graduate from Australia's system that year. George MacGregor was a good student, but very ambitious. He saw the extraordinary leverage a top-notch biotechnology scientist might bring to the commercial marketplace. When he left my lab in England for MIT he already held more than ten million dollars in grants from commercial pharma. He was expert on how to market science."

"You don't sound enthusiastic."

"He was loose with the truth: just a bit too quick to reach a conclusion that favored his point of view, just a shade too willing to endorse an idea that was to his advantage. As he grew intellectually, he wilted ethically. When he left for Boston, I was glad he was out of the lab – someone else's problem."

"So, what are you doing here?"

Winston's face hardened. "Six years ago, my wife was unhappy about her wrinkles. At that time there was a new skin cream on the market, made by a start-up company – Dermatropic Pharmaceuticals. She applied the cream one night before bed, and the next morning I rolled over to find a corpse next to me. Her heart had stopped while she slept. The autopsy showed nothing suspicious …"

Winston's voice broke for a second, but then continued, " …but I was sure there was a connection. So, I made inquiries."

Winston turned to Steve, his sparkling eyes gauging Steve carefully as he spoke. "The active ingredient in the Dermatropic cream was a naturally occurring chemical found in kelp from the Indian Ocean. In essence, the cream was nothing more than concentrated, ground-up seaweed in a neutral cream base. For this reason it qualified as a cosmetic, rather than a drug, and it was not under FDA supervision. However, the active ingredient was a potent angiogenic stimulant, discovered by a group of entrepreneurial scientists who then sold it to Dermatropic. They thought the extract offered anti-aging benefits by stimulating blood vessel growth. However, they never reported the increased rate of heart attacks that they found in the laboratory mice."

"Why didn't you go public? Sue? Expose them?"

"The scientists were insulated – not connected to the product nor to the company. And there was no smoking gun. According to every laboratory record, cardiac complications never occurred. Those lab records of the mice had simply … disappeared. No data. Nothing to review. Nothing to prosecute. No way to hold them liable."

"How did you find out?"

"A cover-up is never a total secret. People talk – at lunch, over a beer, in a hallway at a conference."

"Angiogenesis? Disappearing lab books? You're going to tell me that …"

"Right. The scientists who discovered the seaweed extract were led by my former protégé."

Winston stopped.

Eventually, Steve said, "I'm so sorry." And he slowly lowered the gun.

Winston stared out into the distance. "Thank you."

And they were quiet for a long while.

Winston broke the silence. "I suppose rhere was a certain poetic justice. After all, I'd trained him and then let him loose. But on the other hand, I'd never seen him do anything *wrong*. And as I sorted through these conflicting ideas, I finally put into words a premonition that I had always known but never articulated, a gut principle so deep you can live your entire life without putting it into words. But Maggie's death, and MacGregor's moral guilt, and my tacit role, together forced me to confront a simple truth: facts spring from values. If a man's values aren't solid, as MacGregor's weren't, then his facts aren't solid.'"

Winston paused for a moment for breath. Then he said, with emphasis, "*True values value truth above values.*"

He nodded, as though he were agreeing with himself. "That's the point. My life as a scientist, your life as a doctor, the lives of all who study my science and my ideas and use these to produce more knowledge, the lives of all your patients who rely on your honesty to act in their best interests, all these people rely on our commitment to this bedrock principle: true values value truth above values."

Steve murmured, "'True values value truth above values.' Yes."

Winston smiled.

"After reaching this epiphany," continued Winston, "I decided I would devote my last years to this bedrock truth – or maybe it's a value." He laughed gently. "I can't decide if it's one, or the other, or both, or whether the distinction is unimportant."

"OK, practically speaking, what did you do?"

"Shortly after Maggie's death, I retired from Cambridge and moved to a farm in Yorkshire. Thought I might write memoirs and inspire other scientists in their devotion to the discovery and application of facts and truth.

"About three months after I'd settled in and started writing, two men visited me, an Englishman and an American. The former was Deputy head of the British GCHQ – England's Government Communications Headquarters, its secret code agency – and the other was a high-level spook in the NSA, the U.S. National Security Agency. Over tea they explained that our mutual governments had identified our scientific research base as a matter of utmost national security – I should say, *international* security. They knew my entire history, they knew about Maggie, they knew about MacGregor, and they wanted to make use of my background, experience, sense of guilt, and hunger for revenge. They offered me a job."

Steve's eyes were fixed on Winston, but his hand crept back to the Beretta. "I thought the NSA was a bunch of math-junkie code-breakers?"

"Go ahead, Steve, pull it out, if it makes you feel better. Where'd you get the gun, anyway? But you know I'm no threat. As for the NSA, you're right: it started as a bunch of egghead code-breakers. But over the years it evolved into something more, much more. Its concerns reside in the fundamentals of the American mathematical and scientific enterprises: how the U.S. builds and breaks codes, computers, new technologies, even chemical products and biological organisms. Did you know that our next generation of computers will incorporate DNA as part of their infrastructure? The point is that the NSA does not want American science undermined by foreign or domestic interests. It's an issue beyond the FBI's scope, and it's largely a domestic matter CIA can't touch. Not to mention we've got the budget. So it's ours. You understand?"

Steve's hand was on the Beretta, but he kept his voice steady, "Yes, Professor, I understand."

"Your reaction's common, Steve. This sort of knowledge can upset your worldview. It's unsettling. Pull out the gun, if it helps."

"You're right; it makes me feel better."

Steve hefted the cold blue steel in his hand, noticing the pistol's exquisite balance. He pointed it at a tree near the water's edge, sighting down the barrel.

"Go on," he said.

Winston acted unconcerned about the gun, though Steve thought his face had turned a shade pinker.

"The NSA hired me to run a new division within the Agency, coordinated with GCHQ – a special group focused on the scientific infrastructure shared between our countries. Who better than a Nobel Prize winner, knighted by the Queen, and enraged by the wrongful death of his wife?"

His voice held a hint of bitterness.

Steve focused on Winston's face. "'A special group?'"

"We study the structure of western scientific knowledge, how ideas are developed, how errors are corrected, how innovations occur, how scientists respond to incentives like academic fame, praise from colleagues, financial rewards. We help supervise our two countries' scientific progress. As part of that, we identify bad apples, and then we take steps to render them harmless – prune them off the tree, so to speak."

Steve remained silent.

"We have files on every prominent scientist in the U.S. and the greater U.K. So far, we've identified, beyond any doubt, more than fifty senior members of the scientific Academy who willfully and repeatedly commit fraud to advance their careers. In each instance, we've taken corrective action to prevent further mischief."

"Like what?"

"We get them out of research: line them up with early pensions, forced retirements, administrative positions, virtually anything to make sure they do no further damage."

"OK, sure, good job. And the reason you're telling me all this?"

"I'm sure you can guess. We want MacGregor."

"Why do you need me?"

"His situation's difficult. Believe it or not, we can't get inside his security. He has wiring within the walls of Angion that runs a low level current as a barrier to radio-frequency transmission – making it an electromagnetic fortress. As for the human element, incredibly, none of his scientists seem to think anything's wrong. We monitor their phones and e-mails, their conversations with spouses, friends, significant others, colleagues … nothing! It's as if they've taken loyalty oaths that they *never* break, not even in the privacy of their bedrooms."

Hairs on the back of Steve's neck rose.

"That's some very intimate surveillance you're talking about, Mr. Schmidt."

"Yes, Steve, but this is a high-stakes game. It's almost impossible to prosecute scientific misconduct, unless it's truly gross. This way we can address problems before they become disasters. But so far, George MacGregor represents an ongoing failure. Until you, we've not had an angle for getting inside."

"Mr. Schmidt you sound like a vigilante: convicting people without a judge or jury, making decisions about innocence and guilt that belong in a court of law."

"Steve, you're idealistic and naive, but wrong on a number of counts. For one, I'm not a vigilante – I'm part of your government. Covert operations are part of what your government does routinely."

Steve switched the gun from his right to his left hand, then back again. "Sure."

"Couple of other points," said Winston. "We don't do anything truly illegal – but the NSA has many legal options that are not available to the average citizen. We do respect boundaries, boundaries of all sorts. We have a job to do, and we possess the necessary latitude. We are the watchers. And sometimes we intercede."

"Intercede?"

"Yes, intercede. Make things happen. You used the word 'convict.' But we convict no one. Conviction is a public statement of wrongdoing, a label that has permanent legal implications. With such public legal channels there are safeguards designed to protect the rights of the accused. Otherwise, it would be too easy for the powerful to crush the weak."

"Right, that's my point! You're operating outside of the boundaries of the law."

"Everything I just said applies to our *public* institutions, to the legal system, to the structure of our governments – but scientific knowledge is not a public institution, particularly when we're talking about the frontiers of scientific research. A normal judge and jury would be lost if they tried to wrestle with matters of true and false, good and bad, in scientific work. Because the knowledge is so specialized, you need scientists to evaluate other scientists. But scientists are not *just* scientists, but also people, citizens, who have legal rights. For example, let's say a university president has inside information that a faculty member is publishing questionable work. But that scientist has his rights. If the president takes formal action, the committee meetings, hearings, testimonies, depositions, and so on, might take months or even years. And a sufficiently powerful scientist, one who brings in multi-million dollar grants to the institution – like MacGregor – would *never* be prosecuted. The university administration would be shooting itself in the foot – jeopardizing grants that helped keep the university running. And even if it turned out to be true, the ultimate defense for the scientist, of course, would be to blame his staff: he would deny knowledge of the details and claim that he had been misled by the people running the experiments. The innocent would be called guilty, and the guilty would remain free. No, I'm afraid official avenues work poorly in such situations."

"OK. Let's grant all that, Mr. Schmidt. Still, someone must watch the watchers. Who holds you responsible?"

"The buck's got to stop somewhere, Steve. Who better than a benevolent, Nobel-prize-winning Knight of the Realm? Of course, there are oversight agencies – Congressional committees, that sort of thing. But they know nothing except what they are told, and they do not want to hear about all the operational details."

"Well, how about public accountability rather than a secret police? Democracy instead of decree? Isn't that what a lab's reputation is all about? Word gets 'round, if a lab is putting out shoddy work. Eventually the best students won't go there to study, the best junior faculty leave for other jobs, the best journals won't publish their papers."

"That's idealistic, Steve, but the world isn't that simple. Talk is cheap. There's gossip about every lab. Remember, good science depends on scientific rivals critiquing each other's work. Theories are questioned, and almost all of them discarded, until a very few emerge as solid. And even when the entire world accepts an idea, it only takes one brilliant mind to ask the right question, and the whole edifice gets set on its ear. Look at what Einstein did to Newtonian physics. It's not that Newton was *wrong*, it's just that he wasn't *exactly* right."

Winston continued, "And besides the criticism of rivals, there are always disgruntled employees, bored lab techs, unhappy junior faculty – all of whom spread innuendo daily."

He shook his head, as though to rid himself of a nightmare. "No, gossip is cheap, so common that it's impossible to filter true from false. And the fact is that the merely mediocre, and worse – the malicious – can

hide inside the scientific establishment, once they have acquired sufficient power. No, sadly the answer must be a third party – an indepen-
dent agency that can secretly examine problems, one that can draw a
distinction between the roles of scientist and citizen. Everybody makes
mistakes; every scientist is human. In my NSA branch we aren't looking
for perfection, we're looking for the bad apples, the ones who play fast and
loose and who teach their juniors to do the same. These are the people
we must nail, people like George MacGregor."

"And that's where I come in?"

"Exactly."

"And what if I say 'no?'"

"I'm betting you'll say 'yes.'"

"Yeah, you are."

And they were both silent.

After a while, Winston said, "You realize that's my money you've
been spending?"

"The bum was your guy?"

"You want to meet him?"

"I guess I should say thanks," said Steve, dryly.

"He's parked up the street. Keep the gun out if you want, but please
don't shoot. I'll signal him to come in."

Steve nodded.

Winston opened his jacket, exposing a cell phone at his belt. He
flipped it open: "Jack, we're all set."

About a minute later an old Ford pick-up pulled into the yard. Out
stepped a young man, jet-black hair in a crew cut, wearing an oily T-shirt,
blue denim overalls, and mud-stained work boots. He looked like a farm-
hand, but Steve recognized the laughing eyes: the eyes that had given him
the money on the bridge, the eyes he had noticed at the T-station ages
ago – or had it been only two weeks?

Since then, his world had changed. Irrevocably.

"Hello, Steve, good to see you again," said the man.

Steve kept the gun pointed at Winston sitting on the porch.

"Steve, let me introduce Jack Walker," said Winston.

Steve scrutinized the new arrival. "Don't tell me: you have a cousin
Johnny Daniels, right? I guess I owe you a 'thank you' – sort of. But

before we go further, I'd be more comfortable knowing you fellows are unarmed."

He waived the Beretta at the porch. "Hands against the railing, gentlemen, and please spread your legs."

Jack and Winston obliged. Steve kept the gun level, and with the other hand did his best to frisk them: wallets, keys, cell phones, but no weapons.

"OK," said Steve. "You want some coffee?"

"That'd be mighty fine," said Jack, in a soft Southern accent.

And the three of them went inside.

43.

Shortly, Jack, Winston, and Steve were at the kitchen table with steaming mugs of fresh-brewed coffee.

"So, Steve, why do you think we're here?" asked Winston.

"You want to nail MacGregor. I think you guys like to operate below the radar, outside normal channels, so my guess is you want to blackmail him."

"'Blackmail' is a strong word, Steve. I prefer, 'leverage.' We know he's setting up a clinic at Angion, preparing to test Angiotox in human subjects, which will give him every opportunity to manipulate the clinical data to his liking just as he did in your mice. We must act prior to his treating people with Angiotox. We suspect you can help."

"What makes you think that?"

"MacGregor's silent partner is an old mobster turned financier, Antonio Calibri, Dida Medicia's uncle. He controls several biotech firms around Boston, including Angion. We know that Calibri's head of security, Michael Riker, put together an operation meant to break you – the nastiness you experienced last week. So I see one of two possibilities: Calibri, Riker, and MacGregor are public-spirited citizens who believe you're a menace to society, or – more likely – they think you're a threat to their plan's success. And that means you're holding trump cards. Tell me I'm right."

"Probably."

"But Steve," chimed in Jack, "I still don't understand why you staged the jump? If you've got hard evidence, why didn't you just hand it over and walk away?"

"When your whole world is falling apart," answered Steve, "you don't know whom to trust. I was stuck. The suicide was a way out of MacGregor's trap, and at the same time a cry for help, in a sense."

Winston nodded, "Yes, you *are* crazy – like a fox. You've grabbed the spotlight, which gives *you* leverage: the power to reveal yourself in a public and dramatic way. But of course you know that, if you go public, you must have *conclusive* proof that you're right. Otherwise, you lose."

"I've already revealed myself – Marion Phillips."

Winston and Jack exchanged looks.

"You contacted Phillips? Steve, you're full of surprises." Winston's tone was casual. "When?"

"About two hours ago."

Again, Winston and Jack exchanged glances.

"How?" asked Jack.

"Stolen cell phone."

Winston grunted. "Resourceful. You didn't call from *here*, did you?"

"No. Kennebunkport. Didn't want anyone to trace me back here."

Winston looked relieved. "He didn't believe you, did he?"

"How did you know?"

"He can't afford to," said Winston, almost bitterly. "Universities, hospitals, and research labs depend on the millions they get from industrial contracts, just like an addict going from one fix to the next. Do you think that Phillips – on behalf of All Saints – can follow Nancy Reagan's advice to just say 'no'?"

"The ties are that tight?"

"Angion brings in more than twenty million a year to All Saints," said Winston. "That's a lot of salaries, and a lot of leverage."

It was Steve's turn to whistle.

Winston's tone was serious. "You think Phillips contacted MacGregor after your call?"

Without waiting for a response he pulled out his cell. "Julie, cut the phones to Marion Phillips' house, family's cell phones, everything. Get me a log of all incoming and outgoing calls since Friday, 8 PM." He shot a glance at Steve. "Look particularly for calls to and from George MacGregor. Call me back ASAP."

He slapped the phone closed.

"Say your prayers, brother," said Winston. "If MacGregor finds out you're alive, then the game gets very complicated."

"With no body in the River, I figured he'd assume I was alive."

"No need to confirm his suspicions. Your enemy's uncertainty is your own advantage," said Winston.

"Hmm. You sound like Sun-Tzu's *The Art of War*:

So veiled and subtle,
To the point of having no form;
So mysterious and miraculous,
To the point of making no sound.
Therefore, he can be arbiter of the enemy's fate."

Winston smiled, "We know about your passion for Eastern philosophy. No, not Sun-Tzu, just Winston Schmidt."

"You still haven't said what you want from me?"

"Proof! Give me proof he manufactured data. Then I can engineer his retirement. With MacGregor out of the way we'll get Angion out of Calibri's grip. Good scientists are working there. With the right one at the helm we can steady the ship."

"What about me?"

"Steve, I'm sorry, but did you forget? You're dead. If your existence becomes public, the situation explodes: charges of fraud, countercharges of insanity. It will get very, very, very ugly, involving many lawyers. Frankly, it'd be best if you stayed dead. Instead, you can come work for me. We'll get you a nice spot doing intelligence analysis somewhere in England, where no one will recognize you."

A soft chime sounded. "That was fast," said Winston, pulling out his phone. "Yes?"

He listened, then flipped the phone closed.

"You're a lucky man, Steve August," he said. "He's talked to no one since you phoned him. MacGregor did call Phillips after the police contacted him about your death – presumably to let Phillips know. But nothing since."

"And what if I don't want to work for you? What if I want to take MacGregor down on my own? He may end up hurting thousands of people. He deserves worse than retirement with millions in the bank."

"You must be practical, Steve. Give me the proof. I'll take care of the rest."

"You have a plan, Steve?" drawled Jack.

By now Steve was on high alert with these men.

"I'd hoped Phillips would be more receptive. I still think if I go to him, show him my proofs, that he'll back me up."

"Steve, he can't *afford* to," said Winston.

"He won't be able to afford *not* to. I can go public. *Boston Globe, New York Times.* The public will decide in my favor."

"Unless you have an iron-clad case, they won't print the story," said Winston. "Not how you'd want it. You'd be going up against All Saints Memorial, one of the most famous hospitals in the world. That's a powerful opponent, Dr. August. Many people would be calling you a liar, or worse."

"Well, right now I'm dead. Can't get much worse than that."

"What's the evidence you're holding?" asked Jack.

"Copies of my original lab books in a sealed, post-marked envelope dated April 9. Then, one of the original lab books itself, with edits and changes in the data in Dida Medicia's hand writing, done more recently."

Jack and Winston again exchanged glances.

"That's good, my friend, but maybe not enough," said Winston. "I'll tell you how that'll play out. They'll hang Dida out to dry. Members of the Calibri family do not mind spending a year or two behind bars – it's an occupational hazard. MacGregor, of course, will deny wrongdoing, claim that you made mistakes, that you're unstable and not to be believed, and that Dida was merely trying to fix your errors, trying to save time as well as your reputation and career. It will come out that you and she were lovers, giving her additional motive. By the time it all gets to court, they'll have plenty more proving you wrong. In short, chances are MacGregor can weather that storm. You'll have made his life unpleasant for a while – that's all. With his reputation backing him, with the power of All Saints Hospital at his side, and with Calibri's money and secret organization paving the way, George MacGregor will win. As for the NSA, we can't offer you *public* support. Our involvement *must* remain secret. At the end of the day, you won't stand a chance."

There was silence in the kitchen, marked by the clock ticking on the wall.

"He *can't* get away with this!" exclaimed Steve.

"Then play ball with us."

"I want my life back!"

"Wish that were possible. Can't."

"So I need more evidence?"

"Give it up, Steve. Let me take care of this."

Steve looked at the clock – 1:13 PM.

"Give me forty-eight hours. If I haven't nailed this bastard by one o'clock Monday, then we'll do it your way."

"Now you *are* insane."

"Look, that's my offer. Take it or leave it."

Steve pointed the Beretta.

"First, Steve, tell me where the lab book is. If you die, I don't want to lose the one legacy you could leave the world."

Steve tasted sweat on his upper lip; yet he felt cool, his thinking sharp as a scalpel.

"Then you better pray I don't die."

"OK, Steve. In the interest of keeping you alive, I'm going to do you a favor. Marion Phillips knows me, not as Winston Schmidt, but as Winston Schoenberg. We've served together on committees of the National Academy of Sciences. We will now take advantage of that."

He picked up his cell phone, his eyes on Steve, and hit a button. "Julie, give me a secure line – direct patch to Marion Phillips' home."

For a moment there was silence in the kitchen.

"Hello, Marion? Yes, hello, it's Winston Schoenberg."

Pause.

"Good to hear your voice, too. Last time we spoke was five years ago, at that Washington dinner for the winner of the Presidential Medal for Neuroscience. Afraid, old man, this isn't a social call. I just received a – shall we say – *cryptic* message from a trusted source – highest possible level. Very strange business. I've been asked to relay it to you, though I'm afraid I don't understand any of it."

Pause.

"Here it is: 'The dead remain dead. Do not invoke false dreams. These do no one good. No one. Only absolute silence holds hope – for every living person concerned.' Sounds like a bad Chinese fortune cookie, if you ask me."

Pause.

"Yes, the very highest level imaginable. Not sure what it means. Frankly, I'd rather not know. Seems some knowledge is too dangerous."

Pause.

"Right-o. My best to your lovely wife. Cheers!"

He flipped the phone closed.

This was a side of Schmidt Steve had not seen before – raw, deadly power. The sweat on his neck turned cold, but he held the gun level.

Winston's mouth was set tight. "Well, that should take care of that."

"Thank you," said Steve, his voice a hoarse whisper.

Winston brightened, "Not a problem. Come join us."

Steve shook his head. "By the way, Mr. Schmidt, how did you find me so quickly? I left no clues I was here."

"But you did, Steve – your keys. The police found your clothes when they dredged the River. Your key chain was in your pocket, but two were missing: one to a P.O. Box – whose location we will soon find – and the other to this cabin. You see, a week ago we took the liberty of cataloguing all of your personal effects. But Steve, don't worry about that. Come join us, and I'll take care of the rest."

Moving fast to conceal his fear, Steve kicked his chair back and stood up, the gun steady in his hand.

"Gentlemen, gotta go. I've errands to run."

He backed up to the kitchen door, the gun trained on Winston's chest.

"Steve, don't be stupid. Tell me, where's the lab book?"

"Forty-eight hours, Schmidt. Give me forty-eight hours."

On the kitchen counter was the backpack with his cell phones and cash. Next to the pack was the box of C+H sugar he had just bought. Keeping the gun level, Steve hefted up the pack.

"Gentlemen, empty your pockets. Cell phones and keys on the table."

They complied, but Winston shook his head, "Big mistake."

"You may be right. That's a chance I have to take. Both of you: hands over your heads. Please follow me, slowly. Keep your distance."

He backed up into the hallway between kitchen and living room. Jack and Winston followed, their eyes on the Beretta.

Steve opened the door to the basement and gestured with the gun.

"I'm sure it won't take you fellows long to figure out an escape – but it'll give me time for a head start. Light switch is at the top of the stairs."

He backed away from the door.

The two men walked down the basement steps. Winston tried one more time, "Steve, think about this. For security's sake – *where's your lab book?*"

"Forty-eight hours."

Steve closed the door and turned the old latchkey. He heard the bolt close and tried the door. Solid.

He called out, "Gentlemen, pleasure meeting you both!"

There were shuffling sounds from the other side, but no response.

He scooped their cell phones and keys into his pack, grabbed his jacket and the box of sugar, and ran outside to the water's edge. He tossed the keys and phones into the lake, then turned back to Walker's truck and poured the sugar into the gas tank.

Moments later he was on his bike speeding away from the cabin, thinking through his options.

Unless they have backup right here, I should have a few minutes. Damn, this is getting tough!

Morgan awoke around noon. She called room service, but the airport hotel was no longer serving breakfast. Without showering she packed and left.

Down the street was a Denny's. She ate voraciously: pancakes, hash browns, sausage, bacon, scrambled eggs, and a pot of coffee. It reminded her of childhood with her family vacationing at the cabin, her mother ladling eggs from a giant bowl.

A half hour later, stuffed, she was back in the rental car flying north at eighty-five miles an hour. She no longer cared about rules or laws.

As she pulled up at the cabin shortly after 2:00 P.M., she realized something was wrong. An old Ford pick-up was parked in the yard with a box of sugar spilt next to it. And there were tire tracks in front of the cabin. She bent down to look more closely. These were no more than a few hours old: young blades of grass bent, not yet sprung back erect, the exposed earth moist not yet dried by the sun. The tracks were unpaired – a motorcycle.

She moved to the cabin. The screen door was open. Inside were signs of recent activity: fresh milk in the refrigerator, groceries on the sideboard, three half-full coffee mugs on the table. The door to the basement had been taken off its hinges.

"Hello? Anyone here?"

Silence. She moved to the living room, then one bedroom, then the next, then upstairs to the third. Here was another surprise. The bed had been slept in.

There on the bedside table, in its usual spot, was Steve's watch. He always took it off before going to sleep.

O my God!

She dug her face into the bedclothes.

They smell like him! He's alive!

Maybe a clue in the truck?

She grabbed the watch and ran outside, but stopped short when she reached the porch.

Two unmarked olive green sedans had pulled into the yard, followed by a platform tow truck.

An old bald man with a white beard and rumpled gray suit stepped out of the lead car. He extended his hand. "You must be Morgan Najar. Pleasure to make your acquaintance."

"Hello," she said, stunned at yet another new twist.

"Winston Schmidt, at your service. Why don't we go inside to chat?"

44.

The Honda's 447 cc engine roaring between his legs, Steve sped north along Lake Winnipesauke. He wanted to trust Schmidt, but ...

He has a job to do, and he needs me to do it. The NSA! Sweet Jesus.

They would have the best surveillance: spy satellites that could read license plates, computers that could trace years of credit card charges, microphones that could hear a heartbeat at fifty feet.

Maybe even now?

With Schmidt at his cabin, a spy satellite might have been focused on the place the whole time. Or they might have put a GPS on his cycle. He needed to ditch the bike and disappear. Fast.

Three minutes from the cabin he hit the Pleasant Street intersection. He pulled over and grabbed a cell phone from the backpack.

What was that number?

He dialed.

One ring. "Yeah?"

"Jake, Steve August. Sorry, man, but remember how you said if I ever needed help ...?"

"Name it, doc."

"I'm being chased. They found me at the cabin. I think I've lost them – but maybe not for long. I need to ditch my bike. It might be tagged."

"Where you at?'

"Pleasant Street, close to Route 25."

"Good. Meet me at the bar at Hart's Turkey Farm. I'll call my buddy

Tiny. All the video cams will flip on the fritz. If the Man shows, then just yell out, 'Fuzz bust!' The whole place'll shut down faster than three shakes of a rat's ass. Just stay cool. We're close."

He hit Route 25, the highway running through Laconia, and turned south towards Weir's Beach, the lake still on his left.

If they've tagged me, then their satellites can track me on the highway.

He glanced at his wrist to check the time, only then to realize he'd left the watch at the cabin.

~

Hart's Turkey Farm was a popular diner full with locals, families, tourists, and bikers. The Harley emblem featured throughout the restaurant, on the décor and on the clientele. With his three-day beard, sweat-stained hair, dark sunglasses, black leather jacket, and mud-stained pack, Steve blended well.

Carrying a beer, he retreated to a table in a far corner of the bar, his back to the wall, his eyes wide behind the shades, watching the door. No one came in who looked like a government agent – but then again, the NSA guys seemed to have a talent for the unconventional.

Less than five minutes passed before a biker sporting a familiar earring entered. Jake moved around the bar to sit next to Steve: "Hey Doc."

He gestured around the restaurant.

"Nice spot, huh? Lots of friends here."

Steve smiled, "You want a beer?"

"Thanks, Doc, but we gotta go. This guy MacGregor's on your tail?"

"Worse. Feds. Spooks. Top-gun surveillance."

"Feds? You think they know you're here?"

"Not sure. This guy Schmidt who's looking for me wants to keep a low profile. It's a long story. He hates MacGregor, but I'm not sure he's a friend. I think he's working outside normal channels. And his intel's not perfect. He didn't know I was at the cabin till today, and he was surprised I had a gun."

"You shoot somebody?"

"No! Locked them in the basement. But they're probably out by now."

"OK, Doc, we're gone. Even if they're watching the roads, no one's looking for a Harley gang. Say good-bye to your bike: it's heading to Montreal. I need the key."

Steve peeled it off his keychain.

"Drink up!" Jake put on his glasses and leather cap.

Steve had hardly touched his beer. "I'm all set."

Jake waved the bartender over. "Hey Mooch. You ain't seen us, right?"

Mooch looked at Steve, then at Jake, and nodded. "Right, bro. Never been here."

Jake handed Steve a package.

"Here. Put these on. Toilet's over there."

In the men's room Steve opened the bundle to find a set of black leather chaps. They fit well over his jeans. He now looked the quintessential biker.

When he came back out, there was another biker standing next to Jake.

"Doc, this here's Flash. He's got a girlfriend in Montreal. Wants to drive up there today. You mind if he borrows your ride?"

"No problem."

Flash shook Steve's hand, thumbs and palms clasped. He had a long handlebar moustache and eyes that twinkled.

"Thanks, Doc. Glad to help out. Meanwhile you can borrow my hog."

Flash stepped outside.

"Give him a minute, Doc. Then we're gone."

On the way out Jake threw his arm around the neck of a giant bald man in black T-Shirt and jeans sporting a diamond stud earring.

"You're the best, Tiny."

Tiny, standing six-foot-five and weighing around 350 pounds, grinned at Jake, flashing a gold tooth: "Video's shot. Maintenance guy's supposed to be here real soon. Shame ... we lost the last hour."

"No way to get it back, huh?"

"No way."

"If you were any prettier, I'd kiss you," said Jake.

"Man, don't talk like that. Gives me a hard-on."

Jake patted him on the cheek, then drew on his gloves and stepped outside, Steve close behind. Several others followed, all wearing black biker jackets, sunglasses, chaps, and boots. They looked virtually identical.

Jake gestured at a gleaming blue Harley-Davidson.

"Grab your hog, Doc," said Jake, and then turned to the other bikers. "Let's rock and roll!"

A couple of bikers had been waiting at the cycles, standing watch. The men behind Jake and Steve quickly mounted their bikes. Steve noticed their faces: young, but creased from hard luck, hard riding, and hard living.

"Hellraisers raise hell!" one yelled, and the others whooped, gunning their engines.

Above the roar, Jake shouted, "Keep up, Doc. Stay in the pack."

Steve gave him a thumbs-up, put on his helmet, and mounted Flash's bike.

And the whole crew pulled onto the highway and sped south, away from the inquisitive eyes and ears of Winston Schmidt.

Saturday morning Nathan Spear woke up feeling very fine. Yesterday had been a great adventure: cooling August, cleaning his apartment, collecting five-hundred Benjamins from Smith's boys, and then scoring Valentina – a red hot Cuban chili pepper who liked saying "*si.*"

He looked around his bedroom. Bummer – the chick was gone. No surprise.

He shuffled into the kitchen where he found a pack of Marlboros. He lit a cigarette, inhaled, and enjoyed the power he held over his own life, over that dead bastard Steve August, and over that little Latin bitch who had served his needs so well last night. He had paid her an even thousand, so he still had 490 Benjamins for the Wonderland track this afternoon. *Sweet!*

He pulled a Miller from the frig. Can in hand, cigarette in mouth, he sat at the kitchen table and looked out the narrow window onto the alley.

Steve August – God, what an asshole!

He thought about yesterday's conversation with Smith's muscle.

What'd he say? Something about a notebook?

No. No notebook. Nowhere.

This morning's *Herald* said the body was still missing – only clothes, books, papers, all over the Harbor.

He wondered why they'd be worried about a notebook.

He inhaled more smoke from his cigarette and stared out the window, waiting for an idea. None. Sucking on the Marlboro, he mulled over what he'd heard while listening to August in his apartment over the past several nights.

Why'd Smith care about a notebook?

The answer hit him in the middle of another swig.

The bastard was squeezing Angion! That's why Smith wanted to blast him. And that's why they're so worried about some goddamn notebook. It's gotta have the goods.

Spear figured he understood blackmail.

But never during the surveillance had he pictured August as a blackmailer. The guy was way too white bread. Nathan thought he had watched August long enough to get a feel for the guy: crazy, yeah – but not dirty, not like that.

Nathan smacked his lips together. The beer tasted funny. He swigged another mouthful.

Ain't sour – just don't taste right.

Maybe he was getting a cold. Food always tasted different when he caught a cold.

So, if August's no blackmailer, then what's so important about a lab book? If it ain't blackmail, and he hid it, then maybe … insurance? Maybe he was scared? Maybe he knew something he wasn't supposed to?

Spear noticed the alleyway outside the window was looking blurry. He blinked, squeezed his eyes shut once, twice, three times, but the trashcan down below was no longer distinct – instead, just a smudge. He shook his head, but that just made it worse. He was starting to feel sick.

"Oh hell!" he said.

He smashed the butt into the ashtray, leaned over the table, and grabbed the phone. He had to prop himself up on his elbows as he picked it up. His head and arms and body felt heavy.

Slipped a mickey!

It was the final puzzle piece. August had known something he shouldn't and the notebook had been his insurance. Smith and his buddies were desperate to get it back. They used him, Nathan Spear, as their stooge to get to August. They wanted to break August to make him cough it up. Instead, he'd killed himself.

So now they were cleaning up loose ends, including him, their patsy. They must have known about Mary's brain tumor: played him, made him hate August, made him blame the kid for Mary's death.

And now they're taking me down.

Searching for the notebook, they'd go after the girlfriend next. He remembered the Manhattan area code in August's address book.

He tried to focus on the keypad, but his brain was burning hot. *1-6-4-6-5-5-5-1-2-1-2.*

His head weighed a million tons. His chin hit the table, and his head rolled to one side, but his eyes stayed on the phone by his face.

"What city and state, please," chirped the operator.

"Manhattan, New York," he croaked out. He noticed his voice was very soft.

"And the name?"

"Najar … Morgan … Najar …" He strained to speak up, but his voice ended in a gurgle.

Through thickening fog Spear saw the door open and Bravo and Delta enter the room. In three strides Bravo was at the table. He pulled the receiver out of Spear's hand, turned it off, and put it back in the cradle.

Bravo worked quickly, flipping a piece of rubber hose around Spear's upper arm and exposing a vein. His gloved hands removed a loaded hypodermic from a plastic bag, positioned it under the skin, drew back blood, loosened the tourniquet, and plunged its contents into the vessel. Spear felt his body slump even more, head and shoulders flat on the table. Carefully, Bravo left the needle in place and placed Spear's other hand next to the emptied syringe.

Probably heroin, Spear figured, his brain slowing, slowing, slowing.

Meanwhile, Delta moved to the bedroom. From the closet he pulled out a small paper bag. "Got the cash."

Bending down, he pulled something from the baseboard next to the closet. "And here's the barfly. All set."

Bravo picked up the Marlboros and dropped a replacement box onto the table. He nodded at Spear as he picked up the cigarettes, "These things'll kill ya."

Delta chuckled, "Good one!"

"Yeah. Shame about the Cuban bitch. Nice piece of ass."

"Nobody lives forever."

"You got her prints on the syringe, right?"

"Of course."

Bravo nodded. "Let's go."

They left, closing the unlocked door for the police to find later, the thumbprint on the syringe linking the overdose to the whore's body they would likely find in a trash barrel in Dorchester. Even through the worsening fog, Spear knew there would be no ties to Smith.

Spear focused his gaze one last time, his eyes level with the empty syringe sticking from his arm. Beyond the syringe in the distance he saw Oz, the green Emerald City, but in front of him a blanket of flowering purple poppies. Their perfume grew stronger, sweeping him up in their embrace. His pupils tightened into tiny pinholes, fixing on the million violet flower petals laying a carpet leading to the edge of forever.

It's time.

He stepped onto the petals.

His feet sank into their embrace, and they folded over him, choking off his breath.

45.

For about two hours the bikers headed south, winding their way through the forests along the New Hampshire-Massachusetts border. Their route snaked up into the hills, then eventually back down into a valley where they encountered scattered houses. One turn off the highway took them to a square block of a building with a pink neon sign out front, a couple of its letters burnt out: "Puss 'n' Boots." Four cars and two eighteen-wheelers were parked in the otherwise empty lot.

"Hey, doc, now you're *really* slummin'," yelled out Jake, as the bikers stamped into the club.

It took a minute to get used to the dim light. There was a stripper on stage, randomly gyrating her hips, staring off into the distance while a couple of truckers watched listlessly. The place smelled of stale beer.

Jake walked to the rear and settled behind a high-top table, waving at Steve to join him. The other bikers moved to the bar, where a very fat woman poured them shots from a tequila bottle.

A waitress emerged from nowhere, her cocktail dress a whisper of a nothing. "Hey Jake. You boys want *anything*?"

Her emphasis on the last word seemed to open a world of possibilities.

"Doc, beer for you?"

"Sure."

Jake nodded at the waitress, who vanished, only to re-appear in an instant with two bottles.

"Hey cutie! Hope you like St. Pauli Girl."

She winked at Steve and sashayed off.

Steve looked over to Jake. "Not a lot of business here."

"Picks up later."

Steve took a sip. "Look, Jake, I really appreciate your help. But I don't want to get you into trouble."

Jake raised his bottle to Steve. "Trouble's on you like a junkyard dog smelt a bitch in heat. Doc, trouble don't scare me none. We're in. Talk to me."

Steve looked around the near-empty strip club. His life was not turning out how he had expected.

"OK, here's the scoop."

For the next hour Steve told him the story: what he'd seen in Angion, and the pictures of Alison and him, and Angion pressuring him to capitulate, and his fake suicide, and the lab book, and Phillips's response, and Winston Schmidt and the NSA.

By the end Jake had downed three St. Pauli's, though Steve had just finished his first. "Man! We gotta nail this guy to the wall. You have a plan?"

"Well, I did, but now I don't think Phillips is the solution. Schmidt thinks Phillips can't *afford* to believe me, even if he might want to. And by calling Phillips Schmidt pretty much nailed that coffin shut. But I don't want to play ball with Schmidt, either. He wants to force MacGregor into retirement, but he also wants to protect the system, so he wants to hide me at some desk job in England."

"Doc, what do *you* want?"

"Hell, Jake, I want my life back. And Morgan. And I'd like to see MacGregor go down. Truth, justice, and the American way – that's all."

The waitress put down a fourth beer, and Jake took a long pull.

"So, you wanna go to the cops? You got enough evidence?"

"Schmidt didn't think I did. The lab book doesn't incriminate MacGregor as much as it does Dida. And she's part of Calibri's family. She'd get burned, but not much, and I'd be marked by the Mob for the rest of my short life. Meanwhile, MacGregor would deny all knowledge, and he and Angion would keep going."

"Doc, we need something to nail this dude MacGregor. What was going on in the lab when you saw those guys with the mice?"

"They were fixing the experiment. I checked the mice later. The ones who showed effects with Angiotox were the ones they'd treated with a high-tech machine."

"What was the gadget?"

"A high-precision radiation device. I think they were using it to irradiate the tumors in those mice – making it look like Angiotox was having an effect."

"Any way to prove the mice got radiated?"

"All the brain tissues were melted off after I cast the mouse blood vessels with the gold fixative."

"So, all that was left were these gold models."

"Not exactly. I only worked on the brains. We froze the rest of the body in liquid nitrogen for later study. And then I also . ."

Steve's voice trailed off into silence. His eyes grew round, like a six-year-old boy who had glimpsed a bicycle under a Christmas tree.

"Oh my God!"

"What? You got something?"

"The blood!"

"Doc?"

"The blood will show signs of radiation treatment."

"You just said only the brains got radiated."

"But so did the circulating blood. And even at low doses there can be some changes in the DNA!"

"OK?"

"When I did the castings, I collected each mouse's blood. The irradiated blood samples should show changes in their DNA profiles."

"Hot damn! You're saying the radiation left a footprint."

"Yes."

"Where are the samples?"

"Deep freeze at the lab."

"So, we get the blood samples, and they'll prove the mice were treated wrong. Hot damn!"

"Wait a minute. How can we do that? And even if we *can* steal them, they can't be used in court – stolen evidence, no search warrant."

"Doc, you're no lawyer. Hold on."

Jake waived at the crowd at the bar. "Hey Jimmy!"

A guy peeled away from the cluster of bikers and strippers. Tattoos covered his massive arms, and silver metal chains dangled across his bare hairy chest.

As he sauntered towards them, Jake whispered, "Jimmy was in the pen for five years. He's smart; read a bunch of law books and got his conviction tossed – but he's still real pissed, so don't say nuttin' 'bout that."

Jimmy grunted as he sat down on a bar stool, "What's up?"

"Tell him 'bout your dead mice, Doc," said Jake.

Jimmy listened carefully, asked a couple of questions, and then opined, "Not a problem, Doc. The lab gave you the mice to figure out a problem. You're just doin' your job. If you've got to take your blood samples somewhere else to test 'em, no big deal. Ain't doin' nuthin' wrong."

"But I'm taking them without permission."

"It's your project. You already got permission. You're bringing the samples back once you're done testing them, right?"

"I can't just walk in and take them."

Jake and Jimmy exchanged glances.

"Don't see why not. You're still on their payroll. Not a problem if *you* aren't breaking in," said Jimmy.

Steve was silent. The other two waited. Rod Stewart blasted from the speakers. A woman gyrated on stage.

"OK," said Steve August. "Let's do this. What do you have in mind?"

46.

SUNDAY, APRIL 24

The alarm was set for 4:00 AM, but MacGregor was already awake. He staggered into the bathroom and hit the light. A glance back into the bedroom showed Dida asleep.

Under the shower MacGregor thought about the prior night. Hypnotizing Dida had been surprisingly easy, and her subsequent performance had been nothing less than spectacular.

A hot vixen indeed!

He turned to rinse his shoulders, the steam rising thick.

He thought back to the conversation at the mansion. He had told Calibri that the hypnosis helped speed scientists to their conclusions, but that it could not change someone's fundamental convictions, that it could not get scientists to believe that up was down, true was false, black was white.

Of course, this was not quite accurate.

All depends on the bloody scientist!

If they cared nothing about truth – if ambition, or greed, or simply a love for deceit ruled their passions – then hypnosis could lead them to surrender to any manipulation. He grinned, as he lathered soap across his belly.

And Pieter and Mai are exactly the sort who do not truck with truth.

At times MacGregor marveled at their perversities. They cared nothing about facts absent how the facts affected them; seemed nothing existed outside their appetites.

An unpleasant thought hit him.

Are we all that bloody different – them and me?

But immediately he comforted himself: *No, a world different! I shape the future. I choose my destiny.*

After all, Pieter and Mai were only followers, obedient to his superior will. But *he* – George MacGregor – he obeyed no one. No one dictated *his* thoughts.

For the SS to work, all the participants had to believe its results, eventually reaching unanimity. The group had to be free of known deceit; otherwise, contradictions might arise that would break it apart.

His solution had been simple: find a couple of scientists whose cynicism – born of bad mentors, collapsed ideals, and angry greed – had warped them beyond repair, and then hypnotize them *independently*. Thus, they could affirm with conviction their twisted ideas about Angiotox as actual facts during the Science Service, even while they secretly labored to alter the experiments.

Through Mai and Pieter he could introduce any exaggeration or error, the other scientists then incorporating that into their beliefs as reality. If he had to, MacGregor always had the option of introducing a word or two of support – but he rarely felt the need. The system worked quite smoothly.

He flipped the spigots off, stepped out of the shower, and toweled dry. He studied his pink reflection in the mirror.

21st century god!

As he shaved, he carefully avoided nicking the folds of flesh below his chin.

Unlike Mai and Pieter, the other scientists were not fully corrupted. Most believed they were on a road of discovery, having agreed to the hypnosis because they believed the SS was a tool to intellectual enlightenment. But controlling *them* was easy. Every Sunday he just reinforced in them the same fable he had told Dida last night.

It's all a matter of interpretation.

He grinned at himself in the mirror.

George MacGregor, you're a genius!

He looked down: below his large paunch he could see the tip of his erection. He chuckled, wrapped himself with the towel, and stepped back into the bedroom. Dida 's sexy lines lay exposed.

Shame to waste a perfectly fine hard-on, but what must be …

"Dida, wake bloody up! It's your day: start of a brave new world. The SS awaits!"

She rolled over. "Oh Georgie, I feel delicious. What did you do?"

"Don't worry, joey. More later. Right now we must off to Angion. SS starts soon."

"Mmm. Yummy. OK, bad boy, I'm your guinea pig. Hmm. I like this hypnosis stuff."

She dressed quickly. Soon they were in his car heading towards the lab and their respective destinies.

Steve awoke about the same time MacGregor was rolling out of bed.

He had been lying on a lumpy pullout in the back office of the Puss'n'Boots, but with little sleep. The club had stayed open till past one o'clock, music thumping against the wall. The eventual three hours of silence had been a welcome gift, but now someone was knocking on the door.

Steve threw on jeans and T-shirt. There was another knock.

"Be right there," he called out, pulling on his boots.

With no further notice Jake entered.

"OK, doc, you ready to do this thing?"

Steve's head hurt. "Jake, you could direct a surgical residency. Don't you ever sleep?"

"Yeah, whatever. Shot of tequila wakes me right up. Boys're ready. Java?"

Jake handed him a mug of sludge that smelled like coffee. Steve took a sip.

"Thanks. Next time add some water. Last chance, Jake. You sure you want this nightmare?"

"Nightmare? What the hell! Only live once. You got your piece?"

Steve showed him the Beretta, then stuffed it inside his biker jacket. Jake grinned. "OK, let's bust some ass!"

Outside they joined the other bikers, who were already revving their engines under the dark purple sky and bright silver stars.

Unwashed, with several days' growth across his face, in black leather jacket and chaps, biker boots, jeans, and dirty T-shirt, Steve figured he looked a Hellraiser – in all respects.

About the time Steve was mounting his bike an alarm clock woke Morgan from a troubled sleep.

She flipped on the light. The bunk was standard Army issue, too narrow and too firm, thin cotton sheets with an inadequate olive wool blanket. Against the opposite wall were two chairs and a steel desk with another lamp.

She walked into the bathroom and washed. No make-up. Today would not require make-up.

Shortly before five she stepped into the elevator of Winston Visual Systems. The prior evening Winston had impressed upon her the importance of the hour – "No later than five o'clock!" – but had left the reason a mystery.

The elevator opened on the fifth floor, revealing Winston standing in a dark gray suit, blue striped shirt, shined shoes, and wine red tie – yet somehow still looking slightly disheveled. He beamed at her.

"Happy morning! Pip, pip, Morgan, don't look so glum!"

He stepped inside. "Don't worry! Steve's alive. He'll pop up. Meanwhile, I'm betting we can convince *you* to convince *him* to play ball. We're the good guys."

"Winston, I'm a trained lawyer and the daughter of a federal judge. No matter what you say, I know you're operating outside normal legal channels. Systems do exist to bring people like MacGregor to justice."

"Morgan, my dear, I *am* the system. Here you have a rare glimpse into the secret world of that system's infrastructure. We make the world work. Next time you're in D.C., notice that the power lines run underground."

Morgan digested this, but then continued, "If MacGregor's a bad apple, you should prosecute him and take him down."

"What? And undermine our public's trust in the USA's scientific enterprise? Prosecuting him would take years. And he would bring up a host of counter-allegations – a quagmire of lies. *And* it would open up all sorts of questions into our surveillance methods. No, Morgan, that would not be … shall we say … prudent."

"So, what was it that you want me to witness at this ungodly hour? I'd rather be looking for Steve."

"We'll find him for you. Don't worry about *that*, my dear. The NSA may have means not at your disposal."

The elevator doors opened on the eighth floor, interrupting him. He led her down a corridor.

He continued, "But what you're about to see is the core mystery. In a few minutes several dozen scientists, some quite famous, will walk into Angion. As they enter you'll notice how quiet they are. But come eight o'clock, they'll leave the building animated about their plans, excited about Angion's wonderful progress, delighted to be working for such a wonderful organization.

"But what's even stranger – none talks about it. We've bugged their homes, tapped their phones, deployed undercover agents to chat them up. But the only thing we get is that they're planning experiments. They call it the 'SS' – the Science Service. Quite odd. I need to know what's happening in there. And I suspect Steve knows."

He seemed to be leveling with her.

"Maybe you're right," she said. "Saturday night three weeks ago Steve fell asleep at his desk in Angion. When he awoke a few hours later, he snuck out through an air vent – or at least that's the story he told me. But he said nothing about seeing these scientists, or some kind of meeting, or anything else."

Winston nodded, his eyes narrowing.

"That's it. He knows. Or at least Angion's security boys *think* he knows. I bet that has as much to do with Steve's troubles as do his experiments with Angiotox."

"That's an interesting theory."

"We've put ears in some damn tough places: the White House, Fortune 500 boardrooms, the Vatican. Even the Kremlin isn't the fortress it once was. But so far Angion's been sealed tight. Its plumbers are very, very good – no leaks – at least not till Steve August."

They had reached a door. Winston punched a code on the keypad, then put his right eye against a lens mounted in the wall. The door clicked.

He grinned, "I love retina scanners. Every home should have one."

The room looked like NASA's Mission Control in Houston. About a dozen young men and women in military uniforms were seated at rows of computer consoles. Huge video screens mounted across the walls showed views of the Angion building from a variety of angles, covering all sides and approach roads. One panel even showed a bird's eye view, Angion's skylight and helipad framed by the surrounding streets.

He has his own satellites, Morgan realized. *No matter the Santa Claus beard, this is a scary, scary man.*

A prim, expressionless woman in Army uniform, her brown hair in a sleek bun, turned towards Winston and Morgan.

"Good morning, sir. Good morning, Ms. Najar."

Winston inclined his head. "Morgan, this is Captain Jill Nichols, on loan from U.S. Army Intel. She'll be your immediate contact here at the Center."

"Thank you, chief," said Nichols. "The GPS monitors show the scientists approaching."

"Thanks, Captain. Let's watch, shall we?"

She turned towards the half-dozen uniformed men and women seated at the consoles. "Tillson, monitor two. Audio on speaker."

"Yes, ma'am," said a man at the far-right console.

One of the overhead screens turned black for a split-second, then showed a wide-angle view of Angion and the street extending north toward Massachusetts Avenue.

But the street did not remain empty for long. Soon a few cars were entering the adjacent parking lot and several scientists were walking up Angion's front steps.

The speakers crackled:

"Top of the mornin', Heinrich."

"Hullo, James."

"Michelle, you're alive?"

"Just seems that way, Martin."

For the next fifteen minutes they watched as about four dozen scientists entered Angion.

Unable to hold back her indignation, Morgan blurted out, "Can't you just follow them inside?"

Winston shrugged. "We've tried! Our best surveillance units are tiny combination audio/video transmitters nicknamed 'barflies.' They're as small, silent, and hard to detect as a mosquito. In fact, we've had a couple swatted by their surveillance targets, unaware of the nature of the insect!"

"So what's the problem?"

Nichols looked at her sharply. "This isn't a game. When we fly a barfly into Angion, it flops to the floor inside a strong magnetic field in the entryway. Their metal detectors pick it up, and within seconds the unit's confiscated. Angion security now has a sampling of several of our surveillance toys. Somehow, they are anticipating our technologies and have well-thought out defenses."

"Why not just plant a transmitter inside?"

"Wire nets in the outside walls generate interference fields, making transmission outside impossible."

Winston waved at the screen. "Look! There he is."

Morgan stared at the monitor – a burly, pink-faced man was walking up the steps, a dark, willowy woman at his side. The woman looked familiar.

"That's MacGregor?" she asked. "He looks like a fat pig."

"Maybe," answered Winston, "But he's also a world-class scientific intellect. The sad wrinkle is that the intellect is eclipsed by his world-class lust for power. That's a dangerous combination."

Morgan watched as the couple stepped inside. "Who's the babe?"

"Dida Medicia – President of Angion, Calibri's niece, and MacGregor's mistress. But this morning he's using her as a guinea pig."

"What do you mean?"

"We have both MacGregor's and Medicia's condos wired. Last night MacGregor hypnotized Dida so that she will enter a trance-like state with all these scientists at this meeting. They will give her Angiotox, observe her response, and use her willingness to take the drug as an argument with investors that they are confident the drug is safe. Twisted, isn't it?"

"Very. But why hypnotize her?"

"That's not quite clear. Seems *all* who attend this meeting have undergone hypnosis. In a bedroom conversation between MacGregor and Dida two weeks ago, he suggested that he's influencing reality by controlling the participants' perceptions … but that's so farfetched, I can't believe he was serious. More likely, the SS is the way MacGregor's found to guarantee secrecy. After hypnosis, they don't talk because they can't remember."

"Incredible."

"Yes, indeed."

"So what now?" asked Morgan.

"We wait. I want to make sure Dida emerges in one piece. And I'm always hoping someone will say something revealing as they exit."

"OK. We wait. But I'd rather be looking for Steve."

Winston shrugged, "We'll find him."

He turned to watch the screens.

The minutes ticked by.

Captain Nichols saw it first. She pointed at the monitor of the road running from Massachusetts Avenue to Angion.

"Chief, look!"

Winston's eyes widened. "O my God!"

47.

SUNDAY, APRIL 24

As they walked up the steps to Angion, Dida leaned over, "George, this is scaring me."

The bulge in his crotch stiffened.

Oh, blimey, she'll be cool sugar in the sack tonight.

"Don't worry, my sweet," he murmured, "you're perfectly safe."

She squeezed his hand.

Once inside, he led her to his office. The clock read 5:19 – thirty minutes till daybreak.

He opened the closet and pulled out two robes, one white, the other dark scarlet. He handed the white one to Dida and put on the other: a thick red satin that cascaded from his shoulders to his ankles. It reminded him of simpler times: like a professor at a graduation commencement.

Dida zipped up hers, olive skin a contrast against the white satin. "Beautiful, George!"

"Yes, Dida, pomp and circumstance make for an easier transition into the hypnotic state. They spur the imagination."

She laughed. "You're priceless, Georgie. What's the plan, exactly?"

"You'll be front and center so all can watch. The SS will determine a safe starter dose. Once that's agreed, we'll give you the Angiotox through your IV. All you have to do is lay back and look pretty."

"How will you know it's a safe dose?"

"Dida, relax. These are some of the finest scientific minds in the world. When the SS turns its attention to a question, these minds work together, just like an ultra-fast, parallel-processing super-computer."

"If everyone's hypnotized, George, why don't you just *tell* them I took the Angiotox, without actually administering it? That way everybody wins – I have no side-effects, everyone thinks I took the Angiotox, and the investors are happy!"

"That would be cheating!" George's eyes twinkled, "But even if we considered not playing by the rules – and we'd *never* do that – it would be impossible for them – and you – to believe something directly *contrary* to their perceptions. The SS only allows me the power to control their *interpretations* of reality. *Capisce?*"

She sighed, "OK. One small step for me, one giant leap for Angiotox."

MacGregor smiled, "Here, let me get your IV started. Hold out your arm."

She complied.

He pulled out a cigar box from his desk: rubber tourniquet, alcohol wipes, sterile 18-gauge angiocath, and Band-aid dressing. In a minute there was a capped IV tube in Dida's forearm.

He looked at his watch: 5:40 AM.

"Okay. Showtime. Sunrise in nine minutes."

Inside Angion's Security Control Center, Riker studied the monitor as the scientists walked towards the Arena. Something didn't feel right. He turned to Calibri, sitting at another console. "He doesn't know we're watching?"

Calibri shook his head. "He has no idea. I promised him we wouldn't. I told him we saw all we needed last week."

He puffed on his Cohiba.

They both studied the monitor.

Eventually, Calibri said, "He was insistent we shouldn't. He promised me doom and destruction, if we did. He's crazy."

Riker nodded. "Yes. And incompetent, even though he's very smart."

"There!" Calibri's yellow, crooked finger poked at the screen, "With my sweet niece." He cackled, "She's more of a devil than he is – more than his match!"

Riker chuckled, "They deserve each other."

Calibri glanced over at him, "He does *not* deserve Dida. He is fortunate to kiss her feet."

Riker nodded, but he was sure his assessment of Dida was not as high as Calibri's.

Calibri looked over to Alpha at another console.

"Show us the Arena," he hissed.

The screen flashed black, then re-focused with a wide-angle view of the Arena, a group of white lab coats milling on the floor and first balconies, the podium empty. Next to the podium was a chaise longue, as if waiting for someone to recline, and a small side table with several lab instruments.

"Not much happening," said Riker.

"Watch!" commanded Calibri.

A hooded, red-robed male figure emerged from a side door, carrying a golden globe in his outstretched arms, and set it down on the podium. Suddenly quiet, the white coats moved to form semi-circles facing the dais. From under a fold the robed figure brought out a small, lidded golden bowl, which he set on the side table. Then, he stepped behind the podium and stretched out his arms to the orb.

A low-pitched hum started: "Ooommm." Riker glanced at Calibri, but the old man was focused on the monitor, the tip of his tongue darting out from time to time to wet his lips.

The sound crescendoed. The man in the red robe slowly raised his arms over his head, the chant from the robed voices growing louder, ever louder.

"OOOOOOMMMMM ..."

As the chant swelled to a roar, the figure dropped his arms just as the first light of dawn, a shaft of hot orange-red brilliance, flashed down upon the orb and reflected out into a million bright sparkles, transforming the Arena into a red golden spectacle.

"AD HOMINEM!" shouted the blood-red robe.

Dead silence.

Transfixed, Riker held his breath, his companions likewise quiet, all eyes on the monitor. But for a time there was no motion, no sound from the Arena.

Then MacGregor tapped the podium three times with his finger.

Tap, tap, tap.

A swishing sound could be heard off-screen.

"Back off," said Riker.

Alpha pulled away on the viewing angle, revealing a hooded, white-robed female form beside MacGregor.

"Dida," murmured Riker.

"Yesss," hissed Calibri.

On the screen MacGregor pointed at Dida, then turned to the assembly.

"Now is the dawning of a new day," he declared. "Our day. History will record this the birth of the New Science."

Riker and Calibri glanced at each other.

"Ours is the future," cried MacGregor, his voice resonating to the far reaches of the Arena.

A murmur of assent rose from the robed figures.

"Today you will witness the first administration of Angiotox to a human being. No less than Angion's President, our beloved Dida Medicia, has agreed to this historic role."

The robed figures solemnly applauded. Dida raised her hand.

"We will need assistance!" cried MacGregor. "Alison? Alison! Please come join us."

On the first balcony a woman left her position and walked to the stairs. Meanwhile, MacGregor called out to the assembly, "My first question today is simple. In this initial test of Angiotox, what should be our starting dose?"

After a moment of silence, an uproar ensued as several scientists began to talk loudly, followed by more voices as others joined in, all shouting questions and venturing opinions. Watching the video, Riker found it impossible to understand anything as the din worsened; however, eventually it subsided until only three chattering voices remained: those of Pieter and Mai, whom Riker recognized as part of MacGregor's research group, and that of a man with a young face, though with premature gray at the temples.

"Who's the third wheel?" asked Riker.

Bravo hit several keys on his computer, yielding an Angion company directory. "Volker Luft," he said, "expert in clinical pharmacology – drug development. Two Ph.D.'s. Before joining Angion he patented several biomolecules now in clinical testing. This stuff's his baby."

Riker turned back to the monitor. The three had stopped. All was silent in the Arena but for a harmonious "oommm" from the assembly.

MacGregor called out, "Doctor Luft, what have you concluded?"

Luft spoke slowly, "All we can do is estimate. Unfortunately, the data are inconsistent. The tests in rats suggest a safe but effective dose in humans should be about one thousand to two thousand milligrams, but the tests in mice suggest the dose should be only five or ten milligrams – between the two species the estimates differ by a factor of more than a hundred. My initial conclusion was that in such a situation the safest starting dose would be the lower limit. Instead, Pieter and Mai believe the rat data make good estimates, but that the mouse data are off. They believe Dr. August made mistakes, so they distrust his numbers. They also state they have done their own set of experiments that show the numbers should be much higher in mice. I find this odd, because they have never before mentioned these experiments to the Science Service. Yet, odd or not, they have done these experiments. Therefore, I agree with Pieter and Mai: human dosing should be based on the rat data. A safe, effective starting dose should be one thousand milligrams."

"Thank you, Doctor Luft," said MacGregor. "And the SS agrees?"

"We do," intoned the assembly, in unison.

"Very well," said MacGregor. He turned to Alison, standing next to him. "Alison, the dose will be one thousand milligrams. Please help Dida prepare."

He gestured to an IV pole on the chaise longue from which hung a bag of dextrose 5% and normal saline, D5NS– a balanced mixture of water, salt, and sugar. Alison took Dida by the elbow and guided her to the longue.

Once Dida was settled, Alison attached tubing from the D5NS bag to the angiocath in Dida's arm. She then turned a stopcock, and fluid started dribbling slowly out of the IV bag into the vein.

"Are you ready?" asked MacGregor, his voice echoing in the chamber.

Dida nodded, "I am ready."

On the side table rested the small golden bowl, its lid encrusted with tiny emeralds, rubies, pearls, and diamonds. MacGregor removed the lid, revealing a pile of dark red crystals.

"Behold," he said solemnly. "Angiotox. Our success. Our happiness. Our future!"

The blood red crystals flickered in the Arena's golden light. The ruby crystals, the jeweled bowl, the golden orb, the white-robed woman, the pink sunrise, together created a surreal beauty.

Yet Calibri, Riker, Alpha, and Bravo remained silent, eyes on the monitor, the only sound the hiss of Calibri's breath and his near silent whisper, "*Nipotina.*"

Alison looked to MacGregor, "One thousand milligrams?"

MacGregor nodded.

Alison spooned the red crystals into a beaker on a scale next to the bowl. A digital display registered their weight: *322 ... 635 ... 727 ... 942 ... 958 ... 978 ... 992 ... 1003. ...* She ladled a small crystal back off: *1000.*

MacGregor looked up to the assembly and proclaimed, "One thousand milligrams!"

The entire group nodded.

"Alison, please prepare the Angiotox for injection," he said.

Alison nodded. Slowly she poured saline from a flask into the beaker. The liquid turned a clear, deep, ruby red as it flowed over the Angiotox crystals.

Riker noticed himself sweating.

Why am I nervous?

He *never* lost his cool – not when avoiding snipers in the Vietnam jungle, not when knifing a boy in a Saigon alley, not when shooting a rival on an Afghanistan road. But now he was drenched in sweat.

Something's wrong.

"Back it up," said Riker, referring to the video zoom, but secretly thinking about the entire chain of events. What was wrong? What had they missed?

Alpha hit buttons. The scene zoomed out to include Dida on the chaise, Alison next to her, and MacGregor with the Angiotox.

MacGregor stepped back to the podium and held the beaker over his head, its contents turning darker as the crystals dissolved.

"Behold, Angiotox!" he cried. "Angiotox is the most potent …"

The assembly took up the mantra, " …THE MOST POTENT TREATMENT FOR BRAIN CANCER KNOWN TO MAN."

With everyone else focused on the one screen, it was Alpha who first noticed the activity on his own monitor.

"Look!" he cried.

The others turned, jaws dropping virtually in unison.

"You've got to be kidding," said Riker.

In disbelief they stared at the screen – on which could be seen a dozen leather-clad, bearded and tattooed men crowding through Angion's front door.

"*Dio mio*," breathed Calibri.

48.

SUNDAY, APRIL 24

Around the time MacGregor and Dida were entering Angion, Steve was in the middle of a crowd of Hellraisers, rocketing down Interstate 93 towards Boston.

Shortly before dawn they pulled over at the Somerville exit, their engines roaring.

Jake yelled, "OK, Doc. Break a leg, dude!"

Betty slid off the back of Jake's bike and took hold of Steve's Harley, the one from Flash. Steve didn't hesitate but stepped up to Jake, turned, and put his hands behind his back. Jake slapped a pair of handcuffs onto his wrists and wrapped an oil-stained bandana around Steve's head, covering his eyes.

Steve grimaced, "Thanks a lot."

Jake helped him settle on the back of the Road King. Then he threaded a leather strap around the handcuffs and tied it to the back of the seat.

"OK, Doc, now *no one* will think we're friends. Keep your balance. If we tip, you're road kill."

"Save your breath," Steve retorted. "We're taking this guy. No side trips, no sightseeing, no accidents, no problem."

"*You* the man, Doc."

Jake kicked the starter, and the 1450 cc engine rumbled back to life. He turned to the bikers, "August rocks!"

And they yelled back, "August rocks!"

Steve could see nothing through the oily blindfold. Seated behind Jake, his handcuffed hands holding tight to the seat, the engine roaring between his legs, he imagined the other bikers around him, their hair streaming as they flew free into unknown dangers.

At Winston Visual Systems the monitor filled with a dozen motor-cycles pouring into the Angion parking lot, in the center a giant Harley cruiser on which sat two men, a brute with buzz cut, goatee, and earring, and behind him a grungy, unshaven lean figure, blind-folded, hands behind his back.

Morgan gasped, "Steve!"

"Zoom in," commanded Winston.

The camera displayed handcuffed wrists roped to the bike seat.

Morgan whirled on Winston. "Get him out of there!"

Winston stretched his arm towards her. "Morgan, stay calm. We're watching. We're in control."

But she pushed him away. "Schmidt!! Look at the situation. You're *no way* in control. Some damn biker will slit his throat, and you can do nothing *except* watch. You're not in control. You're crazy!"

Captain Nichols stepped forward, "Now Ms. Najar – Morgan – don't be rash."

"Rash! Rash? I'll show you rash!"

Morgan spun. There was a door next to the elevator. In an eyeblink she was through it.

Yes! Stairs!!

She ran.

Level 7 ... 6 ... 5 ... 4 ... 3 ... 2 ... 1. Out the staircase, then she guessed a left turn, then a right ...

At the end of a corridor she found herself facing a large door, paneled with four plates of frosted glass through which she could see morning light. She contemplated trying to break one open; but they were too nar-row to crawl through.

She hurled her weight against the door's push bar. Didn't budge.

She tried again, slamming against the bar, bruising her hip – again, and then again, and then again. Tears flowed down her cheeks in pain and rage.

The dawn's light taunted her through the frosted panels.

"Morgan, stop! You're hurting yourself."

Winston was walking briskly towards her.

"You bastard," she gasped between sobs and slams. "No! I'm not hurting myself. *You* are. You're hurting me, and you're hurting Steve!"

He grabbed her shoulder.

She stared at the rumpled little old man in the gray suit and red tie. Never before had she considered killing a human being. But she *had* to get to Steve, and Winston was in her way. If she *had* to kill him to reach Steve, to save Steve, then she would.

She readied herself, wincing as she put weight on her bruised right hip, set forwards of her left leg, in preparation for a roundhouse kick to Winston's neck.

But Winston was speaking, "Morgan, listen to me! I'll go with you. But we can't break cover. So here's the story: I'm your attorney, helping you make inquiries into Steve's death. Before he died Steve told you that the senior Angion scientists have a special meeting Sundays at dawn. So you and I are making an impromptu visit to solicit a private audience with MacGregor. Got it?"

Morgan relaxed, if only slightly. She decided not to kill Winston, at least not yet.

"You're coming with me?" she asked.

"Right. We'll go together."

She grabbed his arm. "Wait, what if he recognizes you?"

"It's been more than ten years. I've changed a great deal: clothes, mannerisms, beard, body." He smiled, ruefully. "I used to be thin as a rail."

Morgan looked hard into his eyes. "You *will* help me get Steve out?"

"Yes. My presence gives you a cover story to make your appearance here believable. Anything else, and you're likely dead. Even as stands it's a stretch."

Morgan shrugged, "OK, that's something."

Winston pulled a black object from his pocket, hit a button, and the door chirped. He pressed on the bar.

"After you," he said.

Morgan stepped into the light, her breath steaming in the cold air. Her hip ached.

Winston took her elbow. "Well, my dear, they say improvisation is an art. I hope you're feeling creative."

"I'll paint you a Mona Lisa to save Steve August."

"Screw me sideways," snarled Riker. "How'd they get the door open?"

A dozen bikers were crowding into Angion's entry.

Alpha glanced at his computer. "Thumbprint pass code: Steve August."

"August? How the hell? Zoom in!! Front view – from the hallway."

Alpha's fingers flew across his keyboard. The scene switched to a view of the corridor, the bikers moving fast towards them. At the head was a haggard, blindfolded man, hands behind his back, pushed forwards by a hard-muscled guy with a crew cut holding a gun to his head. Blindfold, leather-jacket, and three-day beard notwithstanding, Riker recognized the blindfolded man.

"Screw me backwards. August!"

He turned to Calibri, "Sir, please stay here with Delta. Safer that way."

He spun on Bravo and Alpha. "Grab automatics. We're nailing these bastards."

He turned to Delta at the security desk, "Lock the Arena. Keep them out at all costs!"

Riker threw on his jacket, covering the holster with the Glock under his left arm. Bravo pulled three AK-47 rifles from the wall cabinet, tossing one to Riker and another to Alpha.

Riker flicked his safety, nodding at Bravo. "Takes me back … Saigon '72. I get August."

Bravo grunted, hefting his rifle, "Mine's Mozambique, May First, '83 – fun war. Their flag always makes me feel cozy. Yeah, you get August. I'll take the rest."

Alpha grinned, revealing small uneven teeth. "Only what I leave behind!"

And they raced out the door.

The Hellraisers put Steve's thumb on the scanner, and he heard the door click open.

He could see nothing. Their boots echoed off the marble hall floor, while Jake's Smith & Wesson kept bumping against the back of his neck.

His other senses sharpened. He tasted salt. He smelled the bikers' sweat. He felt Jake's iron grip on his arm. He heard leather chaps rubbing, guns clinking.

They were moving fast, likely nearing the Arena door.

"Stop!"

He did not know the voice.

Jake spun Steve around, the gun jabbing against his neck.

Jake spat out, "See this asshole? You know who he is? Dead man walkin' – that's who. And he might be a dead man talkin'. What's he worth to ya? What's that drug … Angiotox? What's that worth?"

"Drop your weapons!" said another voice, off to the right.

Steve heard the cock of a rifle, but then the clatter of a dozen guns pulled from Hellraisers' holsters. Now everyone was holding a gun – everyone except for him.

"You can't shoot!" yelled Jake. "Ya don't wanna hurt your boy here. You need to know what he knows, and who knows what he knows. Then you got your plumbers and painters. But you start a war, man, and your boy buys the farm. And then my insurance policy kicks in. Dig it?"

"Why would August tell *you* anything?"

"'Cuz, Big Daddy, he trusted me. Once upon a time I was his patient. I hit my head, and Doc August patches me up. He figures I owe him, so he comes to me for help. And here we are."

A chill went up Steve's spine.

What if he's really selling me out?

"What do you want for August?"

"What do you *think* we want, man?" sneered Jake. "We want a piece."

"Maybe *you're* the dead meat," said a new voice, this one to their left but closer, maybe twenty feet.

Steve heard another rifle cock, and then his hyper-tuned nostrils whiffed the guy's scent, a mix of perspiration and expensive cologne. The scent was only a hint, but it was enough: same as when Miller had let Boston Edison into the apartment.

"Hold on!" yelled Steve, his voice echoing. "Riker, that you?"

"Yes, August. Pleasure to finally meet you."

Steve turned towards the voice.

"Riker, you know you're not the man to cut the deal. Jake needs MacGregor. Or even better: Calibri."

Steve held his breath.

"Goddamn you, August," snarled Riker. "I speak for George MacGregor, and even for Antonio Calibri. You puny punk, you listen when I talk!"

Steve's head snapped back, Jake's grip tight in his hair, the gun's nozzle pushing into his cheek.

"Quiet, asshole!" spat Jake. "I'm doing the talking here."

But an electronic chirp interrupted. Steve heard rustling and a snap.

Riker's voice was flat, "Don Calibri wants to talk directly. Okay, you're on speaker."

Calibri's disembodied voice echoed in the corridor: "Michael ... Michael ... maintain your composure. August is right. I'm the one who can buy him. I can offer these gentlemen the guarantees they need to walk out alive with money in their pockets!"

"Here's the deal, Calibri," replied Jake loudly. "Fifty thousand bucks for each of my buddies here, and a hundred thousand for me. That's about six hundred thousand, chump change for a big-shot like you. I hear Angiotox is worth millions. In return you get August, and your goddamn notebook, and the copies he made of the original numbers. That's the witness and all the evidence. You game?"

There was silence for a time.

Then the hiss was loud over the speaker. "Yessss, I'm game. You're right, Mr. Jake. You have what we want; and the price is reasonable. You know where the lab books are, and the copies of the original data?"

Jake shoved the gun into Steve's cheek. "You know, don't you, Doc? Tell him you know!"

"Of course I know," said Steve quietly. "But that doesn't mean I'm telling."

The speakerphone amplified Calibri's savage whisper, "You are wrong, my boy. You will tell. Oh, yesss, you will most definitely tell."

He then continued, his voice louder, addressing the larger audience. "Gentlemen, I will meet your demands. In fact, I will double them: each one gets a one-hundred thousand dollar bankroll – tax free!" The chuckle was audible over the speaker. "And every year I'll pay each man another hundred thousand, as part of the team. But there's a catch. We must all function as one. Jake, will you lead them? Let us unite!"

Steve sensed the layout. Riker was to his left, maybe with at least one extra gunman, likely another in the corridor to the right, and another directly in front in the corridor through which they had entered. Against these professionals killers were ten very tough but amateur bikers.

Now was the moment.

Without a sound his legs went limp, his body dropping to the floor out of Jake's grip. As he fell, he tucked his legs tight and rolled onto his back, flipping his handcuffed wrists out from under his feet.

He could hear Jake yelling, the other bikers moving, Riker barking commands.

Chaos!

With his wrists in front of him Steve ripped off the blindfold. He was against the wall of the corridor, next to the door leading to the Arena. In front of him were Jake and two other bikers, but beyond them a tall older man in a crew-cut, flak jacket, black turtleneck, black jeans, holding an AK-47, and beside him a stocky muscular brute, also with an assault rifle. To Steve's right were the other Hellraisers, their guns drawn, and beyond them another guy with crew-cut, attitude, and a third AK-47.

Calibri's voice yelled across the speakerphone: "Keep him alive!"

Jake was spinning around, gun at the ready. Steve remembered their earlier conversation: *Make it real.*

Jake was leveling the gun at Steve, but Riker was running towards them, yelling, "Don't shoot!"

Steve's hands were faster than thought. Jake's wrist was in his grasp. In a classic *bagua* move he used Jake's weight against him, leading his wrist in the direction of motion while turning it inexorably out and away. Jake's body had to follow the wrist, twisting backwards, and the Smith & Wesson floated into space. Steve let go as Jake's body completed its flip, and in a smooth continuation he grabbed the gun on its trajectory.

Riker, Alpha, Bravo, the bikers – no one in that instant knew where to point their weapons – at each other, at Jake, at Steve?

Within a breath Steve leveled the gun at the lock and fired, crashing into the Arena moments after the last drops of Angiotox had entered Dida's vein.

As they mounted the steps to Angion, Morgan felt Winston's tug on her arm. He pointed silently.

They caught a glimpse of two bikers disappearing from sight running around the far corner of the building.

Winston shook his head, "Don't think they saw us."

At the top of the steps was a black leather glove propping the inside door open. They could hear voices echoing from the corridor.

Morgan took off her shoes, her bare feet silent on the floor.

Then there was a gunshot and a crash of splintering wood.

Winston pulled out his pistol, but Morgan had already started running – towards Steve, she was sure. She could *feel* him. He was close, and he was in serious trouble.

Ahead, she could see the bikers at the end of the corridor, but between them and Morgan was a man in black fatigues with a nasty-looking gun, looking towards the bikers. He didn't see Morgan.

Her bare feet made no sound.

She grabbed his head, seized the rifle, and ripped his body backwards. Within an instant the AK-47 was in her hands and the man was bent over her knee with her left hand pulling his hair back, ready to break his spine.

A name was sewn into the shirt pocket: "Bravo."

Morgan pushed the rifle butt hard against his neck, closing off his carotids and his airway, and without another sound he went unconscious. She slammed his head against the wall for good measure.

"Bravo!" she said.

She looked up. Winston was leveling his pistol at two flak-jacketed men, who were both aiming their assault weapons back at Winston and Morgan. Between them the leather-clad bikers surrounded a broken door, all with guns, some uncertainly aiming at Winston and Morgan, others at the two men.

But Winston played the hand as planned, "I am the attorney for my client here, Morgan Najar, and she's looking for George MacGregor, because she needs to ask him questions about the disappearance of Steve August. Violence towards us will incriminate all of you. Please stay calm."

She had to admire his chutzpah, staring down firepower that could waste a platoon.

One biker was staggering to his feet in front of the broken door.

"Not them!" he shouted at the others, "That's Doc's girlfriend."

And he pointed at the two men in flak jackets, "Them!"

As a unit, the Hellraisers focused their sights on the two men. One growled, "Dead meat, Jake."

A voice hissed over a speakerphone, "Riker! What's happening?"

Morgan's eyes were on the man with the cell phone, who was ignoring the voice, instead sizing up the situation. Confronting him and his teammate were ten angry bikers, pistols and sawed-off shotguns at the ready, not to mention an old man waving a pistol and Morgan holding Bravo's AK-47.

"Fall back," commanded the man.

They backed up the corridor, their machine guns leveled.

"Where's August?" yelled Winston.

"You'll see August in hell!" yelled Riker. "Let's go."

The two men spun out of sight around the bend of the corridor.

Winston, Morgan, and the bikers exchanged glances.

"By Jove, this feels good," said Winston, hefting his pistol. "So, where is he?"

The biker leader Jake pointed at the splintered door, beyond which they could hear angry voices, then a gunshot. "Ran in there."

"OK!" exclaimed Morgan.

"Wait!" yelled Winston, but Morgan had no time to chat. AK-47 in hand, she crashed through the broken doorway.

49.

MacGregor held up the beaker with its ruby red solution. "Behold, Angiotox – the most …"

And the group responded, " …THE MOST POTENT TREATMENT FOR BRAIN CANCER KNOWN TO MAN."

But even as they spoke the mantra, MacGregor sensed a wrinkle – something *odd*. Maybe Dida? She was a new addition – and never before had a participant simultaneously been a subject. But she lay sedated, oblivious, on the divan.

He had composed a symphony, perfect and harmonious, yet now a violin sounded out of tune.

No matter. I must move ahead.

He placed the beaker on the table and filled a syringe with the crimson fluid.

"Alison, mind the tubing, please."

Dutifully she held the valve assembly, while he attached the syringe.

He turned to his congregation. "Ladies and gentlemen, I give you the world's first administration of Angiotox. Dida, are you ready?"

Her eyes were dull, a combination of School-aid and hypnosis. "Yes, I am. Angiotox – Angiotox is the …"

And the assembly again spoke, " …THE MOST POTENT TREATMENT FOR BRAIN CANCER KNOWN TO MAN."

MacGregor chuckled: humans were *so* predictable.

"Friends and colleagues," he proclaimed, "I give you … Angiotox!"

Pressing on the syringe, he plunged the red liquid into her arm.

An event of worldwide import!

"Dida, share what you are experiencing."

The elixir had emptied into the vein.

"There is burning in my arm …" she murmured. "The Angiotox is everywhere. It is very warm."

The Arena was silent – almost silent. Never before had he noticed how they breathed: a whispered collective breath in, then a soft exhale, then a quiet inhalation, then a gentle expiration.

I even set the tempo of their breathing!

His cock stiffened.

But Dida was saying, "My head hurts. There's a mist. Everything's blue."

MacGregor was fascinated. No mouse could talk.

She continued, "My feet and hands feel like … like pins and needles … My body is tingling."

Her words were slurring, slowing. "I am … numb."

She closed her eyes.

There was silence, except for the bodies breathing.

How different species can be! Neither the mice nor the rabbits ever showed a sedating effect.

The scientists were quiet. Watching. Breathing.

MacGregor waited with them. Alison stood at his side: obedient and silent. All were focused on Dida, strangely peaceful on the longue. But she looked very pale.

Abruptly, the silence was broken – scuffling beyond the Arena's first-floor doorway, then a *thud* against the door. Then several *thumps*, growing louder.

What the hell?

He sensed the S.S.'s attention split: towards him, towards Dida's body, but also towards the noises. Confusion. Even fear!

Damn it to hell, what if we break apart?

Over the banging coming from beyond the door, he cried out, "You hear nothing; you are aware of nothing outside the confines of the Arena. Your focus is here with me. You are safe here with me."

He decided to push the envelope.

Now is the time!

"I am your leader. I am your master. You will obey me, and I will protect you. I AM YOUR GOD."

For a brief moment he sensed the focus of the SS fully back on him.

But then a gunshot sounded outside, and a dirty bearded man in a black leather jacket crashed through the door into the Arena – and then all focus was lost.

Tension erupted like a volcano. The scientists started screaming, chattering gibberish, moving about randomly, some gesturing at each other, some at him, some at Dida, some at the skylight.

Total chaos!

Behind him was a gurgling from the chaise longue, but Alison stepped up, diverting his attention, slack-jawed, spittle dribbling off a corner of her mouth.

"George?" she murmured. "You want me? Please?"

Her arms were outstretched towards him, eyes blank. He took a step back but bumped against the chaise. He looked down.

O god!

Enlarging giant reddish blotches were spreading across Dida's skin. Under the robe her body looked nine months pregnant. Her face was deep violet, pulsing, swelling, her cheeks bulging grossly purple plump, even while her skull seemed unchanged up top. Each eye was a reddish ball with a little central black spot. The gurgling, ever louder, was coming from her gaping mouth. He would have sworn she was staring at him, eyelids pulling back, nostrils flaring.

And then she screamed – one long cry of agony and betrayal. As a child George had seen a cat crushed under the wheel of a truck. It had made exactly that sound. His skin tightened.

The scream lasted only a second, but it was long enough for him to sense the S.S.'s collective energy had turned onto this screeching wretch.

We can save Angiotox! We must!

He cried out, "Listen to me! AD HOMINEM!!! Remember, Angiotox is the …"

And the assembly took up the shout, " …THE MOST POTENT TREATMENT FOR BRAIN CANCER KNOWN TO MAN!"

Yes, he could see it. She had taken another breath. Her skin was less purple, more pink. All he had to do was choose what he willed.

"MacGregor!"

Damn it!

He had forgotten the idiot who had broken in. If this bastard remained alive, then the perceptions of the SS would be forever compromised, and then Dida would die, and then he would lose Angiotox.

Reaching into the folds of his robe, looking for the slit over the .38 strapped to his thigh, he turned to face the leather-clad figure. But then he froze.

Steve August was pointing a pistol at his head.

"August!" he puffed. "You're dead. We left you in the Harbor to rot!"

Where's that bloody slit?

"MacGregor, you're going down. Look at you. You just killed your lady friend."

The gurgling was slowing, but there was something warm at his feet. He looked down to see a pool of blood collecting at his sandals, bubbling up gently from her mouth onto the floor. Another red stain, centered over her inner thighs, was spreading across her white robe.

God damn!

George cried, "You pathetic dingo, if Dida dies, it won't be *me* who goes down. *You* were the one who faked the data. *You* seduced her. *You* enlisted her. Your only redemption is for her to live ... Only the positive will be remembered, the negative will be forgotten, and in being forgotten it will be annihilated!"

His hand kept groping at his robe.

But Steve's gun did not waiver. "You're crazy, man. Angiotox is a disaster. For that mistake Dida paid the ultimate price. You set me up. You know it. I know it. And you're going down."

With a loud, "Faugh!" MacGregor looked at his robe, fanning it away from his body. There was the pocket, where his hand had been searching, but tight, black stitches held the slit shut. The gun was beyond his reach.

"What the bloody hell!"

Turning to the bleeding body, he roared, "Who did this? DIDA!"

The voice echoed from far above – "Wrong again, Georgie. Dida did nothing: never more than a patsy. No, Bossman, you're a loose cannon, so we made sure you wouldn't fire."

MacGregor could see a lone figure up on the fifth floor balcony, the dawn's light glinting off a rifle.

"Riker?" his voice echoed.

"You betcha, Georgie! The punk's right. Your girlfriend's dead, and you killed her, and Don Calibri is very, very upset – you get my drift?"

MacGregor turned to the body on the longue. Blood was welling from its mouth, chest heaving, blood bubbling with every spasm. Suddenly, the muscles seized, shaking her from head to toe, splattering blood everywhere.

And then it was silent, arms and legs at crooked angles – no motion, no breath, no sound.

A murmur arose from the assembly.

He spun back to his congregation.

"My colleagues," he began, "AD HOMINEM!"

He said it with force, and they seemed to respond – shoulders squared, facing him at attention.

"Look at what Steve August has done!" he shouted, pointing at Dida's body. "His unwelcome presence in our hallowed sanctuary, his invasion of the S.S., has created a discord, a contrary perception. We must destroy this blemish to restore our harmony."

He sensed their anger!

"And now," MacGregor shouted, "Now we have *another* intruder! Up there!" And he pointed at Riker on the fifth balcony.

"My colleagues, we can still save Angiotox, but we must purge the S.S. Reality is ours alone!! Those above go up! Those below, come forward! My fellow scientists, *do what you must! ATTACK!!!*"

The hypnotized mobs shifted in unison. MacGregor felt a surge of confidence.

I am their god!

The scientists on the first balcony, maybe about two dozen, turned towards the staircases. But the forty or so at ground level pushed forwards, their full attention on August.

"*ATTACK!*" screamed MacGregor again.

Riker and August, their dead corpses side-by-side – now *that* would be sweet!

"*ATTACK!*" he screamed a third time.

If he joined the mass, then he would be better protected. He started towards the crowd, his legs churning, his robe flapping against his ankles.

August's voice rang out, "MacGregor – stop!"

MacGregor laughed, "You're a dead man!"

He knew the enraged scientists would soon annihilate August.

A weight slammed into his back. He fell forwards, arms outstretched towards the advancing white coats. As quick as bat's wings snaring a moth, August's hands flew across his body, one pulling back on his hair, the other wrapping around his right shoulder. His legs tangled, but then he realized a strong thigh had looped around his left leg and slammed into his crotch. Within a second he was lying immobile on the marble floor, his chin pressed against the ground, August's leg dangerously close to his genitals and August's foot flipped around behind his knee, pinning his hip.

August's hand released his scalp, but only to press the business end of a gun against the back of his head.

"Stop!" bellowed August. "Stop, or your leader dies!"

The scientists had reached the steps leading up to the dais. MacGregor could see their faces: angry, panicked that the S.S. might be destroyed by this evil, evil young man. But there was another …

The voice rang out from above. "That's perfect, August. Hold steady. Say your prayers, assholes. Don Calibri says good-bye!"

MacGregor knew his minions upstairs needed more time to reach the fifth floor. Meanwhile, he and August were in plain sight, easy targets.

That instant wood splintered loud behind them.

August gasped, "Morgan!"

August shifted his weight, rolling the two of them onto his back, the scientist's gargantuan frame on top of the lithe athlete, but MacGregor had no control with August firmly pinning his shoulder, neck, and pelvis. Unsuccessfully he flailed his arms and legs, like a turtle helpless on its back.

"Let me go! Let me go! LET ME GO!"

MacGregor found himself looking straight up. From far above, a flash of morning sunshine glinted off Riker's gun – pointing at them.

In his last glimpse of this world George MacGregor witnessed the muzzle of the AK-47 pour out orange fire as Riker squeezed the trigger.

The first bullet tore into his gut, the searing pain hitting his consciousness just as the second and third punctured his right lung.

But the fourth cut the experience short, slamming into his right eye. Within a millisecond the bullet had buried deeper, crashing into the base of his skull, splintering the bone into fragments that tore into his brain.

The bullet moved forward an inch more, coming to rest in his brainstem, leaving him blind, deaf, and dumb – only to sense more and more pain as more and more bullets crashed into his body, reminding him for a few last seconds, seconds that would stretch out into eternity, that he was dead. Truly.

50.

SUNDAY, APRIL 24

Aghast, Winston watched Morgan barge into the Arena to the sound of rapid gunfire. His eyes locked with Jake's.

"It's a giant open space," Winston said, "five stories up. Give me three men. We'll circle to the top: sniper's view from high ground."

Jake nodded, "Max, Peewee, Duke – this guy's one of us. Do what he says. The rest of you're with me. Haul ass!" And Jake stepped to the doorway, poked his head through, and then rushed in, gun at the ready.

Winston calculated. He had told his people to wait an hour at Winnie's before entering. With no way to contact them and a battle raging, he and this ragtag troop of Hellraisers would have to win this one on their own. He waved at the three bikers – "Follow me!"

They raced up the stairs. Winston knew Angion's layout by heart, having studied its blueprints for hours looking for any vulnerability. The staircase would take them to the balcony overlooking the entire Arena, and also to a quick route to the rooftop, the helipad outside.

No longer a young man, he was panting by the time they reached the fifth floor landing.

"Here we go, boys," he gasped, slamming his weight into the stairwell door.

They raced down the hall towards the nearest entry to the Arena, from which came shouts and gunshots.

At the door Winston paused, pistol at the ready, Duke behind him. Peewee and Max spun to the other side of the doorway, shotguns cocked.

The gunfire had stopped. The four exchanged glances, then burst onto the balcony.

In that split-second Winston saw Riker standing at the opposite end of the Arena, his AK-47 leveled at a score of white coats moving towards him.

"Get down!" shouted Winston, throwing himself onto the balcony floor out of Riker's line of fire. But as he was rolling forwards, a word sounded loud in the Arena. It was just one word, but it seemed to Winston to shake the very foundations, like an earthquake forcing everyone's minds onto bedrock. The word hung in the air, echoing in the sudden silence.

"VERITAS."

The first three bullets hammered MacGregor's body against Steve's. Then the fourth turned the body into a corpse, smashing MacGregor's skull into his face, breaking his nose. No matter. He held the body tight, shielding himself from Riker's onslaught.

Whining bullets ricocheted off the marble as Riker macerated the corpse. Blood was everywhere. Steve's shield would not last long.

Behind him was the cock of a rifle, then the fast staccato of another AK-47, hurling bullets back at Riker.

Morgan!

Riker paused.

That was all he needed. MacGregor's body over him, he kicked against the floor slippery with blood, pushing himself and the corpse back to the chaise. A moment later he was safely underneath the chaise longue, MacGregor's corpse next to him, Dida's above him.

Morgan was behind the podium still firing non-stop. She handled the assault rifle awkwardly, yet the tracer bullets marked their trajectories with unmistakable accuracy. Steve had never seen her so beautiful nor so lethal.

"Morgan," he gasped. "Get out of here!"

"Over my dead body," she grunted, maintaining pressure on the trigger, hurling bullets at Riker. "Good to see you, too!"

"Morgan, stop, he's moved."

"Stephen Leland August, you're a piece of work. I come in here and save your pathetic ass – not even a 'thank you' – and now you're giving me advice."

But she stopped firing.

The Arena was quiet.

Morgan glared at him. "Steve, damn you. You think I've nixed my career, nearly killed an NSA agent, muscled a human ape into submission, and gunned down a trained assassin, just so you can tell me what to do?"

Man, do I love this woman!

But the pleasantries would have to wait.

Steve looked back to see dozens of white coats near the dais, staring at MacGregor's body. They had resumed their chatter: plaintive, desperate, angry. Some were looking up at Riker, but most were looking at Steve. Then more voices joined the din from above: lab coats streaming onto the fifth floor balcony.

There he is!

Riker had shifted to the opposite side of the Arena, up behind the dais. Thinking they would surround him, the white coats had closed in on three sides only to find themselves in his sights.

The chatter crescendoed. Two of the lab coats stepped back towards a door. Riker's rifle barked, and the two bodies fell, white stained with red.

"Quiet!" yelled Riker.

The mob was silent. A couple took a step towards Riker, but stopped at the sound of a fresh clip slamming into his gun.

"Back off – or die!" yelled Riker. "My men have the exits covered, and you have no escape. But all I want is Steve August. Then you can go home, and tomorrow go about your business. It's too bad about your friends," and he waved his gun at the two dead figures, "but that was necessary to teach you an important lesson. Disobey me, and you die. Obey me, and Angion lives. Give me August!"

The mob resumed its chatter.

Steve looked back to see several crouched Hellraisers, including Jake, running into the Arena with pistols and sawed-off shotguns, though at this distance they were no match against Riker's AK-47. Morgan held the firepower.

The scientists' babble took on a frenzied edge. Steve could see their faces, a short distance from the dais, staring at him as though he were an exceptionally peculiar specimen.

Abruptly the chatter stopped. Faces grim, they began advancing towards the dais. He looked up to the fifth balcony and saw the white coats also moving towards Riker, their arms outstretched, fists clenched.

"Come on, you bastards!" screamed Riker.

Steve's memory flashed to an image of Dida, telling him what she knew of MacGregor's SS.

There is a key!

He put all his remaining strength into a word, the single word that might save them. His soul, his heart, his entire being, welled up into this word, as though wrenched from him by a power much greater than his own. The word filled the Arena.

"VERITAS!!!"

Steve held his breath.

Does it mean nothing?

$\sim$

But the effect was profound. In front of him the white coats froze, but then turned to one another, some crying, some chattering, some quiet with mouths agape. They had no further interest in Steve. They huddled – touching, hugging, shaking their heads, their eyes on the bleeding corpses of MacGregor and Dida.

The lab coats on the fifth floor, however, reacted differently. Their eyes opened to see Riker's AK-47 pointing directly at them. As the last syllable of Steve's "VERITAS" echoed within the chamber, they threw up their hands and dropped onto the floor.

Standing at the top of the Arena, Riker waved his gun at the prone scientists. "Goddamn you, August. You saved their asses. But you, you son of a bitch," he yelled, "Your ass is *mine!*"

And he reopened fire at the chaise longue, bullets slapping into Dida's body above Steve's head. In response, Morgan started firing wildly towards the sound of Riker's rifle. And then Jake and his bikers, scattered behind tables and chairs around the periphery of the Arena, were firing at Riker, too – a rain of bullets.

As quickly as he had started his fusillade, Riker stopped. Steve looked around the corner of the chaise. Riker had grabbed a white figure, his arm around her throat, and was holding her in front of him.

The gunfire stopped.

"August, you orphan bastard, talk to me!"

"What do you want, Riker?" yelled back Steve. "Game's over. Angion's history. Medicia and MacGregor are dead. Your scientists are no longer slaves. Give it up!"

"August, you punk idiot, in five minutes the lab blows. All the world will know is there was one little lab fire, a few incendiaries left lying around, and *whamo!* But Calibri *still* has Angiotox – all the files are in the offices downtown."

"You saw what happened to Dida?"

"MacGregor screwed up the dosing. Silverstein's already proved the poison works. Sorry, asshole, you can't stop this train. No evidence! See you in hell!"

He tossed an object high into the air. It floated out over the Arena, then gradually gathered speed falling towards earth.

It took Steve a moment to realize what it was – *Grenade!*

Riker pushed away his human shield and backed out the door, firing indiscriminately at Steve, Morgan, and the bikers. Morgan responded with a spray of bullets, but she was aiming high to avoid the woman. In an instant he was gone.

The grenade hit the dais and bounced high.

"Duck!" shouted Steve.

The white coats threw themselves on the ground as the grenade arced up. It reached its zenith, suspended motionless, and then exploded.

VROOMMM!!!

Steve was under the chaise, Morgan behind the podium, the Hellraisers behind furniture, but the scientists were fully exposed. Shrapnel tore open garments, skin, and flesh, their white coats spotting red, pools of blood forming everywhere. They were screaming, some in pain, some in terror, all flat on the floor.

VROOMMM!!!!!!

Another one! Bastard!!

Before exiting Riker must have rolled a second grenade into the crowd of scientists on the fifth floor balcony.

The explosion had ripped into the balcony floor, and body parts were flying across the Arena. Some dropped through the gaping hole onto the balcony below, while others cascaded into the central space of the Arena, tumbling in grotesque poses until they smashed onto the ground.

Steve rolled out from under the chaise, hurdled over two dying scientists on the dais, and rushed to the podium. Morgan stepped out with the AK-47 under her right arm, her curves barely hidden beneath bloodied T-shirt and jeans.

Steve pulled her close.

"Morgan Najar, I love you!"

She smiled, and he kissed her mouth, their lips meeting after being so many worlds apart. After some time unknown she stepped back.

"And I love you, Steve August, more than you will ever know. But we must leave. You heard the man: the place is rigged to blow."

"Right. Morgan, *you* must leave! There are two guys inside right now getting the evidence that'll stop Angiotox. I've got to get to them! You … you just get out! Jake!"

The biker was looking around the Arena, bleeding bodies everywhere, "Man, you throw one helluva party."

"Listen, Jake, take Morgan and your men, and as many of the wounded as you can. Get away from the building! We've got five minutes."

Jake shook his head, "OK, we're on it. But we won't be able to handle more than one trip."

Steve's face was grim. "Do what you can."

He turned to Morgan. "Babe, please get out. I've got to go back."

"You nuts? You're going nowhere without me …"

Steve grabbed her shoulders, "How did you know I was here? Winston?"

She nodded. "Lab's surrounded with NSA."

He grunted. "No surprise. But without evidence he'll sink me faster than an anchor. Wish me luck. Hey, Jake, help me out!"

She had hoisted the AK-47 onto her shoulder, but the next second Jake was holding her arms, wrapped in a full Nelson.

"Goddamn you, Steve. And Goddamn you, Jake. Twice, you bastards!"

"Morgan, I love you. Jake, stay safe. I'll be back quick."

He flashed her a grin, waived his Baretta in a thumbs-up at Jake, and entered the depths of Angion.

Oh God, let me see her again!

51.

Running past doors marked with names of famous scientists, Steve wondered which were now lying dead in the Arena.

Up the stairs he went, three at a time. The storage freezer was on Level 5. He burst onto the top landing.

Across the hall the door to the freezer was slightly ajar. He checked his Beretta, then whirled through the doorway. Aisles of stacked shelves receded into darkness. The air was brittle, eighty C below zero, cold enough to freeze carbon dioxide gas into dry ice. His breath steamed in the light of a single bulb dangling from the ceiling.

"Bud? … Freddie? …," he called out softly.

SPLANK!

In the next aisle a test tube shattered on the floor.

Bud swore. "Doc! What the hell? You're supposed to be with Jake. We got this under control."

Steve turned the corner to find Freddie filling quart-size plastic bags with dry ice chips from a large wooden crate. Standing next to him, Bud was groping along racks of tubes trying to read their labels. On the floor was a broken test tube, around it small globs of frozen blood.

"Doesn't look under control. Those are the wrong racks. Here!" Steve pointed to the next shelf, loaded with tiny plastic vials. "These are the ones."

"Doc, we'd have figured it out."

"Yeah, but there's no time. A lot's happened in the last few minutes.

MacGregor's dead. Riker's here with heavy firepower. The lab's set to blow. We've got to get you and these samples out – now!"

Freddie whistled, "Blow me!"

Steve grabbed a bag with dry ice, stuffed it with plastic vials till almost full, and then tied it off. "They're all number-coded. Just toss them in, and let's go!"

Within seconds they were done. Steve glanced at his watch: two minutes left.

"Okay, let's fly!"

Three steps across the hall Steve was at the stairwell. He was not prepared for what happened next.

～

An unseen hand pulled him onto the landing, twisting his arm to snap it. Gunfire sounded behind them.

Steve recognized the move – kung fu, Cambodian or Vietnamese variant.

It was Riker. He had grabbed the arm holding the Beretta. Steve let the gun go, relaxing his left shoulder, pivoting his body forwards, following Riker's sweep but pushing his center of gravity inwards.

As his feet left the ground, Steve figured Riker wanted to slam him across the floor into the stairwell's iron railing, smashing his skull.

No way, baby!

At the last instant, just before he hit the ground, he seized Riker's ankle and pulled it against his chest. Riker went down, releasing Steve's arm, trying to break his own fall.

Together they spun across the landing, Steve on top of Riker's legs. It was Riker's left shoulder, not Steve's head, that slammed into the railing. There was a *snap* as Riker's arm left its socket.

Perfect!

If he dislodged the other one, Riker would be incapacitated. He wedged his right arm around Riker's and pulled back at the shoulder, tearing its ligaments. Riker grunted. Within a second the shoulder should pop.

Next to Steve's ear sounded a metal *click*, a pistol's hammer cocked.

"Nice and easy, August. Let go. Any fast moves … you die," hissed the voice.

Steve relaxed his grip.

Where are Bud and Freddie?

Riker wriggled out from under him, holding his useless left arm, grimacing in pain. "Goddamn you, August. I will dance on your grave."

The door behind them opened with the footsteps of another two men.

"Pick him up!" Riker commanded.

Several hands pulled him upright: one holding his scalp, another his neck, another his right arm, another twisting his left wrist. A rifle pushed into his back. Riker stood in front of him, arm dangling.

He picked up the Beretta, hefted its weight, and then slammed it into Steve's face. "Bastard!"

Steve felt a tooth chip and his nose further splinter, shards of bone digging into his cheek, blood flowing into his eyes and mouth.

Breathing hard, Riker stepped back, studying Steve's face with satisfaction.

"Sorry about your friends, August," he grinned. "They weren't ready for our level of competition."

Steve's heart sank.

The gunshots!

"Don't worry, partner," said Riker. "By the time we're done, you'll be wishing you'd died with McGregor. Alpha, hold him! Charlie, help me with this goddamn shoulder!"

Riker knelt. Charlie stood behind him, set his foot into Riker's armpit, wrapped his burly arms around the useless arm, and then with a sudden jerk snapped the shoulder back into the joint. Riker grunted, but his face betrayed intense pain.

"Thanks!" he said, eyes glistening.

Calibri interrupted, "Don't waste time. That crazed woman and her lawyer and their thugs are still out there."

"Hey, what about this?" said Alpha, Freddie's pack in his hand.

"I'll take that," snapped Riker. "If I'm reading this right, that's the reason the Boy Wonder's here. The biker assholes downstairs were a giant diversion."

Calibri turned to Steve, his voice an angry whisper. "I will speak freely, Steve August. You are an idiot. When your men broke into the freezer, we knew. And I watched on camera when you left your lady to run up here with your motorcycle friends. An easy trap. Don't worry: you have *no* power here!"

The old man patted Steve's bloody cheek, and then slowly took his hand to his mouth and licked his fingers. "I am told," he whispered, "that scientists say of their own: 'You eat what you kill.' Indeed, a savage world! Some delicacies, my sweet friend, are indescribable."

"You're going down," choked Steve, mouth thick with blood. "You've run out of time. Lab's about to blow."

"Stupid boy, the lab will explode when I say so. I have the detonator."

His yellow eyes hooded, Calibri licked his lips. "You are mine to play with."

Riker turned to the others, "If he gives you trouble, shoot his feet, knees, wrists, elbows – work your way up. But we need him alive."

Alpha and Charlie, each holding an arm, pushed Steve forwards, Riker and Calibri close behind. They made their way to the access elevator, and seconds later they had reached the rooftop.

Steve remembered the layout. They were in the small glass-walled building facing the helipad, on which now sat a JetRanger helicopter, door open, its rotors slowly turning.

Riker was on his cell phone, "Delta, we're out of here!"

The silhouette of a man at the controls gave them a "thumbs-up," and the rotors started spinning faster.

Riker's face twisted. "Delta didn't respond per protocol. Code yellow, Don Calibri."

Riker's eyes shifted back and forth, hiding a thousand calculations, but then re-focused on Steve. "Pretty boy, you better pray I live, because – I promise you – if I die, you die!"

He winced as he pulled out the Beretta. "Code yellow, gentlemen. We've already lost Bravo, and maybe Delta."

"Michael …" snapped Calibri, "this is very, very bad. Never before have I been in a situation where I am *so* implicated!"

"I'm sorry, Don Calibri," said Riker. "When we started out this morning, I was unaware …"

"Yesss," hissed Calibri. "That's exactly it. You were unaware. Bad intel, Mr. Riker. Bad intel. Bad security."

"Yes, sir," said Riker, sounding shaken. "Don't worry; I can fix this ..."

Calibri interrupted, "I'll hold back with Charlie. When you three get to the helicopter and signal 'all clear,' we will join you."

"Yes, sir."

Riker turned to Charlie. "August stays with me and Alpha. He's our rabbit's foot – they won't shoot the bird with him on board."

Charlie nodded. Alpha grabbed Steve by the hair, his right arm cradling the AK-47 at his hip. Riker stepped forward to the door, left arm dangling, Beretta in his right. Charlie and Calibri held back, Charlie carrying another rifle, Calibri also with a pistol.

"I guess now might be a good time to ask for my gun back," said Steve.

Riker gurgled incomprehensibly, then slammed the Beretta into Steve's gut.

Steve winced, but stifled the cry.

Riker turned into his face, noses almost touching: "Think you're a tough son of a bitch, huh? Just remember – I go down, I'm taking you with me. That's a promise, candy-ass. Damn you *and* your lab books!"

He turned back to Alpha. "Rock and roll!"

The helicopter's rotors were chattering full speed. Through the open cockpit door they could see the man's silhouette.

"OK, I've got your back," said Charlie.

Riker grunted. "See you in hell."

He ran fast, left arm dangling, the Beretta glistening in his other hand. Alpha pushed Steve forwards, holding on to his scalp, his pistol against Steve's back.

The blades were spinning ever faster, anticipating their imminent departure. They were close. They could better see the pilot. Riker waved back at them.

"It's Delta!" he shouted over the beating wind.

Then they were under the blades, the cabin five yards away. Steve could see Delta's silhouette through the open door. But at that moment the profile straightened, and then slumped. An instant later he glimpsed a familiar face: *Jack!*

Riker raised the Beretta.

With the momentum of their run Steve launched himself towards

Riker. Alpha's hand pulled hard at his scalp, but this offered him another fulcrum to finish the kick. His foot crashed into Riker's elbow, the gun firing just as he made contact, the impact sending the Beretta skipping across the helipad.

But the bullet had found a mark, Jack's chest blossoming red.

Alpha's grip on Steve's hair pulled him forward. He let go too late, off-balance even as he was swinging the AK-47 towards Steve.

A barrage of gunfire sounded over the chopper's roar, bullets pouring from the bleachers at the side of the helipad. Alpha tried to regain his balance, but he was too late, falling to his side even as he aimed his rifle vaguely towards the bleachers. Fully exposed, his body was covered by a rain of bullets by the time he hit the ground.

Steve and Riker went down at the copter's door in a tangle of feet and fists, but Riker had the advantage, his hands free. He wedged his left arm under Steve's chin, choking him, pulling them both into the helicopter. Steve kicked with his legs but found no footing.

Inside, Delta was slumped in the pilot's seat, gasping for air, a torn shirt looped around his neck. Steve guessed Delta's earlier "thumbs-up" in actuality had been an attempt to ward off strangulation. Slumped against the door was Jack, breathing labored, blood from his chest oozing onto his combat fatigues.

More gunfire erupted outside. Thirty yards were a long way to run under the line of direct enemy fire, but that did not stop Charlie. He raced across the tarmac, his rifle blazing continuously at the bleachers, and rolled into the copter, firing more rounds. Occasional wild shots responded, but none met its target.

"Where's Calibri?" barked Riker over the engine roar.

"He told me to go ahead," yelled Charlie. "He said he had to go back, he had something to do. He'd give us five minutes before blowing the lab. He said not to worry about him – just worry about us."

Riker looked like he had swallowed one of his grenades. He pulled tight on Steve's throat, making it hard to breathe.

"Charlie, this is code *black*! Live or die. Forget Calibri. We're out of here, now! I've got this asshole. Lighten the load. Dump these bodies! Fly this chopper!!!"

Charlie slid over to the other side of the helicopter and pushed Jack onto the helipad. He unstrapped Delta from the pilot's seat. "Hey, he's still breathing!"

"Lighten up, now!" yelled Riker. "There's no time. Code BLACK!"

Taking the pilot's seat, Charlie pushed Delta onto the tarmac. His hands flew over the switches, then pushed forwards on the control stick. "HOLD ON!"

The spinning blades howled, power surging into the Allison 250C20J turbo engine. The copter barely lifted even as she started flying forwards, cutting tight between the bleachers and the observation room, flinging Riker and Steve back in the cargo space behind the passenger bench, but Riker kept his arm locked tight around Steve's neck. The doors on both sides were open wide, wind blasting over them as they accelerated across the rooftop, then beyond it, Angion's parking lot far below.

Charlie banked sharply, pointing straight towards Massachusetts Bay. "Halifax?"

"Canada! Roger that!" yelled Riker.

As they turned, Steve caught a glimpse of a crowd in the parking lot, some in black biker jackets, some in lab coats, many stained reddish brown, and bodies scattered everywhere. He saw ambulances, red lights flashing, along with motorcycles and plain green sedans. There was only a glimpse, but it was enough: a figure in jeans and T-shirt, long black hair glistening.

Tied up bleeding in this helicopter with men who wanted him dead, Steve smiled, momentarily happy.

Morgan's alive!

Steve assessed his chances. Likely Riker planned to keep the copter below the radar floor. Unless Jack had stashed a GPS device, the NSA would be unable to track them. And once they were in a secluded place, and Riker had his way with Steve, most likely Riker would break him, and Steve would give him the location of the lab book, and reveal the value of the serum samples. And then Riker would kill him.

Now's my best chance – while we can still see land!

Charlie was pouring on the steam, flying low over Chelsea's rooftops, then above Deer Island, its giant egg-shaped towers a white blur, then moments later over Massachusetts Bay, skimming only a few feet above the water, to their right the Graves' Lighthouse on its little outcropping of rock.

"Hey Riker!" yelled Steve over the deafening wind.

"Yeah?"

"Remember what you were saying – if you die – you're taking me with you?"

"So what?" screamed Riker.

"Feeling's mutual!"

His feet against the back bulkhead, Steve kicked, like a coiled spring, firing them sideways. Riker had no leverage. As a unit they skidded across the cargo bay to the edge of the open hatch.

Riker dropped the gun as they slid, his groping right hand just in time finding a grip on the passenger seat frame. The gun bounced once, then twice, firing off a bullet clipping Charlie's forehead.

Dazed, the pilot fell back, his hand on the control stick.

Steve's foot searched for a fresh hold at the hatch door.

Near its top speed the copter responded instantly, arcing up fast, throwing all of them. Charlie swore, wiping blood from his eyes, his other hand trying to regain control of the aircraft. Riker swore, losing his grasp on the seat strut. Steve swore, trying to gain his balance on the doorframe, both his and Riker's weights pushing down on him with the copter's instant ascent.

Just that moment the radio crackled, and the cabin speakers blasted with Calibri's voice: "MICHAEL, JUST WANTED TO BE CLEAR, SO THAT YOU UNDERSTAND. I AM DISAPPOINTED WITH YOUR PERFORMANCE. YOU ARE FIRED. GOOD-BYE."

Steve's foot found leverage. He kicked again, tearing Riker's hand free of its grip. Together they whirled into the air stream outside the copter. Immediately they were ripped backwards, separated from the copter and each other by the hurricane-force wind.

As part of the JetRanger's steep ascent, their bodies floated up over the ocean, while the helicopter leveled as Charlie regained control. Within a second they had reached the zenith of their trajectories, Riker slightly ahead. Far below was the sea, its surface a flat plate of blue steel.

Steve realized – *I'm going to die.*

At that instant, as Steve watched the chopper speeding away … it exploded. One moment it was there; the next it had turned into a giant ball of orange and yellow flame.

And within the split-second the blast slammed Riker through the open air, crashing his body into Steve's. Together, carried by the expanding hot air, they rocketed backwards. Their bodies pressed together, their faces nearly touching, Riker's arms reached up towards Steve's neck.

"I'm going to kill you, you goddamn punk!" Riker screamed, infinite rage in his eyes. "See you in hell!!!"

Though his hands were still tied behind him, Steve's feet were free. As they started falling, Riker scrabbling at his neck, he flipped his legs around Riker's waist and clamped down hard. Riker gasped; his grip loosened; his body spasmed.

They were hurtling downwards, arcing in a faster, ever faster trajectory towards the water. Steve squeezed again. Riker's body shivered, helpless in his grip. "Don't count on it, Riker," he whispered, and kicked him down towards the water, ridding himself of his enemy and slowing his own momentum.

Riker tumbled in a sprawl. His hands balled into fists as his mouth formed soundless obscenities. But then he hit. His body skipped across the ocean surface – one, two, three times – at that speed the water like granite.

In the distance a fire-red light flashed across the morning sky.

Another explosion! Angion!!

A split-second later Steve hit the water. Unlike Riker, he was moving slower, and his body was balanced over his legs. His feet cut clean into the ocean. He held his tied hands close against his back, hoping the impact would not tear his arms from their sockets.

Then he was underwater.

He felt lucky. Had he hit at a shallower angle, he might have bounced, like Riker, in which case he would have been, like Riker, broken into little bits. With some pleasure he found his arms still attached.

But his relief was short-lived. Deep in the ocean, he tried kicking to get back towards the surface ... but nothing happened – only savage pain shooting up from his hips.

My legs won't move!

He had hoped to wrap his arms back around over his legs, to make swimming possible, maybe even to get his wrists free. But his useless back and legs made that impossible.

Too slowly he was floating towards the surface. His lungs ached for oxygen.

Soon, very soon.

He broke the surface, gasping for air. A wave struck, slamming foul water into his mouth. He choked, trying to keep his head up. Swimming was impossible, his legs numb. Agonizing pain ran down his spine. Handcuffed behind his back, his arms were useless.

Another wave hit. He knew the morning should have been bright, but the sky was dark as ink. He gasped for air, but salt filled his mouth. His body dropped back under. Below the surface all was silent, marred only by the beating of his oxygen-starved heart. Everything was slowing down. The water was ice-cold. His whole body was turning numb.

He came up for air one last time. A rush sounded in his ears, crashing waves on sand, normal life so close, somewhere firm earth, but too far to reach. One last time he gasped, but his mouth filled with seawater, again.

Back below the surface, for a brief hope Steve thought he heard a helicopter's blades beating.

No. I'm wrong.

In the deep all was quiet.

He thought of Morgan, how much he loved her, how much he hoped she might be alive.

And he hoped that she might be happy. Some day.

52.

A week later Morgan awoke in a hospital bed, her head wrapped in a bandage, stitches along her chin, her right knee in a brace. A young doctor explained she was not in a Boston hospital, but in a private clinic on the island of Bermuda. She threw her breakfast at him, and he left.

~

A month later, she still was in the hospital bed, her body weak, her mind clear.

Every day a doctor came to visit – pleasantly attentive, yet with nothing to say about how she had arrived there, what had happened at Angion, nor whether Steve, or Winston, or Jake, or anyone else for that matter, was alive.

Eventually, one day she requested a telephone. He politely refused. "You're too unstable," he said in a gentle English accent. "Give yourself time. You've had a bad run of it."

But Morgan had had enough. She was feeling better. She fumed at the young man's implacability, demanded to see his supervisor, and insisted she was well enough to leave, let alone talk on the phone. When she threatened legal action, he turned red-faced and disappeared.

Alone, rage turning into exhaustion, she slept.

~

Later that day she awoke to find Winston Schmidt standing at the foot of the bed, dressed in a wrinkled beige linen suit.

"That's my girl!" he chirped brightly. "Glad to see you're getting your spirits back."

She mustered her energy. "Winston! I figured you were behind this. Bermuda? What the hell? This is kidnapping. Let me go right now – or I'm suing you, and the NSA, and this damn clinic, and the government of Bermuda, and the queen of England, and everyone else!"

"Now, now, Morgan – relax. How can you not like Bermuda? You've yet to get beyond your hospital bed. Take a few days to look around. It's a lovely place. Mark Twain liked it so much, he once wrote, 'You go to heaven if you want to, I'd druther stay here.'"

"Exactly! I might as well be dead. Where's Steve? How's Laurel? I need to be in Manhattan. Damn it, Winston, why are you always in my way?"

She raised her head, but then she felt faint, waves of nausea sweeping over her. She dropped back onto the pillow, angry but helpless.

"When Angion blew up," said Winston, "a lot of people got hurt. Some died. There were ambulances and airlift helicopters everywhere. It took the Cambridge and Boston fire departments more than a day to get the blaze under control. Building next to Winnie's burned down; but we were lucky."

"Hmph. Too bad."

"Shrapnel fractured your skull, causing a nasty subarachnoid bleed. Phillips himself patched you up. Lucky girl – you could have died. Once you were out of the ICU, someone tapped him on the shoulder, but by then he knew not to ask questions, so now you are in my protective custody."

"Outside US jurisdiction? Come on, Schmidt, this stinks!"

"Morgan, while here you are completely safe: it's all our people, tight security, anonymity, limited access. Bermuda's a special place inside the worlds of American and British intelligence. Did you know that during the darkest days of the Second World War, the Yanks and Brits ran Atlantic intelligence from this island? At one point over twelve hundred Allied spies worked here!"

"So I'm under the umbrella of the NSA?"

"Not exactly. I told them I was a good friend of your father's. So you're with a friend of the family."

"And they bought *that*?"

"But Morgan, I *am* a good friend of your father's – or at least a good friend of a good friend. Federal judges value contacts in the intelligence community. Helps avoid embarrassments."

Morgan digested this bit of information. "So, what are you proposing?"

"The rehab doctors say you should take off at least another month. This is a beautiful clinic – really more of a spa. You should take advantage of it, relax, get well. There's an excellent library here. Sorry, no Internet."

Morgan smoldered, "What about a phone?"

Winston frowned, "For now, you must avoid contact with the outside world. Our situation here in Hamilton is extremely … shall we say … delicate. There are *others* here – from time to time. Believe me: you can head home once you're well. But when you're back in the States, you will be on your most solemn honor *not* to reveal the existence of this clinic, nor its location, nor even the island or country. Your being here reflects my trust in your integrity."

His tone was so serious, and his expression so somber, that Morgan chose not to argue.

Maybe this is bigger than me.

"Very well. I will keep your secrets."

They shook hands, and Winston left.

~

Over the next three weeks her body had recovered slowly, but now she felt fine. Yesterday she had even gone for a run around the compound. The walls had gates and sentries, but nowhere any government logo nor a hint of any other patient – quite discrete.

Upon her return she had found a pink box wrapped with a red bow placed on her bed. Attached was a linen envelope with a note inside:

Dear Morgan,

Am looking forwards to our dinner tomorrow. Your questions will be answered.

Please accept these trifles with my compliments. You will lend them grace.

Ever yours,
Winston

He *could* be charming.

She opened the package.

The dress was exquisite – a simple black with discrete neckline and hem, but its lines followed hers as though a seamstress had measured every inch. The material was a luxurious satin, hinting at skilled craftsmanship, discrete wealth, and superlative taste. Also in the box were a pair of heels of black silk and velvet – like the dress, epitomes of understated elegance.

She shook her head. He was eccentric, but the gifts were beautiful.

~

The next morning a doctor declared her fit for discharge.

After lunch two nurses politely escorted her to the clinic's entrance, where a black antique Mercedes sedan was idling. The chauffeur packed her bag in the trunk, opened the door, and tipped his hat, "Mum?"

She settled into the back seat, "Thank you. I don't suppose you have a name?"

"No, mum," he said, with a thick English accent.

Feeling a bit like Alice through the looking glass, Morgan said nothing further. The sedan wound along the curving path to the sentries at the gate, then down through the hills above Hamilton harbor.

Twenty minutes later they arrived at a three-story baby-blue villa surrounded by manicured gardens, terraces, fountains, and sculptures.

A maid escorted her to a bedroom furnished with tasteful Victorian antiques. There she found another note:

Please meet me on the terrace at 6:00 PM for cocktails.
Dinner to follow.

Warmly,
Winston

She unpacked, showered, changed, and waited.

Shortly before six o'clock a butler knocked at her door. Without a word he led her through a maze of hallways, eventually reaching an open veranda along the villa's upper story.

Only then he spoke: "Champagne, mum?"

"Thank you. Do *you* have a name?"

"Of course, mum. Henry."

"Oh, what a relief!"

"*Mum?*"

She smiled, "Sorry, it's unimportant. Yes, thank you, Henry."

He disappeared only to re-surface moments later with a flute on a silver tray. "Bollinger '97, mum."

She took the glass. He bowed slightly and departed.

Morgan looked out onto Hamilton's horseshoe-shaped bay. Picturesque houses, each a different pastel mix of white, pink, orange, yellow, blue, and green, nestled into the tree-covered hillsides. Yachts were moored along clubhouse docks, their lights twinkling in the twilight. The occasional call of a gull overhead, and the sporadic clang of a bell on a buoy, carried softly across the water.

"Hello, Morgan."

She turned. Winston was dressed in white evening jacket, black tie, and cuffed charcoal trousers. For once he did not look rumpled. She had to smile: forty years earlier and forty pounds lighter he must have been quite the lady's man. Even at seventy-five he was dashing.

"You look nice, Winston."

"Thank you."

His blue eyes twinkled as he raised his champagne flute. "To the most beautiful woman on the island of Bermuda."

She raised her glass in demure salute, "And to the most deceitful man on the island of Bermuda."

He smiled, "Touché."

They touched glasses and drank.

"So, Winston. I've promised to keep your secrets. Please, just tell me the truth."

"And I promised to answer your questions, didn't I?"

Morgan looked out on the sunset. She had been thinking about this, her first question, the hardest question.

She took a deep breath. "Winston, what happened to Steve?"

"You really want to know?"

"Yes!"

His words came slowly, "While we were entering Angion, Jack Walker and two other agents went up the fire escape to check Calibri's JetRanger helicopter that had landed earlier that morning. We figured it was Riker's exit strategy. Jack found the doors open. He slipped inside and incapacitated the pilot while the other two staked out a perimeter. But Riker had Steve as hostage, so they didn't fire, and Riker managed to reach the JetRanger and shoot Jack."

Winston looked out to sea, his eyes old and worn, "Riker pushed Jack out, as well as the unconscious pilot. This left only him, his henchman, and Steve on the copter, and they took off for Riker's hideaway in Nova Scotia. Then – and I'm so very, very sorry, Morgan – Antonio Calibri blew up the helicopter."

Morgan pressed a fist to her mouth.

Winston took a deep breath. "We're not sure why. We think Calibri was fed up with Riker, and he was convinced Steve had evidence that would damn Angiotox. He then continued and detonated the whole lab – thereby eliminating any other evidence."

Morgan squeezed her eyes shut.

Talk about something else. Anything else.

Inside she was screaming, but she kept her voice low, "Winston, how is it you're alive?"

"Trying to guess Riker's next move, I had headed to the rooftop with my biker companions. We arrived in time to see Riker fly off, but our people already had a Blackhawk copter set up to follow the JetRanger.

Moments later they picked us up, along with an unconscious Jack Walker and his team."

Why is this old man alive, not Steve? She wanted to strangle him.

"You're a lucky man."

"Morgan, I am so sorry."

"Damn it, Winston. You are *not* going to see me cry."

She turned to the harbor, blinking through her tears.

"Tell me, what was wrong with Angiotox?"

"That's complicated. In the SAGA tests and in the first rabbit experiments, Angiotox worked well. But then in the mouse experiments, run by two of MacGregor's minions, Pieter Ogoranovich and Mai Sachamachi, the mice didn't respond as expected: all died due to massive bleeding. Pieter, Mai, and MacGregor together decided there must have been an error translating the doses from rabbits to mice, so they cut back on the doses in mice. Once they'd done that, they did not get consistent results, but at least the mice weren't bleeding to death. Then enter Steve August."

"How do you know all this? Someone confess?"

"No. Incredibly, the Angion scientists still think that Angiotox is the best drug since penicillin, that MacGregor was a genius, and that Steve was a fraud. Seems the hypnosis was so deep – repeated weekly for many months – that its effects may be lifelong. We've tried, but we don't know how to de-program these people."

"Incredible."

"Our info comes from some of the lab techs, the low-level assistants. Steve's tech, Shiu-Wei Chen, witnessed the switch in dose levels, and the reasons the scientists gave her for the change."

"And then Steve entered the picture …?"

"Yes. Seems MacGregor wanted to make sure Steve would do what he was told. He believed everyone is corruptible; and he tried. But Steve refused. He didn't sleep with Alison – the woman with the black BMW in the photos. Nor did he show interest in money. Instead, he just kept reporting negative results. With his incredible hang-up about truth, Steve was MacGregor's worst nightmare."

"He *didn't* sleep with Alison?"

"No, he didn't. But Morgan, be prepared for a shock."

"OK …"

"MacGregor gave Steve his lab assignment, knowing it was impossible. But MacGregor had set up the scenario so that, once he was convinced Steve *would* play ball, then he'd shape Steve's results into a resounding success."

"How could he do that?"

"Mai and Pieter set up a secret lab inside Angion. They treated some mice from Steve's experiment to show positive results. The technique, using a high-energy radiation applicator, was very delicate and almost undetectable, but Steve discovered it …"

Morgan interrupted, "What Steve was trying to do that last day at Angion was get back the proof that the mice had been tampered with? He died for *that*?"

"Yes. He thought it was *that* important."

Morgan's champagne tasted sour.

"So MacGregor engineered the entire fraud, from its inception, to its promulgation, to its concealment?"

"Well said, counselor."

"Bastard! Didn't he realize he'd be found out?"

"On the contrary. Seems he believed Angiotox would work in human beings. He thought the mouse data represented a species-specific glitch. Furthermore, we *think* he believed that if all of his scientists were convinced of Angiotox's success, then this universal belief would translate into reality. Rather eerie. Seems he was playing God. Megalomaniacal."

"The guy was insane!"

"More precisely: corrupted by greed. But there are many scientists and philosophers who argue MacGregor's point of view – those who think a tree falling in a forest makes no sound, unless someone hears it."

Morgan tried to digest this.

"That Saturday night when Steve overslept in the lab – that night he learned about this fraud?"

"He only saw enough to realize his situation at Angion was dangerous. That's why he pushed you off to New York – to keep you safe. Sadly, he had no idea what he was up against."

Morgan swallowed hard.

"What about the pictures of Steve with Alison? Was Riker trying to make me break up with Steve?"

"Did it work?" asked Winston.

"No. They made me suspicious someone was trying to incriminate him."

"You mean the pictures were evidence of a photographer, even more than their content, because the content didn't make sense?"

"Exactly. So why did they do it?"

"*They* didn't."

Morgan stared at him. "You …?"

"Yes. The NSA knew Calibri had turned Riker on Steve. Those photos were our warning to you both that you were under surveillance. We figured that might be helpful. And if Riker's people learned somebody else was *also* watching Steve, then that might provide him some protection. But we wanted *no one* to suspect the surveillance was friendly."

"Not nice – on their part, or yours."

"Very sorry. But imagine what Riker might have been able to do, had you not been alerted."

Sadly, softly, Morgan murmured, "I see …"

After some time, she asked, "Tell me, Winston, what happened after I left Boston? How could it get so bad that Steve faked suicide?"

"Steve did not know whom to trust, but he knew he was being watched – thanks to those photos. He chose a strategy that was no less difficult than it was dangerous. He decided the best way to understand Angion was to get inside."

"Winston, this is twisted."

"Yes, but true. Knowing you were out of the picture, Dida Medicia, Angion's president and Don Calibri's niece, seduced him. Steve cooperated, intending to break into their inner circle."

But suddenly Morgan was uninterested in Angiotox. "You mean he slept with – not Alison – but … Dida? That woman who bled out in the Arena?"

She put down the champagne, her hand shaking.

"Yes. I'm sorry. He thought it was necessary … a means for getting inside."

"Wait a minute!" She stared at him in disbelief. "*You* were watching him! You showed Steve the photos, scared him into paranoia, and then left him to the sharks. You, you …"

Winston looked away, studying a yacht sailing into the harbor. "We had to warn him, Morgan, and you, too. But we had to remain secret. No choice."

His form blurred through her tears. "So what do you think, Winston? What about Steve? Did you give Steve a choice?"

Indignant, she choked out: "Did he *have* to sleep with her?"

"Morgan, speaking officially, there's always a choice."

But then he paused.

Shocked, Morgan realized that Winston had just damned the NSA, and himself. And then she realized that he had just realized it, too.

"So," he continued flatly, "one might conclude that Steve's sexual interlude with Dida was not only wrong, morally speaking, but also wrong, practically speaking. Riker went after him anyway, and Steve lost. Overall, bad call. The ruse didn't work, and now he's dead. What a waste!"

"You goddamn *bastard*!!"

And she slapped his face. Hard. She meant it to hurt.

"How dare you judge?" she hissed. "Steve was trying to find some advantage, to force Angion to show its hand, to get an edge in a game of life-and-death. *He* was in the line of fire! Where were you? Watching a video screen? *He* had to make the judgment call. Not you. How dare you?"

"You forgive him?" asked Winston.

"Well ... I mean ..."

She gasped at the position he had put her in. How could she defend Steve, yet condemn him? If Winston had no right to judge, how could she?

Morgan blinked through her tears.

His eyes were focused on her face. She met his gaze, challenging him, his view of the situation, of Steve, of her ...

But even as she tried to stare him down ...

Maybe Winston's right?

It was true that Steve *had* been challenged beyond all norms of everyday life.

Extraordinary challenges had required extraordinary ...

Her heart melted.

Steve, I'm so sorry!

"Goddamn you, Winston! I was doing so well. Now you tell me things I never wanted to hear, and then you flip me upside down."

She felt her eyes again filling with tears.

"Morgan, I'm just asking you to be consistent. Human values have a hierarchy of levels. What I'm suggesting is that you go down to bedrock, and then work your way up. I think Steve is exonerated. And I think you think so."

Morgan found herself staring at this strange old man. Should she slap him again, or kiss him? He seemed full of lies, yet he spoke truth. Was she so foolish? Or was he so wise?

Unsure, she picked up her glass, but it was empty. Within the instant Henry appeared carrying the Bollinger. He poured and vanished.

Morgan took a sip and looked out over the harbor.

"More questions?" asked Winston.

She looked at him with wet eyes, shook her head, and then looked back out to sea, wishing the world were different.

"OK, I'll check on dinner," he said.

He stepped inside, leaving her in the company only of her memories.

53.

TUESDAY, MAY 31

The following morning Winston and Morgan walked down the front steps to the waiting antique Bentley, Henry trailing with her bag.

Last night's conversation had been tough, yet Winston had thought it best. An inkling of the "big picture" might help her reach closure. Oh, how Winston liked knowing the big picture, though these days *that* was a mark he never met. Even while a scientist at Cambridge rarely had he reached real insight – how some novel result defied the conventional wisdom yet fit into a much larger truth.

And now? Only spooks and shadows populated his world.

Glimpses, that's all we get. Glimpses.

So, he had given Morgan as much of a glimpse as he could.

Or have I?

With his usual quiet efficiency Henry had stowed Morgan's bag in the boot and opened the door.

"Thanks, Henry. That's fine," said Winston, and Henry walked back to the driver's side.

Other than a noncommittal "Hello, Winston," when he had arrived at her door to walk her downstairs, Morgan had said nothing until now, for the simple reason that she really had nothing to say. She could see inside him. Winston Schmidt was a hollow man. Steve was dead – and Winston Schmidt was as accountable as anyone.

He had so much power at his disposal … yet he did not intervene …

when he could have, when he should have, when Steve might have been saved.

At the limo door Morgan turned to Schmidt.

"You know, Winston, I'm not going to miss you. Steve's dead, and Calibri – the real genius behind Angion – is free as a bird. Rather a colossal failure on your part, wouldn't you say?"

Schmidt took a deep breath.

"Perhaps. But Angiotox is in the hands of Silverstein, and Angion's Board has severed all ties with the Calibri Group. Maybe Silverstein will find some good to do with it. As for Calibri, you're right, he managed to insulate himself. But don't worry: we'll get him."

Winston paused, and then spoke softly, "And you, Morgan, what are you going to do?"

Morgan felt the future weighing down on her like lead. She leaned against the Bentley's door for support.

"I'm resigning from Eddie Mac. I can't work for Edwards, not given what I know."

"What *will* you do?"

She tried to smile. "Think I'll help Laurel with her sexual harassment suit. Who knows? Maybe we can start our own boutique Title IX law firm."

Nodding vigorously, Schmidt managed to surprise her. "Hmmm. Not a bad idea. That fellow Myers may give you ladies a leg up. You do know he's one of the lions of legal liability? Of course, if you take on Edwards, you'll be crossing Calibri again, since Eddie Mac runs Calibri's contractual network."

"You think Calibri will come after me?"

"He wants blood for Dida's death, but he sees your involvement as coincidental. After all, Steve was sleeping with her, not an arrangement to which you would have consented. So, that gives you plausible deniability. And not even Eddie Mac is important to a lizard like Calibri. Cut off his tail, and it grows right back. No, I think Calibri will have more salient matters to focus on than Morgan Najar."

She shook her head, brushed away a tear, and stepped into the Bentley. "Good-bye, Winston. Hope I never see you again."

Winston started shutting the door, but then, almost as an afterthought, pulled it back open.

"One last little thing," he murmured, leaning in. "You do realize – don't you? – that if Steve *were* alive, and this somehow leaked back to Calibri, then your life would be forfeit. Calibri believes in nothing if not revenge – relentless, savage, brutal, absolute revenge. You and your family would be lost. You're much better off with Steve dead."

Her pulse pounded in her ears.

Did he truly say what he just said?

Before she could reply he had stepped away, closed the door, and waved to Henry, who pulled the Bentley out of the driveway, down the winding road, through the iron gates, and then to the nearby helipad for Morgan's return to the USA.

One message *was* clear.

No more questions.

On the drive to the helipad, Steve's voice kept repeating in her head:

The highest good is like water.
Water benefits ten thousand beings,
Yet it does not contend.
Nothing under Heaven is as soft and yielding as water.
Yet in attacking the firm and strong,
Nothing is better than water.